The Best Science Fiction of the Year #11

Once more we present the latest install-
ment of the famous standard anthology of
the best short fiction in the science fiction
field published annually. Reflecting the
themes, styles, and ideas of the top science fiction writers today, this collection
presents the most outstanding short stories, novelettes, and novellas drawn from
a field of astonishing scope and quality.

Books by Terry Carr

Fantasy Annual #3
Fantasy Annual #4
The Best Science Fiction of the Year #10
The Best Science Fiction of the Year #11

Published by TIMESCAPE BOOKS

Most Timescape Books are available at special quantity discounts for bulk purchases for sales promotions, premiums or fund raising. Special books or book excerpts can also be created to fit specific needs.

For details write or telephone the office of the Vice President of Special Markets, Pocket Books, 1230 Avenue of the Americas, New York, New York 10020, 212-245-1760.

THE BEST SCIENCE FICTION OF THE YEAR #11

TERRY CARR, EDITOR

A TIMESCAPE BOOK
PUBLISHED BY POCKET BOOKS NEW YORK

Another *Original* publication of TIMESCAPE BOOKS

A Timescape Book published by
POCKET BOOKS, a Simon & Schuster division of
GULF & WESTERN CORPORATION
1230 Avenue of the Americas, New York, N.Y. 10020

ISBN: 0-671-44483-2

First Timescape Books printing July, 1982

10 9 8 7 6 5 4 3 2 1

POCKET and colophon are trademarks of Simon & Schuster.

Use of the trademark TIMESCAPE is by exclusive license
from Gregory Benford, the trademark owner.

Printed in the U.S.A.

ACKNOWLEDGMENTS

The Saturn Game by Poul Anderson. Copyright © 1981 by Davis Publications, Inc. From *Analog*, February 2, 1981, by permission of the author and his agents, Scott Meredith Literary Agency, Inc., 845 Third Ave., New York, N.Y. 10022.

Walk the Ice by Mildred Downey Broxon. Copyright © 1980 by Mercury Press, Inc. From *Fantasy and Science Fiction*, January 1981, by permission of the author and her agents, Jarvis/Braff Ltd.

Trial Sample by Ted Reynolds. Copyright © 1981 by Davis Publications, Inc. From *Isaac Asimov's Science Fiction Magazine*, June 8, 1981, by permission of the author.

The Pusher by John Varley. Copyright © 1981 by Mercury Press, Inc. From *Fantasy and Science Fiction*, October 1981, by permission of the author and his agents, Kirby McCauley Ltd.

Venice Drowned by Kim Stanley Robinson. Copyright © 1981 by Terry Carr. From *Universe 11*, by permission of the author.

Walden Three by Michael Swanwick. Copyright © 1981 by Michael Swanwick. From *New Dimensions 12*, by permission of the author and his agent, Virginia Kidd.

Second Comings—Reasonable Rates by Pat Cadigan. Copyright © 1981 by Mercury Press, Inc. From *Fantasy and Science Fiction*, February 1981, by permission of the author.

Forever by Damon Knight. Copyright © 1981 by Omni Publications International, Ltd. From *Omni*, November 1981, by permission of the author.

Emergence by David R. Palmer. Copyright © 1980 by Davis Publications, Inc. From *Analog*, January 5, 1981, by permission of the author.

You Can't Go Back by R. A. Lafferty. Copyright © 1981 by Davis Publications, Inc. From *Isaac Asimov's Science Fiction Magazine*, September 28, 1981, by permission of the author and his agent, Virginia Kidd.

Walpurgisnacht by Roger Zelazny. Copyright © 1981 by the Amber Corporation. From *A Rhapsody in Amber*, by permission of the author.

The Woman the Unicorn Loved by Gene Wolfe. Copyright © 1981 by Davis Publications, Inc. From *Isaac Asimov's Science Fiction Magazine*, June 8, 1981, by permission of the author and his agent, Virginia Kidd.

Serpents' Teeth by Spider Robinson. Copyright © 1981 by Omni Publications International, Ltd. From *Omni*, March 1981, by permission of the author.

The Thermals of August by Edward Bryant. Copyright © 1981 by Edward Bryant. From *Fantasy and Science Fiction*, May 1981, by permission of the author.

Going Under by Jack Dann. Copyright © 1981 by Omni Publications International, Ltd. From *Omni*, September 1981, by permission of the author.

The Quiet by George Florance-Guthridge. Copyright © 1981 by Mercury Press, Inc. From *Fantasy and Science Fiction*, July 1981, by permission of the author.

Swarmer, Skimmer by Gregory Benford. Copyright © 1981 by Abbenford Associates. From *Science Fiction Digest*, October/November 1981, by permission of the author.

Contents

THE BEST
SCIENCE
FICTION OF
THE YEAR
#11

INTRODUCTION

≈≈≈≈≈≈≈≈≈≈≈≈≈≈≈≈≈≈≈≈≈≈≈≈≈≈≈≈≈

Terry Carr

A TITLE LIKE *The Best Science Fiction of the Year* strikes me as pretty much self-explanatory, but every now and then, when I get questions from readers or when I see reviews of these books, it seems necessary to comment further on the purposes of such a series.

It goes without saying that a book like this can't include the top full-length novels, but just what is the top limit for the length of stories included? Usually it's about 30,000 words, which allows room to include the best two or three novellas of the year. (There are three this year.) To devote space to longer stories would necessitate leaving out too many of the fine shorter stories; and in any case those few novellas running to, say, 40,000 words have virtually all appeared in book form already.

How about the number of stories—are these the top ten, the best dozen, or what? No, the stories aren't chosen by such a rigid system; instead, this book collects 150,000 words of the best stories, whatever their individual lengths. (This makes it significantly longer and more complete than any other such books.) This year there are seventeen stories.

Most important question: Just who says these are the best SF stories of the year? Answer: I do, and each year I can only hope that you'll agree with my taste. Of course I talk with a great many people about the stories they've liked, but ultimately I have to rely on my own judgment, my own reactions to the stories under consideration, whether or not other people have raved about them.

It might seem more appropriate, in compiling such a

1

"best" anthology, to have the selections made by more people—by a jury of critics, say, or even by open voting from readers at large. But there's an enormous amount of reading time involved in screening all the stories published each year, and these books don't garner sufficient profits to make it worth the time and effort of even a five-person jury. (Besides: Who selects the jurors?) In any case, committees are notorious for inefficiency and inconsistency.

As for selecting the top stories by popular vote, this is already being done in such awards as the Hugos and Nebulas. It's a complicated, time-consuming process, and the books that result from these awards cannot be published promptly. And, again, how many people read enough of the science fiction published to enable them to vote knowledgeably? (Some of the more questionable award winners have reflected this problem.)

So it seems a single editor per book is the most practical answer. Not to worry, though: there is more than one best-of-the-year anthology published, and if you find my taste doesn't agree with yours, you can buy Donald Wollheim's book or others that may be published from time to time. Or, of course, all of them—no two editors' selections overlap very much.

Reassuringly, there *is* noticeable agreement among editors about the top candidates, and best-of-the-year books usually agree to some extent with the Hugos, Nebulas, etc. —proving that truly outstanding stories will usually be recognized by most people.

In fact, a number of people have made a practice of commenting each year on the number of award-winning stories selected by each best-of-the-year editor as if this were some yardstick by which to measure the editor's acumen. To an extent this notion is no doubt correct—an editor whose selections never included any award winners would certainly seem to be out of touch with most readers' preferences. Does this mean, then, that the editors try to choose stories that are likely to win awards?

I doubt it. Predicting award winners is a chancy business even if you know which stories are nominated to the ballots, and it's even harder if you don't have that information. Since each editor's final selections must be made before the end of the year, months before any awards ballots are compiled, obviously none of us has this basic information to influence our choices.

Therefore—taking *The Best Science Fiction of the Year #10*, last year's volume, as an example—the fact that stories in that book subsequently won two Nebula Awards, a Hugo and a World Fantasy Award simply illustrates what I said above, that the cream rises to the top.

There's another curious notion, sometimes put forth by reviewers and even by the editors themselves, that best-of-the-year anthologies reflect trends in science fiction as a whole. If such a book includes several stories written in "experimental" styles, or about ecological doom, or a preponderance of stories longer or shorter than the norm, someone is sure to say that this proves all science fiction is changing. But the stories in any one book comprise less than five percent of the year's science fiction—far less when you count the novels—so clearly they aren't likely to be representative in that sense.

In what ways, then, *does* a "showcase" anthology such as this one represent science fiction? A simple answer: It gathers under one cover a wide sampling of the very best recent SF stories in the shorter lengths, by writers already famous as well as by those first making their mark. Since new writers usually have their first successes in short stories, it gives you an opportunity to discover outstanding new talents early in their careers. And, though as I've said "trend spotting" isn't very appropriate here, when new ideas—scientific or otherwise—make their way into science fiction, they usually appear first in the shorter stories. (I believe the idea of warm-blooded dinosaurs first appeared in SF in Robert Silverberg's 1980 story "Our Lady of the Sauropods," for instance.)

Primarily, though, the purpose of this annual series isn't merely to be "representative," a sampler, or anything of that nature. The purpose is to entertain you, to make you think and feel and live for a while in new worlds and new lives. You have some treats before you.

—TERRY CARR

THE SATURN GAME

Poul Anderson

Poul Anderson is well known as a writer of technologically sophisticated science-fiction adventure, and this absorbing story of an expedition to Saturn's moon Iapetus will delight his many fans. What's less noticed in Anderson's writing (or at least fewer people comment on it) is his sure command of character and human emotions . . . the things that make adventure compelling. The explorers in this story have been playing a game on the long voyage out—a fantasy psychodrama so fascinating that when real dangers threaten they seem oddly remote. But they're real and they're deadly.

I

IF WE ARE TO UNDERSTAND WHAT HAPPENED,
which is vital if we are to avoid repeated and worse trag-
edies in the future, we must begin by dismissing all accusa-
tions. Nobody was negligent; no action was foolish. For
who could have predicted the eventuality, or recognized
its nature, until too late? Rather should we appreciate the
spirit with which those people struggled against disaster,
inward and outward, after they knew. The fact is that
thresholds exist throughout reality, and that things on their
far sides are altogether different from things on their hither
sides. The *Chronos* crossed more than an abyss, it crossed
a threshold of human experience.

> —Francis L. Minamoto, *Death Under Saturn:
> A Dissenting View*
>
> (Apollo University Communications,
> Leyburg, Luna, 2057)

"The City of Ice is now on my horizon," *Kendrick says.
Its towers gleam blue.* "My griffin spreads his wings to
glide." *Wind whistles among those great, rainbow-shim-
mering pinions. His cloak blows back from his shoulders;
the air strikes through his ring-mail and sheathes him in
cold.* "I lean over and peer after you." *The spear in his
left hand counterbalances him. Its head flickers palely with
the moonlight that Wayland Smith hammered into the
steel.*

"Yes, I see the griffin," *Ricia tells him,* "high and far,

6

like a comet above the courtyard walls. I run out from under the portico for a better look. A guard tries to stop me, grabs my sleeve, but I tear the spider silk apart and dash forth into the open." *The elven castle wavers as if its sculptured ice were turning to smoke. Passionately, she cries,* "Is it in truth you, my darling?"

"Hold, there!" *warns Alvarlan from his cave of arcana ten thousand leagues away.* "I send your mind the message that if the King suspects this is Sir Kendrick of the Isles, he will raise a dragon against him, or spirit you off beyond any chance of rescue. Go back, Princess of Maranoa. Pretend you decide that it is only an eagle. I will cast a belief-spell on your words."

"I stay far aloft," *Kendrick says.* "Save he use a scrying stone, the Elf King will not be aware this beast has a rider. From here I'll spy out city and castle." *And then—? He knows not. He knows simply that he must set her free or die in the quest. How long will it take him, how many more nights will she lie in the King's embrace?*

"I thought you were supposed to spy out Iapetus," Mark Danzig interrupted.

His dry tone startled the three others into alertness. Jean Broberg flushed with embarrassment, Colin Scobie with irritation; Luis Garcilaso shrugged, grinned, and turned his gaze to the pilot console before which he sat harnessed. For a moment silence filled the cabin, and shadows, and radiance from the universe.

To help observation, all lights were out except a few dim glows from the instruments. The sunward ports were lidded. Elsewhere thronged stars, so many and so brilliant that they well-nigh drowned the blackness which held them. The Milky Way was a torrent of silver. One port framed Saturn at half phase, dayside pale gold and rich bands amidst the jewelry of its rings, nightside wanly ashimmer with starlight upon clouds, as big to the sight as Earth over Luna.

Forward was Iapetus. The spacecraft rotated while orbiting the moon, to maintain a steady optical field. It had crossed the dawn line, presently at the middle of the inward-facing hemisphere. Thus it had left bare, crater-pocked land behind it in the dark, and was passing above sunlit glacier country. Whiteness dazzled, glittered in sparks and shards of color, reached fantastic shapes heavenward; cirques, crevasses, caverns brimmed with blue.

"I'm sorry," Jean Broberg whispered. "It's too beautiful, unbelievably beautiful, and . . . almost like the place where our game had brought us. Took us by surprise—"

"Huh!" Mark Danzig said. "You had a pretty good idea of what to expect, therefore you made your play go in the direction of something that resembled it. Don't tell me any different. I've watched these acts for eight years."

Colin Scobie made a savage gesture. Spin and gravity were too slight to give noticeable weight, and his movement sent him flying through the air, across the crowded cabin. He checked himself by a handhold just short of the chemist. "Are you calling Jean a liar?" he growled.

Most times he was cheerful, in a bluff fashion. Perhaps because of that, he suddenly appeared menacing. He was a big, sandy-haired man in his mid-thirties; a coverall did not disguise the muscles beneath, and the scowl on his face brought forth its ruggedness.

"Please!" Broberg exclaimed. "Not a quarrel, Colin."

The geologist glanced back at her. She was slender and fine-featured. At her age of forty-two, despite longevity treatment, the reddish-brown hair that fell to her shoulders was becoming streaked with white, and lines were engraved around large gray eyes.

"Mark is right," she sighed. "We're here to do science, not daydream." She reached forth to touch Scobie's arm, smiling shyly. "You're still full of your Kendrick persona, aren't you? Gallant, protective—" She stopped. Her voice had quickened with more than a hint of Ricia. She covered her lips and flushed again. A tear broke free and sparkled off on air currents. She forced a laugh. "But I'm just physicist Broberg, wife of astronomer Tom, mother of Johnnie and Billy."

Her glance went Saturnward, as if seeking the ship where her family waited. She might have spied it, too, as a star that moved among stars by the solar sail. However, that was now furled, and naked vision could not find even such huge hulls as *Chronos* possessed, across millions of kilometers.

Luis Garcilaso asked from his pilot's chair: "What harm if we carry on our little *commedia dell' arte?*" His Arizona drawl soothed the ear. "We won't be landin' for a while yet, and everything's on automatic till then." He was small, swarthy, and deft, still in his twenties.

Danzig twisted his leathery countenance into a frown. At sixty, thanks to his habits as well as to longevity, he kept springiness in a lank frame; he could joke about wrinkles and encroaching baldness. In this hour, he set humor aside.

"Do you mean you don't know what's the matter?" His beak of a nose pecked at a scanner screen which magnified the moonscape. "Almighty God! That's a new world we're about to touch down on—tiny, but a world, and strange in ways we can't guess. Nothing's been here before us except one unmanned flyby and one unmanned lander that soon quit sending. We can't rely on meters and cameras alone. We've got to use our eyes and brains."

He addressed Scobie. "You should realize that in your bones, Colin, if nobody else aboard does. You've worked on Luna as well as Earth. In spite of all the settlements, in spite of all the study that's been done, did you never hit any nasty surprises?"

The burly man had recovered his temper. Into his own voice came a softness that recalled the serenity of the Idaho mountains from which he hailed. "True," he admitted. "There's no such thing as having too much information when you're off Earth, or enough information, for that matter." He paused. "Nevertheless, timidity can be as dangerous as rashness—not that you're timid, Mark," he added in haste. "Why, you and Rachel could've been in a nice O'Neill on a nice pension—"

Danzig relaxed and smiled. "This was a challenge, if I may sound pompous. Just the same, we want to get home when we're finished here. We should be in time for the Bar Mitzvah of a great-grandson or two. Which requires staying alive."

"My point is," Scobie said, "if you let yourself get buffaloed, you may end up in a worse bind than— Oh, never mind. You're probably right, and we should not have begun fantasizing. The spectacle sort of grabbed us. It won't happen again."

Yet when Scobie's eyes looked anew on the glacier, they had not quite the dispassion of a scientist in them. Nor did Broberg's or Garcilaso's. Danzig slammed fist into palm. "The game, the damned childish game," he muttered, too low for his companions to hear. "Was nothing saner possible for them?"

II

Was nothing saner possible for them? Perhaps not.

If we are to answer the question, we should first review some history. When early industrial operations in space offered the hope of rescuing civilization, and Earth, from ruin, then greater knowledge of sister planets, prior to their development, became a clear necessity. The effort started with Mars, the least hostile. No natural law forbade sending small manned spacecraft yonder. What did was the absurdity of using as much fuel, time, and effort as were required, in order that three or four persons might spend a few days in a single locality.

Construction of the *J. Peter Vajk* took longer and cost more, but paid off when it, virtually a colony, spread its immense solar sail and took a thousand people to their goal in half a year and in comparative comfort. The payoff grew overwhelming when they, from orbit, launched Earthward the beneficiated minerals of Phobos that they did not need for their own purposes. Those purposes, of course, turned on the truly thorough, long-term study of Mars, and included landings of auxiliary craft, for everlengthier stays, all over the surface.

Sufficient to remind you of this much; no need to detail the triumphs of the same basic concept throughout the inner Solar System, as far as Jupiter. The tragedy of the *Vladimir* became a reason to try again for Mercury, and, in a left-handed, political way, pushed the Britannic-American consortium into its *Chronos* project.

They named the ship better than they knew. Sailing time to Saturn was eight years.

Not only the scientists must be healthy, lively-minded people. Crewfolk, technicians, medics, constables, teachers, clergy, entertainers—every element of an entire community must be. Each must command more than a single skill, for emergency backup, and keep those skills alive by regular, tedious rehearsal. The environment was limited and austere; communication with home was soon a matter of beamcasts; cosmopolitans found themselves in what amounted to an isolated village. What were they to *do*?

Assigned tasks. Civic projects, especially work on improving the interior of the vessel. Research, or writing a book, or the study of a subject, or sports, or hobby clubs, or service and handicraft enterprises, or more private interactions, or— There was a wide choice of television tapes, but Central Control made sets usable for only three hours in twenty-four. You dared not get into the habit of passivity.

Individuals grumbled, squabbled, formed and dissolved cliques, formed and dissolved marriages or less explicit relationships, begot and raised occasional children, worshipped, mocked, learned, yearned, and for the most part found reasonable satisfaction in life. But for some, including a large proportion of the gifted, what made the difference between this and misery were their psychodramas.

—Minamoto

Dawn crept past the ice, out onto the rock. It was a light both dim and harsh, yet sufficient to give Garcilaso the last data he wanted for descent.

The hiss of the motor died away. A thump shivered through the hull, landing jacks leveled it, and stillness fell. The crew did not speak for a while. They were staring out at Iapetus.

Immediately around them was desolation like that which reigns in much of the Solar System. A darkling plain curved visibly away to a horizon that, at man-height, was a bare three kilometers distant; higher up in the cabin, you could see farther, but that only sharpened the sense of being on a minute ball awhirl among the stars. The ground was thinly covered with cosmic dust and gravel; here and there a minor crater or an upthrust mass lifted out of the regolith to cast long, knife-edged, utterly black shadows. Light reflections lessened the number of visible stars, turning heaven into a bowlful of night. Halfway between the zenith and the south, half-Saturn and its rings made the vista beautiful.

Likewise did the glacier—or the glaciers? Nobody was sure. The sole knowledge was that, seen from afar, Iapetus gleamed bright as the western end of its orbit and grew dull at the eastern end, because one side was covered with whitish material while the other side was not; the dividing line passed nearly beneath the planet which it eternally faced. The probes from *Chronos* had reported the layer was thick, with puzzling spectra that varied from place to place, and little more about it.

In this hour, four humans gazed across pitted emptiness

and saw wonder rear over the world-rim. From north to south went ramparts, battlements, spires, depths, peaks, cliffs, their shapes and shadings an infinity of fantasies. On the right Saturn cast soft amber, but that was nearly lost in the glare from the east, where a sun dwarfed almost to stellar size nonetheless blazed too fierce to look at, just above the summit. There the silvery sheen exploded in brilliance, diamond-glitter of shattered light, chill blues and greens; dazzled to tears, eyes saw the vision glimmer and waver, as if it bordered on dreamland, or on Faerie. But despite all delicate intricacies, underneath was a sense of chill and of brutal mass: here dwelt also the Frost Giants.

Broberg was the first to breathe forth a word. "The City of Ice."

"Magic," said Garcilaso as low. "My spirit could lose itself forever, wanderin' yonder. I'm not sure I'd mind. My cave is nothin' like this, nothin'—"

"Wait a minute!" snapped Danzig in alarm.

"Oh, yes. Curb the imagination, please." Though Scobie was quick to utter sobrieties, they sounded drier than needful. "We know from probe transmissions the scarp is, well, Grand Canyon-like. Sure, it's more spectacular than we realized, which I suppose makes it still more of a mystery." He turned to Broberg. "I've never seen ice or snow as sculptured as this. Have you, Jean? You've mentioned visiting a lot of mountain and winter scenery when you were a girl in Canada."

The physicist shook her head. "No. Never. It doesn't seem possible. What could have done it? There's no weather here . . . is there?"

"Perhaps the same phenomenon is responsible that laid a hemisphere bare," Danzig suggested.

"Or that covered a hemisphere," Scobie said. "An object seventeen hundred kilometers across shouldn't have gases, frozen or otherwise. Unless it's a ball of such stuff clear through, like a comet, which we know it's not." As if to demonstrate, he unclipped a pair of pliers from a nearby tool rack, tossed it, and caught it on its slow way down. His own ninety kilos of mass weighed about seven. For that, the satellite must be essentially rocky.

Garcilaso registered impatience. "Let's stop tradin' facts and theories we already know about, and start findin' answers."

Rapture welled in Broberg. "Yes, let's get out. Over *there*."

"Hold on," protested Danzig as Garcilaso and Scobie nodded eagerly. "You can't be serious. Caution, step-by-step advance—"

"No, it's too wonderful for that." Broberg's tone shivered.

"Yeah, to hell with fiddlin' around," Garcilaso said. "We need at least a preliminary scout right away."

The furrows deepened in Danzig's visage. "You mean you too, Luis? But you're our pilot!"

"On the ground I'm general assistant, chief cook, and bottle washer to you scientists. Do you think I want to sit idle, with somethin' like that to explore?" Garcilaso calmed his voice. "Besides, if I should come to grief, any of you can fly back, given a bit of radio talk from *Chronos* and a final approach under remote control."

"It's quite reasonable, Mark," Scobie argued. "Contrary to doctrine, true; but doctrine was made for us, not vice versa. A short distance, low gravity, and we'll be on the lookout for hazards. The point is, until we have some notion of what that ice is like, we don't know what the devil to pay attention to in this vicinity, either. No, first we'll take a quick jaunt. When we return, then we'll plan."

Danzig stiffened. "May I remind you, if anything goes wrong, help is at least a hundred hours away? An auxiliary like this can't boost any higher if it's to get back, and it'd take longer than that to disengage the big boats from Saturn and Titan."

Scobie reddened at the implied insult. "And may I remind you: on the ground I am the captain. I say an immediate reconnaissance is safe and desirable. Stay behind if you want—In fact, yes, you must. Doctrine is right in saying the vessel mustn't be deserted."

Danzig studied him for several seconds before murmuring, "Luis goes, though, is that it?"

"Yes!" cried Garcilaso so that the cabin rang.

Broberg patted Danzig's limp hand. "It's okay, Mark," she said gently. "We'll bring back samples for you to study. After that, I wouldn't be surprised but what the best ideas about procedure will be yours."

He shook his head. Suddenly he looked very tired. "No," he replied in a monotone, "that won't happen. You see, I'm only a hardnosed industrial chemist who saw this expedition as a chance to do interesting research. The whole way through space, I kept myself busy with ordinary affairs, including, you remember, a couple of inventions I'd wanted the leisure to develop. You three, you're younger, you're romantics—"

"Aw, come off it, Mark." Scobie tried to laugh. "Maybe Jean and Luis are, a little, but me, I'm about as otherworldly as a plate of haggis."

"You played the game, year after year, until at last the game started playing you. That's what's going on this minute, no matter how you rationalize your motives." Danzig's gaze on the geologist, who was his friend, lost the defiance that had been in it and turned wistful. "You might try recalling Delia Ames."

Scobie bristled. "What about her? The business was hers and mine, nobody else's."

"Except afterward she cried on Rachel's shoulder, and Rachel doesn't keep secrets from me. Don't worry, I'm not about to blab. Anyhow, Delia got over it. But if you'd recollect objectively, you'd see what had happened to you, already three years ago."

Scobie set his jaw. Danzig smiled in the left corner of his mouth. "No, I suppose you can't," he went on. "I admit I had no idea either, till now, how far the process had gone. At least keep your fantasies in the background while you're outside, will you? Can you?"

In half a decade of travel, Scobie's apartment had become idiosyncratically his—perhaps more so than was usual, since he remained a bachelor who seldom had women visitors for longer than a few nightwatches at a time. Much of the furniture he had made himself; the agrosections of *Chronos* produced wood, hide, and fiber as well as food and fresh air. His handiwork ran to massiveness and archaic carved decorations. Most of what he wanted to read he screened from the data banks, of course, but a shelf held a few old books—Childe's border ballads, an eighteenth-century family Bible (despite his agnosticism), a copy of *The Machinery of Freedom*, which had nearly disintegrated but displayed the signature of the author, and other valued miscellany. Above them stood a model of a sailboat in which he had cruised Northern European waters, and a trophy he had won in handball aboard this ship. On the bulkheads hung his fencing sabers and numerous pictures—of parents and siblings, of wilderness areas he had tramped on Earth, of castles and mountains and heaths in Scotland where he had often been too, of his geological team on Luna, of Thomas Jefferson and, imagined, Robert the Bruce.

On a certain evenwatch he had, though, been seated before his telescreen. Lights were turned low in order that he might fully savor the image. Auxiliary craft were out in a joint exercise, and a couple of their personnel used the opportunity to beam back views of what they saw.

That was splendor. Starful space made a chalice for *Chronos*. The two huge, majestically counter-rotating cylinders, the entire complex of linkages, ports, locks, shields, collectors, transmitters, docks, all became Japanesely exquisite at a distance of several hundred kilometers. It was the solar sail which filled most of the screen, like a turning golden sun-wheel; yet remote vision could also appreciate its spiderweb intricacy, soaring and subtle curvatures, even the less-than-gossamer thinness. A mightier work than the Pyramids, a finer work than a refashioned chromosome, the ship moved on toward a Saturn which had become the second brightest beacon in the firmament.

The doorchime hauled Scobie out of his exhaltation. As he started across the deck, he stubbed his toe on a table leg. Coriolis force caused that. It was slight, when a hull this size spun to give a full gee of weight, and a thing to which he had long since adapted; but now and then he got so interested in something that Terrestrial habits returned. He swore at his absentmindedness, good-naturedly, since he anticipated a pleasurable time.

When he opened the door, Delia Ames entered in a single stride. At once she closed it behind her and stood braced against it. She was a tall blond woman who did electronics maintenance and kept up a number of outside activities. "Hey!" Scobie said. "What's wrong? You look like—" he tried for levity "—something my cat would've dragged in, if we had any mice or beached fish aboard."

She drew a ragged breath. Her Australian accent thickened till he had trouble understanding: "I . . . today . . . I happened to be at the same cafeteria table as George Harding—"

Unease tingled through Scobie. Harding worked in Ames's department but had much more in common with him. In the game group to which they both belonged,

Harding likewise took a vaguely ancestral role, N'Kuma the Lionslayer.

"What happened?" Scobie asked.

Woe stared back at him. "He mentioned . . . you and he and the rest . . . you'd be taking your next holiday together . . . to carry on your, your bloody act uninterrupted."

"Well, yes. Work at the new park over in Starboard Hull will be suspended till enough metal's been recycled for the water pipes. The area will be vacant, and my gang has arranged to spend a week's worth of days—"

"But you and I were going to Lake Armstrong!"

"Uh, wait, that was just a notion we talked about, no definite plan yet, and this is such an unusual chance— Later, sweetheart. I'm sorry." He took her hands. They felt cold. He essayed a smile. "Now, c'mon, we were going to cook a festive dinner together and afterward spend a, shall we say, quiet evening at home. But for a start, this absolutely gorgeous presentation on the screen—"

She jerked free of him. The gesture seemed to calm her. "No, thanks," she said, flat-voiced. "Not when you'd rather be with that Broberg woman. I only came by to tell you in person I'm getting out of the way of you two."

"*Huh?*" He stepped back. "What the flaming hell do you mean?"

"You know jolly well."

"I don't! She, I, she's happily married, got two kids, she's older than me, we're friends, sure, but there's never been a thing between us that wasn't in the open and on the level—" Scobie swallowed. "You suppose maybe I'm in love with her?"

Ames looked away. Her fingers writhed together. "I'm not about to go on being a mere convenience to you, Colin. You have plenty of those. Myself, I'd hoped— But I was wrong, and I'm going to cut my losses before they get worse."

"But . . . Dee, I swear I haven't fallen for anybody else, and I . . . I swear you're more than a body to me, you're a fine person—" She stood mute and withdrawn. Scobie gnawed his lip before he could tell her. "Okay, I admit it, the main reason I volunteered for this trip was I'd lost out in a love affair on Earth. Not that the project doesn't interest me, but I've come to realize what a big chunk out of my life it is. You, more than any other woman, Dee, you've gotten me to feel better about the situation."

She grimaced. "But not as much as your psychodrama has, right?"

"Hey, you must think I'm obsessed with the game. I'm not. It's fun and—oh, maybe 'fun' is too weak a word— but anyhow, it's just little bunches of people getting together fairly regularly to play. Like my fencing, or a chess club, or, or anything."

She squared her shoulders. "Well, then," she asked, "will you cancel the date you've made and spend your holiday with me?"

"I, uh, I can't do that. Not at this stage. Kendrick isn't off on the periphery of current events, he's closely involved with everybody else. If I didn't show, it'd spoil things for the rest."

Her glance steadied upon him. "Very well. A promise is a promise, or so I imagined. But afterward— Don't be afraid. I'm not trying to trap you. That would be no good, would it? However, if I maintain this liaison of ours, will you phase yourself out of your game?"

"I can't—" Anger seized him. "No, God damn it!" he roared.

"Then goodbye, Colin," she said, and departed. He stared for minutes at the door she had shut behind her.

Unlike the large Titan and Saturn-vicinity explorers, landers on the airless moons were simply modified Luna-to-space shuttles, reliable, but with limited capabilities. When the blocky shape had dropped below the horizon, Garcilaso said into his radio: "We've lost sight of the boat, Mark. I must say it improves the view." One of the relay microsatellites which had been sown in orbit passed his words on.

"Better start blazing your trail, then," Danzig reminded.

"My, my, you *are* a fussbudget, aren't you?" Nevertheless Garcilaso unholstered the squirt gun at his hip and splashed a vividly fluorescent circle of paint on the ground. He would do it at eyeball intervals until his party reached the glacier. Except where dust lay thick over the regolith, footprints were faint under the feeble gravity, and absent when a walker crossed continuous rock.

Walker? No, leaper. The three bounded exultant, little hindered by spacesuits, life support units, tool and ration packs. The naked land fled from their haste, and ever higher, ever clearer and more glorious to see, loomed the ice ahead of them.

There was no describing it, not really. You could speak of lower slopes and palisades above, to a mean height of perhaps a hundred meters, with spires towering farther still. You could speak of gracefully curved tiers going up those braes, of lacy parapets and fluted crags and arched openings to caves filled with wonders, of mysterious blues in the depths and greens where light streamed through translucencies, of gem-sparkle across whiteness where radiance and shadow wove mandalas—and none of it would convey anything more than Scobie's earlier, altogether inadequate comparison to the Grand Canyon.

"Stop," he said for the dozenth time. "I want to take a few pictures."

"Will anybody understand them who hasn't been here?" whispered Broberg.

"Probably not," said Garcilaso in the same hushed tone. "Maybe no one but us ever will."

"What do you mean by that?" demanded Danzig's voice.

"Never mind," snapped Scobie.

"I think I know," the chemist said. "Yes, it is a great piece of scenery, but you're letting it hypnotize you."

"If you don't cut out that drivel," Scobie warned, "we'll cut you out of the circuit. Damn it, we've got work to do. Get off our backs."

Danzig gusted a sigh. "Sorry. Uh, are you finding any clues to the nature of that—that thing?"

Scobie focused his camera. "Well," he said, partly mollified, "the different shades and textures, and no doubt the different shapes, seem to confirm what the reflection spectra from the flyby suggested. The composition is a mixture, or a jumble, or both, of several materials, and varies from place to place. Water ice is obvious, but I feel sure of carbon dioxide too, and I'd bet on ammonia, methane, and presumably lesser amounts of other stuff."

"Methane? Could that stay solid at ambient temperatures, in a vacuum?"

"We'll have to find out for sure. However, I'd guess that most of the time it's cold enough, at least for methane strata that occur down inside where there's pressure on them."

Within the vitryl globe of her helmet, Broberg's fea-

tures showed delight. "Wait!" she cried. "I have an idea—
about what happened to the probe that landed." She drew
a breath. "It came down almost at the foot of the glacier,
you recall. Our view of the site from space seemed to
indicate that an avalanche buried it, but we couldn't understand how that might have been triggered. Well, suppose
a methane layer at exactly the wrong location melted.
Heat radiation from the jets may have warmed it, and
later the radar beam used to map contours added the last
few degrees necessary. The stratum flowed, and down came
everything that had rested on top of it."

"Plausible," Scobie said. "Congratulations, Jean."

"Nobody thought of the possibility in advance?" Garcilaso scoffed. "What kind of scientists have we got along?"

"The kind who were being overwhelmed by work after
we reached Saturn, and still more by data input," Scobie
answered. "The universe is bigger than you or anybody
can realize, hotshot."

"Oh. Sure. No offense." Garcilaso's glance returned to
the ice. "Yes, we'll never run out of mysteries, will we?"

"Never." Broberg's eyes glowed enormous. "At the
heart of things will always be magic. The Elf King rules—"

Scobie returned his camera to its pouch. "Stow the gab
and move on," he ordered curtly.

His gaze locked for an instant with Broberg's. In the
weird, mingled light, it could be seen that she went pale,
then red, before she sprang off beside him.

*Ricia had gone alone into Moonwood on Midsummer
Eve. The King found her there and took her unto him as
she had hoped. Ecstasy became terror when he afterward
bore her off; yet her captivity in the City of Ice brought
her many more such hours, and beauties and marvels unknown among mortals. Alvarlan, her mentor, sent his spirit
in quest of her, and was himself beguiled by what he
found. It was an effort of will for him to tell Sir Kendrick
of the Isles where she was, albeit he pledged his help in
freeing her.*

*N'Kuma the Lionslayer, Béla of Eastmarch, Karina Far
West, Lady Aurelia, Olav Harpmaster had none of them
been present when this happened.*

The glacier (a wrong name for something that might
have no counterpart in the Solar System) lifted off the
plain abruptly as a wall. Standing there, the three could

no longer see the heights. They could, though, see that the slope which curved steeply upward to a filigree-topped edge was not smooth. Shadows lay blue in countless small craters. The sun had climbed just sufficiently high to beget them; an Iapetan day is more than seventy-nine of Earth's.

Danzig's question crackled in their earphones: "Now are you satisfied? Will you come back before a fresh landslide catches you?"

"It won't," Scobie replied. "We aren't a vehicle, and the local configuration has clearly been stable for centuries or better. Besides, what's the point of a manned expedition if nobody investigates anything?"

"I'll see if I can climb," Garcilaso offered.

"No wait," Scobie commanded. "I've had experience with mountains and snowpacks, for whatever that may be worth. Let me work out a route for us first."

"You're going onto that stuff, the whole gaggle of you?" exploded Danzig. "Have you completely lost your minds?"

Scobie's brow and lips tightened. "Mark, I warn you again, if you don't get your emotions under control we'll cut you off. We'll hike on a ways if I decide it's safe."

He paced back and forth, in floating low-weight fashion, while he surveyed the jökull. Layers and blocks of distinct substances were plain to see, like separate ashlars laid by an elvish mason—where they were not so huge that a giant must have been at work. The craterlets might be sentry posts on this lowest embankment of the City's defenses. . . .

Garcilaso, most vivacious of men, stood motionless and let his vision lose itself in the sight. Broberg knelt down to examine the ground, but her own gaze kept wandering aloft.

Finally she beckoned. "Colin, come over here, please," she said. "I believe I've made a discovery."

Scobie joined her. As she rose, she scooped a handful of fine black particles off the shards on which she stood and let it trickle from her glove. "I suspect this is the reason the boundary of the ice is sharp," she told him.

"What is?" Danzig inquired from afar. He got no answer.

"I noticed more and more dust as we went along," Broberg continued. "If it fell on patches and lumps of frozen stuff, isolated from the main mass, and covered them, it would absorb solar heat till they melted or, likelier, sublimed. Even water molecules would escape to space, in this weak gravity. The main mass was too big for that; square-cube law. Dust grains there would simply melt their way down a short distance, then be covered as surrounding material collapsed on them, and the process would stop."

"H'm." Scobie raised a hand to stroke his chin, encountered his helmet, and sketched a grin at himself. "Sounds reasonable. But where did so much dust come from—and the ice, for that matter?"

"I think—" Her voice dropped until he could barely hear, and her look went the way of Garcilaso's. His remained upon her face, profiled against stars. "I think this bears out your comet hypothesis, Colin. A comet struck Iapetus. It came from the direction it did because it got so near Saturn that it was forced to swing in a hairpin bend around the planet. It was enormous; the ice of it covered almost a hemisphere, in spite of much more being vaporized and lost. The dust is partly from it, partly generated by the impact."

He clasped her armored shoulder. "*Your* theory, Jean. I was not the first to propose a comet, but you're the first to corroborate with details."

She didn't appear to notice, except that she murmured further. "Dust can account for the erosion that made those lovely formations, too. It caused differential melting and sublimation on the surface, according to the patterns it happened to fall in and the mixes of ices it clung to, until it was washed away or encysted. The craters, these small ones and the major ones we've observed from above, they have a separate but similar origin. Meteorites—"

"Whoa, there," he objected. "Any sizable meteorite would release enough energy to steam off most of the entire field."

"I know. Which shows the comet collision was recent, less than a thousand years ago, or we wouldn't be seeing this miracle today. Nothing big has since happened to strike, yet. I'm thinking of little stones, cosmic sand, in prograde orbits around Saturn so that they hit with low relative speed. Most simply make dimples in the ice. Lying there, however, they collect solar heat because they're dark, and re-radiate it to melt away their surroundings, till they sink beneath. The concavities they leave reflect incident radiation from side to side, and thus continue to grow. The pothole effect. And again, because the different ices have different properties, you don't get perfectly smooth craters, but those fantastic bowls we saw before we landed."

"By God!" Scobie hugged her. "You're a genius."

Helmet against helmet, she smiled and said, "No. It's obvious, once you've seen for yourself." She was quiet for a bit while still they held each other. "Scientific intuition is a funny thing, I admit," she went on at last. "Considering the problem, I was hardly aware of my logical mind. What I thought was—the City of Ice, made with starstones out of that which a god called down from heaven—"

"Jesus Maria!" Garcilaso spun about to stare at them.

Scobie released the woman. "We'll go after confirmation," he said unsteadily. "To the large crater we spotted a few klicks inward. The surface appears quite safe to walk on."

"I called that crater the Elf King's Dance Hall," Broberg mused, as if a dream were coming back to her.

"Have a care." Garcilaso's laugh rattled. "Heap big medicine yonder. The King is only an inheritor; it was giants who built these walls, for the gods."

"Well, I've got to find a way in, don't I?" Scobie responded.

"Indeed," *Alvarlan says.* "I cannot guide you from this point. My spirit can only see through mortal eyes. I can but lend you my counsel, until we have neared the gates."

"Are you sleepwalking in that fairy tale of yours?" Danzig yelled. "Come back before you get yourselves killed!"

"Will you dry up?" Scobie snarled. "It's nothing but a style of talk we've got between us. If you can't understand that, you've got less use of your brain than we do."

"Listen, won't you? I didn't say you're crazy. You don't have delusions or anything like that. I do say you've steered your fantasies toward this kind of place, and now the reality has reinforced them till you're under a compulsion you don't recognize. Would you go ahead so recklessly anywhere else in the universe? Think!"

"That does it. We'll resume contact after you've had time to improve your manners." Scobie snapped off his main radio switch. The circuits that stayed active served for close-by communication but had no power to reach an orbital relay. His companions did likewise.

The three faced the awesomeness before them. "You can help me find the Princess when we are inside, Alvarlan," *Kendrick says.*

"That I can and will," *the sorcerer vows.*

"I wait for you, most steadfast of my lovers," *Ricia croons.*

Alone in the spacecraft, Danzig well-nigh sobbed, "Oh, damn that game forever!" The sound fell away into emptiness.

III

To condemn psychodrama, even in its enhanced form, would be to condemn human nature.

It begins in childhood. Play is necessary to an immature mammal, a means of learning to handle the body, the perceptions, and the outside world. The young human plays, must play, with its brain too. The more intelligent the child, the more its imagination needs exercise. There are degrees of activity, from the passive watching of a show on a screen, onward through reading, daydreaming, storytelling, and psychodrama . . . for which the child has no such fancy name.

We cannot give this behavior any single description, for the shape and course it takes depends on an endless number of variables. Sex, age, culture, and companions are only the most obvious. For example, in pre-electronic North America little girls would often play "house" while little boys played "cowboys and Indians" or "cops and robbers," whereas nowadays a mixed group of their descendants might play "dolphins" or "astronauts and aliens." In essence, a small band forms, and each individual makes up a character to portray or borrows one from fiction. Simple props may be employed, such as toy weapons, or a chance object—a stick, for instance—may be declared something else such as a metal detector, or a thing may be quite imaginary, as the scenery almost always is. The children then act out a drama which they compose as they go along. When they cannot physically perform a certain action, they describe it. ("I jump real high, like you can do on Mars, an' come out over the edge o' that ol' Valles Marineris, an' take that bandit by surprise.") A large cast of characters, especially villains, frequently comes into existence by fiat.

The most imaginative member of the troupe dominates the game and the evolution of the story line, though in a rather subtle fashion, through offering the most vivid possibilities. The rest, however, are brighter than average; psychodrama in this highly developed form does not appeal to everybody.

For those to whom it does, the effects are beneficial and lifelong. Besides increasing their creativity through use, it lets them try out a play version of different adult roles and experiences. Thereby they begin to acquire insight into adulthood.

Such playacting ends when adolescence commences, if not earlier—but only in that form, and not necessarily forever in it. Grown-ups have many dream-games. This is plain to see in lodges, for example, with their titles, costumes, and ceremonies; but does it not likewise animate all pageantry, every ritual? To what extent are our heroisms, sacrifices, and self-aggrandizements the acting out of personae that we maintain? Some thinkers have attempted to trace this element through every aspect of society.

Here, though, we are concerned with overt psychodrama among adults. In Western civilization it first appeared on a noticeable scale during the middle twentieth century. Psychiatrists found it a powerful diagnostic and therapeutic technique. Among ordinary folk, war and fantasy games, many of which involved identification with imaginary or historical characters, became increasingly popular. In part this was doubtless a retreat from the restrictions and menaces of that unhappy period, but likely in larger part it was a revolt of the mind against the inactive entertainment, notably television, which had come to dominate recreation.

The Chaos ended those activities. Everybody knows about their revival in recent times—for healthier reasons, one hopes. By projecting three-dimensional scenes and appropriate sounds from a data bank—or, better yet, by having a computer produce them to order—players gained a sense of reality that intensified their mental and emotional commitment. Yet in those games that went on for episode after episode, year after real-time year, whenever two or more members of a group could get together to play, they found themselves less and less dependent on such appurtenances. It seemed that, through practice, they had regained the vivid imaginations of their childhoods, and could make anything, or airy nothing itself, into the objects and the worlds they desired.

I have deemed it necessary thus to repeat the obvious in order that we may see it in perspective. The news beamed from Saturn has brought widespread revulsion. (Why? What buried fears have been touched? This is subject matter for potentially important research.) Overnight, adult psychodrama has become unpopular; it may become extinct. That would, in many ways, be a worse tragedy than what has occurred yonder. There is no reason to suppose that the game ever harmed any mentally sound person on Earth; on the contrary. Beyond doubt, it has helped astronauts stay sane and alert on long, difficult missions. If it has no more medical use, that is because psychotherapy has become a branch of applied biochemistry.

And this last fact, the modern world's dearth of experience with madness, is at the root of what happened. Although he could not have foreseen the exact outcome, a twentieth-century psychiatrist might have warned against spending eight years, an unprecedented stretch of time, in as strange an environment as the *Chronos*. Strange it certainly has been, despite all efforts—limited, totally man-controlled, devoid of countless cues for which our evolution on Earth has fashioned us. Extraterrestrial colonists have, thus far, had available to them any number of simulations and compensations, of which close, full contact with home and frequent opportunities to visit there are probably the most significant. Sailing time to Jupiter was long, but half of that to Saturn. Moreover, because they were earlier, scientists in the *Zeus* had much research to occupy them en route, which it would be pointless for later travelers to duplicate; by then, the interplanetary medium between the two giants held few surprises.

Contemporary psychologists were aware of this. They understood that the persons most adversely affected would be the most intelligent, imaginative, and dynamic—those who were supposed to make the very discoveries at Saturn which were the purpose of the undertaking. Being less familiar than their predecessors with the labyrinth that lies, Minotaur-haunted, beneath every human consciousness, the psychologists expected purely benign consequences of whatever psychodramas the crew engendered.

—Minamoto

Assignments to teams had not been made in advance of departure. It was sensible to let professional capabilities reveal themselves and grow on the voyage, while personal relationships did the same. Eventually such factors would help in deciding what individuals should train for what tasks. Long-term participation in a group of players normally forged bonds of friendship that were desirable, if the members were otherwise qualified.

In real life, Scobie always observed strict propriety toward Broberg. She was attractive, but she was monogamous, and he had no wish to alienate her. Besides, he liked her husband. (Tom did not partake of the game. As an astronomer, he had plenty to keep his attention happily engaged.) They had played for a couple of years, and their group had acquired as many characters as it could accommodate in a narrative whose milieu and people were becoming complex, before Scobie and Broberg spoke of anything intimate.

By then, the story they enacted was doing so, and maybe it was not altogether by chance that they met when both had several idle hours. This was in the weightless recreation area at the spin axis. They tumbled through aerobatics, shouting and laughing, until they were pleasantly tired, went to the clubhouse, turned in their wingsuits, and showered. They had not seen each other nude before; neither commented, but he did not hide his enjoyment of the sight, while she colored and averted her glance as tactfully as she was able. Afterward, their clothes resumed, they decided on a drink before they went home, and sought the lounge.

Since evenwatch was approaching nightwatch, they had the place to themselves. At the bar, he thumbed a chit for Scotch, she for Pinot Chardonnay. The machine obliged them and they carried their refreshments out onto the balcony. Seated at a table, they looked across immensity. The clubhouse was built into the support frame on a Lunar gravity level. Above them they saw the sky wherein they had been as birds; its reach did not seem any more hemmed in by far-spaced, spidery girders than it was by a few drifting clouds. Beyond, and straight ahead, decks op-

posite were a commingling of masses and shapes which
the scant illumination at this hour turned into mystery.
Among those shadows the humans made out woods,
brooks, pools, turned hoary or agleam by the light of stars
which filled the skyview strips. Right and left, the hull
stretched off beyond sight, a dark in which such lamps as
there were appeared lost.

The air was cool, slightly jasmine-scented, drenched
with silence. Underneath and throughout, subliminally,
throbbed the myriad pulses of the ship.

"Magnificent," Broberg said low, gazing outward. "What
a surprise."

"Eh?" asked Scobie.

"I've only been here before in daywatch. I didn't anticipate a simple rotation of the reflectors would make it wonderful."

"Oh, I wouldn't sneer at the daytime view. Mighty impressive."

"Yes, but—but then you see too plainly that everything
is man-made, nothing is wild or unknown or free. The
sun blots out the stars; it's as though no universe existed
beyond this shell we're in. Tonight is like being in Maranoa," *the kingdom of which Ricia is Princess, a kingdom
of ancient things and ways, wildernesses, enchantments.*

"H'm, yeah, sometimes I feel trapped myself," Scobie
admitted. "I thought I had a journey's worth of geological
data to study, but my project isn't going anywhere very
interesting."

"Same for me." Broberg straightened where she sat,
turned to him, and smiled a trifle. The dusk softened her
features, made them look young. "Not that we're entitled
to self-pity. Here we are, safe and comfortable till we
reach Saturn. After that we should never lack for excitement, or for material to work with on the way home."

"True." Scobie raised his glass. "Well, skoal. Hope I'm
not mispronouncing that."

"How should I know?" she laughed. "My maiden name
was Almyer."

"That's right, you've adopted Tom's surname. I wasn't
thinking. Though that is rather unusual these days, hey?"

She spread her hands. "My family was well-to-do, but
they were—are—Jerusalem Catholics. Strict about certain
things; archaistic, you might say." She lifted her wine and

sipped. "Oh, yes, I've left the Church, but in several ways the Church will never leave me."

"I see. Not to pry, but, uh, this does account for some traits of yours I couldn't help wondering about."

She regarded him over the rim of her glass. "Like what?"

"Well, you've got a lot of life in you, vigor, a sense of fun, but you're also—what's the word?—uncommonly domestic. You've told me you were a quiet faculty member of Yukon University till you married Tom." Scobie grinned. "Since you two kindly invited me to your last anniversary party, and I know your present age, I deduced that you were thirty then." Unmentioned was the likelihood that she had still been a virgin. "Nevertheless—oh, forget it. I said I don't want to pry."

"Go ahead, Colin," she urged. "That line from Burns sticks in my mind, since you introduced me to his poetry. 'To see ourselves as others see us!' Since it looks as if we may visit the same moon—"

Scobie took a hefty dollop of Scotch. "Aw, nothing much," he said, unwontedly diffident. "If you must know, well, I have the impression that being in love wasn't the single good reason you had for marrying Tom. He'd already been accepted for this expedition, and given your personal qualifications, that would get you in too. In short, you'd grown tired of routine respectability and here was how you could kick over the traces. Am I right?"

"Yes." Her gaze dwelt on him. "You're more perceptive than I supposed."

"No, not really. A roughneck rockhound. But Ricia's made it plain to see that you're more than a demure wife, mother, and scientist—" She parted her lips. He raised a palm. "No, please, let me finish. I know it's bad manners to claim somebody's persona is a wish fulfillment, and I'm not doing that. Of course you don't want to be a free-roving, free-loving female scamp, any more than I want to ride around cutting down assorted enemies. Still, if you'd been born and raised in the world of our game, I feel sure you'd be a lot like Ricia. And that potential is part of you, Jean." He tossed off his drink. "If I've said too much, please excuse me. Want a refill?"

"I'd better not, but don't let me stop you."

"You won't." He rose and bounded off.

When he returned, he saw that she had been observing

him through the vitryl door. As he sat down, she smiled, leaned a bit across the table, and told him softly: "I'm glad you said what you did. Now I can declare what a complicated man Kendrick reveals you to be."

"What?" Scobie asked in honest surprise. "Come on! He's a sword-and-shield tramp, a fellow who likes to travel, same as me; and in my teens I was a brawler, same as him."

"He may lack polish, but he's a chivalrous knight, a compassionate overlord, a knower of sagas and traditions, an appreciator of poetry and music, a bit of a bard. . . . Ricia misses him. When will he get back from his latest quest?"

"I'm bound home this minute. N'Kuma and I gave those pirates the slip and landed at Haverness two days ago. After we buried the swag, he wanted to visit Béla and Karina and join them in whatever they've been up to, so we bade goodbye for the time being." Scobie and Harding had lately taken a few hours to conclude that adventure of theirs. The rest of the group had been mundanely occupied for some while.

Broberg's eyes widened. "From Haverness to the Isles? But I'm in Castle Devaranda, right in between."

"I hoped you'd be."

"I can't wait to hear your story."

"I'm pushing on after dark. The moon is bright and I've got a pair of remounts I bought with a few gold pieces from the loot." *The dust rolls white beneath drumming hoofs. Where a horseshoe strikes a flint pebble, sparks fly ardent. Kendrick scowls.* "You, aren't you with . . . what's his name? . . . Joran the Red? I don't like him."

"I sent him packing a month ago. He got the idea that sharing my bed gave him authority over me. It was never anything but a romp. I stand alone on the Gerfalcon Tower, looking south over moonlit fields, and wonder how you fare. The road flows toward me like a gray river. Do I see a rider come at a gallop, far and far away?"

After many months of play, no image on a screen was necessary. *Pennons on the night wind stream athwart the stars.* "I arrive. I sound my horn to rouse the gatekeepers."

"How I do remember those merry notes—"

That same night, Kendrick and Ricia become lovers. Experienced in the game and careful of its etiquette, Scobie and Broberg uttered no details about the union; they did not touch each other and maintained only fleeting eye contact; the ultimate goodnights were very decorous. After all, this was a story they composed about two fictitious characters in a world that never was.

The lower slopes of the jökull rose in tiers which were themselves deeply concave; the humans walked around their rims and admired the extravagant formations beneath. Names sprang onto lips: the Frost Garden, the Ghost Bridge, the Snow Queen's Throne, *while Kendrick advances into the City, and Ricia awaits him at the Dance Hall, and the spirit of Alvarlan carries word between them so that it is as if already she too travels beside her knight.* Nevertheless they proceeded warily, vigilant for signs of danger, especially whenever a change of texture or hue or anything else in the surface underfoot betokened a change in its nature.

Above the highest ledge reared a cliff too sheer to scale, Iapetan gravity or no, *the fortress wall.* However, from orbit the crew had spied a gouge in the vicinity, forming a pass, doubtless plowed by a small meteorite *in the war between the gods and the magicians, when stones chanted down from the sky wrought havoc so accursed that none dared afterward rebuild.* That was an eerie climb, hemmed in by heights which glimmered in the blue twilight they cast, heaven narrowed to a belt between them where stars seemed to blaze doubly brilliant.

"There must be guards at the opening," *Kendrick says.*

"A single guard," *answers the mind-whisper of Alvarlan,* "but he is a dragon. If you did battle with him, the noise and flame would bring every warrior here upon you. Fear not. I'll slip into his burnin' brain and weave him such a dream that he'll never see you."

"The King might sense the spell," *says Ricia through him.* "Since you'll be parted from us anyway while you ride the soul of that beast, Alvarlan, I'll seek him out and distract him."

Kendrick grimaces, knowing full well what means are hers to do that. She has told him how she longs for freedom and her knight; she has also hinted that elven lovemaking transcends the human. Does she wish for a final time before her rescue? . . . Well, Ricia and Kendrick have neither plighted nor practiced single troth. Assuredly Colin

Scobie had not. He jerked forth a grin and continued through the silence that had fallen on all three.

They came out on top of the glacial mass and looked around them. Scobie whistled. Garcilaso stammered, "I-I-Jesus Christ!" Broberg smote her hands together.

Below them the precipice fell to the ledges, whose sculpturing took on a wholly new, eldritch aspect, gleam and shadow, until it ended at the plain. Seen from here aloft, the curvature of the moon made toes strain downward in boots, as if to cling fast and not be spun off among the stars which surrounded, rather than shone above, its ball. The spacecraft stood minute on dark, pocked stone, like a cenotaph raised to loneliness.

Eastward the ice reached beyond an edge of sight which was much closer. ("Yonder could be the rim of the world," Garcilaso said, and *Ricia replies,* "Yes, the City is nigh to there.") Bowls of different sizes, hillocks, crags, no two of them eroded the same way, turned its otherwise level stretch into a surreal maze. An arabesque openwork ridge which stood at the explorers' goal overtopped the horizon. Everything that was illuminated lay gently aglow. Radiant though the sun was, it cast the light of only, perhaps, five thousand full Lunas upon Earth. Southward, Saturn's great semidisc gave about one-half more Lunar shining; but in that direction, the wilderness sheened pale amber.

Scobie shook himself. "Well, shall we go?" His prosaic question jarred the others; Garcilaso frowned and Broberg winced.

She recovered. "Yes, hasten," *Ricia says.* "I am by myself once more. Are you out of the dragon, Alvarlan?"

"Aye," *the wizard informs her.* "Kendrick is safely behind a ruined palace. Tell us how best to reach you."

"You are at the time-gnawed Crown House. Before you lies the Street of the Shieldsmiths—"

Scobie's brows knitted. "It is noonday, when elves do not fare abroad," *Kendrick says* remindingly, commandingly. "I do not wish to encounter any of them. No fights, no complications. We are going to fetch you and escape, without further trouble."

Broberg and Garcilaso showed disappointment, but understood him. A game broke down when a person refused to accept something that a fellow player tried to put in. Often the narrative threads were not mended and picked up for many days. Broberg sighed.

"Follow the street to its end at a forum where a snow fountain springs," *Ricia directs*. "Cross, and continue on Aleph Zain Boulevard. You will know it by a gateway in the form of a skull with open jaws. If anywhere you see a rainbow flicker in the air, stand motionless until it has gone by, for it will be an auroral wolf. . . ."

At a low-gravity lope, the distance took some thirty minutes to cover. In the later part, the three were forced to detour by great banks of an ice so fine-grained that it slid about under their bootsoles and tried to swallow them. Several of these lay at irregular intervals around their destination.

There the travelers stood again for a time in the grip of awe.

The bowl at their feet must reach down almost to bedrock, a hundred meters, and was twice as wide. On this rim lifted the wall they had seen from the cliff, an arc fifty meters long and high, nowhere thicker than five meters, pierced by intricate scrollwork, greenly agleam where it was not translucent. It was the uppermost edge of a stratum which made serrations down the crater. Other outcrops and ravines were more dreamlike yet . . . was that a unicorn's head, was that a colonnade of caryatids, was that an icicle bower . . . ? The depths were a lake of cold blue shadow.

"You have come, Kendrick, beloved!" *cries Ricia, and casts herself into his arms.*

"Quiet," *warns the sending of Alvarlan the wise.* "Rouse not our immortal enemies."

"Yes, we must get back." Scobie blinked. "Judas priest, what possessed us? Fun is fun, but we sure have come a lot farther and faster than was smart, haven't we?"

"Let us stay for a little while," Broberg pleaded. "This is such a miracle—the Elf King's Dance Hall, which the Lord of the Dance built for him—"

"Remember, if we stay we'll be caught, and your captivity may be forever." Scobie thumbed his main radio switch. "Hello, Mark? Do you read me?"

Neither Broberg nor Garcilaso made that move. They did not hear Danzig's voice: "Oh, yes! I've been hunkered over the set gnawing my knuckles. How are you?"

"All right. We're at the big hole and will be heading back as soon as I've gotten a few pictures."

"They haven't made words to tell how relieved I am. From a scientific standpoint, was it worth the risk?"

Scobie gasped. He stared before him.

"Colin?" Danzig called. "You still there?"

"Yes. Yes."

"I asked what observations of any importance you made."

"I don't know," Scobie mumbled. "I can't remember. None of it after we started climbing seems real."

"Better you return right away," Danzig said grimly. "Forget about photographs."

"Correct." Scobie addressed his companions: "Forward march."

"I can't," *Alvarlan answers*. "A wanderin' spell has caught my spirit in tendrils of smoke."

"I know where a fire dagger is kept," *Ricia says*. "I'll try to steal it."

Broberg moved ahead, as though to descend into the crater. Tiny ice grains trickled over the verge from beneath her boots. She could easily lose her footing and slide down.

"No, wait," *Kendrick shouts to her*. "No need. My spearhead is of moon alloy. It can cut—"

The glacier shuddered. The ridge cracked asunder and fell in shards. The area on which the humans stood split free and toppled into the bowl. An avalanche poured after. High-flung crystals caught sunlight, glittered prismatic in challenge to the stars, descended slowly and lay quiet.

Except for shock waves through solids, everything had happened in the absolute silence of space.

Heartbeat by heartbeat, Scobie crawled back to his senses. He found himself held down, immobilized, in darkness and pain. His armor had saved, was still saving his life; he had been stunned but escaped a real concussion. Yet every breath hurt abominably. A rib or two on the left side seemed broken; a monstrous impact must have dented metal. And he was buried under more weight than he could move.

"Hello," he coughed. "Does anybody read me?" The single reply was the throb of his blood. If his radio still worked—which it should, being built into the suit—the mass around him screened him off.

It also sucked heat at an unknown but appalling rate.

He felt no cold because the electrical system drew energy from his fuel cell as fast as needed to keep him warm and to recycle his air chemically. As a normal thing, when he lost heat through the slow process of radiation—and, a trifle, through kerofoam-lined bootsoles—the latter demand was much the greater. Now conduction was at work on every square centimeter. He had a spare unit in the equipment on his back, but no means of getting at it.

Unless— He barked forth a chuckle. Straining, he felt the stuff that entombed him yield the least bit under the pressure of arms and legs. And his helmet rang slightly with noise, a rustle, a gurgle. This wasn't water ice that imprisoned him, but stuff with a much lower freezing point. He was melting it, subliming it, making room for himself.

If he lay passive, he would sink, while frozenness above slid down to keep him in his grave. He might evoke superb new formations, but he would not see them. Instead, he must use the small capability given him to work his way upward, scrabble, get a purchase on matter that was not yet aflow, burrow to the stars.

He began.

Agony soon racked him. Breath rasped in and out of lungs aflame. His strength drained away and trembling took its place, and he could not tell whether he ascended or slipped back. Blind, half-suffocated, Scobie made mole claws of his hands and dug.

It was too much to endure. He fled from it—

His strong enchantments failing, the Elf King brought down his towers of fear in wreck. If the spirit of Alvarlan returned to its body, the wizard would brood upon things he had seen, and understand what they meant, and such knowledge would give mortals a terrible power against Faerie. Waking from sleep, the King scryed Kendrick about to release that fetch. There was no time to do more than break the spell which upheld the Dance Hall. It was largely built of mist and starshine, but enough blocks quarried from the cold side of Ginnungagap were in it that when they crashed they should kill the knight. Ricia would perish too, and in his quicksilver intellect the King regretted that. Nevertheless he spoke the necessary word.

He did not comprehend how much abuse flesh and bone can bear. Sir Kendrick fights his way clear of the ruins, to

*seek and save his lady. While he does, he heartens himself
with thoughts of adventures past and future—*

—and suddenly the blindness broke apart and Saturn
stood lambent within rings.

Scobie belly flopped onto the surface and lay shuddering.

He must rise, no matter how his injuries screamed, lest
he melt himself a new burial place. He lurched to his feet
and glared around.

Little but outcroppings and scars was left of the sculpture. For the most part, the crater had become a smooth-sided whiteness under heaven. Scarcity of shadows made
distances hard to gauge, but Scobie guessed the new depth
was about seventy-five meters. And empty, empty.

"Mark, do you hear?" he cried.

"That you, Colin?" rang in his earpieces. "Name of
mercy, what's happened? I heard you call out, and saw a
cloud rise and sink . . . then nothing for more than an
hour. Are you okay?"

"I am, sort of. I don't see Jean or Luis. A landslide took
us by surprise and buried us. Hold on while I search."

When he stood upright, Scobie's ribs hurt less. He could
move about rather handily if he took care. The two types
of standard analgesic in his kit were alike useless, one too
weak to give noticeable relief, one so strong that it would
turn him sluggish. Casting to and fro, he soon found what
he expected, a concavity in the tumbled snowlike material,
slightly aboil.

Also a standard part of his gear was a trenching tool.
Scobie set pain aside and dug. A helmet appeared. Broberg's head was within it. She too had been tunneling out.

"Jean!"

"Kendrick!" She crept free and they embraced, suit to
suit. "Oh, Colin."

"How are you?" rattled from him.

"Alive," she answered. "No serious harm done, I think.
A lot to be said for low gravity . . . You? Luis?" Blood
was clotted in a streak beneath her nose, and a bruise on
her forehead was turning purple, but she stood firmly and
spoke clearly.

"I'm functional. Haven't found Luis yet. Help me look.
First, though, we'd better check out our equipment."

She hugged arms around chest, as if that would do any
good here. "I'm chilled," she admitted.

Scobie pointed at a telltale. "No wonder. Your fuel cell's down to its last couple of ergs. Mine isn't in a lot better shape. Let's change."

They didn't waste time removing their backpacks, but reached into each other's. Tossing the spent units to the ground, where vapors and holes immediately appeared and then froze, they plugged the fresh ones into their suits. "Turn your thermostat down," Scobie advised. "We won't find shelter soon. Physical activity will help us keep warm."

"And require faster air recycling," Broberg reminded.

"Yeah. But for the moment, at least, we can conserve the energy in the cells. Okay, next let's check for strains, potential leaks, any kind of damage or loss. Hurry. Luis is still down there."

Inspection was a routine made automatic by years of drill. While her fingers searched across the man's space-suit, Broberg let her eyes wander. "The Dance Hall is gone," *Ricia murmurs*. "I think the King smashed it to prevent our escape."

"Me too. If he finds out we're alive, and seeking for Alvarlan's soul— Hey, wait! None of that!"

Danzig's voice quavered. "How're you doing?"

"We're in fair shape, seems like," Scobie replied. "My corselet took a beating but didn't split or anything. Now to find Luis . . . Jean, suppose you spiral right, I left, across the crater floor."

It took awhile, for the seething which marked Garci-laso's burial was miniscule. Scobie started to dig. Broberg watched how he moved, heard how he breathed, and said, "Give me that tool. Just where are you bunged up, any-way?"

He admitted his condition and stepped back. Crusty chunks flew from Broberg's toil. She progressed fast, since whatever kind of ice lay at this point was, luckily, friable, and under Iapetan gravity she could cut a hole with almost vertical sides.

"I'll make myself useful," Scobie said, "namely, find us a way out."

When he started up the nearest slope, it shivered. All at once he was borne back in a tide that made rustly noises through his armor, while a fog of dry white motes blinded him. Painfully, he scratched himself free at the bottom and tried elsewhere. In the end he could report to Danzig: "I'm afraid there is no easy route. When the rim collapsed where we stood, it did more than produce a shock which wrecked the delicate formations throughout the crater. It let tons of stuff pour down from the surface—a particular sort of ice that, under local conditions, is like fine sand. The walls are covered by it. Most places, it lies meters deep over more stable material. We'd slide faster than we could climb, where the layer is thin; where it's thick, we'd sink."

Danzig sighed. "I guess I get to take a nice, healthy hike."

"I assume you've called for help."

"Of course. They'll have two boats here in about a hundred hours. The best they can manage. You knew that already."

"Uh-huh. And our fuel cells are good for perhaps fifty hours."

"Oh, well not to worry about that. I'll bring extras and toss them to you, if you're stuck till the rescue party arrives. M-m-m . . . maybe I'd better rig a slingshot or something first."

"You might have a problem locating us. This isn't a true crater, it's a glorified pothole, the lip of it flush with the top of the glacier. The landmark we guided ourselves by, that fancy ridge, is gone."

"No big deal. I've got a bearing on you from the directional antenna, remember. A magnetic compass may be no use here, but I can keep myself oriented by the heavens. Saturn scarcely moves in this sky, and the sun and the stars don't move fast."

"Damn! You're right. I wasn't thinking. Got Luis on my mind, if nothing else." Scobie looked across the bleakness toward Broberg. Perforce she was taking a short rest, stoop-shouldered above her excavation. His earpieces brought him the harsh sound in her windpipe.

He must maintain what strength was left him, against later need. He sipped from his water nipple, pushed a bite of food through his chowlock, pretended an appetite. "I may as well try reconstructing what happened," he said. "Okay, Mark, you were right, we got crazy reckless. The game— Eight years was too long to play the game, in an environment that gave us too few reminders of reality. But who could have foreseen it? My God, warn *Chronos*! I happen to know that one of the Titan teams started playing an expedition to the merfolk under the Crimson Ocean

—on account of the red mists—deliberately, like us, before they set off. . . ."

Scobie gulped. "Well," he slogged on, "I don't suppose we'll ever know exactly what went wrong here. But plain to see, the configuration was only metastable. On Earth, too, avalanches can be fatally easy to touch off. I'd guess at a methane layer underneath the surface. It turned a little slushy when temperatures rose after dawn, but that didn't matter in low gravity and vacuum—till we came along. Heat, vibration— Anyhow, the stratum slid out from under us, which triggered a general collapse. Does that guess seem reasonable?"

"Yes, to an amateur like me," Danzig said. "I admire how you can stay academic under these circumstances."

"I'm being practical," Scobie retorted. "Luis may need medical attention earlier than those boats can come for him. If so, how do we get him to ours?"

Danzig's voice turned stark. "Any ideas?"

"I'm fumbling my way toward that. Look, the bowl still has the same basic form. The whole shebang didn't cave in. That implies hard material, water ice and actual rock. In fact, I see a few remaining promontories, jutting out above the sandlike stuff. As for what it is—maybe an ammonia-carbon dioxide combination, maybe more exotic —that'll be for you to discover later. Right now . . . my geological instruments should help me trace where the solid masses are least deeply covered. We all have trenching tools, so we can try to shovel a path clear, along a zigzag of least effort. That may bring more garbage slipping down on us from above, but that in turn may expedite our progress. Where the uncovered shelves are too steep or slippery to climb, we can chip footholds. Slow and tough work; and we may run into a bluff higher than we can jump, or something like that."

"I can help," Danzig proposed. "While I waited to hear from you, I inventoried our stock of spare cable, cord, equipment I can cannibalize for wire, clothes and bedding I can cut into strips—whatever might be knotted together to make a rope. We won't need much tensile strength. Well, I estimate I can get about forty meters. According to your description, that's about half the slope length of that trap you're in. If you can climb halfway up while I trek there, I can haul you the rest of the way."

"Thanks, Mark," Scobie said, "although—"

"Luis!" shrieked in his helmet. "Colin, come fast, help me, this is dreadful!"

Regardless of the pain, except for a curse or two, Scobie sped to Broberg's aid.

Garcilaso was not quite unconscious. In that lay much of the horror. They heard him mumble, "—Hell, the King threw my soul into Hell. I can't find my way out, I'm lost. If only Hell weren't so cold—" They could not see his face; the inside of his helmet was crusted with frost. Deeper and longer buried than the others, badly hurt in addition, he would have died shortly after his fuel cell was exhausted. Broberg had uncovered him barely in time, if that.

Crouched in the shaft she had dug, she rolled him over onto his belly. His limbs flopped about and he babbled, "A demon attacks me. I'm blind here but I feel the wind of its wings." in a blurred monotone. She unplugged the energy unit and tossed it aloft, saying, "We should return this to the ship if we can."

Above, Scobie gave the object a morbid stare. It didn't even retain the warmth to make a little vapor, like his and hers, but lay quite inert. Its case was a metal box, thirty centimeters by fifteen by six, featureless except for two plug-in prongs on one of the broad sides. Controls built into the spacesuit circuits allowed you to start and stop the chemical reactions within and regulate their rate manually; but as a rule you left that chore to your thermostat and aerostat. Now those reactions had run their course. Until it was recharged, the cell was merely a lump.

Scobie leaned over to watch Broberg, some ten meters below him. She had extracted the reserve unit from Garcilaso's gear, inserted it properly at the small of his back, and secured it by clips on the bottom of his packframe. "Let's have your contribution, Colin," she said. Scobie dropped the meter of heavy-gauge insulated wire which was standard issue on extravehicular missions, in case you needed to make a special electrical connection or a repair. She joined it by Western Union splices to the two she already had, made a loop at the end and, awkwardly reaching over her left shoulder, secured the opposite end by a hitch to the top of her packframe. The triple strand bobbed above her like an antenna.

Stooping, she gathered Garcilaso in her arms. The

Iapetan weight of him and his apparatus was under ten kilos, of her and hers about the same. Theoretically she could jump straight out of the hole with her burden. In practice, her spacesuit was too hampering; constant-volume joints allowed considerable freedom of movement, but not as much as bare skin, especially when circum-Saturnian temperatures required extra insulation. Besides, if she could have reached the top, she could not have stayed. Soft ice would have crumbled beneath her fingers and she would have tumbled back down.

"Here goes," she said. "This had better be right the first time, Colin. I don't think Luis can take much jouncing."

"Kendrick, Ricia, where are you?" Garcilaso moaned. "Are you in Hell too?"

Scobie dug his heels into the ground near the edge and crouched ready. The loop in the wire rose to view. His right hand grabbed hold. He threw himself backward, lest he slide forward, and felt the mass he had captured slam to a halt. Anguish exploded in his rib cage. Somehow he dragged his burden to safety before he fainted.

He came out of that in a minute. "I'm okay," he rasped at the anxious voices of Broberg and Danzig. "Only let me rest awhile."

The physicist nodded and knelt to minister to the pilot. She stripped his packframe in order that he might lie flat on it, head and legs supported by the packs themselves. That would prevent significant heat loss by convection and cut loss by conduction. Still, his fuel cell would be drained faster than if he were on his feet, and first it had a terrible energy deficit to make up.

"The ice is clearing away inside his helmet," she reported. "Merciful Mary, the blood! Seems to be from the scalp, though; it isn't running anymore. His occiput must have been slammed against the vitryl. We ought to wear padded caps in these rigs. Yes, I know accidents like this haven't happened before, but—" She unclipped the flashlight at her waist, stooped, and shone it downward. "His eyes are open. The pupils—yes, a severe concussion, and likely a skull fracture, which may be hemorrhaging into the brain. I'm surprised he isn't vomiting. Did the cold prevent that? Will he start soon? He could choke on his own vomit, in there where nobody can lay a hand on him."

Scobie's pain had subsided to a bearable intensity. He

rose, went over to look, whistled, and said, "I judge he's doomed unless we get him to the boat and give him proper care soon. Which isn't possible."

"Oh, Luis." Tears ran silently down Broberg's cheeks.

"You think he can't last till I bring my rope and we carry him back?" Danzig asked.

"'Fraid not," Scobie replied. "I've taken paramedical courses, and in fact I've seen a case like this before. How come you know the symptoms, Jean?"

"I read a lot," she said dully.

"They weep, the dead children weep," Garcilaso muttered.

Danzig sighed. "Okay, then. I'll fly over to you."

"*Huh?*" burst from Scobie, and from Broberg: "Have you also gone insane?"

"No, listen," Danzig said fast. "I'm no skilled pilot, but I have the same basic training in this type of craft that everybody does who might ride in one. It's expendable; the rescue vessels can bring us back. There'd be no significant gain if I landed close to the glacier—I'd still have to make that rope and so forth—and we know from what happened to the probe that there would be a real hazard. Better I make straight for your crater."

"Coming down on a surface that the jets will vaporize out from under you?" Scobie snorted. "I bet Luis would consider that a hairy stunt. You, my friend, would crack up."

"Nu?" They could almost see the shrug. "A crash from low altitude, in this gravity, shouldn't do more than rattle my teeth. The blast will cut a hole clear to bedrock. True, the surrounding ice will collapse in around the hull and trap it. You may need to dig to reach the airlock, though I suspect thermal radiation from the cabin will keep the upper parts of the structure free. Even if the craft topples and strikes sidewise—in which case, it'll sink down into a deflating cushion—even if it did that on bare rock, it shouldn't be seriously damaged. It's designed to withstand heavier impacts." Danzig hesitated. "Of course, could be this would endanger you. I'm confident I won't fry you with the jets, assuming I descend near the middle and you're as far offside as you can get. Maybe, though, maybe I'd cause a . . . an ice quake that'll kill you. No sense in losing two more lives."

"Or three, Mark," Broberg said low. "In spite of your brave words, you could come to grief yourself."

"Oh, well, I'm an oldish man. I'm fond of living, yes, but you guys have a whole lot more years due you. Look, suppose the worst, suppose I don't just make a messy landing but wreck the boat utterly. Then Luis dies, but he would anyway. You two, however, would have access to the stores aboard, including those extra fuel cells. I'm willing to run what I consider to be a small risk of my own neck, for the sake of giving Luis a chance at survival."

"Um-m-m," went Scobie, deep in his throat. A hand strayed in search of his chin, while his gaze roved around the glimmer of the bowl.

"I repeat," Danzig proceeded, "if you think this might jeopardize you in any way, we scrub it. No heroics, please. Luis would surely agree, better three people safe and one dead than four stuck with a high probability of death."

"Let me think." Scobie was mute for minutes before he said: "No, I don't believe we'd get in too much trouble here. As I remarked earlier, the vicinity has had its avalanche and must be in a reasonably stable configuration. True, ice will volatilize. In the case of deposits with low boiling points, that could happen explosively and cause tremors. But the vapor will carry heat away so fast that only material in your immediate area should change state. I daresay that the fine-grained stuff will get shaken down the slopes, but it's got too low a density to do serious harm; for the most part, it should simply act like a brief snowstorm. The floor will make adjustments, of course, which may be rather violent. However, we can be above it —do you see that shelf of rock over yonder, Jean, at jumping height? It has to be part of a buried hill; solid. That's our place to wait . . . Okay, Mark, it's go as far as we're concerned. I can't be absolutely certain, but who ever is about anything? It seems like a good bet."

"What are we overlooking?" Broberg wondered. She glanced down at Luis, who lay at her feet. "While we considered all the possibilities, Luis might die. Yes, fly if you want to, Mark, and God bless you."

But when she and Scobie had brought Garcilaso to the ledge, she gestured from Saturn to Polaris and: "I will sing a spell, I will cast what small magic is mine, in aid of the Dragon Lord, that he may deliver Alvarlan's soul from Hell," *says Ricia.*

IV

No reasonable person will blame any interplanetary explorer for miscalculations about the actual environment, especially when *some* decision has to be made, in haste and under stress. Occasional errors are inevitable. If we knew exactly what to expect throughout the Solar System, we would have no reason to explore it.

—Minamoto

The boat lifted. Cosmic dust smoked away from its jets. A hundred and fifty meters aloft, thrust lessened and it stood still on a pillar of fire.

Within the cabin was little noise, a low hiss and a bone-deep but nearly inaudible rumble. Sweat studded Danzig's features, clung glistening to his beard stubble, soaked his coverall and made it reek. He was about to undertake a maneuver as difficult as a rendezvous, and without guidance.

Gingerly, he advanced a vernier. A side jet woke. The boat lurched toward a nose dive. Danzig's hands jerked across the console. He must adjust the forces that held his vessel on high and those that pushed it horizontally, to get a resultant that would carry him eastward at a slow, steady pace. The vectors would change instant by instant, as they do when a human walks. The control computer, linked to the sensors, handled much of the balancing act, but not the crucial part. He must tell it what he wanted it to do.

His handling was inexpert. He had realized it would be. More altitude would have given him more margin for error, but deprive him of cues that his eyes found on the terrain beneath and the horizon ahead. Besides, when he reached the glacier he would perforce fly low to find his goal. He would be too busy for the precise celestial navigation he could have practiced afoot.

Seeking to correct his error, he overcompensated, and the boat pitched in a different direction. He punched for "hold steady" and the computer took over. Motionless again, he took a minute to catch his breath, regain his nerve, rehearse in his mind. Biting his lip, he tried afresh. This time he did not quite approach disaster. Jets aflicker, the boat staggered drunkenly over the moonscape.

The ice cliff loomed nearer and nearer. He saw its

fragile loveliness and regretted that he must cut a swathe
of ruin. Yet what did any natural wonder mean unless a
conscious mind was there to know it? He passed the lowest
slope. It vanished in billows of steam.

Onward. Beyond the boiling, right and left and ahead,
the Faerie architecture crumbled. He crossed the palisade.
Now he was a bare fifty meters above the surface, and the
clouds reached vengefully close before they disappeared
into vacuum. He squinted through the port and made the
scanner sweep a magnified overview across its screen, a
search for his destination.

A white volcano erupted. The outburst engulfed him.
Suddenly he was flying blind. Shocks belled through the hull
when upflung stones hit. Frost sheathed the craft; the scanner screen went as blank as the ports. Danzig should have
ordered ascent, but he was inexperienced. A human in
danger has less of an instinct to jump than to run. He tried
to scuttle sideways. Without exterior vision to aid him, he
sent the vessel tumbling end over end. By the time he saw
his mistake, less than a second, it was too late. He was out
of control. The computer might have retrieved the situation after a while, but the glacier was too close. The boat
crashed.

"Hello, Mark?" Scobie cried. "Mark, do you read me?
Where are you, for Christ's sake?"

Silence replied. He gave Broberg a look which lingered.
"Everything seemed to be in order," he said, "till we heard
a shout, and a lot of racket, and nothing. He should've
reached us by now. Instead, he's run into trouble. I hope
it wasn't lethal."

"What can we do?" she asked redundantly. They needed
talk, any talk, for Garcilaso lay beside them and his de-
lirious voice was dwindling fast.

"If we don't get fresh fuel cells within the next forty
or fifty hours, we'll all be at the end of our particular
trail. The boat should be someplace near. We'll have to get
out of this hole under our own power, seems like. Wait
here with Luis and I'll scratch around for a possible route."

Scobie started downward. Broberg crouched by the pilot.

"—alone forever in the dark——" she heard.

"No, Alvarlan." She embraced him. Most likely he could
not feel that, but she could. "Alvarlan, hearken to me. This

is Ricia. I hear in my mind how your spirit calls. Let me help. Let me lead you back to the light."

"Have a care," advised Scobie. "We're too damn close to rehypnotizing ourselves as it is."

"But I might, I just might get through to Luis and . . . comfort him. . . . Alvarlan, Kendrick and I escaped. He's seeking a way home for us. I'm seeking you. Alvarlan, here is my hand, come take it."

On the crater floor, Scobie shook his head, clicked his tongue, and unlimbered his equipment. Binoculars would help him locate the most promising areas. Devices that ranged from a metal rod to a portable geosonar would give him a more exact idea of what sort of footing lay buried under what depth of unclimbable sand-ice. Admittedly the scope of such probes was very limited. He did not have time to shovel tons of material aside in order that he could mount higher and test further. He would simply have to get some preliminary results, make an educated guess at which path up the side of the bowl would prove negotiable, and trust he was right.

He shut Broberg and Garcilaso out of his consciousness as much as he was able, and commenced work.

An hour later, he was ignoring pain while clearing a strip across a layer of rock. He thought a berg of good, hard frozen water lay ahead, but wanted to make sure.

"Jean! Colin! Do you read?"

Scobie straightened and stood rigid. Dimly he heard Broberg: "If I can't do anything else, Alvarlan, let me pray for your soul's repose."

"Mark!" ripped from Scobie. "You okay? What the hell happened?"

"Yeah, I wasn't too badly knocked around," Danzig said, "and the boat's habitable, though I'm afraid it'll never fly again. How are you? Luis?"

"Sinking fast. All right, let's hear the news."

Danzig described his misfortune. "I wobbled off in an unknown direction for an unknown distance. It can't have been extremely far, since the time was short before I hit. Evidently I plowed into a large, um, snowbank, which softened the impact but blocked radio transmission. It's evaporated from the cabin area now, and formations in the offing . . . I'm not sure what damage the jacks and the stern jets suffered. The boat's on its side at about a forty-five-degree angle, presumably with rock beneath. But the after part is still buried in less whiffable stuff—water and CO_2 ices, I think—that's reached temperature equilibrium. The jets must be clogged with it. If I tried to blast, I'd destroy the whole works."

Scobie nodded. "You would, for sure."

Danzig's voice broke. "Oh, God, Colin! What have I done? I wanted to help Luis, but I may have killed you and Jean."

Scobie's lips tightened. "Let's not start crying before we're hurt. True, this has been quite a run of bad luck. But neither you nor I nor anybody could have known that you'd touch off a bomb underneath yourself."

"What was it? Have you any notion? Nothing of the sort ever occurred at rendezvous with a comet. And you believe the glacier is a wrecked comet, don't you?"

"Uh-huh, except that conditions have obviously modified it. The impact produced heat, shock, turbulence. Molecules got scrambled. Plasmas must have been momentarily present. Mixtures, compounds, clathrates, alloys—stuff formed that never existed in free space. We can learn a lot of chemistry here."

"That's why I came along . . . Well, then, I crossed a deposit of some substance or substances that the jets caused to sublime with tremendous force. A certain kind of vapor refroze when it encountered the hull. I had to defrost the ports from inside after the snow had cooked off them."

"Where are you in relation to us?"

"I told you, I don't know. And I'm not sure I can determine it. The crash crumpled the direction-finding antenna. Let me go outside for a better look."

"Do that," Scobie said. "I'll keep busy meanwhile."

He did, until a ghastly rattling noise and Broberg's wail brought him at full speed back to the rock.

Scobie switched off Garcilaso's fuel cell. "This may make the difference that carries us through," he said low. "Think of it as a gift. Thanks, Luis."

Broberg let go of the pilot and rose from her knees. She straightened the limbs that had threshed about in the death struggle and crossed his hands on his breast. There was nothing she could do about the fallen jaw or the eyes that glared at heaven. Taking him out of this suit, here, would have worsened his appearance. Nor could she wipe the tears off her own face. She could merely try to stop their flow. "Goodbye, Luis," she whispered.

Turning to Scobie, she asked, "Can you give me a new job? Please."

"Come along," he directed. "I'll explain what I have in mind about making our way to the surface."

They were midway across the bowl when Danzig called. He had not let his comrade's dying slow his efforts, nor said much while it happened. Once, most softly, he had offered Kaddish.

"No luck," he reported like a machine. "I've traversed the largest circle I could while keeping the boat in sight, and found only weird, frozen shapes. I can't be a huge distance from you, or I'd see an identifiably different sky, on this miserable little ball. You're probably within a twenty or thirty kilometer radius of me. But that covers a bunch of territory."

"Right," Scobie said. "Chances are you can't find us in the time we've got. Return to the boat."

"Hey, wait," Danzig protested. "I can spiral onward, marking my trail. I might come across you."

"It'll be more useful if you return," Scobie told him. "Assuming we climb out, we should be able to hike to you, but we'll need a beacon. What occurs to me is the ice itself. A small energy release, if it's concentrated, should release a large plume of methane or something similarly volatile. The gas will cool as it expands, recondense around dust particles that have been carried along—it'll steam —and the cloud ought to get high enough, before it evaporates again, to be visible from here."

"Gotcha!" A tinge of excitement livened Danzig's words. "I'll go straight to it. Make tests, find a spot where I can get the showiest result, and . . . how about I rig a thermite bomb? No, that might be too hot. Well, I'll develop a gadget."

"Keep us posted."

"But I, I don't think we'll care to chatter idly," Broberg ventured.

"No, we'll be working our tails off, you and I," Scobie agreed.

"Uh, wait," said Danzig. "What if you find you can't get clear to the top? You implied that's a distinct possibility."

"Well, then it'll be time for more radical procedures,

whatever they turn out to be," Scobie responded. "Frankly, at this moment my head is too full of . . . of Luis, and of choosing an optimum escape route, for much thought about anything else."

"M-m, yeah, I guess we've got an ample supply of trouble without borrowing more. Tell you what, though. After my beacon's ready to fire off, I'll make that rope we talked of. You might find you prefer having it to clean clothes and sheets when you arrive." Danzig was silent for seconds before he ended: "God damn it, you *will* arrive."

Scobie chose a point on the north side for his and Broberg's attempt. Two rock shelves jutted forth, near the floor and several meters higher, indicating that stone reached at least that far. Beyond, in a staggered pattern, were similar outcroppings of hard ices. Between them, and onward from the uppermost, which was scarcely more than halfway to the rim, was nothing but the featureless, footingless slope of powder crystals. Its angle of repose gave a steepness that made the surface doubly treacherous. The question, unanswerable save by experience, was how deeply it covered layers on which humans could climb, and whether such layers extended the entire distance aloft.

At the spot, Scobie signaled a halt. "Take it easy, Jean," he said. "I'll go ahead and commence digging."

"Why don't we go together? I have my own tool, you know."

"Because I can't tell how so large a bank of that pseudo-quicksand will behave. It might react to the disturbance by causing a gigantic slide."

She bridled. Her haggard countenance registered mutiny. "Why not me first, then? Do you suppose I always wait passive for Kendrick to save me?"

"As a matter of fact," he rapped, "I'll begin because my rib is giving me billy hell, which is eating away what strength I've got left. If we run into trouble, you can better come to my help than I to yours."

Broberg bent her neck. "Oh. I'm sorry. I must be in a fairly bad state myself, if I let false pride interfere with our business." Her look went toward Saturn, around which *Chronos* orbited, bearing her husband and children.

"You're forgiven." Scobie bunched his legs and sprang the five meters to the lower ledge. The next one up was slightly too far for such a jump, when he had no room for a running start.

Stooping, he scraped his trenching tool against the bottom of the declivity that sparkled before him, and shoveled. Grains poured from above, a billionfold, to cover what he cleared. He worked like a robot possessed. Each spadeful was nearly weightless, but the number of spadefuls was nearly endless. He did not bring the entire bowlside down on himself as he had half feared, half hoped. (If that didn't kill him, it would save a lot of toil.) A dry torrent went right and left over his ankles. Yet at last somewhat more of the underlying rock began to show.

From beneath, Broberg listened to him breathe. It sounded rough, often broken by a gasp or a curse. In his spacesuit, in the raw, wan sunshine, he resembled a knight who, in despite of wounds, did battle against a monster.

"All right," he called at last. "I think I've learned what to expect and how we should operate. It'll take the two of us."

"Yes . . . oh, yes, my Kendrick."

The hours passed. Ever so slowly, the sun climbed and the stars wheeled and Saturn waned.

Most places, the humans labored side by side. They did not require more than the narrowest of lanes, but unless they cut it wide to begin with, the banks to right and left would promptly slip down and bury it. Sometimes the conformation underneath allowed a single person at a time to work. Then the other could rest. Soon it was Scobie who must oftenest take advantage of that. Sometimes they both stopped briefly, for food and drink and reclining on their packs.

Rock yielded to water ice. Where this rose very sharply, the couple knew it, because the sand-ice that they undercut would come down in a mass. After the first such incident, when they were nearly swept away, Scobie always drove his geologist's hammer into each new stratum. At any sign of danger, he would seize its handle and Broberg would cast an arm around his waist. Their other hands clutched their trenching tools. Anchored, but forced to strain every muscle, they would stand while the flood poured around them, knee-high, once even chest-high, seeking to bury them irretrievably deep in its quasi-fluid substance. Afterward they would confront a bare stretch.

It was generally too steep to climb unaided, and they chipped footholds.

Weariness was another tide to which they dared not yield. At best, their progress was dismayingly slow. They needed little heat input to keep warm, except when they took a rest, but their lungs put a furious demand on air recyclers. Garcilaso's fuel cell, which they had brought along, could give a single person extra hours of life, though depleted as it was after coping with his hypothermia, the time would be insufficient for rescue by the teams from *Chronos*. Unspoken was the idea of taking turns with it. That would put them in wretched shape, chilled and stifling, but at least they would leave the universe together.

Thus it was hardly a surprise that their minds fled from pain, soreness, exhaustion, stench, despair. Without that respite, they could not have gone on as long as they did.

At ease for a few minutes, their backs against a blue-shimmering parapet which they must scale, they gazed across the bowl, where Garcilaso's suited body gleamed like a remote pyre, and up the curve opposite Saturn. The planet shone lambent amber, softly banded, the rings a coronet which a shadow band across their arc seemed to make all the brighter. That radiance overcame sight of most nearby stars, but elsewhere they arrayed themselves multitudinous, in splendor, around the silver road which the galaxy clove between them.

"How right a tomb for Alvarlan," *Ricia says in a dreamer's murmur.*

"Has he died, then?" *Kendrick asks.*

"You do not know?"

"I have been too busied. After we won free of the ruins and I left you to recover while I went scouting, I encountered a troop of warriors. I escaped, but must needs return to you by devious, hidden ways." *Kendrick strokes Ricia's sunny hair.* "Besides, dearest dear, it has ever been you, not I, who had the gift of hearing spirits."

"Brave darling . . . Yes, it is a glory to me that I was able to call his soul out of Hell. It sought his body, but that was old and frail and could not survive the knowledge it now had. Yet Alvarlan passed peacefully, and before he did, for his last magic he made himself a tomb from whose ceiling starlight will eternally shine."

"May he sleep well. But for us there is no sleep. Not yet. We have far to travel."

"Aye. But already we have left the wreckage behind. Look! Everywhere around in this meadow, anemones peep through the grass. A lark sings above."

"These lands are not always calm. We may well have more adventures ahead of us. But we shall meet them with high hearts."

Kendrick and Ricia rise to continue their journey.

Cramped on a meager ledge, Scobie and Broberg shoveled for an hour without broadening it much. The sandice slid from above as fast as they could cast it down. "We'd better quit this as a bad job," the man finally decided. "The best we've done is flatten the slope ahead of us a tiny bit. No telling how far inward the shelf goes before there's a solid layer on top. Maybe there isn't any."

"What shall we do instead?" Broberg asked in the same worn tone.

He jerked a thumb. "Scramble back to the level beneath and try a different direction. But first we absolutely require a break."

They spread kerofoam pads and sat. After a while during which they merely stared, stunned by fatigue, Broberg spoke.

"I go to the brook," *Ricia relates.* "It chimes under arches of green boughs. Light falls between them to sparkle on it. I kneel and drink. The water is cold, pure, sweet. When I raise my eyes, I see the figure of a young woman, naked, her tresses the color of leaves. A wood nymph. She smiles."

"Yes, I see her too," *Kendrick joins in.* "I approach carefully, not to frighten her off. She asks our names and errands. We explain that we are lost. She tells us how to find an oracle which may give us counsel."

They depart to find it.

Flesh could no longer stave off sleep. "Give us a yell in an hour, will you, Mark?" Scobie requested.

"Sure," Danzig said, "but will that be enough?"

"It's the most we can afford, after the setbacks we've had. We've come less than a third of the way."

"If I haven't talked to you," Danzig said slowly, "it's not because I've been hard at work, though I have been. It's that I figured you two were having a plenty bad time without me nagging you. However—do you think it's wise to fantasize the way you have been?"

A flush crept across Broberg's cheeks and down toward her bosom. "You listened, Mark?"

"Well, yes, of course. You might have an urgent word for me at any minute."

"Why? What could you do? A game is a personal affair."

"Uh, yes, yes—"

Ricia and Kendrick have made love whenever they can. The accounts were never explicit, but the words were often passionate.

"We'll keep you tuned in when we need you, like for an alarm clock," Broberg clipped. "Otherwise we'll cut the circuit."

"But— Look, I never meant to—"

"I know." Scobie sighed. "You're a nice guy and I daresay we're overreacting. Still, that's the way it's got to be. Call us when I told you."

Deep within the grotto, the Pythoness sways on her throne, in the ebb and flow of her oracular dream. As nearly as Ricia and Kendrick can understand what she chants, she tells them to fare westward on the Stag Path until they meet a one-eyed graybeard who will give them further guidance; but they must be wary in his presence, for he is easily angered. They make obeisance and depart. On their way out, they pass the offering they brought. Since they had little with them other than garments and his weapons, the Princess gave the shrine her golden hair. The knight insists that, close-cropped, she remains beautiful.

"Hey, whoops, we've cleared us an easy twenty meters," Scobie said, albeit in a voice which weariness had hammered flat. *At first, the journey through the land of Nacre is a delight.*

His oath afterward had no more life in it. "Another blind alley, seems like." *The old man in the blue cloak and wide-brimmed hat was indeed wrathful when Ricia refused him her favors and Kendrick's spear struck his own aside. Cunningly, he has pretended to make peace and*

*told them what road they should next take. But at the end
of it are trolls. The wayfarers elude them and double back.*

"My brain's stumbling around in a fog." Scobie groaned.
"My busted rib isn't exactly helping, either. If I don't get
another nap I'll keep on making misjudgments till we run
out of time."

"By all means, Colin," Broberg said. "I'll stand watch
and rouse you in an hour."

"What?" he asked in dim surprise. "Why not join me
and have Mark call us as he did before?"

She grimaced. "No need to bother him. I'm tired, yes,
but not sleepy."

He lacked wit or strength to argue. "Okay," he said. He
stretched his insulating pad on the ice, and toppled out
of awareness.

Broberg settled herself next to him. They were halfway
to the heights, but they had been struggling, with occasional breaks, for more than twenty hours, and progress
grew harder and trickier even as they themselves grew
weaker and more stupefied. If ever they reached the top
and spied Danzig's signal, they would have something like
a couple of hours' stiff travel to shelter.

Saturn, sun, stars shone through vitryl. Broberg smiled
down at Scobie's face. He was no Greek god. Sweat, grime,
unshavenness, the manifold marks of exhaustion were upon him, but— For that matter, she was scarcely an image
of glamour herself.

*Princess Ricia sits by her knight, where he slumbers in
the dwarf's cottage, and strums a harp the dwarf lent her
before he went off to his mine, and sings a lullaby to
sweeten the dreams of Kendrick. When it is done, she
passes her lips lightly across his, and drifts into the same
gentle sleep.*

Scobie woke a piece at a time. "Ricia, beloved," *Kendrick whispers, and feels after her. He will summon her up
with kisses—*

He scrambled to his feet. "Judas priest!" She lay un-
moving. He heard her breath in his earplugs, before the
roaring of his pulse drowned it. The sun glared farther
aloft, he could see it had moved, and Saturn's crescent had
thinned more, forming sharp horns at its ends. He forced
his eyes toward the watch on his left wrist.

"Ten hours," he choked.

He knelt and shook his companion. "Come, for Christ's sake!" Her lashes fluttered. When she saw the horror on his visage, drowsiness fled from her.

"Oh, no," she said. "Please, no."

Scobie climbed stiffly erect and flicked his main radio switch. "Mark, do you receive?"

"Colin!" Danzig chattered. "Thank God! I was going out of my head from worry."

"You're not off that hook, my friend. We just finished a ten-hour snooze."

"What? How far did you get first?"

"To about forty meters' elevation. The going looks tougher ahead than in back. I'm afraid we won't make it."

"Don't *say* that, Colin," Danzig begged.

"My fault," Broberg declared. She stood rigid, fists doubled, her features a mask. Her tone was steely. "He was worn out, had to have a nap. I offered to wake him, but fell asleep myself."

"Not your fault, Jean," Scobie began.

She interrupted: "Yes. Mine. Perhaps I can make it good. Take my fuel cell. I'll still have deprived you of my help, of course, but you might survive and reach the boat anyway."

He seized her hands. They did not unclench. "If you imagine I could do that—"

"If you don't, we're both finished," she said unbendingly. "I'd rather go out with a clear conscience."

And what about my conscience?" he shouted. Checking himself, he wet his lips and said fast: "Besides, you're not to blame. Sleep slugged you. If I'd been thinking, I'd have realized it was bound to do so, and contacted Mark. The fact that you didn't either shows how far gone you were yourself. And . . . you've got Tom and the kids waiting for you. Take my cell." He paused. "And my blessing."

"Shall Ricia forsake her true knight?"

"Wait, hold on, listen," Danzig called. "Look, this is terrible, but—oh, hell, excuse me, but I've got to remind you that dramatics only clutter the action. From what descriptions you've sent, I don't see how either of you can possibly proceed solo. Together, you might yet. At least you're rested—sore in the muscles, no doubt, but clearer in the head. The climb before you may prove easier than you think. Try!"

Scobie and Broberg regarded each other for a whole minute. A thawing went through her, and warmed him. Finally they smiled and embraced. "Yeah, right," he growled. "We're off. But first a bite to eat. I'm plain, old-fashioned hungry. Aren't you?" She nodded.

"That's the spirit," Danzig encouraged them. "Uh, may I make another suggestion? I am just a spectator, which is pretty hellish but does give me an overall view. Drop that game of yours."

Scobie and Broberg tautened.

"It's the real culprit," Danzig pleaded. "Weariness alone wouldn't have clouded your judgment. You'd never have cut me off, and— But weariness and shock and grief did lower your defenses to the point where the damned game took you over. You weren't yourselves when you fell asleep. You were those dream-world characters. They had no reason not to cork off!"

Broberg shook her head violently. "Mark," said Scobie, "you are correct about being a spectator. That means there are some things you don't understand. Why subject yourself to the torture of listening in, hour after hour? We'll call you back from time to time, naturally. Take care." He broke the circuit.

"He's wrong," Broberg insisted.

Scobie shrugged. "Right or wrong, what difference? We won't pass out again in the time we have left. The game didn't handicap us as we traveled. In fact, it helped, by making the situation feel less gruesome."

"Aye. Let us break our fast and set forth anew on our pilgrimage."

The struggle grew stiffer. "Belike the White Witch has cast a spell on this road." *says Ricia.*

"She shall not daunt us." *vows Kendrick.*

"No, never while we fare side by side, you and I, noblest of men."

A slide overcame them and swept them back a dozen meters. They lodged against a crag. After the flow had passed by, they lifted their bruised bodies and limped in search of a different approach. The place where the geologist's hammer lay was no longer accessible.

"What shattered the bridge?" *asks Ricia.*

"A giant," *answers Kendrick.* "I saw him as I fell into

the river. He lunged at me, and we fought in the shallows until he fled. He bore away my sword in his thigh."

"You have your spear that Wayland forged," *Ricia says,* "and always you have my heart."

They stopped on the last small outcrop they uncovered. It proved to be not a shelf but a pinnacle of water ice. Around it glittered sand-ice, again quiescent. Ahead was a slope thirty meters in length, and then the rim, and stars.

The distance might as well have been thirty light-years. Whoever tried to cross would immediately sink to an unknown depth.

There was no point in crawling back down the bared side of the pinnacle. Broberg had clung to it for an hour while she chipped niches to climb by with her knife. Scobie's condition had not allowed him to help. If they sought to return, they could easily slip, fall, and be engulfed. If they avoided that, they would never find a new path. Less than two hours' worth of energy was left in their fuel cells. Attempting to push onward while swapping Garcilaso's back and forth would be an exercise in futility.

They settled themselves, legs dangling over the abyss, and held hands.

"I do not think the orcs can burst the iron door of this tower," *Kendrick says,* "but they will besiege us until we starve to death."

"You never yielded up your hope ere now, my knight," *replies Ricia, and kisses his temple.* "Shall we search about? These walls are unutterably ancient. Who knows what relics of wizardry lie forgotten within? A pair of phoenix-feather cloaks, that will bear us laughing through the sky to our home—?"

"I fear not, my darling. Our weird is upon us." *Kendrick touches the spear that leans agleam against the battlement.* "Sad and gray will the world be without you. We can but meet our doom bravely."

"Happily, since we are together." *Ricia's gamin smile breaks forth.* "I did notice that a certain room holds a bed. Shall we try it?"

Kendrick frowns. "Rather should we seek to set our minds and souls in order."

She tugs his elbow. "Later, yes. Besides—who knows?—

when we dust off the blanket, we may find it is a Tarn-kappe that will take us invisible through the enemy."

"You dream."

Fear stirs behind her eyes. "What if I do?" *Her words tremble.* "I can dream us free if you will help."

Scobie's fist smote the ice. "No!" he croaked. "I'll die in the world that is."

Ricia shrinks from him. He sees terror invade her. "You, you rave, beloved," *she stammers.*

He twisted about and caught her by the arms. "Don't you want to remember Tom and your boys?"

"Who—?"

Kendrick slumps. "I don't know. I have forgotten too."

She leans against him, there on the windy height. A hawk circles above. "The residuum of an evil enchantment, surely. Oh, my heart, my life, cast it from you! Help me find the means to save us." *Yet her entreaty is uneven, and through it speaks dread.*

Kendrick straightens. He lays hand on Wayland's spear, and it is as though strength flows thence, into him. "A spell in truth," *he says. His tone gathers force.* "I will not abide in its darkness, nor suffer it to blind and deafen you, my lady." *His gaze takes hold of hers, which cannot break away.* "There is but a single road to our freedom. It goes through the gates of death."

She waits, mute and shuddering.

"Whatever we do, we must die, Ricia. Let us fare hence as our own folk."

"You see before you the means of your deliverance. It is sharp, I am strong, you will feel no pain."

She bares her bosom. "Then quickly, Kendrick, before I am lost!"

He drives the weapon home. "I love you," *he says. She sinks at his feet.* "I follow you, my darling," *he says, withdrawing the steel, bracing the shaft against stone, and lunging forward. He falls beside her.* "Now we are free."

"That was . . . a nightmare." Broberg sounded barely awake.

Scobie's voice shook. "Necessary, I think, for both of us." He gazed straight before him, letting Saturn fill his eyes with dazzle. "Else we'd have stayed . . . insane? Maybe not, by definition. But we'd not have been in reality either."

"It would have been easier," she mumbled. "We'd never have known we were dying."

"Would you have preferred that?"

Broberg shivered. The slackness in her countenance gave place to the same tension that was in his. "Oh, no," she said, quite softly but in the manner of full consciousness. "No, you were right, of course. Thank you for your courage."

"You've always had as much guts as anybody, Jean. You just have more imagination than me." Scobie's hand chopped empty space in a gesture of dismissal. "Okay, we should call poor Mark and let him know. But first—" His words lost the cadence he had laid on them. "First—"

Her glove clasped his. "What, Colin?"

"Let's decide about that third unit—Luis's," he said with difficulty, still confronting the great ringed planet. "Your decision, actually, though we can discuss the matter if you want. I will not hog it for the sake of a few more hours. Nor will I share it; that would be a nasty way for us both to go out. However, I suggest you use it."

"To sit beside your frozen corpse?" she replied. "No. I wouldn't even feel the warmth, not in my bones—"

She turned toward him so fast that she nearly fell off the pinnacle. He caught her. *"Warmth!"* she screamed, shrill as the cry of a hawk on the wing. "Colin, we'll take our bones home!"

"In point of fact," said Danzig, "I've climbed onto the hull. That's high enough for me to see over those ridges and needles. I've got a view of the entire horizon."

"Good," grunted Scobie. "Be prepared to survey a complete circle quick. This depends on a lot of factors we can't predict. The beacon will certainly not be anything like as big as what you had arranged. It may be thin and short-lived. And, of course, it may rise too low for sighting at your distance." He cleared his throat. "In that case, we two have bought the farm. But we'll have made a hell of a try, which feels great by itself."

He hefted the fuel cell, Garcilaso's gift. A piece of heavy wire, insulation stripped off, joined the prongs. Without a regulator, the unit poured its maximum power through the short circuit. Already the strand glowed.

"Are you sure you don't want me to do it, Colin?" Broberg asked. "Your rib—"

He made a lopsided grin. "I'm nonetheless better designed by nature for throwing things," he said. "Allow me that much male arrogance. The bright idea was yours."

"It should have been obvious from the first," she said. "I think it would have been, if we weren't bewildered in our dream."

"M-m, often the simple answers are the hardest to find. Besides, we had to get this far or it wouldn't have worked, and the game helped mightily . . . Are you set, Mark? Heave ho!"

Scobie cast the cell as if it were a baseball, hard and far through the Iapetan gravity field. Spinning, its incandescent wire wove a sorcerous web across vision. It landed somewhere beyond the rim, on the glacier's back.

Frozen gases vaporized, whirled aloft, briefly recondensed before they were lost. A geyser stood white against the stars.

"I see you!" Danzig yelped. "I see your beacon, I've got my bearing, I'll be on my way! With rope and extra energy units and everything!"

Scobie sagged to the ground and clutched at his left side. Broberg knelt and held him, as if either of them could lay hand on his pain. No large matter. He would not hurt much longer.

"How high would you guess the plume goes?" Danzig inquired, calmer.

"About a hundred meters," Broberg replied after study.

"Oh, damn, these gloves do make it awkward punching the calculator. . . . Well, to judge by what I observe of it, I'm between ten and fifteen klicks off. Give me an hour or a tad more to get there and find your exact location. Okay?"

Broberg checked gauges. "Yes, by a hair. We'll turn our thermostats down and sit very quietly to reduce oxygen demand. We'll get cold, but we'll survive."

"I may be quicker," Danzig said. "That was a worst-case estimate. All right, I'm off. No more conversation till we meet. I won't take any foolish chances, but I will need my wind for making speed."

Faintly, those who waited heard him breathe, heard his hastening footfalls. The geyser died.

They sat, arms around waists, and regarded the glory which encompassed them. After a silence, the man said:

"Well, I suppose this means the end of the game. For everybody."

"It must certainly be brought under strict control," the woman answered. "I wonder, though, if they will abandon it altogether—out here."

"If they must, they can."

"Yes. We did, you and I, didn't we?"

They turned face to face, beneath that star-beswarmed, Saturn-ruled sky. Nothing tempered the sunlight that revealed them to each other, she a middle-aged wife, he a man ordinary except for his aloneness. They would never play again. They could not.

A puzzled compassion was in her smile. "Dear friend—" she began.

His uplifted palm warded her from further speech. "Best we don't talk unless it's essential," he said. "That'll save a little oxygen, and we can stay a little warmer. Shall we try to sleep?"

Her eyes widened and darkened. "I dare not," she confessed. "Not till enough time has gone past. Now, I might dream."

WALK THE ICE

Mildred Downey Broxon

We like to think that the first contact between humans and aliens from the stars will be an earthshaking crisis, probably involving the heads of governments. But ours is a large planet, and visitors won't necessarily be able to choose where they land . . . or in what condition. Here's an evocative, moving story of First Contact under tragic conditions, and the result.

Mildred Downey Broxon is best known as the author of *Too Long a Sacrifice*. She lives in Seattle.

THE SCENE DOMINATED ONE WALL: BERGS grumbled on a gray northern sea. A breeze whispered among glittering snow-crystals, and gulls screeched. But the retirement home at Sitka was far from any Arctic shore. This seascape was only a video-sound projection, and the air was warm.

Anagan checked the clock. It was time. She touched a control, and the Bering Sea faded. It was replaced on the video screen by rows of eager young faces: commencement exercises at the Explorers Academy. This first graduating class numbered only twenty. There, in the third row, sat Nakarak, her four-times great-granddaughter. Long had Anagan waited for this day, so long that her age now forbade travel. Well, no matter. As the retired Presidential Advisor of the United North, she could command—and afford—a direct videocast.

This all started many years ago. Anagan mused. I didn't understand what happened then, of course, but I wrote it down. I don't even have the paper anymore. I don't need to read it. I remember everything—

I had seen seven ice breakups. In the winter following my seventh autumn freeze, the stranger came. Earlier, hunting had been good: plenty of seal and walrus lay on the meat rack, and the traps caught many foxes. The women were kept busy scraping and softening the skins.

There were four houses in our winter settlement. In one earth-and-stone house lived Mother, Father, Father's mother, and myself.

Deep winter had passed; we were nearing spring. Sun peeped out for longer periods at midday. One of the men sighted an early-rising polar bear on the sea ice. Sharpboned and ragged after his long sleep, the bear walked with a staggering gait. All four hunters, their half-grown sons, and the dogs went out on the ice to kill him. As happened, though, the bear was not as sleepy as he seemed. Father would have shot him from a safe distance, but he felt a patch of thin ice beneath the snow. He stepped back and slipped. His rifle fell from his grip, broke the ice and sank. Father knelt, looking after it. The only rifle in the settlement—it may as well have never been. Father had gotten it for many foxes from a hunter farther south, who traded skins to the white men.

The others looked away in silence, not to embarrass him. Father laughed: "It seems someone wishes to hunt in the old way." So with nothing but bone-tipped harpoons they went against the bear. It slew three hunters and eight dogs.

Father and the half-grown boys dragged the carcass back to the settlement, where they portioned it out and buried the men. The son of the man who first struck the bear got the choicest meat.

As Father was now the only great hunter, he must go after seal to feed the rest. The young boys hunted also, but they caught little. Father's catch was good. Mother carried portions to the other families and laid the rest on the common meat rack.

Something bad hung over that winter. Perhaps the spirits of the dead men wandered and frightened the animals. Perhaps the woman under the sea wanted her hair combed, and none came to help her, so she held back the game. Who knows? Every time Father had to go farther out on the ice for seals.

One night long after dark, when the Northern Lights flickered, he came back riding the runners behind his sled. His left leg was lashed to a harpoon shaft.

He would not say what had happened—a hole in the ice, a dogfight where the traces wrapped around him and he was dragged—Mother did not ask. She drew off his boots and outer clothing. I saw white and red bone-ends poking through his skin. Mother brought meat around to the other houses, then came home to prepare a meal.

Father lay quiet and did not eat. Father's mother rocked

and crooned—she was very old. Often she thought herself young again, and beautiful. She was able to keep her soapstone lamp burning, however, and she was good for chewing the fat from skins. Toothless, her gums could not tear holes in them.

Now that the settlement no longer had a mighty hunter, the other families thought they might visit friends and relatives. The nearest village was only three days away in good weather. Mother decided to stay with Father and see if he could be made stronger to travel. He was sick, burning, and crazy. Mother could not carry him to the sled, and he could neither walk nor understand why he must try.

So we stayed, Mother, Father, Grandmother, and I. The other families left us meat, taking only what they and their dogs would need on the journey, plus gifts for their hosts.

We stood outside that night and watched the Northern Lights writhe and hiss. Grandmother said it meant someone would die. True, ever since Father came home injured, the Lights had been brighter and noisier than usual. I whistled to see if they would answer me, but they paid no heed.

That night the stranger came. We were still outside looking at the Lights, hearing Father babble in fever, when I saw a dark shape far out on the sea-ice. The Lights were bright enough so that frozen billows and bergs gleamed white, and the stars shone thick where the glow had not blotted them out. The shape walked so clumsily I wondered if it might be a bear. As it came closer I saw it was only a bit taller than man-size. It staggered.

"A young person has noticed that a stranger approaches," I said to Mother. She stood watching. She would not go out to meet him, the man of the house should do that, but she would stand and give greeting. She sighed. "When guests come it is good that there is food to offer." Grandmother mumbled something and went back into the house. I stayed beside Mother.

The stranger saw us, held up his arms, and changed course. When he reached shore he fell to his knees. We waited. If he did not need help, it would be an insult to offer it. He was an adult.

After a time he rose and came closer. "Come visit us," Mother said, as if he had stopped by on a stroll. He made a strange sound. She led him inside.

"Husband," she said to Father, "someone does not wish

to be forward, but it seems a stranger has come across the ice."

Father groaned.

"Anagan," Mother said, "go fetch some meat from the rack." To the stranger she said, "I have, of course, nothing to offer you save some food the dogs scorned, for my husband is not a great hunter. I am ashamed to lay such fare before a guest. Perhaps you would do best to travel on." This showed she wanted me to bring the finest piece, and so I went out under the stars, groped my way to the meat rack, and brought back a seal liver.

All this time the stranger said nothing. Mother and Grandmother made to remove his boots, but he drew back. After I returned with the raw frozen liver, I watched him, when he did not see me. I brushed close; his clothes were smooth and cold, not like furs, and they did not seem thick enough. He must be freezing. And he was thin, so thin, and tall. Never had I seen a living man so thin.

His face was covered with some sort of gut, only more transparent, like ice. Behind it his skin showed blue and rough. His eyes were yellow, very large. I could not see the rest of him, as he was covered in a tight frost-bright garment. His hands must have been frozen at one time, for he was missing some of his fingers. He had only two, and a thumb, on each hand. It must have been a long time past, as his wife had sewn him gloves to fit.

Still he said nothing. He had a box with him, about the size of a sewing box. He worked at it with his poor hands. I thought it impolite to stare. It made a hissing sound, like the Northern Lights.

Mother cut the liver on a flat stone. Her flint knife was sharp, but not as sharp as the metal knives we'd seen. Next year Father had promised to get her one. This year he had needed the rifle. She feigned shame—Mother was very polite—and said, "I regret this piece of offal is all the meat rack held. Perhaps my stupid daughter found it among the dogs' leavings?" Still the stranger said nothing, though he should in turn, praise the fine meat. This would be mannerly. He looked around at the sleeping platform heaped with skins, the stone lamps, Father's bone-tipped harpoon, Mother's flint knife, and made a low sound. He clasped his mutilated hands and stared at the roof.

Mother handed him a piece of seal liver. It was thawing now, and dripped with juice. My own mouth watered. I wondered if the stranger was hungry; he made another low sound and flinched back. Then he quieted, picked up the meat, and looked at it.

Mother waited. He loosed the covering over his face, took one small bite—he had small sharp teeth, like a seal —and set it down. He sat trembling as blood ran down his chin. It made me hungry to see. At last he took his piece of liver and ate it whole.

Then we all could eat. Even Father came out of his raving for a time. He tried to talk with the stranger, man's talk, of hunting, dogs, and weather, but the stranger could only make animal sounds. When we had gorged enough— I made several more trips to the meat rack—Father asked if the stranger would like Mother for the night, since he was traveling without a woman. Our guest did not answer. Perhaps he was deaf-mute. Even in her condition, Mother was very pretty.

In any case, he took the cold place on the side bench, away from the main sleeping platform. In the night we heard him outside being sick. He must have starved a long time, then gorged too quickly. This can happen to anyone. We all went back to sleep.

Over the next few days Father's leg began to stink. He did not know where he was; he babbled. The stranger finally tried to see what he could do. He even took off his gloves.

His poor hands! Not only had they been frozen, but the skin was blue and scaly. Between the scales grew fine golden hairs. I had never known cold that could do that.

He drew back Father's sleeping-skin, looked at the hurt leg, then hissed. He fumbled in his pouch and pulled out a small bladder. When he poured the liquid on the wound, it bubbled, and Father screamed. Steam rose. Quickly the stranger grabbed the water pot and emptied it over Father's leg. The steaming stopped. He stepped back and looked, once again, at his poor mutilated hands. The nails were black claws. He drew the gut-covering back over his face, put his gloves on, and stepped outside.

I should not have followed him. It was plain he wished to be alone. But I was young and discourteous.

He walked around the settlement, peering into the three abandoned houses. He stopped and surveyed the nearly empty meat rack, paused to examine Father's dogsled—it

was a fine one, with bone runners—and stood looking at
our team. They howled and leapt at him, but since they
were tethered they could do no harm. Nonetheless he
stepped back. He was no sled-driver, then. Those were
good dogs.

He stood looking for a long time out over the ice, next
to the stone-heaped hill where we bury our dead. Was he
talking with the ancestors? He had not spoken a word
with us. He'd taken his box along and once again began
to work with it. The Lights danced overhead, and the box
hissed in time to their writhing. Then he put it down and
sat in the snow, curled up, forehead on knees. I was afraid,
after a time, that he would freeze, and so I went up to
him. "Someone sits in the cold snow," I said, "when a
warm house stands nearby." He looked up at me. In the
dark, his yellow eyes had turned green. He blinked. I
held out my hand and led him back indoors. At times he
was as forgetful as Grandmother.

Then the storm struck. Even had Father been well, he
could not have ventured forth to hunt. The meat rack
made empty music with the wind. Once Mother almost got
lost looking for it, though it was only a few steps outside
the door. Beyond, all was white whistling blowing drifts.
The dogs curled beneath the snow, and we huddled inside
and told stories, watching our food run out.

All but the stranger. He had no stories to relate—he
kept mute. At times he would run one scaly blue finger
over the soapstone lamp, or fiddle with the useless box he
carried, but mostly he crouched in the corner, rocking
back and forth like Grandmother did.

After a time we sang to dull the pain in our bellies.
There was nothing else to do. Father did not realize his
singing partner was dead, killed by the bear, and so he
sang his own part and then the other's—the last, using the
dead man's voice. I looked outside to make sure the man
had not thrown off his mound of frozen stones to join us.
But the night held only wind.

The stranger listened and, when Father was done, made
some odd noises of his own. Perhaps that was his sort of
music. It sounded like the creak of thick ice near breakup.

Grandmother, in her turn, sang a lament. At times she
remembered how old she was, and became sad.

Ay-ah, ay-ah, a woman once was young.
Ay-ah, ay-ah, a woman once was beautiful.
Once great hunters fought over a woman,
Once she pleasured many men.
Ay-ah, ay-ah, a woman once could travel.
Ay-ah, ay-ah, a woman once was young. Ay-ah.

Hunger and sickness made Father worse. He fought things only he could see. I do not know how he got up to thrash about the house, staggering, but he knocked over both Mother's and Grandmother's lamps. Mother screamed and beat out the spreading flames with her hands, then put Father back to bed. We sat in the dark.

Kindling a fire is a long, weary task. Mother sighed and began, when a light flared from the stranger's corner. He waited until she refilled the lamp and adjusted the wick, then he touched his flame to the moss. It flared.

I wanted him to do it again. I asked him. He seemed to understand, for he made fire from nothing several times, until he grew tired of child's play and put it back into his pouch.

So the stranger was good for something after all: he could not hunt, sing, or talk, but he *could* light a fire.

When the storm was at its height, Mother's time came. I knew a baby was due soon, but we did not know when. Father could not give a husband's help. The stranger knew nothing. So the task fell to Grandmother and me. I had seen births before, of course. Only last year my baby brother had been born, in the winter. He lived ten days. Mother had little trouble this time, and Grandmother remembered what else must be done. Soon a girl baby was trying to suckle.

Mother did not give much milk. She had been too long hungry. She spoke no name for the baby. I knew what that could mean.

When the storm quieted, Grandmother rose from the sleeping platform and put on her boots, trousers, and parka. "Someone would like to take a walk," she said.

"I'll come along, Grandmother." I was afraid.

"What, am I so old I cannot walk by myself?" Her tone was hard, but her eyes were kind. She patted me on the head, even though I had been impolite. I should have said nothing. Mother, who always had perfect manners, pretended not to notice, and kept trying to nurse the baby.

Should her mother-in-law not go outside if she wished?
Father saw nothing by now. As Grandmother stepped
into the passageway, the stranger put one hand on her arm
as if to detain her. She brushed him aside. I held his hand
to keep him from following. The poor mutilated fingers
were clenched inside his glove. He, too, knew.

The next day we went out and found Grandmother. We
buried her under a heap of stones on the hill and mourned
her for the proper time. During that time, when none of
us went anywhere, or even took off our clothes, Father
died as well. Mother and the stranger carried him out to
lie with the rest of the dead. Again we mourned.

We were all getting thin, but the stranger, I noticed,
was thinning faster than the rest of us, and his mouth was
cracked and bleeding. Mother's milk dried up. She decided
we must kill and eat one of the dogs. The dogs themselves
were starving now, with little meat on them. What there
was made us feel sick. Those were good sled dogs, well
trained. Once we ate them all, of course, there would be
no hope. How could we cross the ice? So we tried to wait
as long as possible between killings. Something might happen, and we would have part of the team left.

New storms blew up. Even had people from the next
village been trying to send help, they could not have
traveled.

Little sister cried and then only whimpered. One day
Mother called me to her. "All my milk is gone. The baby
is starving. It would be cruel to let her suffer. You are
starving too." We had saved some sealskin lines to eat at
the last. I helped her take one and strangle little sister,
as Mother was very weak now. When it would have been
my turn to die, I said, "Life is not yet heavier than death,
Mother. I will try to fend for myself." So she let me live,
even though she was a concerned mother and did not want
to see her children starve.

I decided to go for help. The stranger was very sick,
and of no use. One would think he would walk out on the
ice. Mother was almost too weak to move. We still had
four dogs, and so I killed one for food and harnessed the
other three. That was not enough dogs to pull a normal
load, but I was only a small child, and quite thin by now.
I could run most of the way.

The stranger saw me loading up and made as if to ask
where I was going. By now we could talk by sign, a bit.

So I pointed to Mother and myself, wiggled my fingers to show "many more people," then pointed toward the next settlement. I also pretended to be eating. The stranger offered to come along.

He would be little help, but there would be more dog meat left for Mother, and the stranger was taller than I: he might help right the sled, if it overturned in a drift. So I let him come. He brought his box.

He walked at first, behind the sled. The dogs were weak, even after eating part of their dead teammate, and they only trotted. Soon the stranger became tired and climbed onto the sled to lie atop the sleeping-skins. He weighed very little by then, hardly more than I did. If I ran behind and helped the runners over rough places, the burden did not slow the dogs much.

When night came I tried to build a snow hut. I was not skilled at cutting the blocks—this was men's work, though I had watched—and I never managed to dome the roof, but at least we were sheltered from the wind.

The next day I had to help the stranger onto the sled. Earlier he tried to harness the dogs, but blood seeped through his gloves and stained the snow. The dogs broke loose and licked it, then howled.

Of course we had no food along, but I had Grandmother's lamp. I even had some oil, and we could melt ice for water, which filled the stomach. The stranger should not have been so weak.

Later that day the lead bitch lay down in the traces and was dragged until she died. I loaded her thin body on the sled. When we stopped, I cut off a haunch for ourselves and fed the rest to the two remaining dogs. The stranger would not eat the meat. The next day he could scarcely crawl to the sled.

Fed, the dogs pulled more briskly. I began to feel cheerful. Sun sparkled the snow for a longer time in midday. We might reach the other village after all. One more night on the trail, and we could have food, and warmth, and see other people. If we got there in time we could even send help to Mother. I was learning to build snow huts, too. This night my roof stayed up. I lit the lamp—*my* lamp now, my woman's lamp—and the hut grew warm. I slept well.

I slept so well that I did not hear the stranger rise in

the night. When I woke, his box lay atop the sleeping-skins. I was afraid for him.

Outside, away from the sled, toward the sea ice, I saw his tracks. When I found him he was cold and stiff, his poor hurt hands clasped, his head on his knees. The blood that trickled down his chin was frozen now, and his skin was gray, not blue. So—he'd realized he was a burden, and took the honorable way.

I dragged him back to the snow hut. I had no place to bury him. I loaded his box on the sled—he had left it for me—and set off.

I was not an expert driver. When the dogs overturned the lightly laden sled, the box flew off into a drift and I could not find it. When I loosed the team they ran off, howling, back the way we had come.

I went on afoot. It was not far, now. I would live. A little later, under the crackling Northern Lights, I reached the village just ahead of a ten-day storm.

When the blizzard cleared, help went for Mother, but by the time they reached her she was dead. They stopped at my snow house on the way, to sleep. I had not mentioned the stranger, for he had no name. Inside they found blood and a few shreds of skin and odd-shaped bones. A little farther on, they found my two dogs, dead, their bellies swollen as if with poison.

They never told me the last, but I heard the whispers: when they found Mother they also found the baby's body, and Father's. Pieces were missing. There were human toothmarks on the bones. These things happen, at the extremes of hunger, but people do not speak of them.

So they kept me on in the village, as an orphan. I wore cast-off clothing and ate scraps of food, but no one pitied me. They knew that if I suffered when I was young I would always be resourceful, no matter what life brought. I survived; I neither froze nor starved.

The next year white traders set up a post in the village. That winter I began coughing. The white men called it "tuberculosis." Several in the village had the same cough. They sent me to the mission hospital farther south. There, for the sick children, the missionaries ran a school. At school I learned about other people, white men and the rest who do not have the Inuit speech, even people who live where there is no snow. I learned to read and write, and my world grew large. But I never read of anyone like the stranger.

In the mission school, Anagan bent over the lined yellow paper. Her braids trailed across her desk. She finished her composition and took it forward. "Here, Sister," she said. "You asked us to write how it was at home."

Sister smiled at her star pupil and began to read. When she had finished she frowned and marked the paper with a large red D. "Anagan, come up here!"

Once more, Anagan approached the front of the room. "Yes, Sister?" She bobbed a curtsy.

"You should be ashamed, Anagan. A little girl, telling lies like that. Write me another essay, something that *really* happened." She handed back the pages.

Anagan put them carefully in her desk, coughed, and bent over another sheet of paper. It was impolite to argue. But she kept her essay, over the years.

Had it not been for tuberculosis, she would never have gone on to school; as it was, she was too weak to return to her village. In a few years her people were wiped out by a smallpox epidemic. Anagan stayed south and continued her education.

Eventually Anagan began to suspect who, or what, the stranger might have been. But she kept her own counsel and hid her essay in a safe place.

Years passed.

When the speaker finished, they'd hand out the diplomas and the ceremony would be over. Nakarak sat among her classmates and looked out at the starry backdrop. It resembled a curtain but was really a huge picture window. Far in the distance stood the tiny dome-covered monument at Tranquility Base.

Wait—what was the speaker saying? "Even though we have not yet encountered any alien races, nor have we any assurance that we will, we have already trained our first Xenology graduates." He paused for effect.

Yes, Nakarak thought, *I'm one of them, though sometimes I wonder if I should have gone into planetology or navigation.*

"In addition," the speaker continued, "we have today, in our first graduating class, the many-times greatgranddaughter of a woman who, more than anyone else, made the Explorers Academy possible. Much of our early funding came from the United North. It was Anagan, as Presidential Advisor, who was largely responsible for that funding. Older nations, not to be outdone, also contributed. Perhaps because"—he chuckled—"the North wouldn't sell them oil if they didn't. It was fitting, Anagan said, that since the Arctic had once been called the Last Frontier, it should support exploration of the *real* Last Frontier, Space." He paused again; the audience applauded. "We'd hoped Anagan could be here today, but her health did not permit. She did, however, send something to pass on to her descendant. Nakarak, would you come forward?"

Nakarak could feel herself blushing. She hardly knew Anagan; for years the old woman had been too feeble to travel, and Nakarak herself had spent most of the past five years on the Moon. Light in the one-sixth gravity, she walked to the front of the auditorium, shook the speaker's hand, and took her diploma and sealed envelope. She returned to her seat and opened the latter. It held lined yellow paper, covered with a childish scrawl. The ink was brown and the edges had crumbled.

She'll read it first chance she gets, Anagan knew. *It should make her glad about studying Xenology.*

This was enough. Her own flesh and blood would travel space. She herself had always been too old—sixty-nine at the first Moon landing, eighty-two when the anti-aging drugs were discovered, eighty-five when Alaska and Siberia formed the United North.

The ceremony was over. The graduates filed out to accept congratulations and take assignments. Anagan switched the picture back. On the gray North Sea, bergs still drifted, ice slurry swept the shore, snow sparkled. Some things never changed.

From the Stone Age to the Space Age in my lifetime. When the stranger came, we had neither writing nor metalcraft; Nakarak, child, what will you bring home from the stars? She would never know.

She watched the ice as twilight thickened. She rocked back and forth in her chair and chanted.

Ay-ah, ay-ah, a woman once could travel.
Ay-ah, ay-ah, a woman once was young.

The ice ground on, hundreds of miles away. She could never walk that far. She'd finish here. But Nakarak would walk other worlds, and Anagan had led, on the whole, an interesting life. It was enough. There was really nothing to lament.

When they found her body, she was still smiling at the ice.

TRIAL SAMPLE

Ted Reynolds

Once we've begun to establish contact with alien races among the stars, we'll need to get to know their ways in order to make the most of cultural exchange. Perhaps sending an emissary to live on an alien world, as one of them, would be a practical method of starting. Or maybe *not* so practical, as this risible adventure suggests.

Ted Reynolds has been writing science fiction for only a few years but will be remembered as the author of "Ker-Plop" (in *The Best Science Fiction Novellas of the Year* #2) and "Through All Your Houses Wandering." He works in a hospital in Ann Arbor, Michigan.

PAUL HATED SLEEPTIME WORSE THAN ANY-
thing, even meals. His head swam with dizziness, his bi-
ceps ached abominably, and his hip joints felt on the
verge of parting. He couldn't even balance his weight with
his hands, as the family were still in halfsleep; if they
opened their eyes and saw him clutching the sleeping bar,
it would hardly bode well for trade and diplomatic prospects.

He'd just have to hold out for another half hour till the
others had entered deepsleep; then he could clamber down
from the perch and spread out on the rocky cave floor for
a couple of hours. Just as long as he was back suspended
from the sleeping bar by his knees when the family woke
up.

Sure enough, Pommop opened one eye and looked at
Paul lazily. "We got the Morks corraled just fine, didn't
we, son?"

"Sure, Pamma," squeaked Paul, strumming his translation voder in affection mode.

Pommop closed his eye contentedly and remained swinging slowly back and forth, head downwards on his own
bar.

Halfsleep was always an oscillating time with the Shecklites, entering and leaving. A fair amount of conversation
went on, an almost mindless recapitulation of the past
day's activities, forecasts of the coming one, and general
expressions of mutual esteem and satisfaction.

Now Yoouwee, hanging on the far side of the cave,
rustled his (and/or) her batlike wings, muttering somno-

lently, "Did I tell you today that you're a great sibling, Wayuueo? One of the best."

"You, too, Yoouwee," answered Paul, trying to sound asleep.

There was a short spell of silence. Paul decided it was his turn. "Mappa? Can we have Kabisco for mornmeal tomorrow? I just love your Kabisco." He detested it.

"Mmmmmmm," drowsed Moppom. It sounded gratefully like she, or perhaps he, at least, was nearing deepsleep.

Gradually the talk died away, and the family faded into deepsleep. Paul waited in agony until he was sure they were all quite beyond rewaking. Then he reached up to clutch the perch, painfully brought his legs out from over the sleeping bar, and let himself down to the floor of the cave. Every muscle ached, and he was exhausted. He stretched out his limbs one at a time, working the kinks out of them.

If only sleeping on the floor were an acceptably deviant form of behavior among the Shecklites, Paul wouldn't mind being thought strange. But in the minds of the family, a member who refused to sleep in a properly inverted manner from the sleeping bar would be showing signs of incipient madness, possibly of a homicidal variety. With the best will in the world, such a tendency in one of their children must raise strong instinctive anxiety. After the first few nights on Sheckley, Paul had realized this was one of the activities too close to the border of social acceptance to indulge in.

Paul moved wearily to the far end of the cave, where the Mestoiwe family kept its ancestral altars and computer linkups. He lay down on the floor, straddling as few rocks as possible. He'd have about three and a half hours of sleep before the family rose to midsleep again. They'd better find him swinging from his perch, cozy and content, or there'd be diplomatic trouble.

Paul hated sleeptime with a passion!

And now, to top it all, he couldn't get to sleep at once. His mind kept casting up the same old futile question: *Why me?* With four and a half billion humans to choose from, why couldn't the lottery have fallen on someone else; anyone else? He'd like to see his wife, Marilyn, handle this, for instance.

Not for the first time, he cursed the dumb way the

Galactic races had of arranging interspecies relationships. Surely humans could have worked out a less ridiculous method. But when Earth joined the Galactic community, the scheme had been a set tradition for millions of years; man could join it, or retreat home and sulk, but there was no changing or circumventing it.

Paul knew the technique was necessary. Species across the Galaxy were too diverse, too varied, to expect each of them to get along with all the others. Some were baby-eaters, some held very firm religious convictions. Each new species that entered Earth's purview was a potential diplomatic ally, trade partner, friend—or perhaps far too different, physically, mentally, socially, morally, for humans ever to get along with.

The lottery was the established way to make or break relationships. Paul knew, intellectually, that it made more sense than wars, for example. But for someone forced to carry it out in a given instance, it sure seemed dumb.

The human representative on the planet Sheckley sank into an uneasy doze.

The family squatted on the ledge outside the cave mouth, shuffling tine-loads of morkmeat into their mouths. Paul could be grateful Moppom hadn't come up with the Kabisco, but mork wasn't much more appetizing.

The sky arched pale yellow overhead, flecked by bilious green cloudlets, the corralled Morks shuffled and boomed softly from their pens upslope, and the birdlets flittered busily across the morning sun. Pommop came stretching out of the cave mouth and stood looking out over Kooluuwe Ravine. Ponderously he shook out his delicately ribbed wings and then his long limbs, rubbing the sleep out of them.

"Beautiful day, a really gorgeous day," he said at last, joining the family at their mornmeal. "Isn't it your turn to flap over to Youoory for eggs, Wayuu?" He beamed affectionately at Paul.

A bit of underdone mork caught in Paul's throat and he coughed helplessly. From where he sat, on the rim of the cliff, he could see the tops of the higher planted houses poking over the flametrees. A mere half mile as the bat flies, he thought. Two hours climbing for me, first down and then up. If I make it.

I'm not *one of you,* he thought desperately at the squatting family. *I don't have wings, I can't fly, I* hate *breeir eggs. You know that, why do you pretend?*

It was no use. They were letting Paul know that he was one of them, that they still accepted him. He should feel relieved and flattered. If they ever started coddling him, then he could really start to worry. It was just that all the members of the Mestoiwe family took their turns in shopping at Youoory village, and now it was his turn. As simple as that.

"Sure, Pamma," he squeaked as expected, his fingers racing over the voder keys. "Oh, boy. Can I stay to see a flooel show?" He couldn't abide the local entertainment, but the original Wayuueo, who loved flooel animations, would certainly have asked. Besides, it would give an easily accepted excuse for the extended time he would have to be gone from the family homestead.

"Well, now . . ." drew out Pommop, in his standard role of not-coddling-the-kids, but Moppom broke in at that point. "I don't see any harm in that, Poms. Wayuu's been a good boy for a long time now. He never molts in the cave," she added approvingly. "Not like Yoouwee."

"I'll start right away, then," said Paul, leaping to his feet in haste.

"You sit right down and finish your mork," said Pommop sternly. "No child of mine is going to visit the village in a vitiated condition. What would the olders think?"

"It's not my fault," said Moppom. "That child just picks at his food. I swear, sometimes I don't know what's wrong with him. It must be the mildew itch."

Finally the mornmeal ordeal was over. The family all bid him safe day, Pommop passed him some cash (the dried iridescent underwings of the rock scarab), and then they all assiduously turned to praise the colors of the morning sky to one another. That way they wouldn't have to take notice of the highly unorthodox mode of his departure. When they were all looking upwards, Paul gaily cried out, "Wings up; off, off, and away!" and quietly clambered over the edge of the precipice.

As he cautiously descended from one handhold to another, Paul found himself muttering, "Twenty-seven days of Hell to go, twenty-seven days of Hell. If one of those days should happen to fall . . ."

He stopped humming. He didn't like to think about falling. It was still a long way to the bottom.

Actually, by Earth count it was only twelve days to go, with four hundred twenty passed. Sheckley days were short, though standard galactic years were much too long. It was one of those years he had to hold out.

If he did fall and get killed, would relationships between Earth and Sheckley be established anyway, he wondered. If the Shecklites returned his body to Earth, he supposed not; if they buried him in the family plot and mourned it as one of their own, then everything would be all right. Assuming the real Wayuueo, in his place on Earth, also made out all right.

The walls of the ravine rose higher above him as he descended into the depths. He tried to concentrate on finding firm grasps, and ignoring the sweat that rolled down his neck and soaked the back of his jumper. "I'll bet the real Wayuueo isn't have as much trouble as this," he decided bitterly. A series of rapid visions passed before him; Wayuueo flying to the plant in the morning, working the assembly line, drinking beer at Rod's Grill after work, playing touch football with Paul's sons. Surely he wouldn't find any of that too irksome.

Paul wondered if Wayuueo had to sleep in the same bed with Marilyn. After Paul's wife was asleep, Wayuueo probably crept out of bed and hung upside down from the coatrack. Paul felt an abrupt surge of sympathy for his distant counterpart.

Finally he reached the bottom of the crevice. Far overhead, the narrow sliver of warm lemon sky beamed down upon him. The hollow was full of tangled mockbush and wildweed and cracklethorn; down it ran Kooluuwe Creek, twenty yards across, three deep, and full of mangleworms. He had to plunge through the bushes downstream ten minutes before he found a fallen flametree that bridged the creek.

The fallen log was thick enough, but slippery with oozing sap, and Paul had to inch his way across it sitting down. Halfway across it, he came upon a rogerian. The lizard lay lethargically half out of the water, its long tail streaming in the rapid current. Its tongue flicked meditatively as Paul approached.

"Care to tell me about your problem?" said the rogerian.

"I doubt you'd be any help," said Paul.

"Oh, you doubt I'd be any help?" said the rogerian. "Why is that?"

"Because," answered Paul caustically, "you have about as much intelligence as a tree toad, and you don't understand a word you are saying." He had reached the point where the lizard squatted, and remained straddling the log, waiting for the creature to move.

The rogerian lizard blinked sleepy eyes and regarded Paul steadily. "Is it because I have about as much intelligence as a tree toad, or because I do not understand a word I am saying, that you doubt I would be of any help?" it asked.

"Oh, lord, not another therapy session," said Paul. He drew up his right leg and began to massage the knots out of it. "Your so-called conversation is nothing but a series of evolved tropisms, an eidetic memory and mimic ability. It looks clever, but there's not a thought in your alligator head."

"How do you see this as tying in with your problem?" asked the rogerian.

Paul paused in the midst of switching legs. "You know, that's a good question. If it weren't for you empathic lizards, the pressure on me to hold out the full year wouldn't be nearly so great. Earth dearly wants to be able to import shiploads of you. You may not have an intelligent thought of your own, but you certainly help people solve their own problems. Now move aside."

"Don't you think I could help you solve your own problem?"

Sometimes it was hard to realize that it was a mere tropism.

"No," said Paul.

"Aren't you being a bit negative?"

Paul groaned. "Look, Elijah, or whatever your name is, my problems aren't psychological, they're *real*. If I can't put up with the Shecklites for a full standard year . . . or if they can't put up with me, and kick me out . . . then my name back on Earth is mud. There was a Hungarian a few years back who blew the whole Quatrary exchange within a week of the end of the period, when he refused to impregnate a nubile Quatrary prawn. The Quatrary were vastly disturbed at his dereliction, and expelled him. So now the Quatrarian mungo mines and the sciences of Uxode are closed to humans forever; we will never be able to deal with the Quatrary race. And that man was a social leper on Earth till he blew his brains out last year. I don't want to end up like that!"

"You don't want to end up like that?" the lizard suggested quietly.

"You're damn right I don't. But I also don't want to end up like that Ruwandan who clinched the relation with the Humdingers by serving out his whole term to perfection . . . and then died right after of acute radiation poisoning. He's a human hero now, but he's just as dead . . . a martyr to human desire for Humding microfabrics and the electromagnetic dramas of Cliklick! All I want is to get out of here——" Paul broke off suddenly, drew his legs high out of the water, and said, "I think you should consider your own problem first. There's a mangleworm working his way upstream behind you."

"We were discussing you, not me. What does the mangleworm working his way upstream behind me suggest about your prob——"

Paul sighed and continued along the fallen trunk, carefully keeping his legs well out of the water until he was past the point where small fragments of rogerian spun on the current. *Less* intelligent than a tree toad, he decided. Still, a pleasant break in an otherwise tedious day.

He reached the opposite edge and pushed his way through dried cracklethorn to the facing edge of Kooluuwe Ravine. After one disgusted glance up the vertical face of the cliff, he commenced his climb.

Twelve Earth days, he thought; *only a mere twelve days. If I just can hold out . . . and not make any really deadly faux pas . . . I've got it made. It may not be comfortable, but the Shecklites seem to be as eager to make it work out as I am. I wonder,* he thought, not for the first time, *what in the world they see available from Earth that helps them to put up with me. They're not interested in gold or physics or Beethoven. It all seems to be centered around radishes and tiddlywinks and the works of Phillip James Bailey. That gets them all excited. Now who on Earth was Phillip James Bailey?*

By persistent climbing, and refusal to stop to discuss his problem with three other rogerians, Paul neared the top by midmorn. During the last ten meters, he heard voices from above him; they held a sneering quality not at all to his liking. He looked up. Outlined against the yellow sky stood several Shecklites looking down at him.

He clambered up over the lip of the ravine and sat puffing. The Shecklites moved to encircle him. They were mid-adolescents, six of them, and he began to feel nervous. When he recognized one of them as Noowiioy, the mayor's offspring, he felt really depressed. There was a real bully for you.

Despite his exhaustion, he managed to regain his feet. "Got to get to the village," he said. "Eggs. Can't play now." He took a step towards the flametrees bordering the ravine.

Noowiioy took a sidewise step, blocking Paul's escape. "We saw you climbing," he said nastily, his face scrooching up in gray crinkles. "You want to know something? You're not a Shecklite after all." The other five laughed mockingly.

Paul froze in shock. No one was ever supposed to say that; it could be the sign of the end. The adolescents had been taunting from the beginning, even cruel, but none of them had stepped across that line before.

Noowiioy's face wrinkled again, with the humor of what he was about to say. "You're no Shecklite," he said again. "You're some kind of rockcrab."

Paul's heart picked up where it had left off. He had heard that phrase before among the youthful toughs. It was not a reference to his humanity, but a challenge to his Shecklite manhood . . . or perhaps (Paul had given up trying to differentiate in this area) his womanhood.

"I'm a better Shecklite than you, Noowiioy," he played out on his voder. "Now move aside and let me pass."

Noowiioy looked at his cronies. He raised his wings in a large shrug and let them drop again. "Hear that, guys?" he chewed. "Says he's better than we are! Shall we let him prove it?"

The others chortled unpleasantly and moved the ring in close.

Oh, my God! Not another stupid challenge.

"Some other time," Paul played desperately, "I would be more than delighted to show up your snotty arrogance." He tried, while not cringing utterly, to choose his words carefully from the less provocative ones in use among the youthful gangs. "But as I am on an important mission to Youoory, I cannot paused to engage in your infantile . . ."

Noowiioy bent slowly forward from his upper waist until his beaknose brushed Paul's snub one. "Little rockcrab gotta do what his Mops says; little rockcrab run to store to get eggs; scared to show what a rockcrab he really is."

Paul sighed. He saw no way out. Noowiioy had chosen firm ground. The values were clearly marked; no real Shecklite youth would put parental instructions over a test of 'hoodness; the parents would be ashamed themselves in such a case.

"What did you have in mind, brain-molt?" he asked wearily.

"Rockcrab care to groundplunge?" the other asked bluntly.

Oh, Lord. Scratch one human being.

"Why not?" bluffed Paul. "If it's the only way to stop your asinine yappings."

"Okay. Here and now. I've been waiting months for this. Off the ravine right here, and the last one to lift wing wins."

Paul walked to the edge of Kooluuwe Ravine, the others following. He looked down the sheer drop. Not a chance. He looked at Noowiioy's five cohorts. They seemed nervous, uncertain. But not to the extent they were going to step in and stop this idiocy. His thoughts were running as fast as they ever had before.

"You *are* a cowardly mudworm, Noowiioy," he suggested mildly.

Noowiioy's face blued in rage. "You dare say that!"

Paul pointed down the cliff. "Why lift wing at all? We'll jump together from right here and go all the way to the bottom. If either of us lifts wing before striking bottom, that's being a rockcrab *and* a mudworm."

Noowiioy looked confused. "That's ridiculous. I'll go within ten lengths of the ground before I pull out. Bet you can't do that!"

Paul shook his head disgustedly. "Noowiioy, you're a bully and a boaster, but you just don't have it when it counts. I'm sick of all your ten lengths, five lengths, three, half a length. If you can't face going all the way, then stop bragging about your so-called guts. Put up or shut up."

"But you gotta pull out sometime," choked Noowiioy,

not quite getting it even yet. "Or you'll be smeared all over the bottom!"

"Right. You can't face it, can you?" pressed Paul. *"I'm* willing. It might be fun." He looked at the others. "I'd like to show up this creep for the crabworm he is. If he won't jump with me, let's push him over, and watch him cop out."

"Hey, wait a minute!" Noowiioy was scrabbling rapidly back from the edge. He looked about at his compatriots, but the current of mockery had shifted. They were all in glee at seeing the tables so deftly turned. "Don't you see, he's bluffing—"

"Then call his bluff," said one of his friends mockingly.

"Yeah, Noowy, afraid to go all the way to the ground? Looks like *you're* the rockcrab."

They all chortled.

Noowiioy stared wildly about. "But it's not fair," he said, his voice wobbling. "Don't you see? He's actually trying to *kill* me."

"He's willing to do it," said Geeyuuo. "And you're not."

"But *he's* not . . . I mean, he's not really a . . ." There was a sudden hush as all stared at him, wondering if he would actually break the unspoken taboo.

"Radishes," Paul played rapidly in minor key. "Tiddly-winks. Phillip James Bailey."

Noowiioy glared at him, and suddenly lifted wing. With a down-rush of air on their upturned faces, he mounted to circle above them. "My father the mayor will hear about this," he flung down, and then was rising up toward the pole-mounted houses visible beyond the treetops.

The other youths crowded about Paul, clapping him on the thighs in friendly fashion. "That was beautiful," said Geeyuuo. "Noowy's been flapping for a fall a long time now. Say, would you really have gone through with it?"

Paul shrugged. "Why not?" he said indifferently. "What have I got to lose?"

He started walking toward Youoory village.

The village of Youoory tottered at the top of its tall poles in the wide clearing just west of the ravine. The poles were not intended for climbing, but they could serve the purpose. Paul crossed to the base of the one holding, among other establishments, the Aoweeyo Eggery.

Something massive, floppy, and quite unfamiliar lay sprawled at the base of the pole. As Paul approached, it raised an ursine head above flat flippers, and spoke to him.

" 'Oo 'r 'oo?" A gruff voice, squeezed out between rollers.

"I am Wayuueo of the Mestoiwe lineage," said Paul. "And you?"

" 'M 'oo'a'ee uv 'e 'ee'i'aa 'inea'," said the other.

"Oh," said Paul uncertainly. He had heard that there was another galactic exchange representative in the area, but this was their first encounter. He felt a surge of companionship for the alien. Perhaps here was someone who could feel for his own difficulties; he wondered if he dared venture on a little frank conversation.

A small voice piped from behind him. "Look, Mops; look at those two *funny* animals!"

"Hush, Uyee," answered a female-priority voice. "That is just two Shecklites talking together. They're just like anybody else. Remember that! Animals indeed!"

Paul resignedly smiled at the other alien, and began to climb the post. He couldn't risk bringing trouble to three worlds. He wondered what the temporary 'oo'a'ee of the ee'i'aa would bring to the Shecklites in trade if he managed to fulfill his standard year.

The rough knotted wood, warm in the midday sun, offered good handholds for his climb. Weary as he was, Paul had soon attained the lowest level of Youoory, and paused to rest. The eggery was still five levels above him; this level was crammed with the apparatus servicing the eyrie—power, sewage, computer, and interplanetary teleport equipment. The Shecklites might be simple in their lives, and untechnological in their abilities, but they had very solid trade and diplomatic relations with the rest of the galaxy: they weren't primitives.

Paul crossed to the struts supporting the upper levels, took one glance up at the homes and shops dangling from the second level above him, and began to ascend. The Shecklites wouldn't have done so well in making and keeping Galactic contacts, he thought, if they hadn't been very tolerant of differences. Perhaps he was worrying too much; they wanted him to get through the next few days as badly as he did. Surely, even that idiot Noowiioy couldn't manage to mess up an important interracial relationship. He hoped.

Clutching his embryo sack of breeir eggs, Paul turned from the counter of the Aoweeyo Eggery, and stopped short. Above him towered the tall gray form of Mayor Bleewooe of Youoory.

Mayor Bleewooe looked down thoughtfully at Paul, who gulped helplessly. The mayor's puckered lips chewed slowly sideways in his leathery face—the smooth, lineless face of old age. The wide beak opened and words fell from the heights upon Paul's unwilling ears.

"If it is convenient for you, and no imposition, small one, perhaps you would honor me with a slight conversation. But if it is any trouble, then perhaps some other time."

As on Earth, the elected officials of Sheckley called themselves "public servants." Unlike Earth, they behaved as such.

Paul gulped again and managed to respond, in a combination of vocal and voder, "When I'm good and ready, you lump of obsequiousness." This also was standard format.

Formalities over, the mayor got to the point. "Young one, we have a problem, and I do hope you can spare the time to hear me out. When I speak of a problem, I do not mean only you and I, but the whole village of Youoory. More, this effects the entire province of Iewaooe. In fact, the continent of Eewayow is not exempt from interest in this affair. I dare say that the whole planet—"

"I'm listening," said Paul sullenly. "Spit it out."

Mayor Bleewooe nodded his head wisely for a moment, scratched his left shoulder blade with the tip of his right wing, and then enunciated solemnly:

"Small one, you must be aware of the method by which sentient races make, or fail to make, viable relationships with one another. I refer, of course, to the lottery system, by means of which one randomly chosen individual from a given species is selected to live a standard year as a citizen of another world. . . ."

Paul could say nothing. The mayor's roundabout words certainly sounded like the whiplash of descending doom.

Mayor Bleewooe was methodically continuing. ". . . so if the representative individual and the society he has joined can mutually tolerate each other for one standard year, then trade and diplomatic relationships can be entered into between the two species in question. But . . ."— and the mayor drew himself up austerely—"if for any reason, *not,* then . . . not!"

Paul could not passively wait for the final blow without a last attempt to assert himself. "Sir," he frantically stumbled over his voder keys, "I mean, you bureaucratic underling, servant of the people, what has all this to do with me? No, rather, I do not care to know! I am . . ." He drew himself erect, and glared up at the mayor, "I am Wayuueo of the Mestoiwe lineage, son and daughter of Oyeuuwa and Jooweyu, of the Niiweyoi clan. Do you intend . . . can you possibly dare . . . to impugn my parentage? To cast doubt on my pedigree as a true Shecklite of the Shecklites, a child of my own peoples?"

Mayor Bleewooe gazed down at him for a long, heart-stopping moment, eye-hoods slowly descending over his white orbits, and then snapping up again like a released window shade.

"No," he said mildly at last. "I am sure you are a credit to your Mops and Poms, Wayuueo of the Mestoiwe. A good Shecklite," he muttered, turning away slowly, his aged face shaking as in disbelief. "A fine young Shecklite."

Paul exhaled, and gradually stilled the shaking of his whole body. Carefully planting each foot as he moved, he crossed to the eggery exit.

From behind him came the voice of the mayor. "Please be at home at sunset this evening, young one. You may expect a visit from the Council of Olders."

Paul considered jumping and ending the whole mess at once. But even that would have taken too much effort. He began the long crawl home, his mouth filled with the bilious taste of futility.

"Care to tell me about your problem?" said the rogerian.

Paul slumped weariedly on the ledge and carefully cached the embryo sack of breeir eggs in a safe niche. He looked down into Kooluuwe Ravine. The sun had long passed beyond the rim above him, and the bottom of the cleft was filling with late afternoon shadow. Another twenty minutes' climb should bring him back to the homestead.

"Not particularly," he told the lizard.

"You don't particularly want to tell me about your problem?" the lizard prompted.

Paul rested his chin in his cupped hands. "Don't ask questions," he said. "Give me an answer."

"You want me to give you an answer?"

"Yes," said Paul.

The rogerian was silent a moment. "Why do you want me to give you an answer?"

Paul was silent.

The lizard blinked its large azure eyes, and tried again. "What does your wanting me to give you an answer tell you about your problem?"

Paul was silent.

The lizard twitched nervously. "Why does your problem bother you so, *really?*" it said.

Paul collected his eggs and stood up, thinking. "I think what *really* bothers me most," he said at last, "is that Poms and Mops will be so disappointed in me."

He resumed his climb.

Shortly afterwards he heard the slow beat of wings above him, and saw the full Council of Olders flapping their way across the ravine from the direction of Youoory Village. They circled once above him and passed out of sight in the direction of the Mestoiwe cave. By the time Paul had crawled over the rim to the ledge fronting his home, the whole delegation was squatting in a wide semi-circle, delicately nibbling the Kabisco bars Mops saved for special occasions.

None of them looked in his direction until he crawled drearily up to them and handed the embryo sack to Moppom.

"They have come to talk to you, Wayuueo," Mops told him nervously. "It sounds like it's very important. I'm afraid that . . ." She couldn't finish.

Paul turned to the silent crescent of Olders. He could feel the nails of his hands biting into his palms. This wasn't going to be easy. He took three steps forward and halted, his eyes downcast.

Mayor Bleewooe slowly rose to his feet and stared at Paul a long moment. He scuffed his feet on the ground, kicked at an embedded rock, frowned ponderously.

"I have an official announcement to make," he said. "It is not an easy thing to tell, it is a difficult matter to broach. But it must be said, it cannot be otherwise."

Paul felt a sudden urge to push the garrulous mayor off the cliff, but that would solve nothing. He waited.

Eventually the mayor continued. "It is a very important matter, the lottery system," he said bluntly. "It is at the base of the life of all of us here on Sheckley. Without the economies and arts and sciences we have gained from Galactic contacts, our lives would still be short and narrow and miserable as they were before we reached the stars and joined the lottery exchange system." He looked steadily at Paul. "If it is at all possible, if there is any hope at all, we shall do all in our power to make and keep relationships with the other creatures in the Galaxy. Every Shecklite knows the importance of this." He cleared his throat, looking deeply embarrassed.

Paul considered saving everybody further embarrassment by two steps and a jump into the ravine. But the Shecklites would just catch him on the way down. It was useless.

Slowly the mayor stretched out his leathery wings. "I know you will do well for us, Wayuueo of the Mestoiwe," he was saying huskily. "Tomorrow you will be taken by webship to the world of the Dreffitti. You have been chosen by lottery as Sheckley's representative to those beings."

As the whole delegation and then his family stroked and hugged and ogled him, Paul could hear the mayor's voice ricocheting on: ". . . live in chlorine bubbles under the waters of the muddy estuaries . . . gourmet delicacies and temperature control techniques of huge value to our world . . . far the greatest honor that can befall a Shecklite."

And, oh, were his Poms and Mops proud of him!

A little later, during the formal speeches, Paul *did* step off into the ravine, but they caught him before he fell fifteen feet. Nobody remarked on his awkwardness at such a moment.

After all, such an honor would fluster anybody.

THE PUSHER

John Varley

Star-travelers in a universe of time-dilation effect would necessarily be a breed apart, aging
only a few months while the people on planets
they visit would go through decades of life.
Their relationships with people living in normal
time would have to be very, very strange.
Here's a story of one spaceman's method of
coping.

John Varley won both the Nebula and Hugo
awards for "The Persistence of Vision." He has
published a novel trilogy, *Titan, Wizard,* and
(forthcoming) *Demon.*

THINGS CHANGE. IAN HAISE EXPECTED THAT. Yet there are certain constants, dictated by function and use. Ian looked for those and he seldom went wrong.

The playground was not much like the ones he had known as a child. But playgrounds are built to entertain children. They will always have something to swing on, something to slide down, something to climb. This one had all those things, and more. Part of it was thickly wooded. There was a swimming hole. The stationary apparatus was combined with dazzling light sculptures that darted in and out of reality. There were animals, too: pygmy rhinoceros and elegant gazelles no taller than your knee. They seemed unnaturally gentle and unafraid.

But most of all, the playground had children.

Ian liked children.

He sat on a wooden park bench at the edge of the trees, in the shadows, and watched them. They came in all colors and all sizes, in both sexes. There were black ones like animated licorice jelly beans and white ones like bunny rabbits, and brown ones with curly hair and more brown ones with slanted eyes and straight black hair and some who had been white but were now toasted browner than some of the brown ones.

Ian concentrated on the girls. He had tried with boys before, long ago, but it had not worked out.

He watched one black child for a time, trying to estimate her age. He thought it was around eight or nine. Too young. Another one was more like thirteen, judging from

92

her shirt. A possibility, but he'd prefer something younger. Somebody less sophisticated, less suspicious.

Finally he found a girl he liked. She was brown, but with startling blonde hair. Ten? Possibly eleven. Young enough, at any rate.

He concentrated on her and did the strange thing he did when he had selected the right one. He didn't know what it was, but it usually worked. Mostly it was just a matter of looking at her, keeping his eyes fixed on her no matter where she went or what she did, not allowing himself to be distracted by anything. And sure enough, in a few minutes she looked up, looked around, and her eyes locked with his. She held his gaze for a moment, then went back to her play.

He relaxed. Possibly what he did was nothing at all. He had noticed, with adult women, that if one really caught his eye so he found himself staring at her, she would usually look up from what she was doing and catch him. It never seemed to fail. Talking to other men, he had found it to be a common experience. It was almost as if they could feel his gaze. Women had told him it was nonsense, or if not, it was just reaction to things seen peripherally by people trained to alertness for sexual signals. Merely an unconscious observation penetrating to the awareness; nothing mysterious, like ESP.

Perhaps. Still, Ian was very good at this sort of eye contact. Several times he had noticed the girls rubbing the backs of their necks while he observed them, or hunching their shoulders. Maybe they'd developed some kind of ESP and just didn't recognize it as such.

Now he merely watched her. He was smiling, so that every time she looked up to see him—which she did with increasing frequency—she saw a friendly, slightly graying man with a broken nose and powerful shoulders. His hands were strong, too. He kept them clasped in his lap.

Presently she began to wander in his direction.

No one watching her would have thought she was coming toward him. She probably didn't know it herself. On her way, she found reasons to stop and tumble, jump on the soft rubber mats, or chase a flock of noisy geese. But she was coming toward him, and she would end up on the park bench beside him.

He glanced around quickly. As before, there were few

adults in this playground. It had surprised him when he
arrived. Apparently the new conditioning techniques had
reduced the numbers of the violent and twisted to the
point that parents felt it safe to allow their children to run
without supervision. The adults present were involved with
each other. No one had given him a second glance when
he arrived.

That was fine with Ian. It made what he planned to do
much easier. He had his excuses ready, of course, but it
could be embarrassing to be confronted with the questions
representatives of the law ask single, middle-aged men who
hang around playgrounds.

For a moment he considered, with real concern, how the
parents of these children could feel so confident, even with
mental conditioning. After all, no one was conditioned
until he had first done something. New maniacs were presumably being produced every day. Typically, they looked
just like everyone else until they proved their difference by
some demented act.

Somebody ought to give those parents a stern lecture,
he thought.

"Who are you?"

Ian frowned. Not eleven, surely, not seen up this close.
Maybe not even ten. She might be as young as eight.

Would eight be all right? He tasted the idea with his
usual caution, looked around again for curious eyes. He
saw none.

"My name is Ian. What's yours?"

"No. Not your *name.* Who are *you?"*

"You mean what do I do?"

"Yes."

"I'm a pusher."

She thought that over, then smiled. She had her permanent teeth, crowded into a small jaw.

"You give away pills?"

He laughed. "Very good," he said. "You must do a lot
of reading." She said nothing, but her manner indicated
she was pleased.

"No," he said. "That's an old kind of pusher. I'm the
other kind. But you knew that, didn't you?" When he
smiled she broke into giggles. She was doing the pointless
things with her hands that little girls do. He thought she
had a pretty good idea of how cute she was, but no inkling

of her forbidden eroticism. She was a ripe seed with sexuality ready to burst to the surface. Her body was a bony sketch, a framework on which to build a woman.

"How old are you?" he asked.

"That's a secret. What happened to your nose?"

"I broke it a long time ago. I'll bet you're twelve."

She giggled, then nodded. Eleven, then. And just barely.

"Do you want some candy?" He reached into his pocket and pulled out the pink and white striped paper bag.

She shook her head solemnly. "My mother says not to take candy from strangers."

"But we're not strangers. I'm Ian, the pusher."

She thought that over. While she hesitated he reached into the bag and picked out a chocolate thing so thick and gooey it was almost obscene. He bit into it, forcing himself to chew. He hated sweets.

"Okay," she said, and reached toward the bag. He pulled it away. She looked at him in innocent surprise.

"I just thought of something," he said. "I don't know your name. So I guess we *are* strangers."

She caught on to the game when she saw the twinkle in his eye. He'd practiced that. It was a good twinkle.

"My name is Radiant. Radiant Shiningstar Smith."

"A very fancy name," he said, thinking how names had changed. "For a very pretty girl." He paused, and cocked his head. "No. I don't think so. You're Radiant . . . Starr. With two *r's*. . . . *Captain* Radiant Starr, of the Star Patrol."

She was dubious for a moment. He wondered if he'd judged her wrong. Perhaps she was really Mizz Radiant Faintingheart Belle, or Mrs. Radiant Motherhood. But her fingernails were a bit dirty for that.

She pointed a finger at him and made a Donald Duck sound as her thumb worked back and forth. He put his hand to his heart and fell over sideways, and she dissolved in laughter. She was careful, however, to keep her weapon firmly trained on him.

"And you'd better give me that candy or I'll shoot you again."

The playground was darker now, and not so crowded. She sat beside him on the bench, swinging her legs. Her bare feet did not quite touch the dirt.

She was going to be quite beautiful. He could see it clearly in her face. As for the body . . . who could tell?

Not that he really gave a damn.

She was dressed in a little of this and a little of that, worn here and there without much regard for his concepts of modesty. Many of the children wore nothing. It had been something of a shock when he arrived. Now he was almost used to it, but he still thought it incautious on the part of her parents. Did they really think the world was that safe, to let an eleven-year-old girl go practically naked in a public place?

He sat there listening to her prattle about her friends—the ones she hated and the one or two she simply adored —with only part of his attention.

He inserted um's and uh-huh's in the right places.

She was cute, there was no denying it. She seemed as sweet as a child that age ever gets, which can be very sweet and as poisonous as a rattlesnake, almost at the same moment. She had the capacity to be warm, but it was on the surface. Underneath, she cared mostly about herself. Her loyalty would be a transitory thing, bestowed easily, just as easily forgotten.

And why not? She was young. It was perfectly healthy for her to be that way.

But did he dare try to touch her?

It was crazy. It was as insane as they told him it was. It worked so seldom. Why would it work with her? He felt a weight of defeat.

"Are you okay?"

"Huh? Me? Oh, sure, I'm all right. Isn't your mother going to be worried about you?"

"I don't have to be in for hours and hours yet." For a moment she looked so grown up he almost believed the lie.

"Well, I'm getting tired of sitting here. And the candy's all gone." He looked at her face. Most of the chocolate had ended up in a big circle around her mouth, except where she had wiped it daintily on her shoulder or forearm. "What's back there?"

She turned.

"That? That's the swimming hole."

"Why don't we go over there? I'll tell you a story."

*   *   *

The promise of a story was not enough to keep her out of the water. He didn't know if that was good or bad. He knew she was smart, a reader, and she had an imagination. But she was also active. That pull was too strong for him. He sat far from the water, under some bushes, and watched her swim with the three other children still in the park this late in the evening.

Maybe she would come back to him, and maybe she wouldn't. It wouldn't change his life either way, but it might change hers.

She emerged dripping and infinitely cleaner from the murky water. She dressed again in her random scraps, for whatever good it did her, and came to him, shivering.

"I'm cold," she said.

"Here." He took off his jacket. She looked at his hands as he wrapped it around her, and she reached out and touched the hardness of his shoulder.

"You sure must be strong," she commented.

"Pretty strong. I work hard, being a pusher."

"Just what *is* a pusher?" she said, and stifled a yawn.

"Come sit on my lap, and I'll tell you."

He did tell her, and it was a very good story that no adventurous child could resist. He had practiced that story, refined it, told it many times into a recorder until he had the rhythms and cadences just right, until he found just the right words—not too difficult words, but words with some fire and juice in them.

And once more he grew encouraged. She had been tired when he started, but he gradually caught her attention. It was possible no one had ever told her a story in quite that way. She was used to sitting before the screen and having a story shoved into her eyes and ears. It was something new to be able to interrupt with questions and get answers. Even reading was not like that. It was the oral tradition of storytelling, and it could still mesmerize the nth generation of the electronic age.

"That sounds great," she said, when she was sure he was through.

"You liked it?"

"I really truly did. I think I want to be a pusher when I grow up. That was a really neat story."

"Well, that's not actually the story I was going to tell you. That's just what it's like to be a pusher."

"You mean you have another story?"

"Sure." He looked at his watch. "But I'm afraid it's getting late. It's almost dark, and everybody's gone home. You'd probably better go, too."

She was in agony, torn between what she was supposed to do and what she wanted. It really should be no contest, if she was who he thought she was.

"Well . . . but—but I'll come back here tomorrow and you—"

He was shaking his head.

"My ship leaves in the morning," he said. "There's no time."

"Then tell me now! I can stay out. Tell me now. Please please please?"

He coyly resisted, harrumphed, protested, but in the end allowed himself to be seduced. He felt very good. He had her like a five-pound trout on a twenty-pound line. It wasn't sporting. But, then, he wasn't playing a game.

So at last he got to his specialty.

He sometimes wished he could claim the story for his own, but the fact was he could not make up stories. He no longer tried to. Instead, he cribbed from every fairy tale and fantasy story he could find. If he had a genius, it was in adapting some of the elements to fit the world she knew —while keeping it strange enough to enthrall her—and in ad-libbing the end to personalize it.

It was a wonderful tale he told. It had enchanted castles sitting on mountains of glass, moist caverns beneath the sea, fleets of starships and shining riders astride horses that flew the galaxy. There were evil alien creatures, and others with much good in them. There were drugged potions. Scaled beasts roared out of hyperspace to devour planets.

Amid all the turmoil strode the Prince and Princess. They got into frightful jams and helped each other out of them.

The story was never quite the same. He watched her eyes. When they wandered, he threw away whole chunks of story. When they widened, he knew what parts to plug in later. He tailored it to her reactions.

The child was sleepy. Sooner or later she would surrender. He needed her in a trance state, neither awake nor asleep. That is when the story would end.

*　　*　　*

". . . and though the healers labored long and hard, they could not save the Princess. She died that night, far from her Prince."

Her mouth was a little round *o*. Stories were not supposed to end that way.

"Is that *all?* She died, and she never saw the Prince again?"

"Well, not quite all. But the rest of it probably isn't true, and I shouldn't tell it to you." Ian felt pleasantly tired. His throat was a little raw, making him hoarse. Radiant was a warm weight on his lap.

"You *have* to tell me, you know," she said, reasonably. He supposed she was right. He took a deep breath.

"All right. At the funeral, all the greatest people from that part of the galaxy were in attendance. Among them was the greatest Sorcerer who ever lived. His name . . . but I really shouldn't tell you his name. I'm sure he'd be very cross if I did."

"This Sorcerer passed by the Princess's bier . . . that's a—"

"I know, I *know,* Ian. Go on!"

"Suddenly he frowned and leaned over her pale form. 'What is this?' he thundered. 'Why was I not told?' Everyone was very concerned. This Sorcerer was a dangerous man. One time when someone insulted him he made a spell that turned everyone's heads backwards so they had to walk around with rearview mirrors. No one knew what he would do if he got really angry.

" 'This Princess is wearing the Starstone,' he said, and drew himself up and frowned all around as if he were surrounded by idiots. I'm sure he thought he was, and maybe he was right. Because he went on to tell them just what the Starstone was, and what it did, something no one there had ever heard before. And this is the part I'm not sure of. Because, though everyone knew the Sorcerer was a wise and powerful man, he was also known as a great liar.

"He said that the Starstone was capable of capturing the essence of a person at the moment of her death. All her wisdom, all her power, all her knowledge and beauty and strength would flow into the stone and be held there, timelessly."

"In suspended animation," Radiant breathed.

"Precisely. When they heard this, the people were amazed. They buffeted the Sorcerer with questions, to which he gave few answers, and those only grudgingly. Finally he left in a huff. When he was gone everyone talked long into the night about the things he had said. Some felt the Sorcerer had held out hope that the Princess might yet live on. That if her body were frozen, the Prince, upon his return, might somehow infuse her essence back within her. Others thought the Sorcerer had said that was impossible, that the Princess was doomed to a half-life, locked in the stone.

"But the opinion that prevailed was this:

"The Princess would probably never come fully back to life. But her essence might flow from the Starstone and into another, if the right person could be found. All agreed this person must be a young maiden. She must be beautiful, very smart, swift of foot, loving, kind . . . oh, my, the list was very long. Everyone doubted such a person could be found. Many did not even want to try.

"But at last it was decided the Starstone should be given to a faithful friend of the Prince. He would search the galaxy for this maiden. If she existed, he would find her.

"So he departed with the blessings of many worlds behind him, vowing to find the maiden and give her the Starstone."

He stopped again, cleared his throat, and let the silence grow.

"Is that all?" she said, at last, in a whisper.

"Not quite all," he admitted. "I'm afraid I tricked you."

"Tricked me?"

He opened the front of his coat, which was still draped around her shoulders. He reached in past her bony chest and down into an inner pocket of the coat. He came up with the crystal. It was oval, with one side flat. It pulsed ruby light as it sat in the palm of his hand.

"It shines," she said, looking at it wide-eyed and open-mouthed.

"Yes, it does. And that means you're the one."

"Me?"

"Yes. Take it." He handed it to her, and as he did so, he nicked it with his thumbnail. Red light spilled into her hands, flowed between her fingers, seemed to soak into her skin. When it was over, the crystal still pulsed, but dimmed. Her hands were trembling.

"It felt very, very hot," she said.

"That was the essence of the Princess."

"And the Prince? Is he still looking for her?"

"No one knows. I think he's still out there, and some day he will come back for her."

"And what then?"

He looked away from her. "I can't say. I think, even though you are lovely, and even though you have the Starstone, that he will just pine away. He loved her very much."

"I'd take care of him," she promised.

"Maybe that would help. But I have a problem now. I don't have the heart to tell the Prince that she is dead. Yet I feel that the Starstone will draw him to it one day. If he comes and finds you, I fear for him. I think perhaps I should take the stone to a far part of the galaxy, some place he could never find it. Then at least he would never know. It might be better that way."

"But I'd help him," she said, earnestly. "I promise. I'd wait for him, and when he came, I'd take her place. You'll see."

He studied her. Perhaps she would. He looked into her eyes for a long time, and at last let her see his satisfaction.

"Very well. You can keep it then."

"I'll wait for him," she said. "You'll see."

She was very tired, almost asleep.

"You should go home now," he suggested.

"Maybe I could just lie down for a moment," she said.

"All right." He lifted her gently and placed her prone on the ground. He stood looking at her, then knelt beside her and began to gently stroke her forehead. She opened her eyes with no alarm, then closed them again. He continued to stroke her.

Twenty minutes later he left the playground, alone.

He was always depressed afterwards. It was worse than usual this time. She had been much nicer than he had imagined at first. Who could have guessed such a romantic heart beat beneath all that dirt?

He found a phone booth several blocks away. Punching her name into information yielded a fifteen-digit number, which he called. He held his hand over the camera eye.

A woman's face appeared on his screen.

"Your daughter is in the playground, at the south end

by the pool, under the bushes," he said. He gave the address of the playground.

"We were so worried! What . . . is she . . . who is—"

He hung up and hurried away.

Most of the other pushers thought he was sick. Not that it mattered. Pushers were a tolerant group when it came to other pushers, and especially when it came to anything a pusher might care to do to a puller. He wished he had never told anyone how he spent his leave time, but he had, and now he had to live with it.

So, while they didn't care if he amused himself by pulling the legs and arms off infant puller pups, they were all just back from ground leave and couldn't pass up an opportunity to get on each other's nerves. They ragged him mercilessly.

"How were the swing-sets this trip, Ian?"

"Did you bring me those dirty knickers I asked for?"

"Was it good for you, honey? Did she pant and slobber?"

"*My ten-year-old baby, she's a-pullin' me back home. . . .*"

Ian bore it stoically. It was in extremely bad taste, and he was the brunt of it, but it really didn't matter. It would end as soon as they lifted again. They would never understand what he sought, but he felt he understood them. They hated coming to Earth. There was nothing for them there, and perhaps they wished there was.

And he was a pusher himself. He didn't care for pullers. He agreed with the sentiment expressed by Marian, shortly after lift-off. Marian had just finished her first ground leave after her first voyage. So naturally she was the drunkest of them all.

"Gravity sucks," she said, and threw up.

It was three months to Amity, and three months back. He hadn't the foggiest idea of how far it was in miles; after the tenth or eleventh zero his mind clicked off.

Amity. Shit City. He didn't even get off the ship. Why bother? The planet was peopled with things that looked a little like ten-ton caterpillars and a little like sentient green turds. Toilets were a revolutionary idea to the Amiti; so were ice cream bars, sherberts, sugar donuts, and peppermint. Plumbing had never caught on, but sweets had, and fancy desserts from every nation on Earth. In addition, there was a pouch of reassuring mail for the forlorn human embassy. The cargo for the return trip was some grayish sludge that Ian supposed someone on Earth found tremendously valuable, and a packet of desperate mail for the folks back home. Ian didn't need to read the letters to know what was in them. They could all be summed up as "Get me *out* of here!"

He sat at the viewport and watched an Amiti family lumbering and farting its way down the spaceport road. They paused every so often to do something that looked like an alien cluster-fuck. The road was brown. The land around it was brown, and in the distance were brown, unremarkable hills. There was a brown haze in the air, and the sun was yellow-brown.

He thought of castles perched on mountains of glass, of Princes and Princesses, of shining white horses galloping among the stars.

He spent the return trip just as he had on the way out: sweating down in the gargantuan pipes of the stardrive. Just beyond the metal walls unimaginable energies pulsed. And on the walls themselves, tiny plasmoids grew into bigger plasmoids. The process was too slow to see, but if left unchecked the encrustations would soon impair the engines. His job was to scrape them off.

Not everyone was cut out to be an astrogator.

And what of it? It was honest work. He had made his choices long ago. You spent your life either pulling gees or pushing *c*. And when you got tired, you grabbed some *z*'s. If there was a pusher's code, that was it.

The plasmoids were red and crystalline, teardrop-shaped. When he broke them free of the walls, they had one flat side. They were full of a liquid light that felt as hot as the center of the sun.

It was always hard to get off the ship. A lot of pushers never did. One day, he wouldn't either.

He stood for a few moments looking at it all. It was necessary to soak it in passively at first, get used to the changes. Big changes didn't bother him. Buildings were just the world's furniture, and he didn't care how it was arranged. Small changes worried the shit out of him. Ears, for instance. Very few of the people he saw had earlobes.

Each time he returned he felt a little more like an ape who has fallen from his tree. One day he'd return to find everybody had three eyes or six fingers, or that little girls no longer cared to hear stories of adventure.

He stood there, dithering, getting used to the way people were painting their faces, listening to what sounded like Spanish being spoken all around him. Occasional English or Arabic words seasoned it. He grabbed a crewmate's arm and asked him where they were. The man didn't know. So he asked the captain, and she said it was Argentina, or it had been when they left.

The phone booths were smaller. He wondered why.

There were four names in his book. He sat there facing the phone, wondering which name to call first. His eyes were drawn to Radiant Shiningstar Smith, so he punched that name into the phone. He got a number and an address in Novosibirsk.

Checking the timetable he had picked—putting off making the call—he found the antipodean shuttle left on the hour. Then he wiped his hands on his pants and took a deep breath and looked up to see her standing outside the phone booth. They regarded each other silently for a moment. She saw a man much shorter than she remembered, but powerfully built, with big hands and shoulders and a pitted face that would have been forbidding but for the gentle eyes. He saw a tall woman around forty years old who was fully as beautiful as he had expected she would be. The hand of age had just begun to touch her. He thought she was fighting that waistline and fretting about those wrinkles, but none of that mattered to him. Only one thing mattered, and he would know it soon enough.

"You *are* Ian Haise, aren't you?" she said, at last.

"It was sheer luck I remembered you again," she was saying. He noted the choice of words. She could have said coincidence.

"It was two years ago. We were moving again and I was sorting through some things and I came across that plasmoid. I hadn't thought about you in . . . oh, it must have been fifteen years."

He said something noncommittal. They were in a restaurant, away from most of the other patrons, at a booth

near a glass wall beyond which spaceships were being
trundled to and from the blast pits.

"I hope I didn't get you into trouble," he said.

She shrugged it away.

"You did, some, but that was so long ago. I certainly
wouldn't bear a grudge that long. And the fact is, I thought
it was all worth it at the time."

She went on to tell him of the uproar he had caused in
her family, of the visits by the police, the interrogation,
puzzlement, and final helplessness. No one knew quite
what to make of her story. They had identified him quickly
enough, only to find he had left Earth, not to return for a
long, long time.

"I didn't break any laws," he pointed out.

"That's what no one could understand. I told them you
had talked to me and told me a long story, and then I
went to sleep. None of them seemed interested in what
the story was about. So I didn't tell them. And I didn't
tell them about the . . . the Starstone." She smiled. "Actually, I was relieved they hadn't asked. I was determined
not to tell them, but I was a little afraid of holding it all
back. I thought they were agents of the . . . who were the
villains in your story? I've forgotten."

"It's not important."

"I guess not. But something is."

"Yes."

"Maybe you should tell me what it is. Maybe you can
answer the question that's been in the back of my mind for
twenty-five years, ever since I found out that thing you
gave me was just the scrapings from a starship engine."

"Was it?" he said, looking into her eyes. "Don't get me
wrong. I'm not saying it *was* more than that. I'm asking
you if it wasn't more."

"Yes, I guess it was more," she said, at last.

"I'm glad."

"I believed in that story passionately for . . . oh, years
and years. Then I stopped believing it."

"All at once?"

"No. Gradually. It didn't hurt much. Part of growing
up, I guess."

"And you remembered me."

"Well, that took some work. I went to a hypnotist when
I was twenty-five and recovered your name and the name
of your ship. Did you know—"

"Yes. I mentioned them on purpose."

She nodded, and they fell silent again. When she looked at him now, he saw more sympathy, less defensiveness. But there was still a question.

"Why?" she said.

He nodded, then looked away from her, out to the starships. He wished he was on one of them, pushing *c*. It wasn't working. He knew it wasn't. He was a weird problem to her, something to get straightened out, a loose end in her life that would irritate until it was made to fit in, then be forgotten.

To hell with it.

"Hoping to get laid," he said. When he looked up she was slowly shaking her head back and forth.

"Don't trifle with me, Haise. You're not as stupid as you look. You knew I'd be married, leading my own life. You knew I wouldn't drop it all because of some half-remembered fairy tale thirty years ago. *Why?*"

And how could he explain the strangeness of it all to her?

"What do you do?" He recalled something, and rephrased it. "Who *are* you?"

She looked startled. "I'm a mysteliologist."

He spread his hands. "I don't even know what that is."

"Come to think of it, there was no such thing when you left."

"That's it, in a way," he said. He felt helpless again. "Obviously, I had no way of knowing what you'd do, what you'd become, what would happen to you that you had no control over. All I was gambling on was that you'd remember me. Because that way . . ." He saw the planet Earth looming once more out the viewpoint. So many, many years and only six months later. A planet full of strangers. It didn't matter that Amity was full of strangers. But Earth was home, if that word still had any meaning for him.

"I wanted somebody my own age I could talk to," he said. "That's all. All I want is a friend."

He could see her trying to understand what it was like. She wouldn't, but maybe she'd come close enough to think she did.

"Maybe you've found one," she said, and smiled. "At least I'm willing to get to know you, considering the effort you've put into this."

"It wasn't much effort. It seems so long-term to you, but it wasn't to me. I held you on my lap six months ago."

"How long is your leave?" she asked.

"Two months."

"Would you like to come stay with us for a while? We have room in our house."

"Will your husband mind?"

"Neither my husband nor my wife. That's them sitting over there, pretending to ignore us." Ian looked, caught the eye of a woman in her late twenties. She was sitting across from a man Ian's age, who now turned and looked at Ian with some suspicion but no active animosity. The woman smiled; the man reserved judgment.

Radiant had a wife. Well, times change.

"Those two in the red skirts are police," Radiant was saying. "So is that man over by the wall, and the one at the end of the bar."

"I spotted two of them," Ian said. When she looked surprised, he said, "Cops always have a look about them. That's one of the things that don't change."

"You go back quite a ways, don't you? I'll bet you have some good stories."

Ian thought about it, and nodded. "Some, I suppose."

"I should tell the police they can go home. I hope you don't mind that we brought them in."

"Of course not."

"I'll do that, and then we can go. Oh, and I guess I should call the children and tell them we'll be home soon." She laughed, reached across the table and touched his hand. "See what can happen in six months? I have three children, and Gillian has two."

He looked up, interested.

"Are any of them girls?"

VENICE DROWNED

≋≋≋≋≋≋≋≋≋≋≋≋≋≋≋≋≋≋≋≋≋≋≋≋≋≋≋

Kim Stanley Robinson

We return now to Earth in the not so distant future, when changes in world weather patterns have all but removed the city of Venice from Earth's surface, covering it with Mediterranean waters. Venice is a city rich in history and art —how will its inhabitants live in such a future?

Kim Stanley Robinson's stories have appeared in *Clarion SF, Orbit,* and *Universe.* He lives in California.

BY THE TIME CARLO TAFUR STRUGGLED OUT OF
sleep, the baby was squalling, the teapot whistled, the
smell of stove smoke filled the air. Wavelets slapped the
walls of the floor below. It was just dawn. Reluctantly he
untangled himself from the bedsheets and got up. He
padded through the other room of his home, ignoring his
wife and child, and walked out the door onto the roof.

Venice looked best at dawn, Carlo thought as he pissed
into the canal. In the dim mauve light it was possible to
imagine that the city was just as it always had been, that
hordes of visitors would come flooding down the Grand
Canal on this fine summer morning. . . . Of course, one
had to ignore the patchwork constructions built on the
roofs of the neighborhood to indulge the fancy. Around
the church—San Giacomo du Rialto—all the buildings
had even their top floors awash, and so it had been necessary to break up the tile roofs, and erect shacks on the
roofbeams made of materials fished up from below: wood,
brick, lath, stone, metal, glass. Carlo's home was one of
these shacks, made of a crazy combination of wood beams,
stained glass from San Giacometta, and drainpipes beaten
flat. He looked back at it and sighed. It was best to look off
over the Rialto, where the red sun blazed over the bul-
bous domes of San Marco.

"You have to meet those Japanese today," Carlo's wife
Luisa said from inside.

"I know." Visitors still came to Venice, that was certain.

"And don't go insulting them and rowing off without
your pay," she went on, her voice sounding clearly out

110

of the doorway, "like you did with those Hungarians. It really doesn't matter what they take from under the water, you know. That's the past. That old stuff isn't doing anyone any good under there, anyway."

"Shut up," he said wearily. "I know."

"I have to buy stovewood and vegetables and toilet paper and socks for the baby," she said. "The Japanese are the best customers you've got; you'd better treat them well."

Carlo reentered the shack and walked into the bedroom to dress. Between putting on one boot and the next he stopped to smoke a cigarette, the last one in the house. While smoking he stared at his pile of books on the floor, his library as Luisa sardonically called the collection; all books about Venice. They were tattered, dog-eared, mildewed, so warped by the damp that none of them would close properly, and each moldy page was as wavy as the Lagoon on a windy day. They were a miserable sight, and Carlo gave the closest stack a light kick with his cold boot as he returned to the other room.

"I'm off," he said, giving his baby and then Luisa a kiss. "I'll be back late; they want to go to Torcello."

"What could they want up there?"

He shrugged. "Maybe just to see it." He ducked out the door.

Below the roof was a small square where the boats of the neighborhood were moored. Carlo slipped off the tile onto the narrow floating dock he and the neighbors had built, and crossed to his boat, a wide-beamed sailboat with a canvas deck. He stepped in, unmoored it, and rowed out of the square onto the Grand Canal.

Once on the Grand Canal he tipped the oars out of the water and let the boat drift downstream. The big canal had always been the natural course of the channel through the mudflats of the Lagoon; for a while it had been tamed, but now it was a river again, its banks made of tile rooftops and stone palaces, with hundreds of tributaries flowing into it. Men were working on roof-houses in the early morning light; those who knew Carlo waved, hammers or rope in hand, and shouted hello. Carlo wiggled an oar perfunctorily before he was swept past. It was foolish to build so close to the Grand Canal, which now had the strength to knock the old structures down, and often did; but that was their business. In Venice they all were fools, if one thought about it.

Then he was in the Basin of San Marco, and he rowed through the Piazetta beside the Doge's Palace, which was still imposing at two stories high, to the Piazza. Traffic was heavy as usual; it was the only place in Venice that still had the crowds of old, and Carlo enjoyed it for that reason, though he shouted curses as loudly as anyone when gondolas streaked in front of him. He jockeyed his way to the Basilica window and rowed in.

Under the brilliant blue and gold of the domes it was noisy. Most of the water in the rooms had been covered with a floating dock; Carlo moored his boat to it, heaved his four scuba tanks on, and clambered up after them. Carrying two tanks in each hand he crossed the dock, on which the fish market was in full swing. Displayed for sale were flats of mullet, lagoon sharks, tunny, skates, flatfish, and little red fish packed in crates head up, looking appalled at their situation. Clams were piled in trays, their shells gleaming in the shaft of sunlight from the east window; men and women pulled live crabs out of holes in the dock, risking fingers in the crab-jammed traps below; octopuses inked their buckets of water, sponges oozed foam; beyond them were trays of fish parts, steaks, joints, guts, glistening roe, beady-eyed heads; a slippery field of pink and white and yellow and red and blue.

In the middle of the fish market Ludovico Salerno, one of Carlo's best friends, had his stalls of scuba gear. Carlo's two Japanese customers were there. He greeted them and handed his tanks to Salerno, who began refilling them from his machine. They conversed in quick, slangy Italian while the tanks filled; Carlo paid him and led the Japanese back to his boat. They got in and stowed their backpacks under the canvas decking; Carlo joined them with the scuba gear.

"We are ready to voyage at Torcello?" one asked, and the other smiled and repeated the question. Their names were Hamada and Taku; they had made a few jokes concerning the latter name's similarity to Carlo's own, but Taku was the one with less Italian, so the sallies hadn't gone on for long. They had hired him four days before, at Salerno's stall.

"Yes," Carlo said. He rowed out of the Piazza and up back canals past Campo San Maria Formosa, which was nearly as crowded as the Piazza. Beyond that the canals were empty, and only an occasional roof-house marred the flooded tranquillity.

"That part of city Venice here not many people live," Hamada observed. "Not houses on houses."

"That's true," Carlo replied. As he rowed past San Zanipolo and the hospital, he explained, "It's too close to the hospital here, where many diseases were contained. Sicknesses, you know."

"Ah, the hospital!" Hamada nodded, as did Taku. "We have swam hospital in our Venice voyage previous to that one here. Salvage many fine statues from lowest rooms."

"Stone lions," Taku added. "Many stone lions with wings in room below Twenty-forty waterline."

"Is that right," Carlo said. Stone lions, he thought, set up in the entryway of some expensive Japanese businessman's home around the world. . . . He tried to divert his thoughts by watching the brilliantly healthy, masklike faces of his two passengers as they laughed over their reminiscences.

Then they were over the Fondamente Nuova, the northern limit of the city, and on the Lagoon. There was a small swell from the north. Carlo rowed out a way and then stepped forward to raise the boat's single sail. The wind was from the east, so they would make good time north to Torcello. Behind them Venice looked beautiful in the morning light, as if they were miles away, and a watery horizon blocked their full view of it.

The two Japanese had stopped talking and were looking over the side. They were over the cemetery of San Michele, Carlo realized. Below them lay the island that had been the city's chief cemetery for centuries; they sailed over a field of tombs, mausoleums, gravestones, obelisks that at low tide could be a navigational hazard. . . . Just enough of the bizarre white blocks could be seen to convince one that they were indeed the result of the architectural thinking of fishes. Carlo crossed himself quickly to impress his customers and sat back down at the tiller. He pulled the sail tight and they heeled over slightly, slapped into the waves.

In no more than twenty minutes they were east of Murano, skirting its edge. Murano, like Venice an island city crossed with canals, had been a quaint little town before the flood. But it didn't have as many tall buildings as Venice, and it was said that an underwater river had undercut its islands; in any case, it was a wreck. The two Japanese chattered with excitement.

"Can we visit to that city here, Carlo?" asked Hamada.

"It's too dangerous," Carlo answered. "Buildings have fallen into the canals."

They nodded, smiling. "Are people live here?" Taku asked.

"A few, yes. They live in the highest buildings on the floors still above water, and work in Venice. That way they avoid having to build a roof-house in the city."

The faces of his two companions expressed incomprehension.

"They avoid the housing shortage in Venice," Carlo said. "There's a certain housing shortage in Venice, as you may have noticed." His listeners caught the joke this time and laughed uproariously.

"Could live on floors below if owning scuba such as that here," Hamada said, gesturing at Carlo's equipment.

"Yes," he replied. "Or we could grow gills." He waved his fingers at his neck and bugged his eyes out to indicate gills. The Japanese loved it.

Past Murano the Lagoon was clear for a few miles, a sun-beaten blue covered with choppy waves. The boat tipped up and down, the wind tugged at the sail cord in Carlo's hand. He began to enjoy himself. "Storm coming," he volunteered to the others and pointed at the black line over the horizon to the north. It was a common sight; short, violent storms swept over Brenner Pass from the Austrian Alps, dumping on the Po Valley and the Lagoon before dissipating in the Adriatic . . . once a week, or more, even in the summer. That was one reason the fish market was held under the domes of San Marco; everyone had gotten sick of trading in the rain.

Even the Japanese recognized the clouds. "Many rain fall soon here," Taku said.

Hamada grinned and said, "Taku and Tafur, weather prophets no doubt, make big company!"

They laughed. "Does he do this in Japan, too?" Carlo asked.

"Yes indeed, surely. In Japan rains every day—Taku says, it rains tomorrow for surely. Weather prophet!"

After the laughter receded, Carlo said, "Hasn't all the rain drowned some of your cities too?"

"What's that here?"

"Don't you have some Venices in Japan?"

But they didn't want to talk about that. "I don't understand. . . . No, no Venice in Japan," Hamada said easily, but neither laughed as they had before. They sailed on. Venice was out of sight under the horizon, as was Murano. Soon they would reach Burano. Carlo guided the boat over the waves and listened to his companions converse in their improbable language, or mangle Italian in a way that alternately made him want to burst with hilarity or bite the gunwhale with frustration.

Gradually Burano bounced over the horizon, the campanile first, followed by the few buildings still above water. Murano still had inhabitants, a tiny market, even a midsummer festival; Burano was empty. Its campanile stood at a distinct angle, like the mast of a foundered ship. It had been an island town, before 2040; now it had "canals" between every rooftop. Carlo disliked the town intensely and gave it a wide berth. His companions discussed it quietly in Japanese.

A mile beyond it was Torcello, another island ghost town. The campanile could be seen from Burano, tall and white against the black clouds to the north. They approached in silence. Carlo took down the sail, set Taku in the bow to look for snags, and rowed cautiously to the edge of town. They moved between rooftops and walls that stuck up like reefs or like old foundations out of the earth. Many of the roof tiles and beams had been taken for use in construction back in Venice. This happened to Torcello before; during the Renaissance it had been a little rival of Venice, boasting a population of 20,000, but during the sixteenth and seventeenth centuries it had been entirely deserted. Builders from Venice had come looking in the ruins for good marble or a staircase of the right dimensions. . . . Briefly a tiny population had returned, to make lace and host those tourists who wanted to be melancholy; but the waters rose, and Torcello died for good. Carlo pushed off a wall with his oar, and a big section of it tilted over and sank. He tried not to notice.

He rowed them to the open patch of water that had been the Piazza. Around them stood a few intact rooftops, no taller than the mast of their boat; broken walls of stone or rounded brick; the shadowy suggestion of walls just underwater. It was hard to tell what the street plan of the town would have been. On one side of the Piazza was the cathedral of Santa Maria Ascunta, however, still holding fast, still supporting the white campanile that stood square and solid, as if over a living community.

"That here is the church we desire to dive," Hamada said.

Carlo nodded. The amusement he had felt during the sail was entirely gone. He rowed around the Piazza looking for a flat spot where they could stand and put the scuba gear on. The church outbuildings—it had been an extensive structure—were all underwater. At one point the boat's keel scraped the ridge of a roof. They rowed down the length of the barnlike nave, looked in the high windows: floored with water. No surprise. One of the small windows in the side of the campanile had been widened with sledgehammers; directly inside it was the stone staircase, and a few steps up, a stone floor. They hooked the boat to the wall and moved their gear up to the floor. In the dim midday light the stone of the interior was pocked with shadows; it had a rough-hewn look. The citizens of Torcello had built the campanile in a hurry, thinking that the world would end at the millennium, the year 1000. Carlo smiled to think how much longer they had had than that. They climbed the steps of the staircase, up to the sudden sunlight of the bell chamber, to look around; viewed Burano, Venice in the distance . . . to the north, the shadows of the Lagoon, and the coast of Italy. Beyond that the black line of clouds was like a wall nearly submerged under the horizon, but it was rising; the storm would come.

They descended, put on the scuba gear, and flopped into the water beside the campanile. They were above the complex of church buildings, and it was dark; Carlo slowly led the two Japanese back into the Piazza and swam down. The ground was silted, and Carlo was careful not to step on it. His charges saw the great stone chair in the center of the Piazza (it had been called the Throne of Attila, Carlo remembered from one of his moldy books, and no one had known why), and waving to each other they swam to it. One of them made ludicrous attempts to stand on the bottom and walk around in his fins; he threw up clouds of silt. The other joined him. They each sat in the stone chair, columns of bubbles rising from them, and snapped pictures of each other with their underwater cameras. The silt would ruin the shots, Carlo thought. While they cavorted, he wondered sourly what they wanted in the church.

Eventually Hamada swam up to him and gestured at the church. Behind the mask his eyes were excited. Carlo pumped his fins up and down slowly and led them around to the big entrance at the front. The doors were gone. They swam into the church.

Inside it was dark, and all three of them unhooked their big flashlights and turned them on. Cones of murky water turned to crystal; the beams swept about. The interior of the church was undistinguished, the floor thick with mud. Carlo watched his two customers swim about and let his flashlight beam rove the walls. Some of the underwater windows were still intact, an odd sight. Occasionally the beam caught a column of bubbles, transmuting them to silver.

Quickly enough the Japanese went to the picture at the west end of the nave, a tile mosaic. Taku (Carlo guessed) rubbed the slime off the tiles, vastly improving their color. They had gone to the big one first, the one portraying the Crucifixion, the Resurrection of the Dead, and the Day of Judgment: a busy mural. Carlo swam over to have a better look. But no sooner had the Japanese wiped the wall clean than they were off to the other end of the church, where above the stalls of the apse was another mosaic. Carlo followed.

It didn't take long to rub this one clean; and when the water had cleared, the three of them floated there, their flashlight beams converged on the picture revealed.

It was the Teotaca Madonna, the God-bearer. She stood against a dull gold background, holding the Child in her arms, staring out at the world with a sad and knowing gaze. Carlo pumped his legs to get above the Japanese, holding his light steady on the Madonna's face. She looked as though she could see all of the future, up to this moment and beyond; all of her child's short life, all the terror and calamity after that. . . . There were mosiac tears on her cheeks. At the sight of them Carlo could barely check tears of his own from joining the general wetness on his face. He felt that he had suddenly been transposed to a church on the deepest floor of the ocean; the pressure of his feelings threatened to implode him, he could scarcely hold them off. The water was freezing, he was shivering, sending up a thick, nearly continuous column of bubbles

. . . and the Madonna watched. With a kick he turned and swam away. Like startled fish his two companions followed him. Carlo led them out of the church into murky light, then up to the surface, to the boat and the window casement.

Fins off, Carlo sat on the staircase and dripped. Taku and Hamada scrambled through the window and joined him. They conversed for a moment in Japanese, clearly excited. Carlo stared at them blackly.

Hamada turned to him. "That here is the picture we desire," he said. "The Madonna with child."

"What?" Carlo cried.

Hamada raised his eyebrows. "We desire taking home that here picture, to Japan."

"But it's impossible! The picture is made of little tiles stuck to the wall—there's no way to get them off!"

"Italy government permits," Taku said, but Hamada silenced him with a gesture:

"Mosiac, yes. We use instruments we take here—water torch. Archaeology method, you understand. Cut blocks out of wall, bricks, number them—construct on new place in Japan. Above water." He flashed his pearly smile.

"You can't do that," Carlo stated, deeply affronted.

"I don't understand?" Hamada said. But he did: "Italian government permits us that."

"This isn't Italy," Carlo said savagely, and in his anger stood up. What good would a Madonna do in Japan, anyway? They weren't even Christian. "Italy is over there," he said, in his excitement mistakenly waving to the southeast, no doubt confusing his listeners even more. "This has never been Italy! This is Venice! The Republic!"

"I don't understand." He had that phrase down pat. "Italian government has giving permit us."

"Christ," Carlo said. After a disgusted pause: "Just how long will this take?"

"Time? We work that afternoon, tomorrow; place the bricks here, go hire Venice barge to carry bricks to Venice—"

"Stay here overnight? I'm not going to stay here overnight, God damn it!"

"We bring sleeping bag for you—"

"No!" Carlo was furious. "I'm not staying, you miserable heathen hyenas—" He pulled off his scuba gear.

"I don't understand."

Carlo dried off, got dressed. "I'll let you keep your scuba tanks, and I'll be back for you tomorrow afternoon, late. *Understand?*"

"Yes," Hamada said, staring at him steadily, without expression. "Bring barge?"

"What?—yes, yes, I'll bring your barge, you miserable slime-eating catfish. Vultures . . ." He went on for a while, getting the boat out of the window.

"Storm coming!" Taku said brightly, pointing to the north.

"To hell with you!" Carlo said, pushing off and beginning to row. "Understand?"

He rowed out of Torcello and back into the Lagoon. Indeed, a storm was coming; he would have to hurry. He put up the sail and pulled the canvas decking back until it covered everything but the seat he was sitting on. The wind was from the north now, strong but fitful. It pulled the sail taut; the boat bucked over the choppy waves, leaving behind a wake that was bright white against the black of the sky. The clouds were drawing over the sky like a curtain, covering half of it: half black, half colorless blue, and the line of the edge was solid. It resembled that first great storm of 2040, Carlo guessed, that had pulled over Venice like a black wool blanket and dumped water for forty days. And it had never been the same again, not anywhere in the world. . . .

Now he was beside the wreck of Burano. Against the black sky he could see only the drunken campanile, and suddenly he realized why he hated the sight of this abandoned town: it was a vision of the Venice to come, a cruel model of the future. If the water level rose even three meters, Venice would become nothing but a big Burano. Even if the water didn't rise, more people were leaving Venice every year. . . . One day it would be empty. Once again the sadness he had felt looking at the Teotaca filled him, a sadness become a bottomless despair. "God damn it," he said, staring at the crippled campanile; but that wasn't enough. He didn't know words that were enough. "God *damn* it."

Just beyond Burano the squall hit. It almost blew the sail out of his hand; he had to hold on with a fierce clench, tie it to the stern, tie the tiller in place, and scramble over the pitching canvas deck to lower the sail, cursing all the while. He brought the sail down to its last reefing, which

left a handkerchief-sized patch exposed to the wind. Even
so the boat yanked over the waves and the mast creaked as
if it would tear loose. . . . The choppy waves had become
whitecaps; in the screaming wind their tops were tearing
loose and flying through the air, white foam in the blackness. . . .

Best to head for Murano for refuge, Carlo thought.
Then the rain started. It was colder than the Lagoon water
and fell almost horizontally. The wind was still picking up;
his handkerchief sail was going to pull the mast out. . . .
"Jesus," he said. He got onto the decking again, slid up to
the mast, took down the sail with cold and disobedient
fingers. He crawled back to his hole in the deck, hanging
on desperately as the boat yawed. It was almost broadside
to the waves and hastily he grabbed the tiller and pulled it
around, just in time to meet a large wave stern-on. He
shuddered with relief. Each wave seemed bigger than the
last; they picked up quickly on the Lagoon. Well, he
thought, what now? Get out the oars? No, that wouldn't
do; he had to keep stern-on to the waves, and besides, he
couldn't row effectively in this chop. He had to go where
the waves were going, he realized; and if they missed
Murano and Venice, that meant the Adriatic.

As the waves lifted and dropped him, he grimly contemplated the thought. His mast alone acted like a sail in
a wind of this force; and the wind semed to be blowing
from a bit to the west of north. The waves—the biggest he
had ever seen on the Lagoon, perhaps the biggest *ever* on
the Lagoon—pushed in about the same direction as the
wind, naturally. Well, that meant he would miss Venice,
which was directly south, maybe even a touch west of
south. Damn, he thought. And all because he had been
angered by those two Japanese and the Teotaca. What did
he care what happened to a sunken mosaic from Torcello?
He had helped foreigners find and cart off the one bronze
horse of San Marco that had fallen . . . more than one of
the stone lions of Venice, symbol of the city . . . the entire
Bridge of Sighs, for Christ's sake! What had come over
him? Why should he have cared about a forgotten mosaic?

Well, he had done it; and here he was. No altering it.
Each wave lifted his boat stern first and slid under it until
he could look down in the trough, if he cared to, and see
his mast nearly horizontal, until he rose over the broken,
foaming crest, each one of which seemed to want to break

down his little hole in the decking and swamp him—for a second he was in midair, the tiller free and useless until he crashed into the next trough. Every time at the top he thought, this wave will catch us, and so even though he was wet and the wind and rain were cold, the repeated spurts of fear, adrenaline, and his thick wool coat kept him warm. A hundred waves or so served to convince him that the next one would probably slide under him as safely as the last, and he relaxed a bit. Nothing to do but wait it out, keep the boat exactly stern-on to the swell . . . and he would be all right. Sure, he thought, he would just ride these waves across the Adriatic to Trieste or Rijeka, one of those two tawdry towns that had replaced Venice as Queen of the Adriatic . . . the princesses of the Adriatic, so to speak, and two little sluts they were, too. . . . Or ride the storm out, turn around and sail back in, better yet. . . .

On the other hand, the Lido had become a sort of reef, in most places, and waves of this size would break over it, capsizing him for sure. And, to be realistic, the top of the Ardiatic was wide; just one mistake on the top of these waves (and he couldn't go on forever) and he would be broached, capsized, and rolled down to join all the other Venetians who had ended up on the bottom of the Adriatic. And all because of that damn Madonna. Carlo sat crouched in the stern, adjusting the tiller for the particulars of each wave, ignoring all else in the howling, black, horizonless chaos of water and air around him, pleased in a grim way that he was sailing to his death with such perfect seamanship. But he kept the Lido out of mind.

And so he sailed on, losing track of time as one does when there is no spatial referent. Wave after wave after wave. A little water collected at the bottom of his boat, and his spirits sank; that was no way to go, to have the boat sink by degrees under him. . . .

Then the high-pitched, airy howl of the wind was joined by a low booming, a bass roar. He looked behind him in the direction he was being driven and saw a white line, stretching from left to right; his heart jumped, fear exploded through him. This was it. The Lido, now a barrier reef tripping the waves. They were smashing down on it; he could see white sheets bouncing skyward and blowing to nothing. He was terrifically frightened. It would have been so much easier to founder at sea.

But there—among the white breakers, off to the right—a gray finger pointing up at the black—

A campanile. Carlo was forced to look back at the wave he was under, to straighten the boat; but when he looked back it was still there. A campanile, standing there like a dead lighthouse. "Jesus," he said aloud. It looked as if the waves were pushing him a couple hundred meters to the north of it. As each wave lifted him he had a moment when the boat was sliding down the face of the wave as fast as it was moving under him; during these moments he shifted the tiller a bit and the boat turned and surfed across the face, to the south, until the wave rose up under him to the crest, and he had to straighten it out. He repeated the delicate operation time after time, sometimes nearly broaching the boat in his impatience. But that wouldn't do—just take as much from each wave as it will give you, he thought. And pray it will add up to enough.

The Lido got closer, and it looked as if he was directly upwind of the campanile. It was the one at the Lido channel entrance or perhaps the one at Pellestrina, farther south; he had no way of knowing and couldn't have cared less. He was just happy that his ancestors had seen fit to construct such solid bell towers. In between waves he reached under the decking and by touch found his boathook and the length of rope he carried. It was going to be a problem, actually, when he got to the campanile—it would not do to pass it helplessly by a few meters; on the other hand he couldn't smash into it and expect to survive either, not in these waves. In fact the more he considered it the more exact and difficult he realized the approach would have to be, and fearfully he stopped thinking about it and concentrated on the waves.

The last one was the biggest. As the boat slid down its face the face got steeper, until it semed they would be swept on by this wave forever. The campanile loomed ahead, big and black. Around it waves pitched over and broke with sharp, deadly booms; from behind, Carlo could see the water sucked over the breaks, as if over short but infinitely broad waterfalls. The noise was tremendous. At the top of the wave it appeared he could jump in the campanile's top windows—he got out the boathook, shifted the tiller a touch, took three deep breaths. Amid the roaring, the wave swept him just past the stone tower, smacking against it and splashing him; he pulled the tiller

over hard, the boat shot into the wake of the campanile—
he stood and swung the boathook over a window casement
above him. It caught, and he held on hard.

He was in the lee of the tower; broken water rose and
dropped under the boat hissing, but without violence, and
he held. One-handed he wrapped the end of his rope
around the sailcord bolt in the stern, tied the other end to
the boathook. The hook held pretty well, he took a risk
and reached down to tie the rope firmly to the bolt. Then
another risk: when the boiling soupy water of another broken wave raised the boat, he leaped off his seat, grabbed
the stone windowsill, which was too thick to get his fingers
over—for a moment he hung by his fingertips. With desperate strength he pulled himself up, reached in with one
hand and got a grasp on the inside of the sill, and pulled
himself in and over. The stone floor was about four feet
below the window. Quickly he pulled the boathook in and
put it on the floor, and took up the slack in the rope.

He looked out the window. His boat rose and fell, rose
and fell. Well, it would sink or it wouldn't. Meanwhile, he
was safe. Realizing this he breathed deeply, let out a shout.
He remembered shooting past the side of the tower, face
no more than two meters from it—getting drenched by
the wave slapping the front of it—Christ, he had done it
perfectly! He couldn't do it again like that in a million
tries. Triumphant laughs burst out of him, short and sharp:
"Ha! Ha! Ha! Jesus Christ! Wow!"

"Whoooo's theeeerre?" called a high scratchy voice,
floating down the staircase from the floor above.
"Whoooooo's there? . . ."

Carlo froze. He stepped lightly to the base of the stone
staircase and peered up; through the hole to the next floor
flickered a faint light. To put it better, it was less dark up
there than anywhere else. More surprised than fearful
(though he was afraid), Carlo opened his eyes as wide as
he could—

"Whooooo's theeeeeeerrrrrrrre? . . ."

Quickly he went to the boathook, untied the rope, felt
around on the wet floor until he found a block of stone
that would serve as anchor for his boat. He looked out the
window: boat still there; on both sides white breakers
crashed over the Lido. Taking up the boathook, Carlo
stepped slowly up the stairs, feeling that after what he had

been through he could slash any ghost in the ether to ribbons.

It was a candle lantern, flickering in the disturbed air—a room filled with junk—

"Eeek! Eeek!"

"Jesus!"

"Devil! Death, away!" A small black shape rushed at him, brandishing sharp metal points.

"Jesus!" Carlo repeated, holding the boathook out to defend himself. The figure stopped.

"Death comes for me at last," it said. It was an old woman, he saw, holding lace needles in each hand.

"Not at all," Carlo said, feeling his pulse slow down. "Swear to God, Grandmother. I'm just a sailor, blown here by the storm."

The woman pulled back the hood of her black cape, revealing braided white hair, and squinted at him.

"You've got the scythe," she said suspiciously. A few wrinkles left her face as she unfocused her gaze.

"A boathook only," Carlo said, holding it out for her inspection. She stepped back and raised the lace needles threateningly. "Just a boathook, I swear to God. To God and Mary and Jesus and all the saints, Grandmother. I'm just a sailor, blown here by the storm from Venice." Part of him felt like laughing.

"Aye?" she said. "Aye, well then, you've found shelter. I don't see so well anymore, you know. Come in, sit down, then." She turned around and led him into the room. "I was just doing some lace for penance, you see . . . though there's scarcely enough light." She lifted a tomboli with the lace pinned to it; Carlo noticed big gaps in the pattern, as in the webs of an injured spider. "A little more light," she said and, picking up a candle, held it to the lit one. When it was fired, she carried it around the chamber and lit three more candles in lanterns which stood on tables, boxes, a wardrobe. She motioned for him to sit in a heavy chair by her table, and he did so.

As she sat down across from him, he looked around the chamber. A bed piled high with blankets, boxes and tables covered with objects . . . the stone walls around, and another staircase leading up to the next floor of the campanile. There was a draft. "Take off your coat," the woman said. She arranged the little pillow on the arm of her chair and began to poke a needle in and out of it, pulling the thread slowly.

Carlo sat back and watched her. "Do you live here alone?"

"Always alone," she replied. "I don't want it otherwise." With the candle before her face, she resembled Carlo's mother or someone else he knew. It seemed very peaceful in the room after the storm. The old woman bent in her chair until her face was just above her tomboli; still Carlo couldn't help noticing that her needle hit far outside the apparent pattern of lace, striking here and there randomly. She might as well have been blind. At regular intervals Carlo shuddered with excitement and tension; it was hard to believe he was out of danger. More infrequently they broke the silence with a short burst of conversation, then sat in the candlelight absorbed in their own thoughts, as if they were old friends.

"How do you get food?" Carlo asked, after one of these silences had stretched out. "Or candles?"

"I trap lobsters down below. And fishermen come by and trade food for lace. They get a good bargain, never fear. I've never given less, despite what he said—" Anguish twisted her face like the squinting had, and she stopped. She needled furiously, and Carlo looked away. Despite the draft he was warming up (he hadn't removed his coat, which was wool, after all), and he was beginning to feel drowsy. . . .

"He was my spirit's mate, do you comprehend me?"

Carlo jerked upright. The old woman was still looking at her tomboli.

"And—and he left me here, here in this desolation when the floods began, with words that I'll remember forever and ever and ever. Until death comes. . . . I wish you *had* been death!" she cried. "I wish you had."

Carlo remembered her brandishing the needles. "What is this place?" he asked gently.

"What?"

"Is this Pellestrina? San Lazzaro?"

"This is Venice," she said.

Carlo shivered convulsively, stood up.

"I'm the last of them," the woman said. "The waters rise, the heavens howl, love's pledges crack and lead to misery. I—I live to show what a person can bear and not die. I'll live till the deluge drowns the world as Venice is drowned, I'll live till all else living is dead; I'll live . . ." Her voice trailed off; she looked up at Carlo curiously. "Who are you, really? Oh, I know. I know. A sailor."

"Are there floors above?" he asked, to change the subject.

She squinted at him. Finally she spoke. "Words are vain. I thought I'd never speak again, not even to my own heart, and here I am, doing it again. Yes, there's a floor above intact; but above that, ruins. Lightning blasted the bell chamber apart, while I lay in that very bed." She pointed at her bed, stood up. "Come on, I'll show you." Under her cape she was tiny.

She picked up the candle lantern beside her, and Carlo followed her up the stairs, stepping carefully in the shifting shadows.

On the floor above, the wind swirled, and through the stairway to the floor above that, he could distinguish black clouds. The woman put the lantern on the floor, started up the stairs. "Come up and see," she said.

Once through the hole they were in the wind, out under the sky. The rain had stopped. Great blocks of stone lay about the floor, and the walls broke off unevenly.

"I thought the whole campanile would fall," she shouted at him over the whistle of the wind. He nodded, and walked over to the west wall, which stood chest high. Looking over it he could see the waves approaching, rising up, smashing against the stone below, spraying back and up at him. He could feel the blows in his feet. Their force frightened him; it was hard to believe he had survived them and was now out of danger. He shook his head violently. To his right and left, the white lines of crumbled waves marked the Lido, a broad swath of them against the black. The old woman was speaking, he could see; he walked back to her side to listen.

"The waters yet rise," she shouted. "See? And the lightning . . . you can see the lightning breaking the Alps to dust. It's the end, child. Every island fled away, and the mountains were not found . . . the second angel poured out his vial upon the sea, and it became as the blood of a dead man: and every living thing died in the sea." On and on she spoke, her voice mingling with the sound of the gale and the boom of the waves, just carrying over it all . . . until Carlo, cold and tired, filled with pity and a black anguish like the clouds rolling over them, put his

arm around her thin shoulders and turned her around.
They descended to the floor below, picked up the ex-
tinguished lantern, and descended to her chamber, which
was still lit. It seemed warm, a refuge. He could hear her
still speaking. He was shivering without pause.

"You must be cold," she said in a practical tone. She
pulled a few blankets from her bed. "Here, take these."
He sat down in the big heavy chair, put the blankets around
his legs, put his head back. He was tired. The old woman
sat in her chair and wound thread onto a spool. After a
few minutes of silence she began talking again; and as
Carlo dozed and shifted position and nodded off again,
she talked and talked, of storms, and drownings, and the
world's end, and lost love. . . .

In the morning when he woke up, she wasn't there. Her
room stood revealed in the dim morning light: shabby,
the furniture battered, the blankets worn, the knickknacks
of Venetian glass ugly, as Venetian glass always was . . .
but it was clean. Carlo got up and stretched his stiff
muscles. He went up to the roof: she wasn't there. It was
a sunny morning. Over the east wall he saw that his boat
was still there, still floating. He grinned—the first one in
a few days; he could feel that in his face.

The woman was not in the floors below, either; the
lowest one served as her boathouse, he could see. In it were
a pair of decrepit rowboats and some lobster pots. The
biggest "boatslip" was empty; she was probably out
checking pots. Or perhaps she hadn't wanted to talk with
him in the light of day.

From the boathouse he could walk around to his craft,
through water only knee-deep. He sat in the stern, reliving
the previous afternoon, and grinned again at being alive.

He took off the decking and bailed out the water on the
keel with his bailing can, keeping an eye out for the old
woman. Then he remembered the boathook and went back
upstairs for it. When he returned there was still no sight
of her. He shrugged; he'd come back and say good-bye
another time. He rowed around the campanile and off the
Lido, pulled up the sail and headed northwest, where he
presumed Venice was.

The Lagoon was flat as a pond this morning, the sky
cloudless, like the blue dome of a great basilica. It was
amazing, but Carlo was not surprised. The weather was
like that these days. Last night's storm, however, had been

something else. That was the mother of all squalls; those were the biggest waves in the Lagoon ever, without a doubt. He began rehearsing his tale in his mind, for wife and friends.

Venice appeared over the horizon right off his bow, just where he thought it would be: first the great campanile, then San Marco and the other spires. The campanile . . . Thank God his ancestors had wanted to get up there so close to God—or so far off the water—the urge had saved his life. In the rain-washed air the sea approach to the city was more beautiful than ever, and it didn't even bother him as it usually did that no matter how close you got to it, it still seemed to be over the horizon. That was just the way it was, now. The Serenissima. He was happy to see it.

He was hungry, and still very tired. When he pulled into the Grand Canal and took down the sail, he found he could barely row. The rain was pouring off the land into the Lagoon, and the Grand Canal was running like a mountain river. It was tough going. At the fire station where the canal bent back, some of his friends working on a new roof-house waved at him, looking surprised to see him going upstream so early in the morning. "You're going the wrong way!" one shouted.

Carlo waved an oar weakly before plopping it back in. "Don't I know it!" he replied.

Over the Rialto, back into the little courtyard of San Giacometta. Onto the sturdy dock he and his neighbors had built, staggering a bit—careful there, Carlo.

"Carlo!" his wife shrieked from above. "Carlo, Carlo, Carlo!" She flew down the ladder from the roof.

He stood on the dock. He was home.

"Carlo, Carlo, Carlo!" his wife cried as she ran onto the dock.

"Jesus," he pleaded, "shut up." And pulled her into a rough hug.

"Where have you been, I was so worried about you because of the storm, you said you'd be back yesterday, oh Carlo, I'm so glad to see you. . . ." She tried to help him up the ladder. The baby was crying. Carlo sat down in the kitchen chair and looked around the little makeshift room with satisfaction. In between chewing down bites of a loaf of bread, he told Luisa of his adventure: the two Japanese and their vandalism, the wild ride across the Lagoon,

the madwoman on the campanile. When he had finished
the story and the loaf of bread, he began to fall asleep.

"But, Carlo, you have to go back and pick up those
Japanese."

"To hell with them," he said slurrily. "Creepy little
bastards . . . They're tearing the Madonna apart, didn't I
tell you? They'll take everything in Venice, every last
painting and statue and carving and mosaic and all. . . .
I can't stand it."

"Oh, Carlo . . . It's all right. They take those things all
over the world and put them up and say this is from
Venice, the greatest city in the world."

"They should be here."

"Here, here, come in and lie down for a few hours. I'll
go see if Giuseppe will go to Torcello with you to bring
back those bricks." She arranged him on their bed. "Let
them have what's under the water, Carlo. Let them have
it." He slept.

He sat up struggling, his arm shaken by his wife.

"Wake up, it's late. You've got to go to Torcello to
get those men. Besides, they've got your scuba gear."

Carlo groaned.

"Maria says Giuseppe will go with you; he'll meet you
with his boat on the Fondamente."

"Damn."

"Come on, Carlo, we need that money."

"All right, all right." The baby was squalling. He collapsed back on the bed. "I'll do it; don't pester me."

He got up and drank her soup. Stiffly he descended the
ladder, ignoring Luisa's good-byes and warnings, and got
back in his boat. He untied it, pushed off, let it float out
of the courtyard to the wall of San Giacometta. He stared
at the wall.

Once, he remembered, he had put on his scuba gear and
swum down into the church. He had sat down in one of
the stone pews in front of the altar, adjusting his weight
belts and tank to do so, and had tried to pray through
his mouthpiece and the facemask. The silver bubbles of his
breath had floated up through the water toward heaven;
whether his prayers had gone with them, he had no idea.
After a while, feeling somewhat foolish—but not entirely
—he had swum out the door. Over it he had noticed an
inscription and stopped to read it, facemask centimeters

from the stone. *Around this Temple Let the Merchant's Law Be Just, His Weight True, and His Covenants Faithful.* It was an admonition to the old usurers of the Rialto, but he could make it his, he thought; the true weight could refer to the diving belts, not to overload his clients and sink them to the bottom. . . .

The memory passed and he was on the surface again, with a job to do. He took in a deep breath and let it out, put the oars in the oarlocks and started to row.

Let them have what was under the water. What lived in Venice was still afloat.

WALDEN THREE

Michael Swanwick

The idea of colonizing the space around Earth
in L–5 colonies is very attractive, especially in
recognition of increasing overpopulation on this
planet and the probable loss of opportunity
and freedom that will come with it. Space colonies could be an important part of the solution
—but such closed systems would develop their
own strictures, as Michael Swanwick shows in
this fascinating portrait of a colony in flux.

  Michael Swanwick is one of the best new
writers in science fiction, having published fine
stories in *Universe, New Dimensions, Triquarter-
ly,* and *Penthouse,* among others. He lives in
Philadelphia.

HIGH ABOVE THE EARTH, MAUDE BATALEUR strolled along twisty moonblock paths, almost alone. She was new to the lands that bend up and curve overhead: the orbital colony named Walden and the broken land that had been O'Neil before the terrorist bombing. She gawked and rubbernecked, trying to get the feel of the place.

Change was in the air. Earth's Planners were prepared to risk the global economy a second time. The Waldenites were repairing O'Neil, preparing it for an outmigration of ten thousand people from below. And People's Video had sent Maude up to observe, make sense of the changes, and sum them up in a three-minute stand-up.

Hands behind back, she stalked through Axial Park with her half-companion, feeling gray and dour. The path led under ivied stone arches with cheery slogans and over painted wooden bridges. The lesser gravity made her step light and bouncy. *This is what happens to old revolutionaries,* she thought. *We're dragged out periodically to demonstrate that we're toothless and safe.*

"Look," Sylph said from a nearby telescreen. "A monarch! The hatcheries have released them early." Screens were set into stone steles scattered through the park. A butterfly danced near Sylph's flickering face.

"Very pretty," Maude agreed. Sylph was an *odd* child, but Maude felt better for her half-presence. The oversolicitous nonentities that made up most of Walden set her teeth on edge.

Bailey, her guide, had been panicked by her. She

wouldn't respond to his smiles and frowns, and he was reduced to treating her like an overgrown child. "Please, Ms. Bataleur," he said, "we have a very delicate ecosystem and the grass won't—oh, *please* be careful with that flower." He beamed with approval when her hand hesitated fractionally, then looked horrified as she picked the flower anyway and patted it into her hair.

She favored him with a basilisk glare. "Listen, sonny, if I can't walk on the grass and I can't pick the goddamned posies, just what the hell use *is* this park?"

"Many elders enjoy strolling along the paths just *looking*," he said feebly. "We have benches set up to rest on."

"I'm not an elder, I'm an old woman." She cut defiantly across the park, knowing he would not dare follow her over the grass. "Old enough to be spared this kind of crap," she muttered to herself.

"Ms. Bataleur, we *can't* wade in the stream," Bailey called after her. "The detritus has to be gathered up at the equator and carried back upstream." She ignored him. "You're just making more work for everybody," he wailed, and then she was out of earshot.

Telescreens blinked on and off as Sylph paced her, leapfrogging from stele to stele, now beside her, now ahead. Sylph's chatter was extremely self-absorbed, but Maude found this a positive relief after Bailey.

Maude craned her neck, hoping to see a trout break water in the pond overhead. A swift flew by and she followed its flight admiringly. Then the sun through the axial window caught it in a wash of light and there was a bright glint on the side of its neck. "Even the birds are chained," she muttered with a touch of sour satisfaction.

"Over here!" Sylph exclaimed. Her image winked away, reappeared some distance from the path. "By the oak— this is where Dylan and I first got serious. Fivecreche was by the equator that month, and Westcreche was overhead. So we met here, in between, and he talked me into staying. I was so scared." Maude looked at the oak, a strong tree but preternaturally regular, an effect of the colony's bland weatherlessness. A stone outcrop set just beyond it had HAPPINESS IS CONTAGIOUS carved into its face. "He covered the screen with his blouse so it would be our secret. We were interrupted by a maintenance crew." Her expression was constantly changing, running through a range of expression rare in a girl her age—Maude guessed around seventeen. "They were so disapproving. I cried for hours. Dylan just got angry, though."

Maude waited, but there was no more to the story. "I'd like to meet this young man of yours," she said.

"Oh, yes, you must! He's scheduled to perform at the edge of the park in a half hour. He's *good!* Say you'll go."

"Of course I will."

Sylph directed her to a bicycle shed hidden among the trees, and she cycled to the stage side. Despite her misgivings about the lower gravity and Coriolis effect, Maude found that it was true—you never *do* forget how. Briefly she rode no-handed, and felt pleased with herself all out of proportion with the accomplishment.

The concert stage and surroundings were sculpted to look like a natural amphitheater, though nothing was natural on an orbital colony. Maude chose a cast-slag seat beside one of the ubiquitous steles, so she could chat with Sylph.

Bailey caught up with her there. He presented another bland-faced nobody and said, "This is Laramie Nine-creche Davidson. He's taking over as your guide." Davidson smiled sunnily at Bailey, and Bailey returned the smile with interest. Ignoring Maude completely, they bathed in each other's approval. Then Bailey turned and left, almost hastily.

"I'm most pleased to meet you, Ms. Bataleur." Davidson smiled brightly. "When I heard you were coming to Walden, I punched up your pamphlets and read them all."

"You planning a violent overthrow of the government?" He looked blank.

"Because if you're not, reading my old pamphlets is a waste of your time." He still looked blank. She snorted. "Here. Sit down and keep quiet."

"Dylan's going to be on the dedication-ceremony broadcast just before you," Sylph said. "It'll be his first time on Earth video. First they'll run one of my tapes, and then he'll do a live routine. The video committee wanted to include Walden's art." Then, "There he is—he's about to go on."

Maude looked. She saw a man climb onstage, wearing a traditional clown's suit, white with large bright polka dots, and a clown mask. Strident, wheezing circus music played from a stele as he bounced to center stage, the quintessence of an ancient Saturday-morning clown. He was far too eager, prancing and goofing desperately, obviously under pressure and aware of the poor showing he made. He was, in fact, so bad that it was genuinely funny. He'd pull a stunt, wait for a laugh, and the audience would blink, then realize: *that* was supposed to be a *joke,* and laugh at the incongruity.

Maude barely had time to appreciate that the amateur quality of the performance was deliberate when the music came to an abrupt halt. Caught in mid-caper, the clown froze. He peered about apprehensively, shuffled his feet, and essayed a small leap into the air. No response.

Good mime training there, Maude Bataleur thought.

The clown yanked off the mask, shrugged the clown suit to his feet, and stepped forward. He was a handsome, somewhat overserious-looking young man, dressed conventionally in loose black slacks and silk blouse. "Thank you, that was Coco the Clown," he said. "Let's all give him a big hand." He led the applause himself, drawing attention to the single oversized clown-glove he had somehow retained when shedding the other garments. "I'm Dylan Westcreche Corcoran, and this is a special occasion for me, because it's my last chance to rehearse before the dedication show. So I thought that perhaps this would be a good time to talk about the nature of comedy." The gloved hand came to independent life, capered up and down his side. He appeared not to notice. "Comedy has its roots in ancient Greece." The hand whipped around his back, waved to the crowd from the far side. "Friedrich Nietzsche said—" A laugh made him turn quickly to the side, and the hand retreated. "Said that—" A quick glance to the other side, and still the hand escaped his view. "Friedrich Nietzsche," he began for the third time. The hand hid behind his head, waggled two fingers like horns.

Laughing along with the rest, Maude felt a sudden frisson of recognition. She had seen this man before, on a bootlegged videotape someone had played at a Peep-Vid cast party in Vienna last year. It had been a poor, fragmentary tape, and she had listened totally baffled to the raves of the watchers. Now, though, she saw that they were right, that Corcoran was indeed a comic genius.

The routine ended with the gloved hand trying to strangle him while his face contorted through a rubbery variety of grimaces. Then he moved swiftly on to other bits that ranged from slapstick to subtle sophistication.

The words and situations, however, were of only secondary
importance. His humor lay in the skill with which he
twisted his expression about, the impossible postures his
body fell effortlessly into and out of—the way he made
it all look easy.

By slow degrees, however, Maude came to feel that
something was out of kilter. It was the crowd—her
laughter was ever so slightly out of synch with theirs. She
removed her attention from the comedian. Yes. Their
laughter fell neatly along five-second intervals. There were
four randomly scattered groups in the crowd, roughly
equal in number, each laughing automatically every twenty
seconds. They laughed at all the jokes, but loudest at those
whose punch lines fell on their twenty-second intervals.
When a joke did not fall on their interval, they laughed
anyway.

Maude frowned in puzzlement, then thought, *Of course.
The ceramics.*

On Earth it was known as the Walden Operation. In
Walden it was called Operant Implant Surgery and infor-
mally referred to simply as "instilling a sense of responsibility." The operation was simple. First, the child's abdomen was opened, and a synthetic involuntary muscle with
a piezoelectric crystal sandwiched inside was implanted.
Then the cranium was lifted and a tiny ceramic device
was buried in the pleasure center. Finally, a vein was sliv-
ered from the abdomen to the brain, connecting the two.
It was kiddie surgery in more ways than one; usually it
was handled by interns.

The ceramic was both a transmitter and receiver. When
the pleasure center was active, it ordered the synthetic
muscle to spasm. This fed back the power for a single-
burst short-range broadcast that could be received by any
similar device within ten paces. When it received such a
jolt, it ordered the muscle to provide power again, but
this time it routed the power to the pleasure center. Thus
stimulating it. Result: a feeling of *nice*. Because the muscle
was purposely weak, the signal could not be sent twice
within twenty seconds. This prevented a feedback looping.

No Waldenite could hide his happiness, or overlook
another's. If one makes another happy, he gets an instant
reward: a jolt of joy right between the eyes. It was strictly

in keeping with Skinner's dictum that positive reinforcement is the most effective personality-shaper there is.

If you're happy, let me know.

The crowd was happy. Coco's hands covered his face, the fingers forming the bars of a cage. He was winding up an impression of two songbirds plotting a jailbreak. "Dis had better woik," he growled. "Being cooped up like dis is making me *act funny*." The audience howled.

Corcoran straightened up, made his face serious, waited for the giggles to die down. "I'm here to sound a warning," he said. "Walden is a mockery of all that is sacred, of all we hold true." And he was off and running, explaining that space colonies could not be built, would fall down if they *were* built, and were hell on a farmer trying to dig a root cellar. He did a devastating routine about strolling through the park with sheep constantly falling off the land overhead.

Maude glanced at the stele, saw that Sylph was not laughing. She was staring at the stage with rapt attention, a wistful, adoring expression on her face. *I guess you've just got to be here,* Maude thought

Dylan left the stage to thunderous applause. The air shimmered, and a holoform image of Sylph, life-and-a-half sized, appeared. The technology for holoform imagery was still new, and Maude was not at all surprised to see that all the colors were subtly off. "Thank you," Sylph said. "The flight you're about to see hasn't been performed often. It's—"

Nearby, Sylph said, "It's one Dylan and I did. He used to be quite good, but I almost never got him to agree to be filmed." Maude turned to the stele, then back at the stage where the larger Sylph was still talking.

"Which one of you is live?" she asked.

Sylph's face disappeared from the screen. Maude blinked.

Davidson leaned over to speak solicitously in her ear. "The stage image is a soft-flex program that—"

"Thank you," Maude said coldly. "I don't care to have any of it explained to me." Davidson looked baffled and hurt, but she ignored it. She'd listened to more than enough computer bores in her time, thank you.

There was an *oooh* from the audience. Overstage, a holoform showed two human figures strapped into painted flightframes. They were twisting and spiraling about the invisible colony axis. Behind them, farmland shifted with their flight. Both frames were decorated in red and orange, suggestive of hawks, but the smaller flew more quickly and nimbly.

"Magnificent, isn't it?" Davidson said. "Da Vinci's dream come true—Dylan has a joke about that. It's really kind of sad that there won't be any more flights."

The two wheeled in opposite directions and approached each other, twisting so that they would pass stomach to stomach. They freed their legs on the approach and swung them outward as they neared. Their feet met, toes locked, like golden eagles grabbing talons on a mating flight. Wings closed, they whirled about each other, then released toes and sped off in opposite directions.

"Why no more flights?" Maude asked.

Now Dylan was flying steadily forward, wings pumping regularly, while Sylph spiraled about him. She was incredibly light and graceful, always just a hairsbreadth from tumbling out of control.

"Well, you see, human flight was just an accident. It was possible because we used Walden as a storage tank for the excess air we manufactured against the day we could repair the other colony. Eventually the atmosphere became thick enough for flightframes. But when the air was shipped to O'Neil, the pressure in Walden was halved, so it couldn't hold up a human on flightframes—you have to use powered gliders."

"I see." With sudden snappings-out of their wings, Sylph and Dylan made controlled landings on the colony surface near the axis. The audience applauded and the vision faded. "Hell of a thing to do to Sylph, I'd have to say."

"Beg pardon?"

"Sylph obviously enjoyed flying. You took that away from her."

"I'm sure she didn't mind," Davidson said. Then, at Maude's glare: "It was for the good of the colony. How could she possibly have been upset?"

"Never mind," Maude said. "Where's the comedian? I'd like to talk with him." The audience was filtering away, slowly filing through the exits, pausing to make way for one another and smiling broadly.

Davidson stepped around her, punched a few keys on the stele, and studied the readout. "He's just now entering the cablecar for Skinner."

"Skinner?"

"Well—technically it's still O'Neil. But considering that the dedication ceremony is tomorrow . . ."

"I see. When will he be back?"

"Probably not for some time." The man looked unaccountably embarrassed. "He, uh, has a regular place there."

"What? You mean a home?" Davidson looked away, a hint of revulsion on his face, and nodded. "Maybe there's hope for you guys yet!"

The single feature that most bothered Maude Bataleur about Walden was the fact that nobody had a fixed abode. The small houses—"living units" they were called here— claustrophobically piled into modular villages, were common property of all citizens. They slept in whatever unoccupied unit was closest at day's end. It was explained that this was an integral part of their society, that it transferred territorial instincts from specific locations to the colony as a whole. Maude had snorted and staked a claim on the nearest house. "This one is *mine*," she had said. "For the duration of my stay here. I am *not* going to move about every day, and if I find someone inside when I return, said person shall be thrown out on his or her ass."

"How do I get in touch with him?" she asked.

Davidson looked positively constipated. "You could ask Sylph. Her code is ARIEL."

"What's Mr. Corcoran's code?"

"It's uh, DEADLADY," he said unhappily.

"How downright *negative*," Maude said cheerily. She punched the letters on the stele and Dylan's face appeared. The inside of a cablecar showed behind him. An annoyed expression disappeared as soon as he saw her.

"Ms. Bataleur," he said "A pleasure."

"I saw your performance, and I'd like the chance to talk with you. At your convenience."

"That would certainly be welcome." He looked older than she had expected, in his mid-twenties at least. "Why don't you drop by in two hours? That should give me a chance to recover from the concert."

"I'll do that," Maude said. She cut the connection, feeling vaguely depressed; Dylan seemed as pleasant and over-polite as the rest. She turned to address a question to Davidson, and found that he was not there.

Out by the gate, a lone figure was exiting hurriedly. Davidson had taken the opportunity to slip away from her.

She hooted with laughter.

The cablecar carrying Maude eased through the airlock. She had to stand and simultaneously stoop to peer out the small, thick window, but it was worth it. The stars were bright and thick and rich, and a glimpse of the Milky Way was as sinful as cream. She watched O'Neil grow as the car cranked itself along one of the thick cables connecting the two colonies. Despite an inbred pessimism about technology and its fruits, she had to admit it was a splendid achievement.

She was even regretful that there was no window that would show her Walden dwindling to the rear.

It'll take ten thousand of our best people off the dole back on Earth, she thought. *That's the important thing. Because the choosing of those ten thousand will be the biggest circus the tired old world has ever seen. It'll distract the critics.* Which was indeed the name of the game. Earth's Planners needed time—breathing time that might be stretched out long enough to salvage an economy that still hadn't recovered from the pre-Revolution excesses.

Maude wasn't so sure the Planners deserved breathing time, but as a part of the system, she was committed to making it work.

From behind her a familiar voice said, "Are you going to visit Dylan?"

Maude did not turn around. "Yes. You want to come along?"

"Please," Sylph said.

"Then do." Maude stared at the stars, unaware of the wheels she had just set in motion.

Her first glance showed Maude why O'Neil was called the broken land. Like Walden, the inner surface curved away, slowly at first then quickly—to circle overhead, but there the resemblance ended. A large section not quite overhead was swept clean of everything, even dirt, and gleamed dully of the underlying aluminum. Everywhere were shattered trees, exploded houses, the shards of a thriving society struck down suddenly and violently. Much lay in radiant lines pointing toward the bare spot where the Waldenites had patched the hole created by the ancient thermonuclear device. There was no green.

A quarter mile off stood a lone modular house, obviously patched together from the remains of many others. A path picked clean of trash led to it. Light leaked from the house's window wall, making Maude conscious of how gloomy it was inside O'Neil. A faulty mirror alignment, surely, and the lack of any urgency to its correction.

A bluish light winked on to one side. A thin voice called out, and Maude saw Sylph appear on the single working face of a battered stele. She hiked over to it, said, "What was that?"

"I said there aren't many screens still intact out here, so I'll just meet you in Dylan's house."

"Thanks heaps," Maude said. She picked her way back to the trail, followed it to the house, and knocked on the door.

It opened. "Welcome to the House of Usher." Dylan winked, gestured her inside. "I'm a bit of a recluse, I'm afraid. I prefer solitude when I can get it and—" He shrugged. "Have a chair."

"Thank you." It was a warm, pleasant place. The furnishings were sparse, and the layout identical to her own Walden apartment, but it was cluttered with knickknacks and mementoes, and they made the cramped rooms feel like a home.

Sylph appeared on a telescreen. "Hello, Dylan," she said. "We haven't seen each other for some time."

"Damn!" Dylan exploded from his chair and slapped the screen's keyboard. Sylph disappeared.

Maude gaped at him. "Mr. Corcoran! That was—I've never seen such . . ." Her voice trailed off as she saw that his face was contorted with rage.

His eyes blazed for an instant, then changed. Almost magically his expression went from anger to bleak sorrow. He collapsed into a chair. "I see," he said. "You didn't— no, of course you didn't." His hands moved, started to make a gesture, didn't complete it. He clasped them, let them fall into his lap. He didn't look at her. "When did you first encounter Sylph?"

"Why—I'm not really certain. Sometime during the welcome-aboard tour."

He nodded. "That makes sense. Ms. Bataleur, Sylph has been dead for over seven years."

"But—"

"I built the construct myself, about a month after she died. I was assigned to computers then; that was before they decided my comedy was valuable enough to the colony to be listed as a career.

"I realize now—I realized as soon as it was done—that it was a stupid thing to do. It just drags up unpleasant memories. But while I was working on the program—it had to take everything the cameras had recorded and let it combine naturally and fluidly—it took up all my energy. I just thought about the *program*, you see. Then, when it was done, I saw what I'd created and buried it. I couldn't destroy it." He put a hand to the back of his neck and massaged gently, as if he had a headache. "Somebody must have dug it up and let it loose as a plaything. It *is* a nice bit of programming. I don't think anything exactly like it's been done before."

"How did she die?" Maude asked.

"They killed her," he said bitterly. "She was just too reliant on their goddamned *approval*." The last word came out with too much force and he paused to calm himself. "No, no," he said. He rose unsteadily, went to a cabinet, and removed a bottle. "Would you like some wine?" He didn't look at her.

"Yes," she lied.

He slowly poured two glasses, gave her one, using the time to compose himself. "Chateau O'Neil," he said. "Not very good, but quite rare." Then: "The truth of it is that she was an addict. She *needed* approval. It's something a performer can fall into quite easily, I suppose. When they took half the air away and she couldn't fly anymore, they cut off her largest source of approval. They might as well have taken away all the air. I—loved her, but it wasn't enough. She needed more than I could provide.

"So she went flying again. She must have known the air couldn't hold her. But she wasn't thinking rationally by that time. She gave me a call just before the flight, and I couldn't talk her out of it. She was acting—ah, Christ. I saw her land."

Maude leaned forward, took his hand. It clenched hers tightly. He lifted his free arm to his face and cried into it. He rocked gently, weeping.

"Change—" his voice choked. He struggled on, "—the subject. Tell me something about yourself, about Earth, anything." So she did.

Maude Bataleur owed her fame to a faulty safety pin. She had been radical as hell during the Revolution. She'd dropped out of college to join Women Without Fear, slept in attics, printed her pamphlets, got involved in any number of riots. In the Wall Street Riot, she had been in the forefront of the group that tore down the doors of a brokerage house, screaming and hysterical, none of them really in control. When they surged in, she had turned to urge some friends forward. As her arm swept up in a beckoning gesture, the safety pin holding together the left shoulder strap of her dress had given and one breast had popped free. A photographer had been present.

"Shades of the Bastille," Dylan said. He smiled weakly.

"That was it exactly," Maude said. "Flesh and violence. All the attention the pamphlets got—that was just an excuse to run the photo as often as possible. I understand that even *Pravda* ran it, before the Kremlin was taken."

Dylan freshened their glasses, reentered the conversation by slow degrees. Eventually the only traces of his sorrow were the salt tracks of tears that had dried on his cheeks. Maude posed the question that had brought her to O'Neil to see him in the first place: "What is your real opinion of the kind of society that's been set up on Walden? Objectively?"

"Objectively? I'm *agin* it," he said in a quaint hillbilly accent. Then: "There. You didn't laugh."

"Should I have?"

"You would have if you were a Waldenite. It's a catchphrase—I've used that line so often that people laugh without hearing the joke. I must have hundreds of catchphrases. I say them, and get a cheap laugh. In a way I've conditioned them as thoroughly as they've conditioned me. There are times when I wonder if I'm actually a comedian, or just shrewd at manipulating their conditioning."

"I heard you. You're actually very good."

"That's reassuring to know." He swirled the dregs of his wine, stared down into the glass. "The thing is, though, when you laugh at a catchphrase, that's a conditioned reaction. You don't actually *feel* it. And on Walden everyone is conditioned to behave in a quote socially beneficial manner. Endquote. So your every action is suspect. You don't feel emotions, you react to having your buttons pushed. It's like being a marionette."

Maude smiled. "Ah now. You've just lapsed into rhetoric, my friend. I'm an old hand at propaganda, and I know." She held up her glass for more wine.

He poured. "You think so? Then let me tell you about my childhood."

He told her of being the creche clown—the kid who capers and pulls faces and does pratfalls while his compatriots stand in a circle about him, laughing at what a jerk he is, and *approving*. Of endless hours humiliating himself because their gleeful childish cruelty expressed itself in an irresistible wave of positive reinforcement. And for all the underlying currents of resentment (which Maude could identify with only too well), she was impressed with how calmly, how objectively he could speak of experiences that must have wounded him deeply.

"I was half-crazy," he said. "But I got through it okay, because there was always Goldstein, right? She was this old computer programmer, dated back to before the ceramics. And she was always willing to listen to me. She never laughed at me, never forced me to do anything I didn't want to do. So it was okay, because there was always at least *one* adult who was on my side."

Dylan fell silent. "What happened?" Maude asked. Because there was clearly more to come.

"Eventually she decided to do something. She spoke out. Told everyone who would listen that the ceramics were a mistake and that the whole society needed to be changed."

"Good for her!"

"Not so good. She wasn't very popular to begin with." He smiled fondly. "She was an immodest old bird. She was very good at what she did and she let everybody know it. That raised a certain amount of resentment."

Maude nodded. "So what happened?"

"They shunned her. For over a year, nobody would talk to her. Nobody would acknowledge her presence. They'd turn away if she spoke, they'd walk away if they saw her coming. She could walk through a crowd and not a soul would come within a yard of her. Eventually, she died. Natural causes, supposedly, though I've always imagined she'd have had a lot more time if she hadn't been so damned *alone*."

"I can't imagine it," Maude said. "Shunning! It's like hearing that someone's been burned at the stake for witchcraft."

"You have to understand," Dylan said, "that Waldenites don't know how to handle negative feelings. Walden runs on positive reinforcement. There aren't any negative sanctions. So when the system breaks down, they don't know how to handle it. They were—embarrassed. They didn't want to hear what she had to say. So they simply didn't."

"Where were you when all this was going on?" Maude asked.

Dylan lowered his eyes. "I'm not proud of myself," he said. Then, when Maude continued to wait silently: "They moved Westcreche to the far side of Walden from wherever she happened to be—they'd gotten my name, they knew I was involved. They thought she was a bad influence. So I was watched. When I tried to see her, they withdrew their approval. I was just a kid!" He poured some more wine.

"You could have done something."

"Could I? I was born and programmed in Walden. Look. There's a game I made up when I was an adolescent. You go up to people in the street, give them your sunniest smile and say something like, 'You smell like a goat.' I used to play it all the time. You know what happens? They smile back at you. Then they stop and look puzzled—something's wrong and they can't quite figure out what. And then they smile again, because that's what they've been conditioned to do."

"That," Maude said, "is a horrid mockery of the soul."

"That's how I feel. I try to be rational about it, but deep down inside I hate them all. For what they've done to me and to Sylph and to Goldstein."

An evil thought occurred to Maude. "O'Neil will operate on the same basis, won't it?"

Dylan looked at her, uncomprehendingly. "Why else would they rename it Skinner? I expect it won't be exactly the same; there have been advances in technology. But in essence—yes. I've seen the reports claiming that cooperative Earthsiders can be turned into Waldenites in two, maybe three years."

Maude stood, began restlessly pacing, the way she always did when ideas were adding up. "First Walden, then —Skinner. Then all the new colonies, won't they? Oh, yes, they will. The human race will spread out into space and give up its identity to do so. And sooner or later this poison will seep back down to Earth, won't it?"

"I hadn't thought of it before," Dylan said, "but you're probably right. I don't see anything else happening."

"Well, I won't have it!" Maude's hands clenched tightly at her sides. She was outraged and angry and the old fires burned hot within her. "I won't let it happen! I have my three minutes. I can sound a warning. I'll write them a speech they won't be able to ignore, I'll—" She stopped.

Dylan's eyes were bright, unblinking, almost animal. "Can you do it?"

She opened her fists, raised her hands, stared at them. "No," she said. "I can't. I'd have my three minutes of glory and they'd go ahead and do it all anyway. They'd set me quietly aside, ban me from broadcasting, and that would be it. Maybe there'd be a few who—but no, nothing that would do any good."

" 'Tyranny creates the means of its own destruction,' " Dylan quoted. "That was in one of your own pamphlets. Walden *is* a tyranny and it *can* be destroyed."

" 'A people gets the government it deserves.' Tom Jefferson said that. The people decide. Not one person; not two. And the people are not about to overthrow Walden."

"But they can!"

"But they won't!" Maude could taste the bitterness in her voice. It hurt to admit to herself that she was indeed toothless, ineffective—safe. "I've been through all this before. I watched how quickly the bright shiny ideals of the Revolution tarnished. So now Earth has Assemblies and Planners instead of governments and politicians. Big whoop. Ninety-nine percent of the population is still property. We just traded in our owners for a new set.

"I thought a lot about the why and how of it, and the problem is the same down below as it is here—the enemy is too abstract. I say that Walden is evil over the video and what can I show the watchers? A lot of happy, polite people who don't curse, smoke, use drugs, or void their bowels in public. You have to let people *see* the problem. You have to show it to them in concrete terms."

Dylan pulled at one of his fingers, stared at it without seeing. In a tentative voice, he said, "I had a plan once."

Maude said nothing. "I figured I could topple the whole corrupt structure. I did all the spadework, spent years building it up. But I gave up on it because I thought I didn't have the right to impose my values on everyone else."

"Well, I'm impressed." Maude was feeling angry and frustrated and powerless, and perhaps the wine had loosened her tongue a bit too much. At any rate, she spoke intemperately. "You can do it all by yourself, can you? Listen, friend, I've encountered your kind before, and it's always the same tired line. You moan about how badly life treats you, and you never do anything about it. Sure, you've got grandiose plans, but does anything ever come of them? No. It's always life treats *me* bad. I could do something about it if *I* only wanted to, *I*—"

"I—"

"It's your kind that's always stood in the way of every useful change that's come along—the kind that simply *sits* there and doesn't *do* anything. Well, there's an old saying, kiddo: *Shit or get off the pot!*" She swayed weakly, moved toward the door. "I think I'm drunk."

Everything on Walden was movable. Maude spent the morning watching an entire village be dismantled and its component units scattered throughout the colony to make room for the dedication-ceremony grounds. The grounds were huge because every Waldenite who could be spared from vital duties wanted to be present.

It's so nice when a *lot* of people are happy together.

For a while Maude amused herself by playing Dylan's game on the workers. "You're a fool," she told one, smiling. "Get stuffed," she told another. "Shithead," to a third. They smiled, nodded, looked puzzled, smiled again. Just like Dylan had said they would; just like little robots.

When Maude tired of the game, she retreated to the gigantic boulder—ten yards across—that had been set up overlooking the ceremony stage. A camera cluster was grafted to a stele on the side away from the stage, just above the stone face with SHARE YOUR SMILES carved into it. She punched TECHCREW on the stele, and a young, bearded face appeared. "I'd like to try taping my stand-up from here," she said. "Having any trouble with the linkages?"

"None at all, Maude. These people are wizards. You should see their setup."

"Let's go, then." She faced the stele, smiled. "Walden is an evil little world," she began.

Three minutes later, she finished. "Jesus, Maude," the tech said in awe. "You really planning on using that?"

"No," she said slowly. "It wouldn't do much good, would it? Erase it all, will you?" And tried not to dwell on the relief that spread over his face.

The speeches were about what you'd expect from "leaders" who were rotated from committees selected by weighted lottery. In all fairness, Maude had to admit that the offerings of Earth's Planners were little better. They droned on and then they ended. Sylph appeared. She introduced a tape of herself on a solo flight. It was an incredibly graceful performance, an almost perfect summation of every human dream of flight ever imagined. Maude noted that no mention was made that such flights were things of the past. Then Dylan came onstage.

Tinny music played briefly, trailed down to nothing as he strode to stage center. He was wearing the clownsuit, but not the mask or gloves. His feet capered, and his face was dead serious. The audience, prepared for him, laughed uproariously.

"I am here to sound a warning," he said. "Walden is a mockery of all that is sacred, of all that is human." The audience laughed, and applauded. "Ten thousand human animals live in this cage." His hands briefly formed bars over his face. "This cage not of the body, but of the soul." The audience caught the gesture and the word "cage" and howled.

"Jesus." Maude punched TECHCREW and a young woman appeared. "What the hell is going on?" Maude demanded. The woman shrugged helplessly. "Can you route what's being broadcast through this stele?" The woman nodded, and Dylan's face appeared on the screen.

The suit is solid black, Maude realized. Onscreen, the suit was somehow transformed from a cheery clownsuit to a plain, somber costume. *Programmed animation?* she wondered, and then the screen went from a medium shot to a close-up. Comedians never play to close-ups.

There was nothing humorous about what was going out. Dylan was playing on all networks, live, to almost a *billion* people, as close to a captive audience as makes no differ-

ence, and he wasn't being funny. He was throwing his
career down the tubes.

"You may have been surprised by the fact that there
are only two entertainment portions to this broadcast. Or
then again, you may not have noticed." The audience
laughed. "The fact is that Sylph—who died years ago—
and I are the only two individuals in Walden who are *best*
at anything. Because being better than somebody else does
not make them happy. And on Walden, if *they're* not
happy, you're not happy." More laughter.

"Why haven't they cut into this?" Maude demanded.
The image on the screen divided, and the woman from the
techcrew appeared on one half, while Dylan held the other.
"None of the colony people are on duty. They've got all
their equipment preprogrammed."

"Who's responsible for the close-ups?"

"It's all programmed," the woman said. The bearded
tech appeared onscreen briefly, whispered in the woman's
ear. "Oh yeah, and the Peep-Vid people downstairs are on
the line. They want to know what's going on."

I think I'm just beginning to catch on, myself. Dylan had
said he worked with computers, and apparently he was
very good at it. "Stall them," she said. "And give me the
situation here. Who has the authority to say whether we
cut into this or not?"

The woman looked confused. "I don't know, I—I guess
it's your decision, Maude. You're the ranking Peep-Vid
person here."

Maude chose sides swiftly. "I'm with you, kid," she
muttered to herself. "Let it play," she said aloud.

The laughter continued at regular five-second intervals.
Dylan spoke bitterly, with his catchphrases cleverly woven
into his invective so they hit on the ceramics' intervals.
Knowing they were there, watching for them, Maude
could only catch one out of three phrases, they were so
smoothly woven into his speech.

"A friend—a very close friend—of mine was destroyed
by her conditioning. Or addiction. There's a very thin
line between addiction and conditioning; both destroy any
semblance of free will."

"Free will" was apparently the punchline to one of
Dylan's better jests.

Dylan told Sylph's story, as the audience convulsed with

laughter. He went into excruciating detail, and he carried the story further than he had when telling it to Maude.

"I stood over her shattered body and I felt that I should make a gesture, the sort of thing you see in old movies: Hold it in my arms and cry, maybe—*something*.

"But I couldn't. Because it wasn't nice. Because it wouldn't make anybody happy. Because I was as thoroughly conditioned as any of the zombies in this Skinner box. *I couldn't even cry.* I just stood there.

"And while I was standing there, a maintenance crew came along to remove the body. They scooped Sylph up, slid her into an orange body bag, and dumped her into an electric sanitation cart. But the horrible, the really unbearable part of all this was their attitudes. They were *cheerful*. Just as they were leaving, one of them winked, and smiled at me.

"And, God help me, I smiled back."

Dylan's voice choked with tears. Even so, he delivered his every word with the power and careful placement of a Shakespearean actor. But it was not the words *per se*, Maude realized, that would have the greatest impact on the world below. It was the sound, caught by the video microphones, of all of Walden assembled laughing gleefully at what he had to say.

He had conditioned them to laugh, and they did, impelled by pulses of pleasure the Earthsiders could not sense. The meaning of his speech simply could not penetrate. He controlled them like so many thousands of puppets, and they happily danced at the ends of his strings.

"How could this happen? Why would every human being on Walden allow a personality to disintegrate before their eyes without even *trying* to do something?"

"Because they are no. Longer. Human." He dropped the words like heavy bricks, and the audience shrieked joyfully. "They're little robots, just like Sylph was, and as long as everything went smoothly, they smiled and let her be." He took a jerky stride forward. Seen from the audience, the motion was a flash of comic genius. Onscreen, it registered as a somber shift of position. "They did not care that her mind was being eaten away. They were not capable of caring."

The pain it cost Dylan to speak was obvious. Even without the laughter, it would have been a moving, even tragic, performance.

"I—" Dylan halted, looked lost, tried again. "I—I can't go on." He stumbled from the stage to uproarious applause.

"Maude!" the stele said.

She ignored it, lost in what she had just seen.

"Maude!" The voice was insistent. "We've got an extra five minutes to fill. Can you stretch your stand-up?"

"Switch it over," she said.

Then she spoke. "It begins something like this . . ."

Space colonies are vulnerable. A single malcontent, saboteur, suicide, has the potential of destroying ten thousand people at a shot. External controls don't work. Repressive government creates its own enemies.

As was demonstrated in 2058 when a jerry-rigged thermonuclear device punched a rather spectacular hole in the side of O'Neil. All of Walden watched on closed-circuit television as air, trees, homes, and citizens were ejected into space, a gory spume of garbage that lacked the velocity to escape O'Neil's orbit and formed a diffuse halo around the two colonies.

What was needed were responsible citizens. People who would willingly act in socially responsible ways. People incapable of endangering the colony because they recognized that its survival was more important than their own. People who would be happy under constant supervision, and who would ask only that their lives be of use to their society.

The survivors decided to build such citizens. After a few false starts and a number of unfortunate incidents, they succeeded. They inserted ceramics and engineered out private space. They made parenthood communal and rotational. They built people who were clean and wholesome and cooperative.

In flat, even sentences, Maude did her best to explain. She didn't pass judgment, but she knew that judgment was being passed. Hundreds of millions were watching her, had seen Dylan's performance. And the audience's reaction.

Small red lights on the camera cluster counted down the final seconds of the last minute, and Maude wound down her talk on cue. ". . . the rebellion of a lone clown," she said, letting her voice trail off ever so slightly, and held for a beat. The camera shut down and she sagged slightly.

God, I love that, she thought. *I'm as much an addict as*

anyone here. She looked down on the stage and didn't see Dylan. He had left.

The crowd was stirring angrily, a swarm of hornets about its broken nest. The clean, wholesome people were waking up and realizing that they had just laughed their way through a prolonged cry of agony. That they had exposed themselves as fools to the world below. That they were not happy.

They were intelligent people, most of them. They could see that Dylan's performance would bring changes, changes they would not like, and that there was nothing they could do about it. But they were also angry, and they were not used to anger, did not know how to handle it.

Maude reached past the camera equipment and punched DEADLADY on the keyboard. A printed message appeared: System Overload Please Wait Before Trying Again. Obviously a lot of people wanted to say something to Dylan at this point. *Think,* she told herself. She punched ARIEL. Sylph's face appeared.

"Hello, Ms. Bataleur," she said.

"Sylph, I have to get in touch with Dylan and I can't. He's in serious trouble, I think. Can you connect me with him?"

Sylph frowned prettily. Maude found it hard to react to her as a set of programmed responses, lacking any self-awareness. A ghost, or less than a ghost. "I'm sure Dylan couldn't be in any trouble," she said.

"Sylph! Those people are angry. They might kill him!"

"Oh, no," Sylph said. "That couldn't possibly happen." She smiled.

Maude caught herself. "I'd like to speak with him anyhow," she said. "Do you know where he might be?"

"Dylan likes to go off by himself after a performance. Have you tried the other colony?"

"No, but I doubt that's where he's going." The crowd was moving. Long arms of people streamed in the direction of the window axis, away from the nearest cablecar station.

"Then he's going to the axis. There's a platform there we used to jump from when we flew. It's the most isolated place in the colony. Nobody likes to go there."

All of the crowd was moving now, spreading out, extenuating itself. They pushed things aside, broke saplings and trod them underfoot in their haste.

Maude made some quick calculations. "Tell the tech

crew to focus their equipment on the axis," she snapped.
She hurried toward the nearest bicycle shed—she could
see it some five minutes' walk spinwards. If she peddled
hard and circled around the crowd, and if she had a lot of
luck, she just might reach the axis behind Dylan and
ahead of the crowd. It would be dicey. Almost, she wished
she were younger.

"Say hello to Dylan for me," Sylph cheerily called after
her.

Maude Bataleur ran for the shed, knowing she would
be too late.

Dylan stood on the platform, holding the faded paper-
and-bamboo wings he had flown on years before. He
clutched the wings to himself and cried. People were
gathering at the foot of the platform, circling it, re-forming
the crowd, and they hated him. Their ceramics were silent.
JUMP one of them shouted and there was a shiver of approval in the air. JUMP somebody echoed.

Coco strapped on the wings, looking dazed, crying.
JUMP, the people screamed. JUMP. And JUMP and
JUMP and JUMP and JUMP, JUMP, JUMP, until it
was sheer pleasure to leap into the air, spread the wings
that found no purchase, and fall, slowly at first, almost
floating, then faster and faster, curling down in a long arc,
and shedding bitter tears all the way to the ground.

The clown was dead.

Maude Bataleur lived a few years more, then moved on
to greener pastures.

Sylph cheerfully searched for Dylan for several centuries more. Somehow her program was duplicated and
spread throughout all of colonized space, and it is hard
to separate the last legitimate sighting of her from the
numerous hoaxes that popped up later.

For the rest of her life, Maude felt guilty that she had
taken the time to order her crew to tape Dylan's final
flight. But it was effective, an old propagandist couldn't
kid herself about *that*—and it got a tremendous amount of
play on Earth. After Maude's death, when the inevitable
retrospectives of her turbulent life were aired, it was again
played worldwide, inevitably accompanied by Coco's mono-
logue, and her own angry stand-up spot.

The broken land was patched and restored, and the

thousands came up from Earth to people it. But public sentiment had its effect, and the new colonists were not subjected to Walden-style social conditioning. Without the ceramics, they evolved a totally different kind of social order, and came to call their colony Dickens rather than Skinner.

Dickens and Walden made uneasy, and not always peaceful, neighbors.

The battle for control of the human spirit had begun.

SECOND COMINGS— REASONABLE RATES

Pat Cadigan

If we should develop the means to bring back the dead, their relatives and loved ones might have mixed reactions to these revenants. Not to mention the reactions of some people who might not want to be revived . . . Here Pat Cadigan, another of the many fine new writers in SF, tells a story rich in characterization and irony.

HUMPHREY HATED FUNERALS. HATED THEM. *Hated* them.

He slipped the bright purple tunic over his head, wound a belt around his waist and yanked it tight. It cut into his skin sharply, but he left it that way. If he was going to do something he didn't like, he might as well be uncomfortable. The intercom in the wall chimed.

"Almost ready, Hum?" asked his brother-in-law's voice.

"Just about. Gotta comb my hair." He could hear his wife speaking indistinctly in the background. "Tell Rita I'll be down directly." He put on his shoes and went into the bathroom.

"Funerals are sick. I hate them," he whispered to his reflection in the full wall mirror as he brushed his shoulder-length black hair into a semblance of order. Stepping back to survey his appearance, he frowned even more sourly. The tie-belt made him look like a sack of something unpleasantly lumpy, and there was a stain on one knee of his white pants. Rita would be too distraught to notice, but his brother-in-law would. He shrugged. Daniel's disapproval was something he could live with. Stabbing the light button off, he went down to the living room.

Rita was holding a handkerchief over her mouth and nose as she rocked gently in the waterchair. Daniel's wife Aleene stood nearby as though she were a servant waiting for instructions, while Daniel himself paced back and forth in front of the door, flipping his credit card nervously. Aleene bent over and touched Rita's shoulder. "Hum's ready, dear. We can go now."

Steeling himself, Humphrey walked over to her and helped her to her feet. She looked up at him, red-eyed, tears still rolling down her cheeks.

"Do you want a BeCalm?" he asked lamely.

With a sob, she flung herself into his arms, crying a large wet spot into his shoulder. He held her awkwardly, patting her hair. Aleene watched, shaking her head sadly. Daniel cleared his throat.

"We really should go," he said apologetically. "If we wait any longer, they'll have to hold up the service. Mom will be very upset."

Humphrey nodded, hoping he didn't look as revolted as he felt. His wife's brother didn't look like someone who had just lost his father. Rita, on the other hand, was crying harder than ever, twisting the soft cloth of his tunic in her fists.

"She's getting hysterical. Get her a sedative," he told Aleene.

"But—"

God, how he hated furnerals. *Hated* them! "Just get her one or we'll never be able to get her into the car."

"What about afterwards?"

"Bring along a counteractive. A *mild* one. Too much excitement will be bad for her."

Between the two of them, they managed to get the pill down her while Daniel looked on, all but tapping his foot. It was five minutes before the pill took effect, and another five before they could put her in the car.

"Name?" asked the car.

"Daniel Greyson," said Daniel, slipping his credit card into the slot on top of the dashboard.

"Scanning," the car said and chimed softly. "Please look into the binocular eyepiece located just in front of you." Daniel leaned forward and did so to let the car check his retina pattern. "Affirmative. Destination, please."

"Allardyce Non-Specific Religious Temple and Crematorium."

The car lifted soundlessly and began circling in preparation for entering the air traffic. Humphrey stared distractedly out the window, fidgeting with a strap of the shoulder harness. Below, rows and rows of houses diminished to the size of dice, freckling a landscape divided regularly by narrow roadways for pedestrians and the few necessary ground vehicles.

He twisted around to look at his wife. She was lying down in the back seat with her head pillowed on Aleene's slender thighs. "Make her sit up and strap in," he said irritably. "That isn't safe."

"She's asleep. Besides, what can it hurt this one time? We're not out joy-riding, we're going to a funeral. Anyway, you were the one who made her take the BeCalm. It blanked her right out."

Humphrey suppressed a sigh and looked at his brother-in-law. Daniel was staring straight ahead with his arms folded over his chest. He seemed put-upon.

"How far away is the temple?" he asked.

Daniel didn't look at him. "About twenty minutes, if we don't hit any heavy traffic. That's why I wanted to get started before this. We could get caught in a holding pattern for I don't know how long. Mom will be down there by herself—" His voice started to shake a little.

"Won't Veronica be there?"

Daniel laughed bitterly. "Oh, undoubtedly. And she'll probably be good and drunk, too. Poor Mom. I don't know why they put up with her all these years, they sacrificed to give her—to keep her—and she'll be making a spectacle of herself—" He took a deep breath. "Bitch. I'd have her barred if I could."

"Daniel!" Aleene was shocked. "Your own sister. I'm just glad Rita isn't awake."

"It's Rita I'm thinking of as well as Mom. How do you think it's going to be for her to see Veronica like that at a time like this? Rita was always Poppa's favorite," he added to Humphrey. "We all knew it, but it didn't matter. He was such a grand old guy. He loved us all—" Daniel fished a handkerchief out of the pouch on his belt and blew his nose. Aleene reached out awkwardly to touch his shoulder, trying not to disturb Rita, who had begun to snore.

"It's okay, Danny boy," she said softly. "It's okay to cry for Poppa. I loved him, too. I know."

Daniel broke down completely. Aleene began sniffing sympathetically. Rita continued to snore. Humphrey rested his head against the door window and closed his eyes.

Funerals were horrible. He hated them, hated them, *hated* them.

A policeman strapped to a flying platform was directing air traffic over the temple; otherwise, they might have been caught in a holding pattern indefinitely. Humphrey peered down at the cars stacked triple and quadruple on top of each other. Parking attendants on platforms smaller than the policeman's were guiding the cars coming in, cutting dizzying paths through the air, lighting and taking off like insects.

"God," breathed Humphrey. "How many people are coming to this?"

"It's a big family," Daniel said nasally. He had managed to bring himself under control. In the back seat, Rita was semiconscious and stirring a little, but still prone and spilling tears into Aleene's lap.

"I'm sure a lot of Poppa's friends are here, too," said Aleene. "Poppa has miles of friends."

The car descended, following electronic signals from one of the parking attendants, who guided them to a clear patch of ground marked with a large white X. Daniel rolled down his window. "Do I leave the car here?"

"Yeah. I park it for you. Leave your card in. Mine goes in next to it. It's an authorized temple card." She held it up for Daniel's inspection.

"All right. Give us a minute. We're the immediate family, and one of us is sedated."

"Take your time, sir. The service has been delayed because of the large volume of traffic, anyway."

"Poor Mom," Daniel muttered as he got out of the car. Humphrey was already out and trying to pull Rita's limp form from the back seat. Eyes closed, she allowed herself to be pulled forward and then slumped over the folded-down front seat.

"Maybe we should have rented a four-door," said Aleene, her hands fluttering helplessly. Humphrey pinched his wife's cheek several times.

"Come alive, now, honey. We have to get out of the car."

"Where are we?" she sighed wearily.

"We're at the temple. Come on."

"Poppa!" she wailed and slid onto the floor in an untidy heap. Daniel hurried around to help Humphrey extricate her. They got her standing unsteadily between them with her arms around their shoulders and their arms twined about her waist.

"Let's walk her some," said Humphrey. "Fresh air might rouse her a little."

"We're going to look like hell entering with her in this condition," Aleene said primly. She still hadn't forgiven Humphrey for sedating her.

"Would you rather we brought her in screaming like a psycho?" he snapped as he and Daniel struggled to keep the sagging woman upright.

"She can't help it. She's never had anyone die in the family before. She was only a baby when——"

"That's enough," Daniel barked, surprising them all, including himself. "We've got plenty to be concerned about without you two going for each other's throats. He's my father, too, you know."

"I'm sorry, Danny boy. I was just—well, never mind." She glowered briefly at Humphrey before she controlled her expression long enough to give him a cold little apology. Humphrey didn't reply. His wife seemed to be waking up, but reluctantly, fighting it. Maybe the BeCalm had been a mistake, but he wasn't about to admit it to Aleene.

When they reached the front steps of the temple, an usher waiting at the open door rushed down, offering to take Rita. Daniel waved him off. "Aleene, see if you can comb her hair any and wipe off some of that smeared makeup."

Startled, Aleene looked down at herself. "Oh, God, it's all over my pants!" She groaned, but made an attempt to arrange her sister-in-law's mashed and flattened hairdo. "Maybe if I put my scarf over her head——"

"Never mind. Wipe her face and we'll go in."

"Wipe her face with what?"

"With your *scarf*," growled Humphrey, snatching it from around her neck and doing it himself. He gave it back to her ruined with mascara, and he could see her toting up the cost of the scarf and the pants. No doubt she'd send him a bill.

"Are we ready now?" asked Daniel impatiently.

"Are we ever." Humphrey avoided looking at Aleene as they half dragged Rita up the steps.

*   *   *

The temple was filled almost to capacity. Under the soft synthesized music, whispers rustled like papers in a wind as they went slowly down the center aisle to the front pew. Rita's mother Adelle stood up when she saw them, relief washing over her face like a storm. She embraced each of them with a fluttery little moan. Over her shoulder, Humphrey saw Veronica Greyson, dressed shockingly in black from head to foot, sprawled lazily in the pew with her ankles crossed on the kneeler.

"Oh, God, Veronica *is* drunk," whispered Aleene to no one. "How *could* she?"

Humphrey was tempted to tell her. He could have used a drink himself, or at least a BeCalm.

There was a shuffle of people, a flurry of whispered directions, and he found himself in the pew behind them, next to a middle-aged couple who introduced themselves as the Swanwicks. Humphrey nodded and told them who he was, feeling mildly annoyed at their approving murmurs. Veronica had moved so that she was directly in front of him, and she was twisted around regarding him through half-closed, bloodshot eyes. Humphrey could see she was drunker than usual. She wore a thick layer of pale makeup that made the rouge on her cheeks stand out like clown paint. Her eyes were thickly lined in black and fringed with a veritable forest of false eyelashes.

Hi, she mouthed at him.

Hi, he mouthed back.

She beckoned him with a black-gloved hand; he bent forward obligingly as the Swanwicks bristled.

"I hate these fucking *things,*" she whispered hoarsely, and Humphrey realized the redness in her eyes wasn't totally due to heavy drinking. She had been crying. He patted her arm reassuringly.

"It'll all be over soon."

She swung her head from side to side, her loose brown hair falling in her face. "It's never gonna be over. Never, never, never."

Daniel reached behind Rita and Adelle Greyson and tapped her hand warningly. She jabbed her black middle finger at him but turned around to slouch down in her seat.

Humphrey sat back, pushing his tight belt lower. A small roll of fat hung over it and he folded his arms to hide it. Veronica had really done it this time, he thought grimly.

Black at a funeral—she might as well have stood up and shouted her feelings to the entire congregation. Even the Swanwicks, stodgy as they seemed, were bright in greens and yellows.

"Too bad," whispered Mr. Swanwick.

"Isn't it?" Humphrey answered vaguely, unsure of what the man meant. Rita was groping behind her mother for his attention. He gave her his hand automatically, surprised at the vigorous squeeze she gave it.

"Sit with me," she begged.

"Honey, there isn't room for all of us. I'll be right here."

She looked pained, her tongue flicking around her mouth as though she were thirsty. He felt a surge of anger. That damned Aleene must have given her a counter and then a stimulant besides. He'd strangle her with her own scarf.

"Hum, what's wrong? Why are you frowning?"

Not ten minutes before she'd been weeping and wailing, barely able to stand up. He wanted to tear his hair in frustration. "Nothing, Rita. It's all right. They're going to start any moment now. I'm right here if you need me." He knew she wouldn't.

She turned around reluctantly, saying, "Okay. Okay. Okay," as though it were a chant.

Mrs. Swanwick was beaming at him. "How long have you been married?" she asked him sweetly.

"Two years next month."

"Lovely. Just lovely."

He managed a weak grin. He hated, hated, *hated* funerals.

"Too bad," Mr. Swanwick said again.

"Pardon?"

Mr. Swanwick jerked his chin at Veronica. "The things they've put up. Gerald and Adelle. Gerald is my cousin, and I've never understood why he keeps trying with—" he jerked his chin at Veronica's back again. "Totally unnecessary. She—"

The soft organ music became a flourish of trumpets and the entrance of the minister and her two acolytes marked the beginning of the service. Humphrey stood up with everyone else, listening through a hymn he didn't know as the celebrants took their places on the altar steps above the flower-draped coffin. Under the spotlights, their white robes seemed to glow phosphorescently. At the end of the

hymn, the minister offered an elaborate blessing, and the
spotlights changed to pink. Humphrey restrained himself
and didn't groan. He half expected a song-and-dance team
to come out next.

The congregation sat down on a cue from the minister
he didn't get and he was left momentarily standing alone.
Embarrassed, he sat down quickly and stared at his lap,
too mortified to listen to the service. It must have been
very nice; both the Swanwicks were sniffing, as were most
of the people in the temple. It sounded, he thought sourly,
like a convention of the last hayfever incurables. Veronica
was not sniffing, he noticed. She was bent forward with
her elbows on her knees, shaking a little. His wife, by con-
trast, was sitting up stiffly, as though she were having trouble keeping from jumping up. He wondered what Aleene
had given her.

The synthesized music, which had died down to an un-
dertone of accompaniment, was beginning to swell in
imitation of a gigantic pipe organ, but with trills and
embellishments no organ could ever have given it. He
looked up at the altar. The minister had acquired a
cordless microphone and was winding up for a big finish.
The spotlights were writhing through a spectrum of colors.
Funerals, he thought sourly.

"The hand of God has touched our Gerald Greyson and
called him from our midst," intoned the minister, with
feeling. "But the goodness that is the essence of Gerald
Greyson—that will always be with us!"

The spotlights went blindingly to white as the casket
sank slowly into the floor. As the flowers disappeared, the
lights went out and then snapped on again, focused on
some curtains to the immediate right of the altar. Humphrey rubbed his forehead tiredly. The organ music was
nearly unbearable, the vibrations penetrating bone-deep. In
spite of himself, he felt the desired sensation: anticipation.

At the height of the earthshaking crescendo, a man
stepped through the curtains. He was tall, gray-haired, with
a trim little mustache and beard, wearing white robes identical to the minister's. He smiled at the congregation and
held out his arms.

"Poppa!" screamed Rita. She fought her way out of the
pew, ran up to the altar and threw herself into the man's
arms. Adelle Greyson and Daniel followed, Aleene trailing
them and turning around to look at Humphrey, indicating

he should go up, too. He sighed and stood up, touching Veronica's shoulder tactfully. She shrugged away from him.

"That isn't my father," she said huskily. "My father's dead."

He went up to the altar to take his place for the wedding ceremony that would reunite the Greysons, so recently parted by death.

The reception, held next door at a temple annex, was a large, noisy, crowded affair. Adelle and Gerald Greyson sat at the head table with Daniel, Rita, and Aleene in the place of the prodigal Veronica. Humphrey found himself seated at a table with four women and three men he'd never seen before, wondered briefly why he wasn't sitting with the Greysons and decided he was better off. He looked around for Veronica, who would have been conspicuous in her black outfit, but she didn't seem to be there. At the next table, the Swanwicks thought he was looking for them and kept waving to him, calling, "Here we are!" to which he would reply, each time, "There you are!"

The meal kept him busy. He couldn't count the number of courses served nor could he seem to empty his wineglass. Every other minute, the room toasted the Greysons, who toasted each other and then toasted the room, while waiters (in a departure from the usual servant mechanisms) rushed to fill everyone's glass before the level in each went down below the halfway mark. Eventually he was in worse shape than Veronica had been in, unable to do much more than hunker over his plate and wonder what was on it. Electronic music began to play a medley of the latest holo hits, adding to the pandemonium.

". . . look lifelike?" asked the woman next to him, dipping her sleeve in his wineglass accidentally. He removed it, squeezed the wine out and picked up the glass.

"Pardon?" he asked, having a sip of wine.

"I said, doesn't old Gerry look lifelike?"

Humphrey twisted around to look at him. Old Gerry was on his feet, giving a speech no one could hear but everyone was applauding anyway.

"Yes," someone else answered for him. "It's amazing what they can do, isn't it?"

"I'd swear it was him," said the woman. "Looks like him, sounds like him, acts like him."

"I don't understand how they do it," said another woman, almost with disapproval.

Gerald Greyson was leading his wife out into the middle of the floor as "Anniversary Waltz," for no discernible reason, flowed out of the speakers in the ceiling, liquid with ersatz violins.

"Technology," said the first woman vaguely.

"Well, I know that, but how can they make them so they can eat and drink and—and so on?"

"Haven't you ever seen those antique dolls? My grandmother had one, we found it in the attic, cleaned it up, and you wouldn't believe what we sold it for."

"Probably not."

"Well, those old dolls could drink water, cry real tears, and wet. Of course, that's all they could do. These days—well, look at old Gerry!"

Old Gerry was now dancing with a beaming Rita. Mrs. Greyson was partnered with Daniel. Several other couples were rising to join them.

"You know," the woman went on, "I told my daughter she ought to get something like that instead of having a baby. Less trouble." Everyone laughed.

Humphrey turned around to look at her. She was staring past him, smiling and craning her neck to get a glimpse of Gerald Greyson.

"I heard that Rita, the daughter he's dancing with now, took it so badly they had to dope her up," said the second woman. Or was it a third woman? Humphrey put his elbows on the table and propped up his chin in his hands.

"Didn't she *know?* It's been, what, ten years?"

"Closer to fifteen, I think, before they were on the open market. Well, of course, she must have known, but I guess it was still a blow for her. My ex and I used to party-hop with the Greysons, and it was no secret Rita was his favorite. Then, too, she was only a baby when Daniel died."

Humphrey frowned woozily, not sure that he had heard right.

"Oh, come on," said a man. "You aren't saying—"

"That's what I'm saying. Daniel was eight. He hit his head in, of all places, the bathtub and drowned."

"Look, I know they can make them do a lot of things, but they can't make them grow."

"No. The Greysons just traded up for a bigger model every few years."

"That's impossible," Humphrey heard himself saying, as if from very far away. "His wife—"

"His wife is one lucky woman, friend." All the women giggled.

"I'll bet she is," said one of the men.

"Can he cry real tears?" Humphrey asked of no one. "And wet?"

"Who is that?" he heard someone ask.

"I saw him talking to Veronica in church, some friend of hers, I guess."

"No, he came in with Rita and the others."

"He's Rita's husband, nit, don't talk so loud."

"Oh." Everyone shut up.

Humphrey sighed and stood up. "Guess I'm not going to hear anything interesting at this table," he said and walked unsteadily into the crowd of dancers, thinking that he had seen an exit on the other side of the room. Suddenly, he wanted fresh air very much.

Rita seemed to materialize in his arms, laughing and talking excitedly. "Hum! Hum! Here's Poppa! Look! Here's Poppa! It's so wonderful, Hum, he's back, I knew he wasn't dead, I just knew it!"

Humphrey frowned, opened his mouth to correct her, realized it would be bad form with her father's replacement standing right there and shut up again. Gerald Greyson was pumping his hand in a familiar grip, and he saw how Rita would be confused by it. It really did look and feel like her father.

"Good to see you here," Greyson said. "Are you having a good time?"

Humphrey blinked.

"Rita, I think you've been neglecting your husband." He tried to push them together. "Why don't you two—"

"No, thanks, but why don't *you* two keep on dancing? I've just got to have some air. Have to get out. Side. Outside. Stuffy." He fanned himself with one hand and then shouldered his way past them.

". . . not electronics, exactly, but biochemicals," someone crooned almost in his ear. "And electricity. Or something like that."

"And it works?"

Humphrey turned around and found a couple deep in conversation as they danced, nearly rubbing up against him without noticing him.

"Marvelously. You know Ted and George Simons? Can you guess which one of them is—"

Humphrey fled, looking over people's heads for any sign of a door leading out. People bumped into him, stepped on his feet, elbowed his ribs. He might have been invisible.

"When you die, Ed, I think I'll just have you stuffed."

"You're awful."

"No, you're awful."

"You're all awful," muttered Humphrey, and spotted a door marked PATIO. He struggled against the current of dancers, trying to make his way toward it.

". . . Jody died, I just let them take over. We had advance arrangements. They're so reasonable, too, I was surprised."

". . . hated to break up a good foursome, so they used their own money and replaced *her*, too, and they weren't even related. Now the four of them . . ."

". . . came home from school and asked me was the President dead. What could I say? I didn't know, I told him to ask . . ."

". . . last year. You didn't know? Good Lord, I was fifty-four. A heart attack. Terrible shame if I do say so myself . . ."

He reached the door and fell through it, gasping with relief. It swung to behind him, cutting off the music and voices. Grimacing, he undid the knot of his belt and let it fall. He rubbed his sagging stomach and immediately felt better. The air was surprisingly cool for a late afternoon in midsummer, and he took great, deep breaths of it as though he had just emerged from underwater.

"Care to join me?"

He looked around. Veronica was reclining on a chaise lounge with a bottle of vodka. He shuffled over and sat down by her feet. "Wondered where you were."

"Been in this bottle." She held it up; it was three-quarters empty. "Want a hit?"

He shook his head. She shrugged, tilted it up and drank deeply.

"Uh-huh." She smacked her lips. "Enjoy the funeral?"

"I hate funerals."

"Yeah? How many you been to?"

"Three. four. Friends of our family. Both my parents are still alive." He shuddered. "I suppose some day—"

"Do you know," asked Veronica, "Daniel is dead?"

"I didn't, until a few minutes ago."

"Had to grow up with that *thing* in the house. Now Mom has another *thing*. They said treat it like your brother. Be goddamned if *I* would. Rita was only two. She didn't care."

"Aleene married it. Him." He still couldn't believe it.

"That's a ballbuster, ain't it? Plenty of live men, she marries a *thing*."

"Is it legal?"

"Mom just married a *thing*."

"Yes, but she was already married to him. Sort of."

"Well, it isn't *il*legal. A lot of people prefer *things* to other people."

"Less trouble," Humphrey said, echoing the woman at the table.

"Damn right on. They eat, sleep, make love—I'd sooner do it with a 'lectric cord. A live 'lectric cord. Anything. But it screws on command. You don't bother it, it won't bother you. That's what I call perfection. Build a better screwing machine, and the world will beat a path to your door." She tilted the bottle up again. "When Mom goes, that's the end. I'm through with all of them. There'll be two *things* living in a house together. For Rita's benefit. Daniel, as you know, has already attained *thing*ship. Three *things*, one live idiot woman, scuse me, she's my sister and I know what she is, and one disgusting drunk, and that's what *I* am." She leered at him suddenly. "Hey, baby, whaddaya say we run off together?"

Humphrey's mouth dropped open. "Ah . . . why?" He laughed nervously.

"We may be the only two live people left around here in the not-too-distant future. Hell, we may be the only two live people now. Rita doesn't count."

He was aware of feeling like he should say something in Rita's defense, but his mind was still foggy, and there was something else he was curious about. "I don't understand why they never told me about Daniel."

"Why should they? If you're happy with a syntho-heart, or a glass eye, or a dildo, why mention it?" Veronica looked troubled. "I'm not drunk enough. Why aren't I drunk enough?"

Humphrey thought of asking her why she didn't tell him and changed his mind. It didn't matter. He stood up.

"Where are you going?"

"Back inside. I ought to check on Rita. Aleene gave her a stimulant and it's made her awfully hyper."

"That means you're not running off with me, I take it?" He laughed again, weakly.

"Same to you, buddy." She toasted him with the bottle before killing it and flinging it away. It landed with a nerve-jangling crash. "Olé!"

Humphrey turned away from her and walked back to the door to the reception hall. Just as he put his hand on the knob, Rita and her father spilled through it and took hold of his arms.

"Darling, are you all right?" Rita ran her hand through his hair and felt his face concernedly.

"Fine. Just needed some air." He tried to pull away.

"You looked pretty woozy," said Greyson.

"Too much to drink."

"Ah. Rita, see about getting this fine husband of yours a glass of water."

She nodded and hurried away, leaving them alone together. Humphrey suddenly felt very awkward, unsure of what to do or say. What could he say to this *thing*—father-in-law, he corrected himself. Father-in-law, in spirit. Sort of.

"I've been talking to Veronica," he said, glancing back to the chaise lounge. It was empty, Veronica nowhere in sight.

"Poor dear. Someday, we'll get through to her," Greyson said serenely. "Then we can put her troubled soul to rest."

Humphrey frowned in puzzlement. "Put her troubled soul to rest?" It didn't make any sense at first. And then, it did, horribly.

"She killed herself when she was twenty-one, already a hopeless alcoholic. That was ten years ago. My wife felt such profound failure as a mother that we chose to have her reproduced and replaced as she was, without the knowledge that she'd died, of course. Adelle refuses to give it up. It *has* gotten expensive—every so often, somebody slips up and she finds out she's dead. Then she shuts herself off, and we have to replace her again. But no parent wants to be left feeling that a child has been let down. So we endure the scenes, the embarrassments, the occasional disgrace or scandal. Just so we can keep trying to help her. I remember the beautiful child that she was, and I think, someday—well." He smiled at Humphrey, who began to feel dizzy.

"Don't you ever get the feeling that it's, ah, hopeless?" he asked after several moments had passed.

"Where there's life, there's hope, eh, Hum?" Greyson clapped him on the shoulder. "Let's go see what's become of your ice water. That Rita."

Humphrey allowed himself to be pulled back into the reception, back into the place where he could not tell the live people from the replacements, where there would be no need for him to grow or change or do anything, really at all. After a little more wine, it didn't make any difference anyway.

FOREVER

≈≈≈≈≈≈≈≈≈≈≈≈≈≈≈≈≈≈≈≈≈≈≈≈≈

Damon Knight

Every year human life and history is diminished
by the deaths of great scientists, artists . . .
people. But what if someone had discovered a
real "elixir of life"—say a hundred years ago?
The world would certainly have followed a different course, as Damon Knight details in this
slyly funny short story.

Damon Knight is one of the preeminent authors, anthologists, critics, and teachers of science-fiction writing. He lives in Oregon with his
wife, Kate Wilhelm.

IN 1887, IN WIESBADEN, GERMANY, HERR Doktor Heinrich Gottlieb Essenwein discovered the elixir of life. The elixir, distilled from pigs' bladders, was simple to manufacture and permanent in its effects. After taking one dose of the clear reddish liquid, colored and flavored with cinnamon, one no longer aged. It was as simple as that. A chicken to which the Herr Doktor fed a dose of the elixir in January, 1887, was still alive in 1983 and had laid an estimated 25,860 eggs, of which 7,000 had double yolks.

An unfortunate side effect of this discovery was that Essenwein's son Gerd, to whom the good Doktor gave a dose of the elixir in 1888, remained twelve years old for the remainder of his life. Gerd, a talented piccolo player, had a sunny disposition and was loved by all, but he was pimply and shy.

Once the Herr Doktor had discovered his error, he recommended that the elixir not be taken until a suitable age, which varied according to the talents and wishes of the individual: an athlete, for example, might take his dose at twenty-three, when he was at the height of his physical powers; a financier perhaps at forty-five or so, and a philosopher at fifty.

Encouraged by Essenwein's example, the British physicist John Tyndall discovered penicillin in 1895. Three years later, Louis Pasteur announced his so-called universal bacteriophage, one injection of which would destroy any marauding germ whatever, at the cost of making the recipient feel out of sorts for about a year and a half.

As a result, the population of the world expanded dramatically during the years 1890-1903, the birthrate remaining the same or even advancing a trifle, while the death rate had fallen to a negligible figure. Fortunately, in 1897 the American physician Dr. Richard Stone perfected an oral contraceptive, which worked on both men and women, and also slowed down cats and dogs a great deal.

Partly because of the unbearable crankiness of children who had had their bacteriophage shots, the new contraceptive was adopted with enthusiasm all over the world, and the habit of having children fell into disrepute. Occasional infants still came into the world, by accident or inattention, but so rarely that as early as 1953, when a year-old infant was displayed to Queen Victoria as a curiosity, she started in horror and exclaimed, "What is that?"

As a consequence, a number of famous people were never born. These included Yogi Berra, George Gershwin, Aldous Huxley, Leonid Brezhnev, and Marilyn Monroe. On the other hand, a number of famous people *were* born, such as McDonald Wilson Slipher, the founder of the Church of Self-Satisfaction; the song-writer Sidney Colberg ("I'll Be Good When You're Gone"); and Harriet Longworth Tubman, the first woman president of the United States.

Early in the twentieth century, armies all over the world were plagued by mutiny and desertion; hardly anyone was crazy enough to risk a life which might last for centuries, or even, with luck and reasonable care, for thousands of years. When the Archduke of Austria-Hungary was killed by an assassin at Sarajevo, Emperor Franz Josef wanted to declare war on Serbia, but Conrad von Hötzendorf told him he would merely embarrass the nation by doing so. Kaiser Wilhem consulted von Moltke and was told the same thing. Both rulers gloomily asented to an international conference to resolve the issue; the war never took place.

Thus the world entered an era of lasting peace and prosperity. A network of electric railways covered the earth; Count Zeppelin's airships, which went into service in 1898, carried freight and passengers to the farthest parts of the globe. Thomas Edison, the wizard of Menlo Park, together with Nikola Tesla, Lee De Forest, and other

giants of modern invention, poured out a steady stream of
scientific marvels for the enrichment of human life.

Albert Einstein, of the Kaiser Wilhelm Institute in Berlin, published his equation $E = mc^2$ in 1905, demonstrat-
ing that the release of nuclear energy was possible, but the
world already had abundant electrical power, thanks to
Edison and Tesla, and nobody paid any attention.

In 1931 the astronomer Schiaparelli persuaded Gugli-
elmo Marconi to attempt communication with the planet
Mars. Marconi built a signaling apparatus, in effect a giant
spark coil, in the Piedmont near Turin, and during the
opposition of 1933 he fired off electric impulses into space
every night; the sounds he produced were so terrific that
sheep and cattle lost their bowel control for miles around.
Marconi's message, repeated over and over, was a simple
one: "Two plus one are three. Two plus two are four. Two
plus three are five."

At the end of six months the hopes of the two Italians
were realized when they received a return message: it
said, "Eight plus seven are fourteen." Critics pointed out
that this was not quite right, but the achievement captured
the world's imagination nevertheless. The popular author
Jules Verne, in collaboration with the German Hermann
Oberth, immediately began to draw plans for a cosmobile
in which to visit the Martians. The task proved difficult,
and more than two decades passed before the designers
were ready to test their first cosmic vehicle. Because of
technical difficulties, no attempt was to be made to reach
Mars at this time; the vehicle was to swing around the
Moon and take photographs, then return to Earth. Even
so, the rocket could carry only one passenger, who must
weigh no more than one hundred pounds. Gerd Essenwein, the son of the discoverer of the elixir of life, volunteered to go, and so did a double amputee named
Brunfels, who had lost both legs in a streetcar accident in
Berlin, but a midget was selected instead. This midget was
Walter Dopsch, a popular circus performer; he was a perfectly formed little fellow who stood only three feet nine
inches tall and weighed seventy-five pounds. Because this
was twenty-five pounds less than the allowed weight,
Dopsch was able to take along on the voyage a large supply of cognac, cigars, paperbound novels, and the bonbons
to which he was addicted.

The flight took place on April 23, 1956; the space vehi-

cle was raised to a height of thirty miles by means of a
balloon designed by the Piccard brothers; then it was cut
free and ascended by rocket power. The whole world listened to Dopsch's radio transmissions as he soared through
space and looped around the Moon, which he described as
"like a very large Swiss cheese." On the return journey,
however, the parachute which was to lower the vehicle to
Earth proved defective; it collapsed in the tropopause and
Dopsch plunged flaming into the North Sea. His last radio
message was, "I love you, Helga." Helga, it was later as-
certained, was the fat lady in the circus in which Dopsch
had been employed.

This tragedy put a damper on space exploration, and,
since no further messages were received from the Martians, the whole enterprise was forgotten.

Public opinion, anyhow, was turning against such dangerous pursuits. The internal combustion engine, for example, which had enjoyed a brief vogue early in the century,
was everywhere replaced by safe, quiet electric trains and
interurban trolleys. The Safety Prize, instituted in 1944 by
Count Alfred Nobel, was awarded every year to such inventions as no-slip shoe soles and inflatable pantaloons.

In 1958 a snydicate headed by John D. Rockefeller and
J. P. Morgan constructed a graceful steel and glass enclosure, 225 feel tall, over the entire island of Manhattan.
By an ingenious use of wind vanes and filters, fresh air
was kept circulating inside the enclosure while smoke and
grime from the industrial areas of Queens and New Jersey
were kept out. Inside this enclosure, dubbed "The Crystal
Matterhorn" by journalists, ever taller and more fanciful
buildings were constructed throughout the sixties; beginning
in 1970, many were joined by spiral walkways. All vehicular travel in Manhattan was by subway and electric cars;
horses, gasoline engines, and other sources of pollution were
strictly banned. In the winter, the enclosure was kept at a
comfortable temperature by electrical heaters and by the
calories generated by the island's 300,000 inhabitants.
Thus, winter or summer, the Manhattanites could stroll
the pavements in perfect comfort and safety.

In literature and the arts, unwholesome innovation was
forestalled by the taste of the public, who knew what they
liked, and by the survival of many of the great figures of
the late nineteenth century. In 1983 the sensations of the
opera season were Enrico Caruso in Puccini's *I Malavoglia*

and Lillian Russell in Tchaikovsky's *Nicolas Negorev;* the best-selling novels were Mark Twain's *Life in an Iceberg, The Borderland* by Robert Louis Stevenson, and *The Society of Ink-Tasters* by Arthur Conan Doyle. A traveling exhibition of new works by James McNeill Whistler, at the Metropolitan Museum, was seen by hundreds of thousands.

A man in East Orange, New Jersey, found a painting by Paul Cézanne in his grandmother's attic; it was obviously old, and he took it to a dealer, who informed him regretfully that it was worthless.

Centuries passed. In 2250 it was discovered that the population was declining, but the world took little notice at first, although it mourned the increasingly frequent deaths of great men and women. The elixir and the bacteriophage, although one kept people from aging and the other made them immune to disease, could not protect them against fatal ailments such as cancer, heart failure, and hardening of the arteries, or against poison, fire, drowning, and other accidents.

By 2330, when the decline became alarming, it was too late; the youngest living women, although they were as little as nineteen years old in appearance, had a chronological age of more than two hundred, and they were no longer fertile.

One by one, the smaller inhabited places of the world were abandoned and their former citizens moved into the great domed cities. Eventually even these became depopulated. Forests again covered the continents, effacing the works of man; for the first time in two thousand years, there were bears in Britain and giant elk in Russia. Six centuries after the discovery of the elixir of life, there were only two human beings left on the surface of the planet.

One of these was Gerd Essenwein, the Herr Doktor's son, who was then living in a villa overlooking Lake Lucerne, where he had collected all the sheet music for piccolo in the Lucerne and Zürich libraries. The other was a Japanese woman, Michi Yamagata, who at the time she took the elixir had been sixteen years of age. The two got into communication with each other by shortwave radio, and although they could not understand each other very well because of static, they agreed to meet. Michi found a serviceable small boat in Takatsu, crossed the Sea of Japan, and made her way across Asia and Europe by bicycle, stopping frequently to rest and replenish her stocks of dried food. The trip took her eleven years.

It was an emotional moment when at last she appeared on Gerd's doorstep. Neither had seen another human face, except in photographs and films, for over a century. Gerd played his piccolo for her and showed her his collection of autographs of famous musicians; he took her on a walking tour around the lake, and then they had a picnic in the country. It was a warm day, and Michi took off her dress. Speaking in German, which was their only common language, she said, "Essenwein-san, do you rike me?"

"I like you very much," said Gerd. "However, what you have in mind is not possible." In turn, he removed his clothing, and she saw that although he had lived for more than six centuries, his body was still twelve years old. They looked at each other ruefully and then put their clothes back on. The next day Michi got on her bicycle and started home. This time she was not in a hurry, and the trip lasted fifteen years.

After her return, they continued to communicate by shortwave radio on their birthdays for some years. In 2510 Michi told him that she was about to leave on a visit to Fujiyama; that was her last message.

A few years later, Gerd put a few prized possessions in a handcart and made his way into the mountains of Unter Walden, where he found a herd of Hartz Mountain goats, a hardy and affectionate breed. When he discovered that the goats liked his piccolo playing, he built a hut on the mountainside and moved in. Besides his sheet music and his autographs, he had a small harmonium, which he also played, but not as well; also, the goats did not care for it.

It was here, one morning in the spring of 2561, that the Arcturians found him. The Arcturians had received Marconi's signals, intended for Mars, and they had also received radio transmissions of voices singing "Yes, Sir, She's My Baby," stock-market reports, and "Amos 'n' Andy."

Three of the Arcturians disembarked from their landing vehicle and approached Gerd, who was sitting beside his hut, dressed in goatskins. The Arcturians were large gray worms, or, more properly, millipedes. They wore hemispherical dark covers over their eyes to protect them from

the unaccustomed glare of our sun, and looked like bug-
eyed monsters.

During their long voyage they had had plenty of time to
learn Earth languages from radio and television broadcasts, but they didn't know which one Gerd spoke. "¿Es
usted el ultimo?" they asked him. "Are you the last? Etes-
vous le dernier?"

Gerd looked at them and played the opening bars of the
Fantasia for Unaccompanied Piccolo by Deems Taylor.

"We come from another world," they told him in Hindi,
Swedish, and Italian. Gerd went on playing.

"Do you want to come with us? Doni të vij me neve?
Wollen Sie gehen mit uns?"

Gerd lowered the piccolo. "Nein, danke," he said.
"Glück auf," said the Arcturians politely, and went away
forever.

EMERGENCE

David R. Palmer

When international tensions increase, the problems of survival in the event of full-scale war return to the forefront of our consciousness. Here a new writer takes his turn, with a story told by a twelve-year-old girl who finds herself alive after the bombs drop. It's a grim setting, but as she discovers more and more facts about her startling destiny there's room for hope.

David R. Palmer, after working in his youth as an insurance salesman, school-bus driver, and managing a pet store, became a court reporter in 1976. He is married and lives in Florida.

NOTHING TO DO? NOWHERE TO GO? TIME hangs heavy? Bored? Depressed? Also badly scared? Causal factors beyond control?

Unfortunate. Regrettable. Vicious cycle—snake swallowing own tail. Mind dwells on problems; problems fester, assume ever greater importance for mind to dwell on. Etc. Bad enough where problems minor.

Mine aren't.

Psychology text offers varied solutions: Recommends keeping occupied, busywork if necessary; keep mind distracted. Better if busywork offers challenge, degree of frustration. Still better that I have responsibility. All helps.

Perhaps.

Anyway, keeping busy difficult. Granted, more books in shelter than public library; more tools, equipment, supplies, etc., than Swiss Family Robinson's wrecked ship— all latest developments: lightest, simplest, cleverest, most reliable, non-rusting, Sanforized. All useless unless—correction, *until* I get out (and of lot, know uses of maybe half dozen: Screwdriver for opening stuck drawer; hammer to tenderize steak, break ice cubes; hacksaw for cutting frozen meat . . .).

Oh, well, surely must be books explaining selection, use.

Truly, surely are books—thousands! Plus microfilm library—even bigger. Much deep stuff: classics, contemporary; comprehensive museum of man's finest works: words, canvas, 3-D and multi-view reproductions of statuary. Also scientific: medical, dental, veterinary, entomology, genetics, marine biology; engineering, electronics, physics (both nuclear and garden variety), meteorology, astronomy; carpentry, agriculture, welding (equipment, too), woodcraft, survival, etc., etc., etc.; poetry, fiction, biographies of great, near-great; philosophy—even complete selection of world's fantasy, new and old. Complete Oz books, etc. Happy surprise, that.

Daddy was determined man's highest achievements not vanish in Fireworks; also positive same just around corner. (Confession: Wondered sometimes if was playing with complete deck; spent incalculable sums on shelter and contents. Turns out was right; is probably having last laugh Somewhere. Wish were here to needle me about it—but wouldn't if—could; was too nice. Miss him. Very much.)

Growing maudlin. Above definitely constitutes "dwelling" in pathological sense as defined by psychology text. Time to click heels, clap hands, smile, Shuffle Off to Buffalo.

Anyhow, mountains of books, microfilm of limited benefit; too deep. Take classics: Can tolerate just so long; then side effects set in. Resembles obtaining manicure by scratching fingernails on blackboard—can, but would rather suffer long fingernails. Same with classics as sole remedy for "dwelling": Not sure which is worse. May be that too much culture in sudden doses harmful to health; perhaps must build up immunity progressively.

And technical is worse. Thought I had good foundation in math, basic sciences. Wrong—background good, considering age; but here haven't found anything elementary enough to form opening wedge. Of course, haven't gotten organized yet; haven't assimilated catalog, planned orderly approach to subjects of interest. Shall; but for now, can get almost as bored looking at horrid pictures of results of endocrine misfunctions as by wading through classics.

And am rationing fantasy, of course. Thousands of titles, but dasn't lose head. Speed-reader, you know; breach discipline, well runs dry in matter of days.

Then found book on Pitman Shorthand. Changed everything. Told once by unimpeachable source (Mrs. Hartman, Daddy's secretary and receptionist) was best, potentially fastest, most versatile of various pen systems. Also most difficult to learn well. (Footnote, concession to historical accuracy: Was also her system; source possibly contaminated by tinge of bias.) However, seemed promising; offered challenge, frustration. Besides, pothook patterns quite pretty, art form of sorts. Hoped would be entertaining.

Was—for about two days. Then memory finished absorbing principles of shorthand theory, guidelines for briefing and phrasing; transferred same to cortex—end of challenge. Tiresome being genius sometimes.

Well, even if no longer entertaining for own sake, still useful, much more practical than longhand; ideal for keeping journal, writing biography for archeologists. Probably not bother if limited to longhand; too slow, cumbersome. Effort involved would dull enthusiasm (of which little present anyway), wipe out paper supply in short order. Pitman fits entire life story on line and a half. (Of course, helps I had short life—correction: Helps brevity; does nothing for spirits.)

Problem with spirits serious business. Body trapped far underground; emotional index substantially lower. Prospects not good for body getting out alive, but odds not improved by emotional state. Depression renders intelligent option assessment improbable. In present condition would likely overlook ten good bets, flip coin over dregs. Situation probably not hopeless as seems, but lacking data, useful education, specialized knowledge (and guts), can't form viable conclusion suggesting happy ending. And lacking same, tend to assume worst.

So journal not just for archeologists; is therapeutic. Catharsis: Spill guts on paper, feel better. Must be true— psychology text says so (though cautions is better to pay Ph.D.-equipped voyeur week's salary per hour to listen. However, none such included in shelter inventory; will have to make do).

First step: Bring journal up to date. Never kept one; not conversant with format requirements, Right Thing To Do. Therefore will use own judgment. One thing certain: Sentence structure throughout will have English teachers spinning in graves (those fortunate enough to have one).

English 60 percent flab, null symbols, waste. Suspect massive inefficiency stems from subconsciously recognized need to stall, give inferior intellects chance to collect thoughts into semblance of coherence (usually without success), and to show off (my $12-dollar word can lick your $10-word). Will not adhere to precedent; makes little sense to write shorthand, then cancel advantage by employment of rambling academese.

Keep getting sidetracked into social criticism. Probably symptom of condition. Stupid; all evidence says no society left. Was saying:

First step: Bring journal up to present; purge self of neuroses, sundry hangups. Then record daily orderly progress in study of situation, subsequent systematic (brilliant) self-extrication from dire straits. Benefits twofold:

First, will wash, dry, fold, put away psyche; restore mind to customary genius; enhance prospects for successful escape, subsequent survival. Second, will give archeologists details on cause of untimely demise amidst confusing mass of artifacts in shelter should anticipated first benefit lose rosy glow. (Must confess solicitude for bone gropers forced; bones in question *mine!*)

Enough maundering. Time to bear down, flay soul for own good. Being neurotic almost as tiresome as being genius. (Attention archeologists: Clear room of impressionable youths and/or mixed company—torrid details follow.)

Born 11 years ago in small Wisconsin town, only child of normal parents. Named Candidia Maria Smith; reduced to Candy before ink dried on certificate. Early indications of atypicality: Eyes focused, tracked at birth; cause-effect association evident by six weeks; first words at four months; sentences at six months.

Orphaned at ten months. Parents killed in car accident. No relatives—created dilemma for baby-sitter. Solved when social worker took charge. Was awfully cute baby; adopted in record time.

Doctor Foster and wife good parents: loving, attentive; very fond of each other, showed it. Provided good environment for formative years. Then Momma died. Left just Daddy and me; drew us very close. Was probably shamelessly spoiled, but also stifled:

Barely five then, but wanted to *learn*—only Daddy had firm notions concerning appropriate learning pace, direction for "normal" upbringing. Did not approve of precocity; felt was unhealthy, would lead to future maladjustment, unhappiness. Also paternalistic sexist; had bad case of ingrown stereotypitis. Censored activities, reading; dragged heels at slightest suggestion of precocious behavior, atypical interests.

Momma disagreed; aided, indulged. With her help I learned to read by age two; understood basic numerical relationships by three: could add, subtract, multiply, divide. Big help until she had to leave.

So sneaked most of education. Had to—certainly not available in small-town classroom. Not difficult; developed speedreading habit, could finish high school text in 10, 20 minutes; digest typical best-seller in half, three-quarters of hour. Haunted school, local libraries every opportunity (visits only; couldn't bring choices home). But town small; exhausted obvious resources three years ago. Have existed since on meager fruits of covert operations in friends' homes, bookstores, occasional raids on neighboring towns' libraries, schools. Of course not all such forays profitable; small-town resources tend to run same direction: slowly, in circles. Catalogs mostly shallow, duplicated; originality lacking.

Frustrating. Made more so by knowledge that Daddy's personal in-house library rivaled volume count of local school, public libraries put together (not counting shelter collection, but didn't know about that then)—and couldn't get halfway down first page of 95 percent of contents.

Daddy pathologist; books imperviously technical. So far over head, couldn't even tell where gap lay (ask cannibal fresh off plane from Amazon for analysis of educational deficiencies causing noncomprehension of commercial banking structure). Texts dense; assumed reader already possessing high-level competency. Sadly lacking in own case—result of conspiracy. So languished, fed in dribbles as tireless prospecting uncovered new sources.

Single bright exception: Soo Kim McDivott, son of American missionary in Boxer Rebellion days, product of early East-West alliance. Was 73 when retired, moved next door two years ago. Apparently had been teacher whole life but never achieved tenure; tended to get fired over views. Did not appear to mind.

Strange old man. Gentle, soft-spoken, very polite; small seemed almost frail. Oriental flavoring lent elf-like quality to wizened features; effect not reduced by mischief sparkling from eyes.

Within two weeks became juvenile activity focus for most of town. Cannot speak for bulk of kids, but motivation obvious in own case: Aside from intrinsic personal warmth, knew everything—and if exception turned up would gleefully drop everything, help find out—and had *books*. House undoubtedly in violation of Fire Code; often wondered how structural members took load.

Fascinating man: could, would discuss anything. But wondered for a time how managed as teacher; never answered questions but with questions. Seemed whenever I had question, ended up doing own research, telling *him* answer. Took a while to catch on, longer before truly appreciated: Had no interest in teaching knowledge, factual information—taught learning. Difference important; seldom understood, even more rarely appreciated. Don't doubt was reason for low retirement income.

Oh, almost forgot: Could split bricks with sidelong glance, wreak untold destruction with twitch of muscle. Any muscle. Was Tenth-Degree Master of Karate. Didn't know were such; thought ratings topped at Eighth—and heard rumors *they* could walk on water. (But doubt Master Mac would bother. Should need arise, would politely ask waters to part—but more likely request anticipated, unnecessary.)

Second day after moving in, Master was strolling down Main Street when happened upon four young men, early 20s, drunk, unkempt—Summer People (sorry, my single ineradicable prejudice)—engaged in self-expression at Miller's Drugstore. Activities consisted of inverting furniture, displays; dumping soda-fountain containers (milk, syrup, etc.) on floor; throwing merchandise through display windows. Were discussing also throwing Mr. Miller when Master Mac arrived on scene.

Assessed situation; politely requested cease, desist, await authorities' arrival. Disbelieving onlookers closed, averted eyes; didn't want to watch expected carnage. Filthy Four dropped Mr. Miller, converged on frail-looking old Chinese. Then all fell down, had subsequent difficulty arising. Situation remained static until police arrived.

Filthies taken into custody, then to hospital. Attempted investigation of altercation unrewarding: Too many eye-witness accounts—all contradictory, disbelieving, unlikely. However, recurring similarities in stories suggested simultaneous stumble as Filthies reached for Master; then all fell, accumulating severe injuries therefrom: four broken jaws, two arms, two legs, two wrists; two dislocated hips; two ruptured spleens. Plus bruises in astonishing places.

Single point of unanimity—ask *anyone:* Master Mac never moved throughout.

Police took notes in visibly strained silence. Also took statement from Master Mac. But of dubious help: Consisted mostly of questions.

Following week YMCA announced Master Mac to teach karate classes. Resulted in near riot (by small-town standards). Standing room only at registration; near fistfights over positions in line.

Was 16th on list to start first classes but deserve no credit for inclusion: Daddy's doing. Wanted badly—considering sociological trends, self-defense skills looked ever more like required social graces for future survival—but hesitated to broach subject; seemed probable conflict with "normal upbringing" dictum.

So finally asked. Surprise! Agreed—granted dispensation! Was still in shock when Daddy asked time, date of registration. Showed article in paper: noon tomorrow. Looked thoughtful maybe five seconds; then rushed us, outdoors, down street to Y. Already 15 ahead of us, equipped to stay duration.

Daddy common as old slipper: warm, comfortable, folksy. But shared aspects with iceberg: Nine-tenths of brains not evident in everyday life. Knew was very smart, of course. Implicit from job; pathologist knows everything any other specialist does, plus own job. Obviously not career for cretin—and was *good* pathologist. Renowned.

But not show-off; was easy to forget; reminders few, far between. Scope, foresight, quick reactions, Command Presence demonstrated only in time of need.

Such occurred now: While I stood in line with mouth open (and 20 more hopefuls piled up behind like Keystone Cops), Daddy organized friends to bring chairs, cot, food, drink, warm clothing, blankets, rainproofs, etc. Took three minutes on phone. Was impressed. Then astounded—spent whole night on sidewalk with me, splitting watches, trading off visits to Little Person's room when need arose.

Got all choked up when he announced intention. Hugged him breathless; told him Kismet had provided better father than most workings of genetic coincidence. Did not reply, but got hugged back harder than usual; caught glimpse of extra reflections in corners of eyes from streetlight. Special night; full of warmth, feelings of belonging, togetherness.

After Daddy's magnificent contribution, effort to get me into class, felt slight pangs of guilt over my subsequent misdirection, concealment of true motivation. True, attended classes, worked hard; became, in fact, star pupil. But had to—star pupils qualified for private instruction—yup!—at Master's home, surrounded by what appeared to be 90 percent of books in Creation.

Earned way though. Devoted great effort to maintain favored status; achieved Black Belt in ten months, state championship (for age/weight group) six months later. Was considered probable national championship material, possibly world. Enjoyed; great fun, terrific physical conditioning, obvious potential value (ask Filthy Four), good for ego due to adulation over ever-lengthening string of successes, capture of state loving cup (ironic misnomer—contest was mock combat: "killed" seven opponents, "maimed" 22 others for life or longer).

But purely incidental; in no way distracted from main purpose:

With aid of Master (addressed as Teacher away from *dojo*) had absorbed equivalent of advanced high school education, some college by time world ended: Math through calculus, chemistry, beginnings of physics; good start on college biology, life sciences—doing well.

Occasionally caught Teacher regarding me as hen puzzles over product of swan egg slipped into nest; making notes in "Tarzan File" (unresolved enigma: huge file, never explained; partially concerned me, as achievements frequently resulted in entries, but was 36 inches thick before I entered picture), but definitely approved—and his approval better for ego than state cup.

Regarding which, had by then achieved Fifth Degree; could break brick with edge of hand, knee, foot. But didn't after learned could. Prospect distressed Daddy. Poor dear could visualize with professional exactitude pathological consequences of attempt by untrained; knew just what each bone splinter would look like, where would be driven; which tendons torn from what insertions; which nerves destroyed forever, etc. Had wistful ambition I might follow into medicine; considered prospects bleak for applicant with deformed, calloused hammers dangling from wrists.

Needless concern; calluses unnecessary. With proper control body delivers blow through normal hands without discomfort, damage. Is possible, of course, to abuse nature to point where fingers, knuckles, edge of hands, etc., all turn to flint, but never seen outside exhibitions. Serves no purpose in practice of art; regarded with disdain by serious student, Master alike.

So much for happy memories.

Not long ago world situation took turn for worse. Considering character of usual headlines when change began, outlook became downright grim. Daddy tried to hide concern but spent long hours reading reports from Washington (appreciated for first time just how renowned was when saw whom from), watching news; consulting variety of foreign, domestic officials by phone. Seemed cheerful enough, but when thought I wasn't looking, mask slipped.

Finally called me into study. Sat me down; gave long, serious lecture on how bad things were. Made me lead through house, point out entrances to emergency chute leading down to shelter (dreadful thing—200 foot vertical drop in pitch dark, cushioned at bottom only by gradual curve as polished sides swing to horizontal, enter shelter). Then insisted we take plunge for practice. Although considered "practice" more likely to induce physic block, make subsequent use impossible—even in time of need— performed as requested. Not as bad as expected; terror index fell perhaps five percent short of anticipation. But not fun.

However, first time in shelter since age three. Scenic attractions quickly distracted from momentary cardiac arrest incurred in transit. Concealed below modest small-town frame house of unassuming doctor was Eighth Wonder of World. Shelter is three-story structure carved from bedrock, 100 feet by 50; five-eighths shelves, storage compartments. Recognized microfilm viewer immediately; identical to one used at big hospital over in next county. Film-storage file cabinets same, too—only occupied full length of two long walls, plus four free-standing files ran almost full length of room. Rest bookshelves, as is whole of second floor. Basement seems mostly tools, machinery, instrumentation.

Hardly heard basic life-support function operation lecture: air regeneration, waste reclamation, power production, etc. Was all could do to look attentive—books drew me like magnet. However, managed to keep head; paid sufficient attention to ask intelligent-sounding questions. Actually learned basics of how to work shelter's vital components.

. . . Because occurred to me: Could read undisturbed down here if knew how to make habitable. (Feel bad about that, too; here Daddy worried sick over my survival In The Event Of—and object of concern scheming about continuing selfish pursuit of printed word.)

Tour, lecture ended. Endless spiral staircase up tube five feet in diameter led back to comfortable world of small-town reality. Life resumed where interrupted.

With exception: Was now alert for suitable opportunity to begin exploration of shelter.

Not readily available. As Fifth was qualified assistant instructor at formal classes; took up appreciable portion of time. Much of rest devoted to own study—both Art (wanted to attain Sixth; would have been youngest in world) and academics, both under approving eye of Master. Plus null time spent occupying space in grammar school classroom, trying not to look too obviously bored while maintaining straight-A average (only amusement consisted of correcting teachers, textbooks—usually involved digging up proof, confrontations in principal's office). Plus sundry activities rounding out image of "normally well-rounded" 11-year-old.

But patience always rewarded. If of sufficient duration. Daddy called to Washington; agreed was adult enough to take care of self, house, Terry during three days' expected absence. Managed not to drool at prospect.

Terry? True, didn't mention before, by name; just that had responsibility. Remember? First page, fourth paragraph. Pay attention—may spring quiz.

Terry is retarded, adoptive twin brother. Saw light of day virtually same moment I emerged—or would have had opened eyes. Early on showed more promise than I: Walked at nine weeks, first words at three months, could fly at 14 weeks. Achieved fairly complex phrases by six months but never managed complete sentences. Peaked early but low.

Not fair description. Actually Terry is brilliant—for macaw. Also beautiful. Hyacinthine Macaw, known to lowbrows as Hyacinth, pseudo-intellectuals as *anodorhynchus hyacinthinus*—terrible thing to say about sweet baby bird. Full name Terry D. Foster (initial stands for Dactyl). Length perhaps 36 inches (half of which is tail feathers); basic color rich, glowing hyacinth blue (positively electric in sunlight), with bright yellow eye patches like clown, black feet and bill. Features permanently arranged in jolly Alfred E. Neuman, village-idiot smile. Diet is anything within reach, but ideally consists of properly mixed seeds, assorted fruits, nuts, sprinkling of meat, etc.

Hobbies include getting head and neck scratched (serious business, this), art of conversation, destruction of world. Talent for latter avocation truly awe-inspiring: 1,500 pounds pressure available at business end of huge, hooked beak. Firmly believe if left Terry with four-inch cube of solid tungsten carbide, would return in two hours to find equivalent mass of metal dust, undimmed enthusiasm.

Was really convinced were siblings when very young. First deep childhood trauma (not affected by loss of blood parents; too young at time, too many interesting things happening) induced by realization was built wrong, would never learn to fly. Had stubbornly mastered perching on playpen rail shortly after began walking (though never did get to point of preferring nonchalant one-legged stance twin affected—toes deformed: stunted, too short for reliable grip), but subsequent step simply beyond talents.

Suspect this phase of youth contributed to appearance of symptoms leading to early demise of Momma Foster. Remember clearly first time she entered room, found us perched together on rail, furiously "exercising wings." Viewed in restrospect, is amazing didn't expire on spot.

(Sounds cold, unfeeling; is not. Momma given long advance notice; knew almost to day when could expect to leave. Prepared me with wisdom, understanding, love. Saw departure as unavoidable but wonderful opportunity, adventure; stated was prepared to accept, even excuse reasonable regret over plans spoiled, things undone—but not grief. Compared grief over death of friend to envy of friend's good fortune: selfish reaction—feeling sorry for self, not friend. Compared own going to taking wonderful trip; "spoiled plans" to giving up conflicting movie, picnic, swim in lake. Besides, was given big responsibility —charged me with "looking after Daddy." Explained he had formed many elaborate plans involving three of us— many more than she or I had. Would doubtless be appreciably more disappointed, feel more regret over inability to carry out. Would need love, understanding during period it took him to reform plans around two remaining behind. Did such a job on me that truly did not suffer loss, grief; just missed her when gone, hoped was having good time.)

Awoke morning of Daddy's trip to startling realization—didn't want him to go. Didn't like prospect of being alone three days: didn't like idea of *him* alone three days. Lay abed trying to resolve disquieting feeling. Or at least identify. Could do neither; had never foreboded before. Subliminal sensation: below conscious level but intrusive. Multiplied by substantial factor could be mistaken for fear —no, not fear, exactly; more like mindless, screaming terror.

But silly; nothing to be scared about. Mrs. Hartman would be working in office in front part of house during day; house locked tight at night—with additional security provided by certain distinctly non-small-town devices Daddy recently caused installed. Plus good neighbors on all sides, available through telephone right at bedside or single loud scream.

Besides, was I not Candy Smith-Foster, State Champion, Scourge of Twelve-and-Under Class, second most dangerous mortal within 200-mile radius? (By now knew details of Filthy Four's "stumble," and doubt would have gotten off so lightly had I been intercessor.)

Was. So told feeling to shut up. Washed, dressed, went down to breakfast with Daddy and Terry.

Conduct during send-off admirable; performance qualified for finals in stiff-upper-lip-of-year award contest. Merely gave big hug, kiss; cautioned stay out of trouble in capital, but if occurred, call me soonest—would come to rescue: split skulls, break bones, mess up adversaries something awful. Sentiment rewarded by lingering return hug, similar caution about self during absence (but expressed with more dignity). Then door of government-supplied, chauffeur-driven, police-escorted limousine closed; vehicle made its long, black way down street, out of sight around corner.

Spent morning at school, afternoon teaching at Y, followed by own class with Master. Finally found self home, now empty except Terry (voicing disapproval of day's isolation at top of ample lungs); Mrs. Hartman done for day, had gone home. Silenced twin by scratching head, transferring to shoulder (loves assisting with household chores, but acceptance means about three times as much work as doing by self—requires everything done at arms' length, out of reach).

Made supper, ate, gave Terry whole tablespoon of peanut butter as compensation for boring day (expressed appreciation by crimping spoon double). Did dishes, cleaned house in aimless fashion; started over.

Finally realized was dithering, engaging in busywork; afraid to admit was really home alone, actually had opportunity for unhindered investigation of shelter. Took hard look at conflict; decided was rooted in guilt over intent to take advantage of Daddy's absence to violate known wishes. Reminded self that existence of violation hinged upon accuracy of opinion concerning unvocalized desires; "known wishes" question-begging terminology if ever was one. Also told self firmly analysis of guilt feeling same as elimination. Almost believed.

Impatiently stood, started toward basement door. Terry recognized signs, set up protest against prospect of evening's abandonment. Sighed, went back, transferred to shoulder. Brother rubbed head on cheek in gratitude, gently bit end of nose, said, "You're so bad," in relieved tones. Gagged slightly; peanut-butter breath from bird is rare treat.

Descended long spiral stairs down tube to shelter. Ran through power-up routine, activated systems. Then began exploration.

Proceeded slowly. Terry's first time below; found entertaining. Said, "How 'bout that!" every ten seconds. Also stretched neck, bobbed head, expressed passionate desire to sample every book as pulled from shelf. Sternly warned of brief future as giblet dressing if so much as touched single page. Apparently thought prospect sounded fun, redoubled efforts. But was used to idiot twin's antisocial behavior; spoiled fun almost without conscious thought as proceeded with exploration.

Soon realized random peeking useless; was in position of hungry kid dropped in middle of Willy Wonka's Chocolate Factory: Too much choice. Example: Whole cabinet next to microfilm viewer was *catalog!*

Three feet wide, eight high; drawers three feet deep, six inches wide (rows of six); ten titles per card (*thin* cards) —72 cubic feet of solid catalog.

Took breath away to contemplate. Also depressed; likelihood of mapping orderly campaign to augment education not good. Didn't know where to start; which books, films within present capacity; where to go from there. Only thing more tiresome than being repressed genius is being ignorant genius recognizing own status.

Decided to consult Teacher; try to get him to list books he considered ideal to further education most rapidly from present point, cost no object. (Was giving consideration to Daddy's ambition to see me become doctor; but regardless, no education wasted. Knowledge worthwhile for own sake.) Didn't feel should report discovery— would be breach of confidence—but could use indirect approach. Not lie; just not mention that any book suggested undoubtedly available on moment's notice. Ought to fool him all of ten seconds.

Started toward switchboard to power-down shelter. Hand touching first switch in sequence when row of red lights began flashing, three large bells on wall next to panel commenced deafening clangor. Snatched hand back as if from hot stove; thought had activated burglar alarm (if reaction included thought at all). Feverish inspection of panel disclosed no hint of such, but found switch marked "Alarm Bells, North American Air Defense Command Alert." Opened quickly; relieved to note cessation of din, but lights continued flashing. Then, as watched, second row, labeled, "Attack Detected," began flashing.

Problem with being genius is tendency to think deep, mull hidden significance, overlook obvious. Retrieved Terry (as usual, had gone for help at first loud noise), scratched head to soothe nerves. Twin replied, "That's *bad!*" several times; dug claws into shoulder, flapped wings to show had not really been scared. Requested settle down, shut up; wished to contemplate implications of board.

Impressive. Daddy must be truly high-up closet VIP to rate such inside data supplied to home shelter. As considered this, another row flashed on, this labeled, "Retaliation Initiated." Imagine—blow-by-blow nuclear-war info updates supplied to own home! Wonderful to be so important. Amazing man. And so modest—all these years never let on. Wondered about real function in government. With such brains was probably head of super-secret spy bureau in charge of dozens of James Bond types.

Don't know how long mindless rumination went on; finally something clicked in head: Attack? Retaliation?

Hey . . . ! Bolted for steps. Terry dug in claws, voiced protest over sudden movements.

Stopped like statue. Daddy's voice, tinny, obviously recording: "Red alert, radiation detected. Level above danger limit. Shelter will seal in 30 seconds—29, 28, 27 . . ." Stood frozen; listened as familiar voice delivered requiem for everything known and loved—including probably self. Interrupted count once at 15-second mark to repeat radiation warning, again at five seconds.

Then came deep-toned humming; powerful motors slid blocks of concrete, steel, asbestos across top of stairwell, did same for emergency-entry chute. Sealing process terminated with solidly mechanical clunks, thuds. Motors whined in momentary overload as program ensured was tight.

Then truly alone. Stood staring at nothing for long minutes. Did not know when silent tears began; noticed wet face when Terry sampled, found too salty. Shook head; said softly, "Poo-oor bay-bee-ee . . ."

Presently found self sitting in chair. Radio on; could not remember turning switch, locating CONELRAD frequency. Just sat, listened to reports. Only time stirred was to feed, water Terry; use potty. Station on air yet, but manned only first three days.

Was enough, told story: Mankind eliminated. Radiation, man-made disease. International quick-draw ended in tie.

Final voice on air weakly complained situation didn't make sense: Was speaking from defense headquarters near Denver—miles underground, utterly bombproof, airtight; self-contained air, water—so why dying? Why last alive in entire installation? Didn't make sense . . .

Agreed, but thought objection too limited in scope. Also wondered why *we* were still alive. Likewise didn't make sense.

If invulnerability of NORAD headquarters—located just this side of Earth's core under Cheyenne Mountain—proving ineffective, how come fancy subcellar hidey-hole under house in small town still keeping occupants alive? And for how long? Figured had to be just matter of time.

Therefore became obsessed with worry over fate of retarded brother. Were safe from radiation (it seemed), but plague another matter. Doubted would affect avian biochemistry; would kill me, leave poor baby to starve, die of thirst. Agonized over dilemma for days. Finally went downstairs; hoped might turn up something in stores could use as Terry's Final Friend.

Did. Found Armory. Thought of what might have to do almost triggered catatonia; but knew twin's escape from suffering dependent on me, so mechanically went ahead with selection of shotgun. Found shells, loaded gun. Carried upstairs, placed on table. Then waited for cue.

Knew symptoms; various CONELRAD voices had described own, those of friends. Were six to syndrome. Order in which appeared reported variable; number present at onset of final unconsciousness not. Four symptoms always; then fifth: period of extreme dizziness—clue to beginning of final decline. Was important, critical to timing with regard to Terry. Desperately afraid might wait too long; condemn poor incompetent to agonizing last days. And almost more afraid might react to false alarm, proceed with euthanasia; then fail to die—have to face scattered, blood-spattered feathers, headless body of sweetest, jolliest, most devoted, undemandingly loving friend had ever known.

Which was prospect if acted too soon—intended to stand 20 feet away, blow off head while engrossed in peanut butter. Pellet expansion sufficient at that distance to ensure virtually instantaneous vaporization of entire head, instant kill before possibility of realization, pain. Would rather suffer own dismemberment, boiling in oil than see innocent baby suffer, know was me causing.

Thus, very important to judge own condition accurately when plague sets in.

Only hasn't yet. Been waiting three weeks, paralyzed with grief, fear, apprehension, indecision. But such emotions wearisome when protracted; eventually lose grip on victim. I think perhaps might have—particularly now that journal up to date, catharsis finished. Book says therapy requires good night's sleep after spilling guts; then feel better in morning. Suspect may be right; do feel better.

Okay. Tomorrow will get *organized* . . . !

Good morning, Posterity! Happy to report I spent good night. Slept as if already dead—first time since trouble began. No dreams; if tossed, turned, did so without noticing. Appears writer of psychology text knew stuff (certainly should have; more letters following name than in). Catharsis worked—at least would seem; felt good on waking. Wounds obviously not healed yet, but closed. A beginning—scabs on soul much better than hemorrhage.

Situation unchanged; obviously not happy about fact (if were would know had slipped cams), but this morning can look at Terry without bursting into tears; can face possibility might have to speed birdbrained twin to Reward before own condition renders unable. Thought produces entirely reasonable antipathy, sincere hope will prove unnecessary—but nothing more.

Despairing paralysis gone; mind no longer locked into hopeless inverse logarithmic spiral, following own tail around ever-closer, all-enveloping fear of ugly possibility.

Seems have regained practical outlook held prior to Armageddon; i.e., regard worry as wasteful, contra-productive if continued after recognition, analysis of impending problem, covering bases to extent resources permit. Endless bone-worrying not constructive exercise: if anything, diminishes odds for favorable outcome by limiting scope of mind's operation, cuts down opportunities for serendipity to lend hand. Besides, takes fun out of life— especially important when little enough to be had.

Time I rejoined world of living (possibly not most apt choice of words—hope do not find am in exclusive possession). First step: consider physical well-being. Have sadly neglected state of health past three weeks; mostly just sat in chair, lay abed listening to airwaves hiss.

And speaking of physical well-being—has just occurred: am ravenous! Have nibbled intermittently without attention to frequency, content—mostly when feeding, watering Terry. (Regardless of own condition, did *not* neglect jovial imbecile during course of depression. Even cobbled up makeshift stand from chair, hardwood implement handle; found sturdy dishes secured firmly to discourage potential hilarity. Granted, diet not ideal—canned vegetables, fruits, meat, etc.—but heard no complaints from clientele, and would be no doubt if existed: Dissatisfaction with offerings usually first indicated by throwing on floor; if prompt improvement not forthcoming, abandons subtlety.)

Have also noticed am *filthy!* Wearing same clothes came downstairs in three weeks ago. Neither garments nor underlying smelly germ farm exposed to water, soap, deodorant since. (Can be same fastidious Candy Smith-Foster who insists upon shower, complete change of clothing following any hint of physical exertion, contact with

even potentially soiled environment? Regrettably is.) And
now that am in condition to notice—*have!* Self-respecting
maggot would take trade elsewhere.

So please excuse. Must rectify immediately. Bath (probably take three, four complete water changes to do job);
then proper meal, clean clothes. Then get down to business. Time to find out about contents of shelter—availability of resources relevant to problems.

Be back later . . .

Apologies for delay, neglect. But have been so *busy!*
Bath, resumption of proper nutrition completed cure.
Spirits restored; likewise determination, resourcefulness,
curiosity (intellectual variety; am not snoop—rumors to
contrary). Also resumed exercises, drills (paid immediate
penalty for three-week neglect of Art—first attempt at
usual *kata* nearly broke important places, left numerous
sore muscles.)

Have systematically charted shelter. Took pen, pad
downstairs to stores, took inventory. Then went through
bookshelves in slow, painstaking manner; recorded titles,
locations of volumes applicable to problems. Project took
best part of three days. Worth effort; variety, volume of
equipment simply awesome. Together with library probably
represents everything necessary for singlehanded founding
of bright new civilization—from scratch, if necessary. (Not
keen on singlehanding part, however; sounds lonely. Besides, know nothing about Applied Parthenogenesis; not
merit-badge topic in scouts. Only memory of subject's discussion concerned related research—was no-no; leader
claimed caused myopia, acne, nonspecific psychoses. Oh,
well, considering age, prospects for achieving functional
puberty, seems less than pressing issue.)

Speaking of pressing issues, however—found *food.*
Founder of civilization will certainly eat well in interim.
Must be five-year supply of frozen meat, fruit, fresh vegetables in deep-freeze locker adjoining lower level (huge
thing—50 feet square). Stumbled upon by accident; door
wasn't labeled. Opened during routine exploration expecting just another bin. Light came on illuminating scenery—
almost froze tip of nose admiring contents before realized
was standing in 50-degree-below-zero draft. Also good
news for Terry: Daddy anticipated presence; lifetime sup-

ply of proper seed mix in corner bin. Will keep forever; too cold to hatch inevitable weevil eggs, etc.

Actually haven't minded canned diet; good variety available—but sure was nice to drop mortally-peppered steak onto near-incandescent griddle, inhale fumes as cooked; then cut with fork while still bleeding inside charred exterior. Of course had to fight Terry for share; may be something likes better, but doesn't come readily to mind.

Is regrettable this could be part of Last Words; means must exercise honesty in setting down account. Bulk of organized theologies I've read opine dying with lie upon lips bodes ill for direction of departure. Since can be no doubt of Terry's final Destination, must keep own powder dry. Twin would be lonely if got There without me—besides, without watching would announce presence by eating pearls out of Gate.

So despite self-serving impulses, must record faithfully shameful details of final phase in monumental inventory: assault upon card file. Intended to make painstaking, card-by-card inspection of microfilm catalog (vastly more extensive than bound collection), recording titles suggesting relevance to problems. Grim prospect; 72 cubic feet holds dreadful quantity of cards—each with ten titles. Even considering own formidable reading speed, use of Pitman for notes, seemed likely project would account for substantial slice of remaining lifespan—even assuming can count upon normal duration.

However, could see no other way; needed information. So took down first drawer (from just below ceiling, of course; but thoughtful Daddy provided rolling ladder as in public stacks), set on table next to notepad. Sighed, took out first card, scanned—stopped, looked again. Pulled out next 20, 30; checked quickly. Made unladylike observation regarding own brains (genius, remember?). Reflected (after exhausted self-descriptive talents) had again underestimated Daddy.

Humble healer, gentle father was embodiment of patience—but had none with unnecessary inefficiency. Obviously would have devised system to locate specifics in such huge collection. Useless otherwise; researcher could spend most of life looking for data instead of using.

First 200 cards index of *index*. Alphabetically categorized, cross-referenced to numbered file locations. Pick category, look up location in main file; check main file for specific titles, authors; find films from specific location number on individual card. Just like downtown.

So after settled feathers from self-inflected wounds (ten well-deserved lashes with sharp tongue), got organized. Selected categories dealing with situation; referred to main index; decided upon specific films, books. Cautioned Terry again about giblet shortage, dug out selections. Settled down to become expert in nuclear warfare, viral genocide; construction details, complete operation of shelter systems.

Have done so. Now know exactly what happened. Every ugly detail. Know which fissionables used, half-life durations; viral, bacterial agents employed; how deployed, how long remain viable threats without suitable living hosts. Know what they used on us—vice versa. Found Daddy's papers dealing with secret life.

Turns out was heavyweight government consultant. Specialty was countering biological warfare. Privy to highest secrets; knew all about baddest bugs on both sides. Knew how used, countermeasures most effective—personally responsible for development programs aimed at wide-spectrum etiotropic counteragents. Also knew intimate details of nuclear hardware poised on both sides of face-off. Seems had to; radiation level often key factor: In many cases benign virus, bacteria turned instantaneously inimical upon exposure to critical wavelengths. Only difference between harmless tourist and pathogen: Soothing counsel transmitted from pacific gene in DNA helix to cytoplasmic arsenal by radiation-vulnerable RNA messenger. Enter energy particle flood, exit restraint; hello Attila the Germ. Clever, these mad scientists.

Undoubtedly how attack conducted—explains, too, fall of hermetically sealed NORAD citadel. Entire country seeded over period of time with innocuous first-stage organisms until sufficiently widespread. Then special warheads—carefully spaced to irradiate every inch of target with critical wavelength—simultaneously detonated at high altitude across whole country. Bombs dropping vertically from space remained undetected until betrayed by flash—by which time too late; radiation front travels just behind visible light. Not a window broken but war already over: Everybody running for shelter already infected, infectious with at least one form of now-activated, utterly lethal second-stage plague. Two, three days later—all dead.

Supposed to be another file someplace down here detailing frightful consequences to attackers; haven't found yet. Only mention in this one suggests annihilation even surer, more complete among bad guys—and included broken windows.

Tone of comment regretful. Not sure can agree. True, most dead on both sides civilians—but are truly innocent? Who permitted continuing rule by megalomaniacs? Granted, would have been costly for populace to throw incumbent rascals out, put own rascals in—but considering cost of failure in present light . . .

Must give thought before passing judgment.

Enough philosophy.

Have learned own tactical situation not bad. No radiation detectable on surface, immediate area (instrumentation in shelter; sensors upstairs on roof of house—part of TV antenna). Not surprising: According to thesis, nuclear stuff to be used almost exclusively as catalyst for viral, bacterial invaders. Bursts completely clean—no fallout at all—high enough to preclude physical damage. Exception: Direct hits anticipated on known ICBM silos, SAC basis, Polaris submarines, bomber-carrying carriers, overseas installations—and Washington. . . .

Where Daddy went. Hope was quick, clean.

Plague another question entirely. Daddy holds opinion infection of target country self-curing. No known strain in arsenals of either side capable of more than month's survival outside proper culture media; i.e., living human tissue (shudder to contemplate where, how media obtained for experimentation leading to conclusion). Odds very poor such available longer than two, three days after initial attack; therefore should be only another week before is safe to venture outside, see what remains of world. However, wording, ". . . should be . . ." erodes confidence in prediction; implies incomplete data, guesswork—*gamble*. Considering stake involved is own highly regarded life, placing absolute reliance on stated maximum contagion parameters not entirely shrewd policy.

So shan't. Now that can get out whenever wish, no longer have such pressing need to; claustrophobic tendencies gone. Shelter quite cozy (considering): Dry, warm, plumbing, furniture; great food (brilliantly prepared), safe water; good company, stimulating conversation ("Hello, baby! What'cha doin'? You're so bad! Icky *pooh!*"); plus endless supply of knowledge. Delay amidst such luxury seems small price for improved odds. So will invest extra two months as insurance.

Figure arbitrary; based on theory that treble safety factor was good enough for NASA, should be good enough for me. (Of course theory includes words "should be" again, but must draw line somewhere.)

And *can* get out when ready. Easy: Just throw proper switches. All spelled out in detailed manual on shelter's systems, operation. Nothing to it. Just pick up book, read. After finding. After learning exists in first place. (Daddy could have reduced first three weeks' trauma had bothered to mention, point out where kept—on other hand, had learned how to get out prior to absorbing details on attack, would doubtless be dead now.)

Makes fascinating reading. Shelter eloquent testimonial to wisdom of designer. Foresight, engineering brilliance embodied in every detail. Plus appalling amount of money, shameless level of political clout. Further I got into manual, more impressed became. Is NORAD headquarters miniaturized, improved: hermetically sealed; air, water, wastes recycled; elaborate communications equipment; sophisticated sensory complex for radiation, electronics, detection, seismology, medicine. Power furnished by nuclear device about size of Volkswagen—classified, of course (talk about clout?). Don't know if works; supposed to come on automatically when municipal current fails. But according to instruments am still running on outside power.

Let's see—nope; seems to be about everything for now. Will update journal as breathtaking developments transpire.

Hi. One-month mark today. Breathless developments to date:

1. Found stock of powdered milk: awful. Okay in soup, chocolate, cooking, etc., but alone tastes boiled.

2. Discovered unplugged phone in hitherto-unnoticed cabinet. Also found jack. Plugged in, found system still working. Amused self by ringing phones about country— random area codes, numbers. But no answers, of course; and presently noticed tears streaming down face. Decided not emotionally healthy practice. Discontinued.

3. Employed carpentry tools, pieces of existing make-shift accommodation to fabricate proper stand for brother. Promptly demonstrated gratitude by chewing through perch (which had not bothered for whole *month*!). Re-

placed with thick, hardwood sledge handle; sneered, dared him try again. Have thereby gained temporary victory: Fiend immediately resumed game but achieving little progress. Wish had stands from upstairs in house. Are three, all 11 years old—still undamaged (of course, perches consist of hard-cured, smooth-cast concrete—detail possibly relevant to longevity).

Guess that's it for now. Watch this space for further stirring details.

Two months—hard to believe not millenia. Einstein correct: Time *is* relative. Hope doesn't get more so; probably stop altogether. Have wondered occasionally if already hasn't.

Not to imply boredom. Gracious, how could be bored amidst unremitting pressure from giddy round of social activities? For instance, just threw gala party to celebrate passing of second month. Was smash, high point of entombment, sensation of sepulchral social schedule. Went all out—even invited Terry (desperately relieved to find invitee able to squeeze event into already busy whirl of commitments).

First-class event: Made cake, fried chicken thighs, broiled small steak; even found ice cream. All turned out well. Preferred steak, cake myself; honored guest chose ice cream (to eyebrows), chicken bones (splits shafts, devours marrow—possibly favoritest treat of all). No noisemakers in inventory (gross oversight), but assemblage combined efforts to compensate. At peak of revelry birdbrain completed chewing through perch. Was standing on end at time, of course; accepted downfall with pride, air of righteous triumph. Then waddled purposefully in direction of nearest chair leg. Had to move fast to dissuade.

Replaced perch.

Also have read 104 microfilmed books, regular volumes. Am possibly world's foremost living authority on everything.

As if matters.

Later.

Ever wanted something so bad could almost taste, needed so long seemed life's main ambition? Finally got—wished hadn't?

You guessed: Three months up—*finally!*

Went upstairs, outside. Stayed maybe two hours. Wandered old haunts: familiar neighborhood, Main Street shopping area, Quarry Lake Park, school, Y, etc.

Should have quit sooner: would, had understood nature of penalty accruing. By time got back was already too late; trembling all over, tears running down face. Scabs all scraped from wounds; worms awake, gnawing soul. In parlance of contemporaries—past: Was bad trip.

However, conditions outside are fact of life, something must face. Must overcome reaction unless intend to spend balance of years simulating well-read mole. Nature works slowly, methods unesthetic; tidying up takes years. Inescapable; must accept as is; develop blind spot, immunity. Meanwhile will just have to cope best I can with resulting trauma each time crops up until quits cropping.

Well, coping ought be no problem. Catharsis worked before, should again. But wish were some other way. No fun; hurts almost as much second time around. But works —and already learned cannot function with psyche tied in knots. So time to quit stalling. "Sooner started, sooner done; sooner outside, having fun."—Anon. (Understandably.)

Only just *can't* right now. Not in mood; still hurting too bad from initial trauma. Guess I'll go read some more. Or pound something together with hammer.

Or apart.

Later.

Okay. Feel no better yet, but feel less bad. Is time got on with therapy.

Suspect current problems complicated by *déjà vu*. Still retain vivid mental picture of body of Momma Foster minutes after pronounced dead. Bore physical resemblance to warm, wise, vital woman whose limitless interests, avid curiosity, ready wonderment, hearty enjoyment of existence had so enriched early years.

But body not person—person *gone*. Resemblance only underscored absence.

So too with village: Look quick, see no difference. Bears resemblance to contentedly industrious, unassuming, small farm town of happy childhood. Same tall, spreading trees shade same narrow streets; well-kept, comfortably ageless old homes. Old-fashioned streetlights line Main Street's storefront downtown business district, unchanged for 50 years, fronting on classic village square. Hundred-year-old township building centered in square amidst collection of heroic statues, World War I mementos, playground equipment; brightly painted, elevated gazebo for public speakers. Look other direction down street, see own ivy-covered, red-brick school at far end, just across from Y. Next door, Teacher's house looks bright, friendly, inviting as ever in summer-afternoon sunshine.

But open door, step out onto porch—illusion fades. Popular fallacy attends mystique of small towns: Everyone knows are "quiet." Not so; plenty of noise, but right kind—comfortable, unnoticed.

Until gone.

Silence is shock. Is wrong, but takes whole minutes to analyze *why* wrong; identify anomalous sensation, missing input.

Strain ears for hint of familiar sound: Should be faint miasma of voices, traffic sounds drifting up from direction of Main Street; chatter, squeals, laughter from schoolyard. Too, is truly small town, farmlands close at hand; should hear tractors chugging in fields, stock calling from pastures. Should catch frequent hollow mutter as distant semi snores down highway past town; occasional, barely-perceptible rumble from jet, visible only as fleecy tracing against indigo sky. Should be all manner of familiar sounds.

But as well could be heart of North Woods; sounds reaching ear limited to insect noises, birdcalls, wind sighing through leaves.

Visual illusion fades quickly, too. Knee-deep grass flourishes where had been immaculately groomed yards; straggly new growth bewhiskers hedges, softening previous mathematically-exact outlines. Houses up and down street show first signs of neglect: Isolated broken windows, doors standing open, missing shingles. Partially uprooted tree leans on Potters' house, cracking mortar, crushing eaves, sagging roof. Street itself blocked by car abandoned at crazy angle; tire flat, rear window broken, driver's door hanging open. Closer inspection shows Swensens' pretty yellow-brick Cape Cod nothing but fire-gutted shell; roof mostly gone, few panes of glass remain, dirty smudge marks above half-consumed doors and windows; nearby trees singed.

And the smell . . . ! Had not spent last three months sealed in own atmosphere, doubt could have remained in vicinity. Still strong enough outside to dislodge breakfast within moments of first encounter. And did. Happily, human constitution can learn to tolerate almost anything if must. By time returned to shelter, stench faded from forefront of consciousness—had other problems more pressing:

Learned what knee-deep lawns conceal. Three months' exposure to Wisconsin summer does little to enhance cosmetic aspects of Nature's embalming methods: Sun, rain, insects, birds, probably dogs, too, have disposed of bulk of soft tissues. What remains is skeletons (mostly scattered, incomplete, partially covered by semi-cured meat, some clothing). Doubtless would have mummified completely by now in dry climate, but Wisconsin summers aren't. At best, results unappealing: at worst (first stumbled over in own front yard), dreadful shock.

Yes, I know; should have anticipated. Possibly did, in distant, nonpersonally-involved sort of way—but didn't expect to find three bodies within ten feet of own front door! Didn't expect to confront dead neighbors within three minutes after left burrow. Didn't expect so *many!* Thought most would be respectably tucked away indoors, perhaps in bed. That's where I'd be. I think.

Well, lived through initial shock, continued foray. Was not systematic exploration; just wandered streets, let feet carry us at random. Didn't seem to matter; same conditions everywhere. Peeked into houses, stores, cars; knocked on doors, hollered a lot.

Wasn't until noticed twin digging in claws, flapping wings, protesting audibly that realized was running blindly, screaming for somebody—*anybody!*

Stopped then, streaming tears, trembling, panting (must have run some distance); made desperate attempt to regain semblance of control. Dropped where stood, landed in Lotus. Channeled thoughts into relaxation of body, achievement of physical serenity; hoped psyche would heed good example.

Did—sort of. Worked well enough, at least, to permit deliberate progress back to shelter, deliberate closing door, deliberate descent of stairs, deliberate placing of Terry on stand—all before threw screaming fit.

Discharged lots of tension in process, amused Terry hugely. By end of performance fink sibling was emulating noises. Ended hysteria in laughter. Backwards, true, but effective.

Recovered enough to make previous journal entry. Granted, present (therapeutic) entries beyond capacity at that point; but after spent balance of day licking wounds, night's rest, was fit enough to make present update, discharge residual pain onto paper.

Amazing stuff, therapy; still not exactly looking forward to going outside again, but seem to have absorbed trauma of dead-body/deserted city shock; adjusted to prospect of facing again. Forewarned, should be able to go about affairs, function affectively in spite of surroundings.

Which brings up entirely relevant question: Exactly what *are* my affairs, functions . . . ? Now that am out, what to do? Where to go? What to do when get there? Why bother go at all?

Okay, fair questions. Obviously prime objective is find Somebody Else. Preferably somebody knowing awful lot about Civilizations, Founding & Maintenance Of—to say nothing of where to find next meal when supplies run out.

Certainly other survivors. Somewhere. So must put together reasonable plan of action based on logical extension of available data. Sounds good—uh, except, what *is* available data?

Available data: *Everybody* exposed to flash, to air at time of flash, to anybody else exposed to flash or air exposed to flash or to anybody exposed to anybody, etc., either at time of flash or during subsequent month, anywhere on planet, is dead. Period.

Shucks. Had me worried; thought for moment I had problem. Ought be plenty survivors; modern civilization replete with airtight refuges: nuclear submarines, hyperbaric chambers, space labs, jet transports, "clean assembly" facilities, many others (not to forget early-model VW beetles, so long as windows closed). Ought be many survivors of flash, initial contagion phase.

But—loaded question—how many knew enough; stayed tight throughout required month? Or got lucky, couldn't get out too soon despite best efforts? Or with best intentions, had supplies, air for duration? Or survived emotional ravages; resisted impulse to open window, take big, deliberate breath?

Could employ magnet to find needle in haystack; easy by comparison. Real problem is: *Is needle in there at all?*

Well, never mind; leave for subconscious to mull. Good

track record heretofore; probably come up with solution, given time.

Other, more immediate problems confronting: For one, must think about homestead. Can't spend balance of years living underground. Unhealthy; leads to pallor. Besides, doubt is good for psyche; too many ghosts.

Where—no problem for short term; can live just about anywhere warm, dry. Adequate food supplies available in shelter, stores, home pantries, etc.; same with clothing, sundry necessities. Can scavenge for years if so inclined.

However, assuming residential exclusivity continues (and must take pessimistic view when planning), must eventually produce own food, necessities; become self-sufficient. Question is: Should start now or wait; hope won't prove necessary?

Not truly difficult decision: longer delayed, more difficult transition becomes. Livestock factor alone demands prompt attention. Doubtless was big die-off over summer. Too stupid to break out of farms, pastures, search for water, feed, most perished—"domestic" synonym for "dependent." But of survivors, doubt one in thousand makes it through winter unaided. Means if plan to farm, must round up beginning inventory before weather changes. Also means must have food, water, physical accommodations ready for inductees beforehand.

Means must have farm.

However, logic dictates commandeering farm relatively nearby. Too much of value in shelter: must maintain reasonable access. Availability of tools, books, etc., beneficial in coming project: provisioning, repairing fences, overhaul well-pumps, etc.

Plus work needed to put house in shape for winter. Wisconsin seasons rough on structures; characteristic swayback rooflines usually not included in builders' plans, zoning regulations. After summer's neglect buildings of farm selected apt to need much work—none of which am qualified to do. Expect will find remainder of summer, fall highly educational, very busy.

So perhaps should quit reflecting on plans, get move on. Best reconnoiter nearby farms. Be nice to find one with buildings solid, wells pumping, fences intact, etc.; be equally nice to meet jolly red-dressed, white-bearded gentlemen cruising down road in sleigh pulled by reindeer.

*   *   *

Hi, again. Surprised to see me? Me too. Thinking of changing name to Pauline, serializing journal. Or maybe just stay home, take up needlepoint. Seems during entombment character of neighborhood changed; deteriorated, gotten rough—literally gone to dogs. Stepped out of A & P right into— Nope, this won't do. Better stick to chronology; otherwise sure to miss something. Might even be important someday. So:

Awoke fully recovered—again (truly growing tired of yo-yo psychology). Since planned to be out full day, collected small pile of equipment, provisions: canteen, jerky, dried apricots, bag of parrot mix; hammer, pry bar (in case forcible investigation indicated). Went upstairs, outside.

Retained breakfast by force of will until accustomed to aroma.

Took bike from garage, rode downtown (first ride in three months: almost deafened by twin's manic approval). After three months' neglect, tires a tad soft (ten-speed requires 85 pounds); stopped at Olly's Standard, reinflated. And marveled: Utilities still on, compressor, pumps, etc., still working—even bell still rang when rode across hose.

Started to go on way; stopped—had thought. Returned, bled air tanks as had seen Big Olly do. Had explained: Compression, expansion of air in tanks "made water" through condensation; accumulation bad for equipment. Found was starting to think in terms of preserving everything potentially useful against future need. (Hope doesn't develop into full-blown neurosis; maintaining whole world could cramp schedule.)

Set about conducting check of above-ground resources: Eyeball-inventoried grocery stores, hardware, seed dealers; took ride down to rail depot, grain elevators. Found supplies up everywhere; highly satisfactory results. Apparently business conducted as usual after flash until first symptoms emerged. No evidence of looting; probably all too sick to bother.

And since power still on, freezers in meat markets maintaining temperature; quantity available probably triple that in shelter. If conditions similar in nearby towns, undoubtedly have lifetime supply of everything—or until current stops. (Personally, am somewhat surprised still working; summer thunderstorms habitually drop lines, blow transformers twice, three times a year—and *winter . . . !* One good ice storm brings out candles for days; prime reason why even new houses, designed with latest heating systems, all have old-fashioned Franklin-type oil stoves in major rooms, usually multiple fireplaces. Doubt will have electricity by spring.)

OH HELL! Beg pardon; unladylike outburst—but just realized: Bet every single farm well in state *electrically* operated. I got *troubles . . . !*

Well, just one more problem for subconscious to worry about. Can't do anything about it now—but must devote serious thought.

Back to chronology: Emerged from A & P around ten; kicked up stand, prepared to swing leg over bike. Suddenly Terry squawked, gripped shoulder so hard felt like claws met in middle. Dropped bike, spun.

Six dogs: lean, hungry; visibly exempt from "Best Friend" category.

Given no time to consider strategy; moment discovered, pack abandoned stealth, charged. Had barely time to toss twin into air, general direction of store roof, wish Godspeed. Then became very busy.

Had not fought in three months but continued *kata;* was in good shape. Fortunate.

First two (Shepherd, Malamute) left ground in formation, Doberman close behind. Met Malamute (bigger of two) in air with clockwise spin-kick to lower mandible attachment. Felt bones crunch, saw without watching as big dog windmilled past, knocking Shepherd sprawling. Took firm stance, drove forward front-fist blow under Doberman's jaw, impacting high on chest, left of center. Fist buried to wrist; felt scapula, clavicle, possibly also humerus crumble; attacker bounced five feet backwards, landed in tangle. Spun, side-kicked Shepherd behind ear as scrambled to rise; felt vertebrae give. Took fast step, broke Malamute's neck with edge-hand chop. Spun again, jumped for Doberman; broke neck before could rise.

Glanced up, body coiling for further combinations—relaxed; remaining three had revised schedule; were halfway across parking lot.

Looked wildly about for Terry; spotted twin just putting on brakes for touchdown on shopping cart handle 20 feet away. Wondered what had been doing in interim; seemed could have flown home, had dinner, returned to watch outcome.

Retrieved; lectured about stupidity, not following orders —suppose had been flankers? Would have been lunch before I got there.

Birdbrain accepted rebuke; nuzzled cheek in agreement, murmured, "You're so icky-poo!"

Gave up; continued sortie.

Wondered briefly at own calmness. First blows ever struck in earnest; halfway expected emotional side-effects. But none; only mild regret had not met attackers under favorable circumstances. Doberman in particular was beautiful specimen, if could disregard gauntness.

Decided, in view of events, might be best if continued explorations in less vulnerable mode. Decided was time I soloed. Had driven cars before, of course; country kids all learn vehicular operation basics soonest moment eyes (augmented by cushions) clear dashboard, feet reach pedals.

Question of which car to appropriate gave pause. Have no particular hangups: familiar (for nondriver) with automatics, three-, four-speed manuals, etc. But would be poking nose down vestigial country roads, venturing up driveways more accustomed (suitable) to passage of tractor, horses; squeezing in, out of tight places; doubtless trying hard to get very stuck. Granted, had been relatively dry recently; ground firm most places, but—considering potential operating conditions, physical demands . . .

Would take Daddy's old VW. Happy selection: Answered physical criteria (maneuverable, good traction, reliable, etc.); besides, had already driven—for sure could reach pedals, see out. Did give thought to Emerson's Jeep, but never had opportunity to check out under controlled conditions. Further, has plethora of shift levers (three!). True, might be more capable vehicle, but sober reflection suggested unfamiliar advantages might prove trap; seemed simpler, more familiar toy offered better odds of getting back.

Pedaled home quickly, keeping weather eye out for predators (can take hint). Arrived without incident. Found key, established blithe sibling on passenger's seatback: adjusted own seat for four-foot-ten-inch stature, turned key.

Results would have warmed ad-writer's heart: After standing idle three months, Beetle cranked industriously about two seconds; started.

Gauge showed better than three-quarters full, but

wanted to make sure; lonely country road frequented by
hungry dog packs wrong place to discover faulty gauge.
So backed gingerly down drive (killed only twice), navi-
gated cautiously to Olly's. Stuck in hose, got two gallons
in before spit back. Beetle's expression seemed to say,
". . . *told* you so," as capped tank, hung up hose.

Went about tracking down suitable farm in workmanlike
fashion, for beginner. Picked up area USGS Section Map
from Sheriff's office. Methodically plotted progress as went;
avoided circling, repetition. Drove 150 miles; visited 30,
35 farms; marked off on map as left, graded on one-to-ten
basis. Were many nice places; some could make do in
pinch. But none rated above seven: nothing rang bell until
almost dark.

Found self at terminus of cow-path road. Had wound
through patchy woods, hills; felt must go somewhere so
persevered to end, where found mailbox, driveway. Turned
in; shortly encountered closed gate. Opened, drove through;
resecured. Followed drive through woods, over small rise,
out into clearing, farmyard. Stopped abruptly.

Knew at once was *home*. . . .

To right stood pretty, almost new, red-brick house; to
left, brand-new, modern steel barn, henhouse; two silos
(one new), three corncribs—all full.

Got out, walked slowly around house, mouth open, heart
pounding. No broken windows, doors closed, shingles all
in place—*grass cut!* For glorious moment heart stopped
altogether; thought had stumbled on nest of survivors.
Then rounded corner, bumped into groundskeepers—
sheep.

Owners quite dead. Found remains of man in chair on
porch. Apparently spent last conscious moments reflecting
upon happy memories. Picture album in lap suggested four
impromptu graves short distance from house were wife,
three children; markers confirmed. Fine looking people;
faces showed confidence, contentment, love; condition of
farm corroborated, evidenced care, pride.

Grew misty-eyed looking through album. Resolved to
operate farm in manner founders would approve. Had
handed me virtual "turn-key" homestead; immeasurably advanced schedule, boosted odds for self-sufficiency, survival. Least I could do in return.

Farm nestles snugly in valley amidst gently rolling,

wooded countryside. Clean, cold, fast-running brook meanders generally through middle, passes within hundred yards of house; and by clever fence placement, zigs, zags, or loops through all pastures. Perimeter fence intact; strong, heavy-gauge, small-mesh fabric. Probably not entirely dog-proof, but highly resistant; with slight additional work should be adequate.

Contents of silos, cribs, loft product of season's first planting; second crop still in fields—primary reason stock alive, healthy. Internal gates open throughout; allowed access to water, varied grazing (includes nibbling minor leakages from cribs, silos). Beasties spent summer literally eating "fat of land"; look it.

Besides five sheep are nine cows (two calves, one a *bull*), two mares, one gelding, sundry poultry (rooster, two dozen chickens, motley half-dozen ducks, geese). No pigs, but no tears; don't like pigs, not wild about pork either.

From evidence, losses over summer low: Found only two carcasses: two cows, one horse. Bones not scattered, doubt caused by dogs; more likely disease, injury, stupidity —salient characteristic of domestic ruminants: Given opportunity, will gorge on no-no, pay dearly later.

Wandered grounds, poked through buildings until light gone. Found good news everywhere looked. Nothing I can't use as is, put right with minor work.

Clocked distance on return: 17 miles by road. Not too bad; can walk if necessary—should breakdown occur while commuting—but perhaps wiser to hang bike on bumper. Still, machines can't last forever; only matter of time before forced back to horseback technology. Will still have occasion to visit shelter often. Map shows straight-line distance only nine miles; guess better learn bulldozer operation, add road-building to skills. (Goodness—future promises such varied experiences; may vary me to death. . . .)

Was late when finally got back to shelter, tired but glowing all over at prospect. Can hardly wait for morning, start packing, moving in; start of new life.

Demented twin shares view; hardly shut up whole time were at farm. Or since. Lectured stock, dictated to poultry, narrated inspection tour throughout. Hardly took time out for snack, drink. Must be country boy at heart. So urbane, never suspected.

Hey—am really *tired!*
Good night.

Oh! Hurt places didn't even know I had. Suspect must have come into being just for occasion.

Six trips to farm. Count 'em.

Light failed just before self. Packing stuff from house no problem: Eight, ten trips to car; all done. Stuff in shelter is rub. Aye.

Two hundred feet straight up, arms loaded. Repeatedly. *Must* be better way.

Good night.

This is embarrassing; guess is time quit posing as genius. Proof in pudding. What matters 200-plus IQ if actions compatible with mobile vegetable?

Occurred this morning to ponder (after third trip up stairs) how excavated material removed during construction. Hand-carried in buckets? Counting stairwell, material involved amounts to 200,000 cubic feet plus. At half cube per bucket, assuming husky lad carrying doubles, 15-minute round trips, that's 32 cubic feet every eight hours. Would take ten-man crew 625 days—not counting down time due to heart attacks, hernias, fallen arches. . . .

And what about heavy stuff? Doubt nuclear generator carried down by hand—must weigh couple tons.

Okay. Obviously done some other way. But how? Oh—shelter manual; had forgotten. Thumbed through quickly, found answer: *elevator!* Of course. Missed significance of small, odd-shaped, empty storeroom during first inspection. Other things on mind; didn't notice controls.

Balance of day much easier. Still tired tonight but not basket case.

Tomorrow is another day . . . !

STOP THE PRESSES! Strike the front page! Scoop! I'm not me—I'm something else. No—we're not us—no—Oh, bother; not making *any* sense. But can't help it: hard to organize thoughts—so *DAMNED* excited . . . ! Will try, *must* try. Otherwise will end up leaving out best parts, most important stuff. Then, by time get feathers settled, blood pressure reduced, will have forgotten *everything!* *Oh*, must stop this *blithering!* Must get back to chronology. So . . .

Deep breath . . . release slow-oo-ow-ly . . . heart slowed to normal. physical tranquillity . . . serenity . . . ohm-m-m . . .

Amazing, worked again.

Okay, resumed packing this morning. Took two loads over, returned for third. Finished; everything in car, at farm that felt would need. But still fidgeting; couldn't decide why. No question of something forgotten; farm only short drive away, omission not crisis.

Finally recognized source of unscratchable itch: Was time I did duty. Had avoided at first; knew couldn't face prospect. Then got so busy, slipped mind. But now remembered: Soo Kim McDivott. Teacher. Friend.

To friend falls duty of seeing to final resting place.

Generally inured now to face of death *per se;* unaffected last few days by myriad corpses have stepped over during course of running errands. Had no problem, for instance, removing Mr. Haralsen from porch to proper place beside wife, children; even finished job with warm feeling inside. (Suspect original trauma caused by sudden shock of events; enormity, completeness of isolation.) Condition improved now; felt could perform final service for old friend—more, felt need to.

Went next door, looked for body. Checked entire house: upstairs, downstairs, basement—even stuck head in attic.

Finally returned to library. Teacher had used as study; desk located there, most of favorite dog-eared references close at hand. Hoped might find clue regarding whereabouts amidst clutter.

First thing to catch eye was "Tarzan File" standing on desk. Large envelope taped to top, printing on face. Glanced at wording. Blood froze.

Was addressed to me!

Pulled loose, opened with suddenly shaking fingers. Teacher's meticulous script, legible, beautiful as Jefferson's on Declaration, read:

> *Dearest Candidia,*
> *It is the considered opinion of several learned men familiar with your situation, among them Dr. Foster and myself, that you will survive the plague to find and read this. The viral complex employed by the enemy cannot harm you, we know; it was created as a specific against Homo sapiens.*

Almost dropped letter. Surely required no genius to note implications. Took deep breath, read on:

I know, my child, that that statement must sound like the ramblings of an old man in extremis . . .

Ramble? *Teacher?* Ha! True, was old; condition intrinsic to amount of water over dam—of which lots (all deep, too). Probably also in extremis; lot of that going around when wrote this. But ramble? *Teacher?* Comes the day Teacher rambles, Old Nick announces cooling trend, New Deal, takes up post as skiing instructor on glorious powder slopes of Alternate Destination. *I* ramble; Teacher's every word precise, correct.

Precise, correct letter went on:

. . . but please, before forming an opinion, humor me to the extent of reading the balance of this letter and reviewing the supporting evidence which documents 25 years of painstaking investigation by me and other.

Note that of 1,284 incidents wherein wild animals of varying descriptions "adopted" human children, none (with the exception of the very youngest—those recovered from the wild below age three) developed significantly beyond the adoptive parents. They could not be taught to communicate; they evinced no abstract reasoning; they could not be educated. IQ testing, where applicable, produced results indistinguishable from similar tests performed on random members of the "parents'" species. Further, except for the 29 cases where the adoptive parents were of a species possessing rudimentary hands (apes, monkeys, the two raccoon incidents; to a lesser degree the badger and the wolverine), the children possessed no awareness of the concept of grasping, nor did it prove possible to teach them any manual skills whatever.

Finally, most authorities (note the citations in the file) are agreed that Man is born devoid of instincts, save (a point still in contention) suckling; therefore, unlike lesser animals, human development is entirely dependent upon learning and, therefore, environment.

This principle was deeply impressed upon me during the years I spent studying a number of these children; and it occurred to me to wonder what effect

*this mechanism might have within human society—
whether average parents, for instance, upon producing
a child possessing markedly superior genetic potential, might raise such a child (whether through ignor-
ance, unconscious resentment or envy, deliberate
malice, or some unknown reason) in such a manner as
to prevent his development from exceeding their own
attainments; and if such efforts took place, to what
extent the child would in fact be limited.*

Then followed narrative of early stages of investigation,
solo at first, but producing preliminary findings so startling
that shortly was directing efforts of brilliant group of associates (including *Daddy!*), whole project funded by bottomless government grant. Object of search: reliable
clues, indicators upon which testing program could be
based enabling identification of gifted children (potential
geniuses) shortly after birth, before retardation (if such
truly existed) began operation.

Efforts rewarded: Various factors pinpointed which, encountered as group, were intrinsic to genetically superior
children. Whereupon study shifted to second phase. As
fast as "positives" found, identified, were assigned to study
group. Were four:

AA (positive/advantaged), potentially gifted kids whose
parents were in on experiment; guided, subsidized, as-
sisted every way possible to provide optimum environment for learning, development. AB (positive/nonadvan-
taged), potential geniuses whose parents weren't let in on
secret; would have to bloom or wither, depending on qualities of vine. BA (negative/advantaged), ordinary babies,
random selection, whose parents were encouraged (for
which read "conned") to think offspring were geniuses;
also received benefit of AA-type parental coaching (and
coaches didn't know whether were dealing with AA or BA
parents), financial asistance. And BB (negative/nonad-
vantaged), control group: ordinary babies raised ordinary
way. Whatever that is.

As expected, AA did well in school; average progress
tripled national norm. Further, personality development
also remarkable: AA kids almost offensively well adjusted;
happy, well-integrated personalities. BAs did well, too,
but beat national figures by only 15 percent. Were also
generally happy, but isolated individuals demonstrated

symptoms suggesting insecurity; perhaps being pushed close to, even beyond capabilities.

ABs also produced spotty results: Goods very good, equaling AA figures in certain cases; however, bads *very* bad: ABs had highest proportion of academic failures, behavioral problems, perceptibly maladjusted personalities.

BBs, of course, showed no variation at all from national curves; were just kids.

Study progressed cozily; all content as confirming evidence of own cleverness emerged from statistical analysis, continued to accumulate (Teacher, in particular, basking in glow emanating from vindication of theory), when suddenly Joker popped from deck:

It became obvious that AA and AB children lost vastly less time from school through illness. Further breakdown, however, showed that approximately one third of the positives had never lost any time, while the balance had attendance records indistinguishable from the norm. Detailed personal inquiry revealed that these particular children had never been sick from any cause, while the balance had had the usual random selection of childhood illnesses. It was also determined that these unfailingly healthy positives were far and away the highest group of achievers in the AA group and constituted the best, worst, and most maladjusted of the AB group.

At that time study blessed by convenient tragedy: AA "healthy" child died in traffic accident. Body secured for autopsy.

Every organ was examined minutely, every tissue sample was scrutinized microscopically and chemically, and chromosome examination was performed. Every test known to the science of pathology was performed, most three, four, and five times, because no one was willing to believe the results.

And thereafter, quickly and by various subterfuges, complete physicals, including X rays, and biopsy samples of blood, bone, skin, hair, and a number of organs, were obtained from the full test group and compared.

The differences between "healthy" positives and the

balance proved uniform throughout the sample, and were unmistakable to an anthropologist . . .

Shock upon shock: Folksy, humble, simple Teacher was Ph.D.—three times over! Was physician (double-barreled —pediatrician, psychiatrist) plus anthropologist. Predictably, renowned in all three—qualities leading to Tenth Degree not confined to Art.

. . . but none of themselves were of a character to attract the notice of a physician not specifically and methodically hunting for an unknown "common denominator," using mass sampling techniques and a very open mind; nor would they attract notice by affecting the outcome of any known medical test or procedure. The single most dramatic difference is the undisputed fact, still unexplained, that "healthy" positives are totally immune to the full spectrum of human disease.

Differences proved independent of race, sex: Makeup of AA, AB "healthy" kids 52 percent female; half Caucasoid, one-third Negroid, balance apportioned between Oriental, Hispanic, Indian, other unidentifiable fractions. Breakdown matched precisely population area from which emerged.

The conclusion is indisputable: Although clearly of the genus Homo, AA and AB "healthy" children are not human beings; they are a species distinct unto themselves.

Quite aside from the obvious aspect of immunity and the less obvious anatomical characteristics which identify them, these children possess clear physical superiority over Homo sapiens children of like size and weight. They are stronger, faster, more resistant to trauma, and demonstrate markedly quicker reflexive responses. Visual, aural, and olfactory functions operate over a broader range and at higher levels of sensitivity than in humans. We have no data upon which to base even a guess as to the magnitude, but all evidence points toward a substantially longer lifespan.

A study was begun immediately, a search for clues which might help to explain this phenomenon of uni-

formly mutated children being born to otherwise normal, healthy human couples. And these couples were *normal: To the limits of our clinical capabilities to determine, they were indistinguishable from any other Homo sapiens.*

However, it was only very recently, after years of the most exhaustive background investigation and analysis, that a possible link was noticed. It was an obvious connection, but so removed in time that we almost missed its significance, due to the usual scientific tendency to probe for the abstruse while ignoring the commonplace.

The grandmothers of these children were all of a similar age, born within a two-year span: All were conceived during the rampage of the great influenza pandemic of 1918-19.

This "coincidence" fairly shouts its implications: Sweeping genetic recombination, due to specific viral invasion, affecting either of the gametes before, or both during, formation of the zygotes which became the grandmothers, creating in each half of the matrix which fitted together two generations later to become the AA and AB "healthy" children.

Personally I have no doubt that this is the explanation; however, so recently has this information come to light, that we have not had time to study the question in detail. And suspecting that something may be true—even a profound inner conviction—is not the same as proving it. I hope you will one day have the opportunity to add this question to your own studies. It needs answering.

After much reflection we named this new species Homo post hominem, meaning "Man Who Follows Man," for it would appear that this mutation is evolutionary in character; and that, given time and assuming it breeds true (there is no reason to suspect otherwise—in fact, chromosome examination suggests that the mutation is dominant; i.e., a sapiens/hominem pairing should unfailingly produce a hominem), it will entirely supplant Homo sapiens.

Wonderful thing, the human nervous system; accustoms quickly to mortal shocks. Didn't even twitch as other shoe landed—or perhaps had anticipated from buildup; just wondering how would be worded: Very nice; no fanfare, just matter-of-fact statement:

> *You, my child, are a Homo post hominem. You are considerably younger than your fellows among the study group, and were never involved in the study itself. Your identification and inclusion in our sample came about late and through rather involved and amusing circumstances.*
>
> *The Fosters, as you know, had long desired a child and had known equally long that they could never have one. When your natural parents died, it was entirely predictable that they lost no time securing your adoption (which is certainly understandable; you were a most winning baby).*

Neither Daddy nor rest of staff thought to have me tested; had been exposed to ten months' "unmonitored parentage"; was "compromised subject." Besides, Daddy wasn't interested in studying me; wanted to enjoy raising "his little girl." Professional competence crumbled before gush of atavistic paternalism. Most reprehensible.

Momma disagreed; felt determination of potential would provide useful child-rearing information. In keeping with formula long established for maintaining smooth marriage, kept disagreement to self; however, took steps: Prevailed upon staff to test me—all unbeknownst Daddy.

Tests proved positive, but follow-up determination as to "healthy" status not performed—didn't occur to discipline-blindered scientists, and Momma didn't know any better so didn't insist.

> *You were a genius; she was content. And she thereupon took it upon herself to see that you were raised in the same "advantaged" manner as the rest of the AAs—with the exception of the fact that the doctor did not know this was taking place. He continued to enjoy his "daddy's little girl" as before, prating endlessly about the advantages of "sugar and spice," etc. And as for the rest of us, after swearing each other to secrecy about your test results and our involvement, we forgot you. You were, after all, a "compromised subject."*

Was almost five when next came to their attention. Had soured "sugar and spice" by glancing up, commenting living-room wall ". . . looks awful hot." Was, too—result of electrical fault. Would have burned down house shortly.

Remember incident clearly. Not that caused any particular, immediate fuss, but Daddy spent balance of evening trying not to show was staring at me.

The doctor had spent much time during the previous few years observing children whose visual perception extended into the infrared and ultraviolet; and as shortly thereafter as possible, without letting Mrs. Foster know, he had you examined and tested.

Oho! Finally—explanation what triggered Daddy's reaction that day—and of friends' inexplicable night-blindness, even during summer. Of course, could understand difficulty seeing at night during winter; is *dark* outside on cold night. Only perceptible glow comes from faces, hands; and after short exposure to cold, cheeks, noses dim perceptibly.

And remember also that testing session. Salient feature was expressions of other staff as repeated tests done on previous (conspicuously unmentioned) occasion: utterly deadpan.

It was only after the tests (performed fully this time) identified you as a Homo post hominem; after the doctor had diffidently broached this fact to Mrs. Foster and she, giggling helplessly, confessed to him, and finally, we also came clean, that further testing demonstrated that you were substantially more advanced in intellectual development than the profile developed by our studies suggested you should be at that age.

How nice. Even as superkid can't be normal; still genius. Is no justice.

Detailed analysis of this phenomenon brought forth two unassessable factors: One, you had experienced ten months of unmonitored BB parentage; and two, your subsequent upbringing had been AA from your mother but BB from your father. Since we could

*neither analyze nor affect the first of these, we chose
to continue the second factor unaltered, observing you
closely and hoping that in some way, then unknown,
the whipsaw combination of indulgent spoiling and
accelerated, motivational education you had received
to this point would continue to produce these outstanding results.*

Momma's death terminated experiment; but before she
left, made Teacher promise would take over overt manage-
ment of education, keep pushing me hard as would accept
while Daddy (apparently) continued classic BB father role.
Momma felt hunger for knowledge already implanted;
abetted by Daddy's careful negative psychology, seeding
of environment with selected books (*Ha!* Always suspected something fishy about circumstances surrounding
steady discovery of wanted, needed study materials, always
just in time, just as finishing previous volume—not complaining; just wish planting had gone faster), would carry
on through interim without lost momentum. Was right,
too—but now know how puppet must feel when wires too
thin to discern.

Phase Two of scheme hit snag, though; was not anticipated would take four years for Teacher to extricate self
from complications attendant profession(s), "retire."

*Fortunately the delay appeared to be without con-
sequences. Mrs. Foster's opinion of you was borne
out; Dr. Foster reported that you located every book
he planted—and not a few that he didn't. He said it
was rarely necessary to "steer" you; that you were
quite self-motivated, distinctly tenacious, and could be
quite devious when it came to tracking down knowledge in spite of the "barriers" he placed in your way.*

*By the time I managed to delegate all my other
responsibilities to my successors and devote my entire
attention to you, your advantage over other AAs had
increased impressively. There were only a very few
individuals showing anywhere near as much promise.
And by the time the blunderings of our late friends
behind the Iron Curtain put an end to all such research, you were—for your age—quite the most advanced of our hominems.*

If I seem to harp on that point, it is because you

must remember that this study was initiated some 20 years ago. You are ten years younger than the next youngest in our group; and as advanced as you are for your age, you still have considerable catching up to do—see that you keep at it.

Yes, I know; the exigencies of solo survival will occupy much of your time, but do not neglect your studies entirely. Cut back if you must, but do not terminate them.

Now, if I may presume to advise a singularly gifted member of an advanced species, there is security and comfort in numbers. You will doubtless find the preservation and extension of knowledge more convenient once a group of you have been assembled. Within the body of the Tarzan File you will find a complete listing of known Homo post hominems. I can anticipate no logical reason why most should not be alive and in good health.

Pawed through file with shaking hands. Found listing referred to: collection of mini-dossiers. One had small note attached. Read:

Dear Candy,

It is now almost time for me to leave, and a number of things still remain undone, so I must be brief.

The subject of this dossier, Peter Bell, is the direct, almost line-bred descendant of Alexander Graham Bell (would that I could have tested him). A measure of his intellect is the fact that he, alone of our hominems, deduced the existence and purpose of our study, the implications regarding himself, and most of the characteristics of his and your species.

To him, not long ago, I confided your existence, as well as my impressions of your potential.

As well as probably being your equal (after you reach maturity, of course), he is also nearest to your own age, at 21; and of all our subjects, I predict he is the most likely to prove compatible with you as you continue your unrelenting search for knowledge in the future—in fact, he may give you quite a run for it; he is a most motivated young man.

However, I was unable to reach him following the attack; therefore he does not know that you are alive

and well in the shelter. The burden is upon you to
establish contact, if such is possible—and I do urge
you to make the attempt; I feel that a partnership
consisting of you two would be most difficult to op-
pose, whatever the future may bring you.

> *Love,*
> *Teacher.*

Hands shook, blood pounded in head as turned back to
first letter. Balance consisted of advice on contacting other
hominems—AAs from study.

Cautioned that, based on (terribly loose) extrapolation
of known data, should be perhaps 150,000 of us on North
America continent— but virtually *all* must be considered
ABs, replete with implications: High proportion of maladjusted, discontents, rebels, borderline (or worse after
shock of depopulation) phychotics, plus occasional genius.
Plus rare occurrences of surviving Homo sapiens.

Teacher suggested moving very deliberately when meeting strangers: Evaluate carefully, rapidly, selfishly. If decide is not sort would like for neighbor, hit first; kill without hesitation, warning. No place in consideration for
racial altruism. Elimination of occasional bad apple won't
affect overall chances for lifting species from endangered
list; are enough of us to fill ranks after culling stock—
but only one *me*. Point well taken.

Letter continued:

Well, time grows short. So much remains to be ac-
complished before I leave, so I had best hurry.

I leave with confidence; I know the future of the
race is in hands such as yours and Peter's. You will
prosper and attain levels of development I cannot
even envision; of that I am certain. I hope those
heights will include much joy and contentment.

I might add this in parting: When your historians
tell future generations about us, I hope they will not be
unduly severe. True, we did not last the distance; also
true, we did exterminate ourselves, apparently in a
display of senseless, uncontrolled aggression; equally
true, we did many other things that were utterly
wrong.

But we did create a mighty civilization; we did
accumulate a fund of knowledge vast beyond our ca-

*pacity to absorb or control; we did conceive and
aspire to a morality unique in history, which placed
the welfare of others ahead of our own self-interest—
even if most of us didn't practice it.*

And we did produce you!

*It may well be that we were not intended to last more
than this distance. It may even be that your coming
triggered seeds of self-destruction already implanted
in us for that purpose; that our passing is as necessary
to your emergence as a species as was our existence to
your genesis.*

*But whatever the mechanism or its purpose, I think
that when all are judged at the end of Time, Homo
sapiens will be adjudged, if not actually a triumph,
then at least a success, according to the standards
imposed by the conditions we faced and the purposes for which we were created; just as the Cro-
Magnon, Neanderthal, and Pithecanthropus—and even
the brontosaur—were successful in their time when
judged in light of the challenges they overcame and
the purposes they served.*

Single page remained. Hesitated; was final link with living past. Once read, experienced, would become just
another memory. Sighed, forced eyes to focus:

*Candy, my beloved daughter-in-spirit, this is most
difficult to bring to a close. Irrationally I find myself
grieving over losing you; "irrationally," I say, because
it is obviously I who must leave. But leave I must,
and there is no denying and little delaying of it.*

*It will be well with you and yours. Your growth
has been sound, your direction right and healthy; you
cannot fail to live a life that must make us, who discovered and attempted to guide you this far, proud of
our small part in your destiny, even though we are not
to be permitted to observe its fulfillment. I think I
understand something of how Moses must have felt as
he stood looking down that last day on Nebo.*

*Always know that I, the doctor, and Mrs. Foster
could not have loved you more had you sprung from
our own flesh. Remember us fondly, but see that you
waste no time grieving after us.*

The future is yours, my child; go mold it as you see the need.

Goodbye, my best and best-loved pupil.

> Love forever,
> Soo Kim McDivott

P.S.: *By the authority vested in me as the senior surviving official of the United States Karate Association, I herewith promote you to Sixth Degree. You are more than qualified; see to it that you practice faithfully and remain so.*

Read, reread final page until tears deteriorated vision, made individual word resolution impossible. Placed letter reverently on desk, went upstairs, outside onto balcony porch. Was Teacher's favorite meditation setting. Settled onto veranda swing, eased legs into Lotus.

Terry understood; moved silently from shoulder to lap, pressed close, started random-numbers recitation of vocabulary in barely audible, tiny baby-girl voice. Held twin nestled in arms as pain escalated, tears progressed to silent, painful, wracking sobs. Sibling's uncritical companionship, unquestioning love all that stood between me and all-engulfing blackness, fresh awareness of extent of losses threatening to overwhelm soul.

Together we watched early-afternoon cumulonimbus form up, mount into towering thunderheads, roil and churn, finally develop lightning flickers in gloom at bases, arch dark shafts of rain downward to western horizon; watched until fading light brought realization how long had sat there. Brighter stars already visible in east.

Reviewed condition with mounting surprise: Eyes dry, pain gone from throat, heart; blackness hovering over soul mere memory. Apparently had transcendentalized without conscious intent, resolved residual grief. All that remained was sweet sadness when contemplated Daddy, Momma, Teacher; were gone along with everything, everybody else, leaving only memories. Suddenly realized was grateful being permitted to keep those.

Cautiously moved exploratory muscle, first in hours. Terry twitched, fretted; then woke, set up justifiable protest over starved condition. Arose, shifted twin to shoulder; went inside, downstairs.

Picked up Tarzan File, Teacher's letter, went back to

Daddy's house. Fed birdbrain, self; settled down, skimmed file's contents.

Presently concluded Teacher correct (profound shock, that): Peter Bell doubtless best prospective soul mate of lot. Very smart, very interested, very conscious; educational credits to date sound like spoof (*Nobody* that young could have learned that much, except, uh . . . perhaps me —okay); very strong, quick; very advanced in study of Art (Eighth Degree!); plus (in words of Teacher): "Delightfully unconcerned about his own accomplishments; interested primarily in what he will do *next*." And, ". . . possessed of a wry sense of humor." Sounds like my kind of guy. Hope turns out can stand him.

Sat for long moments working up nerve. Then picked up phone, deliberately dialed area code, number. Got stranded after a few moments' clicking, hissing when relay somewhere Out There stuck. Tried again; hit busy circuit (distinct from busy number: difference audible—also caused by sticky relay). Tried again, muttering in beard. Stranded again. Tried again. Failed again.

"That's *bad*," offered Terry enthusiastically, bobbing head cheerfully.

Took deep breath, said very bad word, tried again.

Got ring tone! Once, twice, three times; then: "Click. Hello, is that you, Candy? Sure took you long enough. This is Peter Bell. I can't come to the phone right now; I'm outside taking care of the stock. But I've set up this telephone answering machine to guard my back. It's got an alarm on it that'll let me know you've called so I can check the tape.

"When you hear the tone at the end of my message, give me your phone number if you're not at home—*don't forget the area code* if it's different from your home— and I'll call you back the moment I get back and find your message. Boy, am I glad you're all right.

"Beep!"

Caught agape by recording. Barely managed regroupment in time to stutter out would be home; and if not, would be at farm, give number before machine hung up, dial tone resumed.

Repeated bad word. Added frills tailored specifically for answering machine.

Did dishes, put away. Refilled twin's food dish, changed

water; moved stand into study, placed next to desk, within convenient head-scratching range.

Settled into Daddy's big chair, opened journal, brought record up to date. Have done so. Now up to date. Current. Completely. Nothing further to enter. So haven't entered anything else. For quite a while.

Midnight. Might as well read book.

Stupid phone.

Awoke to would-be rooster's salute to dawn's early light. Found self standing unsteadily in middle of study, blinking sleep from eyes, listening to echoes die away. Glared at twin; received smug snicker in return.

Took several moments to establish location, circumstances leading to night spent in chair with clothes on. When succeeded, opened mouth, then didn't bother—realized bad word wouldn't help; no longer offered relief adequate to situation.

Casual approach had worn out about one A.M.—by which time had read possibly ten pages (of which couldn't remember single word). Featherhead snored on stand; nothing within reach to disassemble, had lost interest.

Yawning prodigiously myself by time abandoned pretense, grabbed phone, dialed number.

Got through first try. But was *busy!*

Repeated attempt at five-minute intervals for two hours or until fell asleep—whichever came first.

Have just tried line again. Still busy. Better go make breakfast.

Contact problem no longer funny. In two months since last entry have averaged five tries daily. Result: Either (usually) busy signal or transistorized moron spouts same message. One possible explanation (among many): Recorded message mentions no dates; could have been recorded day after Armageddon, yesterday—anytime.

Not that am languishing, sitting wringing hands by phone, however; have been *busy*. Completed move to farm; padded supply reserves; shored weaknesses; collected additional livestock, poultry. Have electrified fences, augmented where appeared marginally dogproof; trucked in additional grain (learned to drive semi, re-re-re-replete with 16-speed transmission—truly sorry about grain company's gatepost, but was in way; should have been moved long ago); located, trucked in two automatic diesel generators, connected through clever relay system so first comes on line (self-starting) if power fails, second kicks in if first quits. So far has worked every time tested, just as book said.

Have accumulated adequate fuel for operation: Brought in four tankers brim full of diesel (6,000 gallons each); rigged up interconnecting hose system guaranteeing gravity feed to generators—whichever needs, gets. At eight gallons hourly (maximum load) should provide over four months' operation if needed. (However, farm rapidly taking on aspect of truck lot. Must think about disposing of empties soon; otherwise won't be able to walk through yard.)

Overkill preparations not result of paranoia. Attempting to make place secure in absence; improve odds of finding habitable, viable farm on return, even if sortie takes longer than expected. Which could; is over 900 miles (straight-line) to file's address on Peter Bell. And he's only first on AA list; others are scattered all over.

Have attempted to cover all bets, both home and for self on trip. Chose vehicle with care: Four-wheel-drive Chevy van. Huge snow tires bulge from fenders on all four wheels, provide six inches extra ground clearance, awesome traction. Front bumper mounts electric winch probably capable of hoisting vehicle bodily up sheer cliff. Interior has bed, potty, sink, stove, sundry cabinets—and exterior boasts dreadful baroque murals on sides.

Though might appear was built specifically to fill own needs (except for murals—and need for build-ups on pedals), was beloved toy of town banker. When not pinching pennies, frittered time away boonies-crawling in endless quest for inaccessible, impassable terrain. Bragged hadn't found any. Hope so; bodes well for own venture.

Personal necessities, effects aboard. Include: Ample food, water for self, Terry; bedding, clothing, toiletries; diverse tools, including axe, bolt cutters, etc.; spares for van; siphon, pump, hose for securing gas; small, very nasty armory, including police chief's sawed-off riot gun, two Magnum revolvers, M-16 with numerous clips and scope. Not expecting trouble, but incline toward theory that probably won't rain if carry umbrella.

Leaving this journal here in shelter for benefit of archeologists; keep separate book on trip. Can consolidate on return, but if plans go awry this account still available for posterity.

Well, time to go: unknown beckons.

But have never felt so small. Awfully big world waiting out there.

For me.

YOU CAN'T GO BACK

R. A. Lafferty

R. A. Lafferty has, in his twenty years as a science-fiction writer, told many unusual and droll tales of things others have rarely imagined. Here he suggests that Earth may have more than one moon—White Cow Moon, for instance, which is little known because it's comparatively small and orbits only a few feet over Earth's surface. Of course it would have been "colonized"—but by whom?

I

A note, a musty smell, a tune,
Some bones and pebbles from the moon!
Today they set a-flow a spring,
Remembering, remembering.
　　　　　—*The Helen Horn-Book*

ONE EVENING IN THE LATTER DAYS HELEN
brought over some bones and rocks that had belonged to
her late husband John Palmer. She brought the Moon
Whistle too. And she left those things with us.

Helen had married again, and to a man who hadn't
known John. And she thought that she'd better get some
of those funny old things out of her house.

"The Moon Whistle will be no good without you to
blow it, Helen," Hector O'Day said. She blew it then,
very loudly, with her too-big mouth; and there was laughing lightning in her eyes, still undiminished. Then she was
away and down the stairs and out of the building with
that rush of hers that was a sort of breakneck tumble.

And she left behind her a tumble of memories of the
times when we, decades before this, had gone to White
Cow Town four times. It had never been crowded in White
Cow Town when we were there. It wasn't a place you
stumbled over, not unless you were a pretty high stepper.

In Osage County there were some pretty small towns:
Bigheart, Hulah, Okeas, Wild Horse, Shidler, White Eagle,
Horseshoe, Kaw City, Hog Shooter, Rock Salt, Bluestem,
each of these towns being smaller than its fellows. But

232

smaller than any of them was White Cow Town. There just weren't many people there, and those that were there were pretty narrow. There was a saying: "There are no fat people in White Cow Town."

(An informant has just told me that Hog Shooter isn't in Osage County, that it's over the line in Washington County. Not in memory it isn't! The informant must be wrong.)

In these latter days it was Barry Shibbeen, Grover Whelk, Caesar Ducato, Hector O'Day, and myself who were together in our cardplaying and discussion den when Helen had brought those mementos over.

But back in the old days John Palmer had been with us, and Helen had been there too for the events at White Cow Town, and some of the Bluestems.

That first time, we had ridden up to Bluestem Ranch Number One with Tom Bluestem and his mother in her Buick sedan. The Number One was the oldest of the Bluestem Ranches and was run by Tom's grandparents. They were wonderful people and they said that the place was ours.

The Moon Whistle was hanging on the wall in the ranch house, and Helen, who was a horn-blower and whistle-blower, asked if she could blow it.

"Oh, we'll give it to you," Tom's grandmother said, and she handed it to Helen. And Helen blew it loudly.

"Don't blow that damned thing in here!" Grandfather Bluestem shouted. "Take it down to Lost Moon Canyon if you want to blow it. We'll have White Cow Rock breaking in our roof here if it hears it. Oh, that damned whistle!"

This was a surprising outburst, for Grandfather Bluestem was always a friendly and soft-spoken man.

Well, that Moon Whistle did have an eerie and shrill and demanding tone, even a little bit insulting. It was a "call," and somebody had better answer it.

"I don't know where Lost Moon Canyon is," Helen said.

"Oh, I'll take you all over there," Grandmother Bluestem told us. Barry, Grover, Caesar, Hector, John, Helen, myself, and Tom Bluestem, we all got in the ranch truck and Grandmother Bluestem drove us to Lost Moon Canyon. We were all nine years old except John Palmer who had recently had his tenth birthday, and Grandmother Bluestem who said that she was either fifty or a hundred years old, she forgot which, she was weak at numbers.

Lost Moon Canyon, through which ran Hominy Creek, was the roughest place on the Bluestem Ranches. There were large and dangerous-looking overhanging rocks, unnaturally large for a canyon no bigger than that, absolutely threatening in their extreme overhang. There was the feeling that one of them was about to fall right now. Then the biggest of those rocks moved, and we howled in near fear.

"Oh, that's only White Cow Rock," Grandmother Bluestem said. "It's different from the other rocks. It's a moon. And it won't fall. It moves slowly. Blow the Moon Whistle, Helen, and it'll come on down."

Helen blew the Moon Whistle (oh, that damned shrill whistle!), and White Cow Rock descended a hundred feet, with a slow and wobbling motion, and hung right over the ranch truck. There was an upside-down goat standing on the bottom of the big rock, but it didn't seem as if it were going to fall off. There were also some ducks walking upside down on the bottom of White Cow Rock.

"Let's go up," Tom Bluestem said. "There's a shaft or channel right here in the middle of it, and you can climb through it all the way to the top. You can if you're not afraid. It's scary, but that's all."

"I'm not afraid of anything," Caesar said, "but some things make me kind of nervous. I don't know when anything's made me as nervous as that big, bobbling rock does."

From the top of the cab of the truck we could get to the bottom of the shaft in the rock. Tom Bluestem climbed up that shaft followed by John Palmer, Barry Shibbeen, Grover Whelk, Caesar Ducato, Hector O'Day, myself, and Helen.

"Aren't you coming up too, Grandmother Bluestem?" Helen asked.

"No, I can't," that lady said. "Since I've gotten older I can't do it. There are no fat people on White Cow Rock or in White Cow Town."

As we climbed up the shaft we could see why there were no fat people on top of that rock. That shaft got pretty narrow in some places. It was tricky climbing up it, but not as dangerous as it might seem. There was no place so wide that we couldn't put one hand on each side of the shaft, and there were no smooth or slippery places in it. But it was a very high and long climb and it was pretty dark in there. We had climbed about fifty yards when we came to a short tunnel leading into a little cave.

"We can crawl in here and rest for a little while," Caesar said.

"No, we can't either," Tom Bluestem contradicted. "There's some real mean and peculiar people who live in that nook, and the gnawed bones on the floor of their cave are real weird. Some of them are bones of kids about our age. Let's keep climbing."

"What lives in that cave are gnomes and trolls," Helen said.

"How'd you know?" Barry asked her. "You've never been up here before."

"Every moon everywhere has a family of gnomes or trolls or whatever their local name is living in the exact center of it," Helen said. "And all the caves have real weird bones in them, dire wolf bones, woolly rhinocerous bones, human bones, things like that."

There was a sharp, strong smell there. It was the most characteristic smell on the whole of White Cow Moon. We climbed the rest of the way to the top. And then we were in the middle of White Cow Town and in the brightest and friendliest sunshine ever anywhere.

White Cow Rock was a rough, rock-and-clay sphere about a hundred yards in diameter. White Cow Town on the top of the rock had thirteen houses and one store in it. Nine of the houses had outhouses behind them; but the outhouses that had been behind the other four houses had fallen off that rock or moon in times gone by. Of necessity, for there wasn't much level space on White Cow Rock, those outhouses had been built quite a ways down the slope, and sometimes the whole rock wobbled. It had never been very safe to use any of those outhouses on the rears of those lots in White Cow Town.

"I tell you though," said an elderly citizen of the town, "there comes times, at least once a day, when it's not very safe *not* to use them either."

Listen, it was plain magic up on top of that rock or moon. There were never such bright colors or such nourishing air anywhere. The rock was free-floating. It had now drifted about five hundred feet higher in the air and about half a mile to the north. It gave us a good view of both Lost Moon Canyon and the Bluestem Ranch House far below, and you could even see the towers of Pawuska off in the misty distance northeast. This was much more magical than being up in a balloon even.

All of us had been up in a balloon once, at the Barton's Show Grounds in T-Town. But that balloon was held by three cables worked by winches, and it rose only about seventy-five feet up in the air. This moon had it beat by a sky mile.

All those houses up on the moon were old-looking and unpainted, but they had a sharpness of outline and a liveliness of detail that isn't to be found in the houses down on Earth. This was like being in really bright daylight for the first time in our lives.

The only animals that the people up on White Cow had were chickens and ducks and goats. The saying about the place should have been amended to "There are no fat people *nor no big animals* on White Cow either." The goats were native to that moon, a man said, and so were the chickens. The ducks had come there about five hundred years before this, and the people had come about a thousand years ago. But big animals wouldn't have been able to go up that shaft.

The delight and magic of White Cow was just the "living in the sky" that was the condition there. There was an immediacy, a wininess, a happiness, an exhilaration, a music, a delight about "living in the sky."

Four of the men on White Cow worked for the Bluestem Ranches down below, mowing and baling hay, mending fences, moving cattle from one pasture to another, doing whatever workers do on a ranch. One of the women taught at the consolidated school that was between Bluestem and Gray Horse. And nine of the children of White Cow went to that same country school down on Earth. One of the men up there had a still and made moonshine.

"You show me a law that says you can't make moonshine on a moon," he used to challenge people. His still gave a sour-mash smell to the whole moon, but it wasn't the strongest or sharpest smell that they had.

"How can the goats and the ducks walk straight out or even upside down on this rock?" Hector O'Day puzzled to us. "They walk on every part of this sphere."

"It's all a question of gravity," John Palmer said. "A weak gravity will hold little things but not big things. It'll hold goats or ducks on a moon maybe, but it might not hold the people on. One of you lighter kids try walking around this moon to the bottom and up again if you want to. If you don't fall off, then the heavier of us will try it."

"The mathematics of the gravity here is really rum," Barry Shibbeen cut in, but he had that crooked grin on his funny-looking face that meant that he couldn't be trusted. "Recall Foxley's Formula Five, and you'll understand the gravity a little bit better. Think about Edwardson's Elliptical Equation. Remember Mumford's Monotreme!"

"That sounds like a good battle-cry slogan: 'Remember Mumford's Monotreme!'" Grover Whelk giggled. "I wonder what it means."

"I know what Foxley's Formula Five means," Helen contributed, "and it doesn't have anything to do with gravitation. It's for women's sickness and it comes in blue bottles. Mama takes it sometimes."

There was one "wanted" man who lived in White Cow Town, and the sheriff wouldn't go up there to get him.

"The sheriff is afraid of me," the man said.

"I'm not afraid of any man on Earth," the sheriff answered when that was reported to him, "and I'll go anywhere on Earth to get a man. But White Cow Town isn't on Earth. I'm not afraid of that man. I'm just spooked of those off-Earth places."

In the general store they had a little radio, homemade, and superior to anything that might be bought. It would get station KVOO fifty miles away in Bristow. It would get it clear and loud whenever White Cow Moon went up more than five hundred feet in the air.

They had Nehi pop in that store, but it cost six cents a bottle instead of a nickel.

"That's because of the transportation," the lady said. "We have to get a penny more for it up here than they get for it down on Earth."

The kids in White Cow Town had a rope and they were playing tug-of-war, but they were playing it like a bunch of sissies. They didn't show us much pull at all.

"Look," Barry Shibbeen told them, "there are eight of us and nine of you, and I bet we can out-pull you all over the place."

"No, there are just seven of you, Barry," Tom Bluestem said. "Count me out of it." That was odd. Tom had always been very competitive in all games and sports. Well, there were *seven* of us then, and there were nine of the White Cow kids, and some of them were quite a bit bigger than we were. And we still pulled them all over the place. We pulled them oll over the place until—

Well, we pulled them until, if they had let go of that rope, we would have fallen clear off of White Cow Moon. We were that far down on the slope of the sphere.

"Help, Tom, what'll we do?" we called to our friend, our friend who had been acting a little bit funny in not joining in the game.

"When you play tug-of-war up here, the name of the game isn't checkers," Tom said. "The name of the game is 'give-away.' "

"Don't let them give us away," we wailed.

The kids finally dug in and held the rope fast, with the aid of a loop around "Last chance tree." We climbed up the rope to safety then. But those moon kids sure laughed and hooted at us a lot after that. We had been beaten about as bad as anybody can be beaten at any game; and we were the smart kids and they were just a bunch of sky bumpkins.

Helen said she was going to stay up on that moon forever since they had plenty of the two things she loved most, duck eggs and goat milk.

"You'll want to go back home and get your cornet," John Palmer told her. "And you can always come back here."

"That's right. I can always come back here," Helen said.

We were adopted by several nations of birds. They gathered on White Cow Moon like clouds, black clouds of crows and blackbirds, gray clouds of doves, brown and yellow clouds of larks. There were congregations of catbirds up there, and of nighthawks, even of kingbirds and mockingbirds, and of hawks and eagles. Most of these birds had a contempt for the people of Earth, but they were friendly and genial to the people on the moon.

And there were other things up there that were *not quite* birds. We didn't know what to call them, but they were things of a different wing. And the bones in their nests were as strange and varied as those in the trolls' cave.

Seedling clouds nested on White Cow Moon, and some of them glittered like jewels from all the sparkling water in them. When they wanted to start a shower down below, one of them would say "now," another one would say "now," and a third one would say "now." Then they would zoom down and start a shower and spill all over the place.

From a hundred feet down in the shaft you could see the stars in the daytime sky.

And this moon was the place where the "mysterious night lights" nested in the daytime. Almost every rural neighborhood in Osage County has had its own special ghost light for at least a century. These things draw notice, and they scare people. Sometimes they are written up in the newspapers, and there is no explanation of them. But, as to where they come from, they come from White Cow Moon. "Mysterious Night Lights" look funny in the daytime though. You'd hardly recognize them as lights when you see them nesting and confabbing together in the sunlight.

And there were the millions of wonderful jumping fleas on White Cow Moon. Fleas can always jump a little bit further on a moon than they can on Earth. It's a question of gravity.

We played up there till almost dark, and it was one of the finest days of our entire lives. Then we heard Grandmother Bluestem honking the horn of the ranch truck far below and to the south of us. From the top of White Cow Moon when it's high in the sky you can hear a long ways.

Helen blew *"Go down, go down!"* on the Moon Whistle. She could really blow that thing! And White Cow Moon settled down over Lost Moon Canyon again. We climbed down through the shaft once more (it was a pretty dark and spooky go of it there), and we finally dropped out of it and onto the top of the cab of the truck. Then we all went back to the Bluestem ranch house.

"But what is it *really?*" Hector O'Day asked them when we were back in the ranch house and eating a ranch-house supper. *"Really,* I mean."

That Heck! What did he mean by "really"? We had been up into reality, up into blue-sky reality almost all day long. Why the grubby question?

"Oh, it's just one of the Earth's moons," Grandfather Bluestem said.

"How, how?" Hector asked like a gooney. "What *one* of the Earth's moons?"

"I don't have the comparative measures or masses,"

Grandfather Bluestem smiled, "but I'd say that it was the *smaller* of the Earth's two moons."

"But where'd it come from?" Hector still asked.

"Oh, it used to hang out up in Missouri, about a hundred miles southwest of St. Louis," Grandfather Bluestem said. "Then, when some of the Osage Indians came down here from Missouri in 1802, that moon just followed along after them and came down here too. It had always got along with the Osage people, but it didn't like most people at all."

Grandfather Bluestem was a full-blooded Osage, of course.

That hardly touched it. Life on a moon has so many things that just aren't to be found on Earth at all. It has a special magic. Oh, there are plenty of magics on Earth, but moon-magic is in a different category completely. Every group of kids should have a moon of its own.

But there were *other* activities and delights. There was an endless tumble of delights for us in those years. In such cases, it is good to keep one particular treasure-house-full of delights in reserve. So we went back to White Cow Moon only three more times in that wonderful old decade.

We went once the summer we were ten years old; once the summer we were eleven; and once when we were twelve years old (we stayed up there three days that time).

It was on that last and longest visit that John Palmer and Barry Shibbeen were able to fill up a gunnysack with stones and bones from the cave of the gnomes or trolls who lived right at the center of that moon.

Barry made a chloroform bomb and he tossed it into that cave and knocked all those strange folks out. And John Palmer had made gas masks for himself and Barry. So they put them on and crawled in and loaded up the sack. A study of those stones and bones was to raise questions that aren't all answered yet.

But, though it was the most magical place on the world, or just *off* the world, we didn't get back there in those early years after that long special visit when we were all twelve years old. There were just too many other things to do. We nearly forgot it, the pervading magic of the place, and the strong sharp odor. But it was a buried treasure that the pack of us owned henceforth, a treasure buried a little ways up in the sky.

II

In skies unhigh it still is set.
It's as it's always been. . . . And yet
There's thinnish magic that does cling,
Diminishing, diminishing.
            —Barry's Shibbeens

Into these Latter Days again where we have all been adults for many aeons.

"Who faked them, who faked them? And how did they do it?" Hector O'Day asked on that latter-day evening when Helen had brought the bones and stones and the Moon Whistle over to us. Many years had gone by since we had last gone up onto White Cow Moon.

"It had to be you and John Palmer, Barry," Hector said. "Both of you were smart as well as book-learned, but how did you fake the bones and stones from that rock, from that rock that you conned us into thinking was a moon?"

"I didn't fake them, and I don't believe that John did," Barry said. "Well yes, they were an odd lot of things. The gnawed bones that we took from that cave were those of human children, of bear cubs, of crested eagles, and of certain extinct dog-sized rhinos. They were just the sort of bones, Heck, that you are likely to find in any trolls' cave on any moon. And the fossil stones, they are somewhat stranger. They record a life on that little moon that was quite different and somewhat older than anything on Earth."

"Exquisite fakeries, that's what some of the savants have called the things, Barry. But they haven't been able to explain how the fakeries were done. Why have they not, exquisite faker Barry?"

"Because they're not fakes. At least I don't think that they are."

"Just what is the 'core of facts' in the whole business?" Caesar Ducato asked the bunch of us. "Just what *was* the thing that we psyched our young selves into believing was a moon? Well, I guess that there was a large and nearly spherical rock in the Lost Moon Canyon area of the Blue-stem Ranches. And it did have a fissure in it by which we climbed up onto the top of the rock. And it did have a dangerous wobble to it, or at least some kind of motion. And so we were hypnotized into believing that it was a little moon hanging in a low sky. We believed that easily when we were nine years old. What puzzles me is that we still believed it when we were twelve years old and were capable of conceptual thinking. What hypnotism!"

"Who could have hypnotized us and turned our wits moony?" Barry asked. "Several of us were types almost impossible to hypnotize. Who could have conned us into believing that it was a moon, if it wasn't? But it was."

"Helen could have hypnotized us into it, Barry. John Palmer could have done it. You could have done it a little bit yourself. The three of you together could certainly have done it—"

"What, what, *what?* Did you just say 'But it was,' Barry? But it *wasn't,* man. It couldn't have been."

"It could have been, yes," Barry Shibbeen maintained. "The best argument that it was is that it still is. I fly over it sometimes in my helicopter. And I still fly *under* it sometimes, which is more to the proof. How about all of you flying there with me in the copter in the morning and landing on the little moon? Will that be proof that it's still there, Hector?"

"Man, it can't be! It's physically and psychologically impossible. None of us has even thought that he saw it since we were twelve years old."

"Wrong, Hector. Tom Bluestem and Julia Flaxfield spent their honeymoon on White Cow Moon ten years after that."

"But they're both Indian. And they hadn't really grown up then, however old they were. They were high on each other then, and it would have seemed to them that they were on a moon wherever they were. Dammit, Barry, there is just no way that a thinking person can accept that there's a little moon there."

"Oh, Caesar, and you too, Hector O'Day, I say that if you can accept the Earth's regular or big moon, it's a million times as easy to accept that little moon in the low sky in Osage County. *Do* you fellows accept the regular or big moon of the Earth? That so-called moon is an anomaly and the father of anomalies. It's irrational and it's impossible. The only reason we have for believing in its existence is that we've seen it, and that several persons have attested to having been on it. And there is plenty of instrumental

evidence for it. But we have better reason to believe in the
existence of the little moon. We have seen it at much
closer range. Several persons that we know much better
(ourselves) have been on it. We have even traversed its
dark inner tract. And if electronic waves have been
bounced off the larger moon, we have bounced baseballs
off the smaller moon. And baseballs are more tangible.
Yes, that little moon is real."

"In its psychological involvement with our childhoods it
was real, I suppose," Grover Whelk said, "but it wasn't
real in any other sense. I'm not sure whether its psychological effect on us was good or bad."

"Somebody should be smart enough to settle this matter," Hector said, "especially to settle your pigheadedness
in still believing in it, Barry."

"Oh, I'm smart enough to settle it," Barry proposed.
"I've already offered the way to do it, and I offer it again.
Let's all get into my copter in the morning and go find
that little moon. We'll fly under it and we'll fly over it and
we'll land upon it. If we can do these things, then it's real.
If we can't do them, then it isn't real. Let's all be ready
to take off at the reasonable time of eight-thirty in the
morning. Agreed, Cease, Grove, Heck, Al?"

"Agreed," we all said. And that is where we made our
mistake.

We called Helen the next morning, but she said that she
didn't want to go. "It'd spoil it for me," she said. But her
daughter Catherine Palmer ("the child of my old age,"
Helen always called Catherine) told her mother that she
wanted to go, and Helen conveyed the message over the
phone. "It will be all right with Catherine," Helen said.
"She was born an adult, so it won't do her any harm to
know that the moon is a crummy place. But I'm eternally
a child and it would shatter me. *You can't go back,*' you
know."

So Catherine Palmer, a seventeen-year-old mature adult
and a major in psychological anthropology, came with us.
She was a cheerful kid.

"Oh yeah, I've been up on the little moon before," she
said. "I went up there with some of the Bluestem kids the
summer before last, but it didn't do much for me. I hadn't
yet become psychologically oriented the summer before
last. Now I'll have to discover why that little moon once

did something for you old fogies, and why some of you think about it and mumble 'magic!' "

If Catherine hadn't been so pretty and so seventeenish, she couldn't have gotten away with that psychological patter.

We took off from the Jenks airport, which is closer to T-Town than the T-Town airport is. It also has better facilities for stabling private planes and copters, not being obsessed with all those scheduled commercial flights. It was no more than thirty miles to our destination. Oh, it is plea- ant to rattle in a copter over the Green Country on a fine morning in late spring!

"Catherine, I want you to realize that White Cow Moon *is* a magic place," Barry almost sang. "I don't believe that young people have nearly enough magic in their lives now- a-years. Drink deep of it when we get there, Cat."

"All right."

"Catherine, yes, it was enchanting," Hector O'Day said. "I only wish that it was *real,* that it had been real, that it could be real again. I wish that you could experience the enchantment of it, but I don't even know how we were able to experience it once. We'd like to offer it to you, but I'm afraid that we don't have it to offer."

"Thanks anyhow," young Catherine said.

"Ah, it was wonder, it was *sortilège,* it was delight," Caesar Ducato murmured. "It was a special place. It was the elegance and the charm. And at the same time it was tall magic with all the hair on it. It was the 'world of our own,' the 'moon of our own.' It was the place that only the secret masters knew about. So we belonged to the secret masters. It's a pity that the little moon didn't exist except in our imaginations."

"Mr. Ducato, your wattles wobble when you get intense about something," Catherine said.

"It was the thirst and the slaking at the same time," Grover Whelk declaimed. "It was the 'promise fulfilled.' It's too bad that it never was. But even thinking that we re- member it is wonderful."

"Why not let it stand on its own two abscissae?" Cath- erine said. She sounded like her mother Helen when she made cracks like that.

"See, it isn't there!" Hector O'Day cried out, half sad, half gloating, when we had come to the region.

"See, it *is* there!" Barry Shibbeen countered. "It's there, with its little bit different color green, snuggled down almost to Earth over Lost Moon Canyon, nearly invisible among other rocks almost as big and almost the same color. Blow the Moon Whistle, Catherine. Blow the *'Rise up, rise up!'* sequence and let's get it up into the sky a ways."

Catherine Palmer blew the Moon Whistle. She had almost as big a mouth as her mother Helen had, and she had an equal talent for blowing all horns and whistles. She blew the sequence, and White Cow Moon wobbled a few hundred feet up into the sky.

"It isn't as big as it used to be," Grover Whelk said sadly.

"Yes it is, Grove," Caesar said with sudden animation. "And it does have that peculiar green color in its topping boscage. It has it yet. I don't quite know the name of that color of green."

"Bilious green, sour bilious green," young Catherine said. She was right, of course. White Cow Moon had risen about five hundred feet into the air. Barry Shibbeen flew the copter under it several times, and then he hovered it at standstill under it so we could look up through the old fissure that ran through it from top to bottom. Yes, it sure did look as though White Cow Moon was real and present.

"Well, are you fellows convinced that it's real?" Barry jibed.

"Not entirely convinced," Hector O'Day mumbled thoughtfully. "You have to admit, Barry, that it doesn't look very convincing."

"No, it doesn't," Barry admitted. "I wonder why it doesn't. But it *is* as big as it used to be. It's still about a hundred yards in diameter."

"Yes, but the yards aren't as long as they used to be," Whelk complained.

We climbed around and above White Cow Moon. Then we landed in the middle of the top of it. Yes, that strong and sharp odor was still as permeating a presence on White Cow Moon as it had been when we were children. We hadn't realized then that it was an unpleasant odor, but we realized it now.

"It smells like a badly kept zoo," Catherine said. "I think it's the smell of the Greater Yeti or Stinking Yeti. I'll interview him in the interests of science."

There were only four houses left on White Cow Moon, and only one outhouse.

"When the last outhouse falls off White Cow Moon, I just don't know what will happen to us," an old citizen said. "Extinction, I guess. People without outhouses just would not be people any longer."

"I discern the true and unmemorable quality of White Cow Moon now," Barry Shibbeen said, "but I just can't set my tongue to the name of it."

" 'Dingy' is the word for it," Catherine said. She was right, of course. I felt a sort of constriction in my throat and chest, and I believe that the rest of them felt it too.

"This moon is full of swamp gas or worse," Caesar said. "Is Magic itself made of nothing better than swamp gas?"

Catherine took the drinking gourd that was hanging on the town pump and milked it full from one of the she-goats there. The goats all had the mange. The chickens had the mange. Even the ducks on White Cow Moon had the mange now.

"Mother and I both drink a lot of goat milk for our health," Catherine said. "Oh, it's sour!"

"Maybe it's the gourd that's sour and gives a sour taste to the milk," Barry said hopefully.

"Nah, it's the goat herself who's sour and gives a sour taste to the milk," Catherine said. "I suppose that the Greater Yeti or Stinking Yeti lives down in that hole that runs through this moon. I'd better go see." And Catherine Palmer disappeared down the shaft that ran clear through White Cow Moon.

"Well, how does it go on this moon?" Barry asked one of the citizens.

"Badly," that person said. "The main thing wrong is our shrinking population. There's only seven people left. A century ago there were a hundred of us here."

"What's the *next* main thing wrong here?" Grover Whelk asked.

"The corruption," the citizen said. "The trolls or Yeti in the middle of our moon have corrupted our children, both of them. They've taught them immorality and dis-obedience and smart talk. It's those befuddling mushrooms that they grow down there and give our kids to eat that do the damage. Yeah, there goes the future of White Cow Moon, blown, completely blown. And the third main thing wrong on this moon is the fleas."

Fleas! Yes, there were lots of fleas on that moon, and they got all over you and set you to scratching. Well, there had always been lots of fleas there, but they hadn't seemed so demanding in the old days.

"If you have trolls or yetis, you're going to have fleas," a citizen said. "There's no way you can miss it."

Catherine came up out of the shaft then, and a Yeti followed her out. He was eight feet tall, shaggy, quite stringy and spare (there were no fat Yetis on White Cow Moon), and smelly. He was roughly thirty-three and one-third percent of the strong, sharp odor of that moon.

"He's a genuine *Homo yeti putens* or Stinking Yeti," Catherine said, "and there's two more of them: another gentleman one, and a lady one. Even in the interest of science there's nothing to be got from the Yetis. Nothing, nothing. This one is the least interesting creature I ever saw. I guess he's harmless though."

"I'm not so sure of that," Hector O'Day growled. "How about all those knawed bones down in your hole, tall fellow? Some of them were bones of human children."

"If more people gnawed more bones they'd have better teeth," the Yeti said.

"Ugh, platitudes yet!" Catherine shuddered. And we all felt a bit glum.

"How our great memories have shrunken!" Caesar Ducato lamented.

"It is and it isn't," Hector said cryptically. "The moon, I mean. And the way it is, it wouldn't matter much if it was."

"Not only has the magic gone out of it, but nothing else has taken its place," Barry Shibbeen mourned. "What's the word for this place? Oh yes, 'dingy.' I could cry."

"If you cry a tear down into the fissure, it will fall all the way through, and if a sky person should look down and see it through the hole it'd look like a star in the day-time," Catherine said with sudden poetic insight.

Young Catherine Palmer blew *"Retreat"* on the Moon Whistle. We all got into the copter and rattled away from there.

"You can't go back," the proverb says.

And it's a good thing you can't.

WALPURGISNACHT

Roger Zelazny

Walpurgisnacht, the night when the dead return for a time of partying and revelry, is an
ancient and somehow dignified legend. Like
other "fantasies" of the past, it may one day
become a reality, through laser-holograms of
the departed, kept up to date by programming
them with news of new developments. But traditions change as people change . . . especially
some unusual individuals.

Roger Zelazny is best known as a novelist,
author of *This Immortal, Lord of Light,* and the
Chronicles of Amber, but he's also very deft in
the art of the short-short, as he shows in this
wry tale, whose only previous publication was
in a small-circulation chapbook.

SUNNY AND SUMMER. HE WALKED THE SWEEP-
ing cobbled path beside the fringe of shrubbery, map in
one hand, wreath in the other, passing from rest aisle to
funerary glade. Grassy mounds with embedded bronze
plaques lay along the way; beds of flowers, pale and
bright, alternated with gazebos, low stone walls, fake Gre-
cian ruins, stately trees. Occasionally, he paused to check
a plate, consult the map.

At length he came to a heavily shaded glade. Recorded
birdsongs were the only sounds in the low, cool area. The
numbers were running higher here. Yes!

He put aside the chart and wreath and he knelt. He
ran his fingers across the plate that read "Arthur Abel
Andrews" above a pair of dates. He located the catch and
sprung the plate.

Within the insulated box beneath was a button. He
pressed it and a faint humming sound began. It vanished
as he snapped the plate shut.

"Well now, it's been awhile since I've had any visitors."

The young man looked up suddenly, though he had
known what to expect.

"Uncle Arthur . . ." he said, regarding the suddenly
materialized form of the ruddy, heavyset man with the
shifty eyes who now occupied the space above the mound.
"Uh, how are you?"

The man, dressed in dark trousers, a white shirt,
sleeves rolled up to the elbows, maroon tie hanging loose-
ly about his neck, smiled.

" 'At peace.' I'm supposed to say that when you ask. It's in the program. Now, let's see . . . You're . . ."

"Your nephew Raymond. I was only here once before, when I was little. . . ."

"Ah, yes. Sarah's son. How is she these days?"

"Doing fine. Just had her third liver transplant. She's off on the Riviera right now."

Raymond thought about the computer somewhere beneath his feet. Programmed with photos of the departed it could produce a life-sized, moving hologram; from recorded samples of his uncle's speech, it could reproduce his voice patterns in conversation; from the results of a battery of tests and a series of brainwave readings, along with a large block of information—personal, family and general—it could respond in character to anyone's queries. Despite this knowledge, Raymond found it unnerving. It was far too real, far too much like that shrewd, black-sheep relative last seen through the eyes of youth with a kind of awe, and wrapped now in death's own mysteries— the man he had been told had a way of spoiling anything.

"Uh . . . Brought you a nice wreath, Uncle. Pink rose-buds."

"Great," the man said, glancing down at them. "Just what I need to liven things up here."

He turned away. He was seated upon a high stool which swiveled. Before him was the partial image of a bar, complete with brass rail. A stein of beer stood before him upon it. He took hold of it and raised it, sipped. Raymond recalled that, the cooperation of the person being memorialized being necessary, the choice of a favorite location for the memorial photographs was generally left up to the soon-to-be-departed.

"If you don't like the flowers, Uncle, I can always exchange them or just take them back."

His uncle set down the mug, belched gently and shook his head.

"No, no. Leave the damned things. I just thought of a use for them."

Arthur got down from the stool. He stooped and picked up the wreath. Raymond stumbled backward.

"Uncle! How did you do that? It's a material object and—"

Arthur strolled toward a mound across the way, carrying the pink circlet.

"It's a laser-force field combination," he commented. "Produces a holographic pressure interface. Latest thing."

"But how did you come by it? You've been—"

Arthur chuckled.

"Left a little trust account, to keep updating my hardware and such."

He stooped and pried up a brass headplate.

"What's your range, anyway?"

"About twenty meters," his uncle replied. "Then I start to fade out. Used to be only ten feet. There!"

He pressed a button and a tall, pale-haired woman with green eyes and a laughing mouth materialized beside him.

"Melissa, my dear. I've brought you some flowers," he said, passing her the wreath.

"What grave did you get them from, Arthur," she said, taking it into her hands.

"Now, now. They're really mine to give."

"Well, in that case, thank you. I might wear one in my hair."

"—Or upon your breast, when we step out tonight."

"Oh?"

"I was thinking of a party. Will you be free?"

"Yes. That sounds—lively. How will you manage it?"

Arthur turned.

"I'd like you to meet my nephew, Raymond Asher. Raymond, this is Melissa DeWeese."

"Happy to meet you," Raymond said.

Melissa smiled.

"Pleased," she replied, nodding.

Arthur winked.

"I'm sure I can arrange everything," he said, taking her hand.

"I believe you can—Arthur," she answered, touching his cheek.

She drew loose a rosebud and set it in her hair.

"Till then," she said. "Good evening to you, Raymond," and she faded and was gone, dropping the wreath upon the center of the mound.

Arthur shook his head.

"Husband poisoned her," he said. "What a waste."

"Uncle, death does not seem to have improved your morals a single bit," Raymond stated. "And chasing dead women, that's necro—"

"Now, now," Arthur said, turning and moving back toward the bar. "It's all a matter of attitude. I'm sure you'll see these things in a totally different light one day." He raised his mug and smacked his lips. "Nepenthe," he observed. "Necrohol."

"Uncle . . ."

"I know, I know," Arthur said. "You want something. Why else would you come here after all these years to visit me?"

"Well, to tell the truth . . ."

"By all means, tell it. It's a luxury few can afford."

"You always were considered a financial genius . . ."

"True." He made a sweeping gesture. "That's why I can afford the best life has to offer."

"Well, a lot of the family money is tied up in Cybersol stock and—"

"Sell! Damn it! Get rid of it quick!"

"Really?"

"It's going to take a real beating. And it won't be coming back."

"Wait a minute. I was going to brief you first and hope—"

"Brief me? I have abstracts of all the leading financial journals broadcast to my central processor on a regular basis. You'll lose your shirt if you stay with Cybersol."

"Okay. I'll dump it. What should I go into?"

His uncle smiled.

"A favor for a favor, nephew. A little *quid pro quo* here."

"What do you mean?"

"Advice of the quality I offer is worth more than a few lousy flowers."

"It looks as if you'll be getting a good return on them."

"Honi soit qui mal y pense, Raymond. And I need a little more help along those lines."

"Such as?"

"You come by here about midnight and push everybody's buttons in this whole section. I'm going to give a big party.

"Uncle, that sounds positively indecent!"

"—And then get the hell out. You're not invited."

"I—I don't know . . ."

"Do you mean that in this modern, antiseptic age you're afraid to come into a graveyard—pardon me, cemetery—

no, that's not it either. Memorial park—yes. At midnight. And press a few buttons?"

"Well—no . . . That's not it, exactly. But I've got a feeling you carry on worse than the living. I'd hate to be the instigator of a brand new vice."

"Oh, don't let that bother you. We thought it up ourselves. And as soon as we get the timers installed we won't need you. Look at it as contributing to the sum total of joy in the world. Besides, you want to preserve the family fortune, don't you?"

"Yes . . ."

"See you at twelve then."

"All right."

". . . And remember I've got a heavy date. Don't let me down, boy."

"I won't."

Uncle Arthur raised his mug and faded.

As Raymond walked back along the shaded aisles, he had a momentary vision of the *Todentanz*, of a skeletal fiddler wrapped in tattered cerements and seated atop a tombstone, grinning as the mournful dead cavorted about him, while bats dipped and rats whirled in the shadows. But for a moment only. And then it was replaced by one of brightly garbed dancers, mirrors, colored lights, body paint, where a disco sound rolled from overhead amplifiers. Death threw down his fiddle, and when he saw that his garments had become very mod he stopped smiling. His gaze focused for a moment upon a grinning man with a stein of beer, and then he turned away.

Uncle Arthur had a way of spoiling anything.

THE WOMAN
THE UNICORN LOVED

Gene Wolfe

The future of genetic engineering is very much
in doubt, largely because many people mistrust
such research and are legislating against it.
But it could provide us with fascinating things:
it ought to be possible even to engender such
mythical beasts as unicorns.

Gene Wolfe has won the Nebula Award for
his novella "The Death of Doctor Island," the
Rhysling Award for science fiction poetry, the
Chicago Foundation for Literature Award for
his mainstream novel *Peace*, and the World
Fantasy Award for his novel *The Shadow of
the Torturer.*

AT THE WESTERN EDGE OF THE CAMPUS THE parkway sent a river of steel and rubber roaring out of the heart of the city. Fragrant pines fringed the farther side. The unicorn trotted among them, sometimes concealed, sometimes treading the strip of coarse grass that touched the strip of soiled gravel that touched the concrete. That was where Anderson, looking from his office window, first saw him.

Drivers and passengers saw him too. Some waved; no doubt some shouted, though their shouts could not be heard. Faces pale and faces brown pressed against glass, but no one stopped. Possibly some trucker with a CB informed the police.

The unicorn was so white he gleamed. His head looked Arabian, but his hooves were darkly red, like pigeon's-blood rubies, and his tail was not like a horse's tail at all, but the kind of tail—like the tail of a bull, but with an additional guidon of hair halfway to the tip—that is seen only in heraldic beasts. His horn shone like polished ivory, straight as the blade of a rapier and as long as a man's forearm. Anderson guessed his height at fourteen hands.

He turned away to lift his camera bag down from the top of the filing cabinet, and when he got back to the window the unicorn was in the traffic. Across two hundred yards of campus lawn he could hear the squealing of brakes.

> *"Pluto, the grisly god, who never spares,*
> *Who feels no mercy, who hears no prayers."*

Anderson recited the couplet to himself, and only as he pronounced the words *prayers* was he aware that he had spoken aloud.

Then the unicorn was safe on the other side, cantering across the shaven grass. (Pluto, it appeared, might hear prayers after all.) As the armed head lifted to test the wind, Anderson's telephone rang. He picked it up.

"Hello, Andy? Dumont. Look out your window."

"I am looking," Anderson said.

"Dropped right into our laps. Can you imagine anybody letting something like that go?"

"Yes, pretty easily. I can also imagine it jumping just about any fence on earth. But if we're going to protect it, we'd better get on the job before the kids run it off." Anderson had found his telephoto zoom and coupled it to the camera body. With the phone clamped between his shoulder and his ear, he took a quick picture.

"I'm going after it. I want a tissue specimen and a blood sample."

"You can get them when the Army shoots it."

"Listen, Andy, I don't want to see it shot any more than you do. A piece of work like that? I'm going out there now, and I'll appreciate any help I can get. I've already told my secretary to phone some members. If the military comes in —well, at least you'll be able to get some stills to send the TV people. You coming?"

Anderson came, a big, tawny man of almost forty, with a camera hanging from his neck. By the time he was out of the Liberal Arts Building, there were a hundred or so students around the unicorn. He must have menaced them; their line bent backward, then closed again. His gleaming horn was lifted above their heads for a moment, half playful, half triumphant. Anderson used his size and faculty status to elbow his way to the front of the crowd.

The unicorn stood—no, trotted, almost danced—in the center of a circle fifty feet wide; while the students shouted jokes and cheered. A little group who must have known something of his lore grabbed a blonde in a cheerleader's sweater and pushed her forward. He put his head down, a lancer at the charge; and she scampered back into the jeering crowd, breasts bobbing.

Anderson lowered his camera.

"Get it?" a student beside him asked.

"I think so."

. A Frisbee sailed by the unicorn's ears, and he shied like a skittish horse. Someone threw it back.

Anderson yelled, "If that animal gets frightened, he's going to hurt somebody."

Dumont heard him, whether the students did or not. He waved from the farther side of the circle, his bald head gleaming. As the unicorn trotted past him, he thrust out a loaf of bread and was ignored.

Anderson sprinted across the circle. The students cheered, and several began running back and forth.

"Hi," Dumont said. "That took guts."

"Not really." Anderson found he was puffing. "I didn't come close. If he was angry, none of us would be here."

"I wish none of them were—nobody but you and me. It would make everything a hell of a lot simpler."

"Don't you have that tranquilizer gun?"

"At home. Our friend there would be long gone by the time I got back with it. Maybe I should keep one in the lab, but you know how it is—before this, we've always had to go after them."

Anderson nodded, only half listening as he watched the unicorn.

"We had this bread to feed to mice in a nutrition project. I put some stuff in it to quiet him down. On the spur of the moment, it was the best I could do."

Anderson was wondering who would arrive first—their Mythic Conservationists with protest signs or the soldiers and their guns. "I doubt that it's going to be good enough," he told Dumont.

A young woman slipped between them. "Here," she asked, "can I try?" Before Dumont could object, she took the bread and jogged to the center of the circle, the wind stirring her short, brown hair and the sunlight flashing from her glasses.

The unicorn came toward her slowly, head down.

Dumont said, "He'll kill her."

The students were almost quiet now, whispering. Anderson had to fight the impulse to dash out, to try to hold back the white beast, to knock him off his feet and wrestle him to the ground if he could. Except that he could not; that a dozen like him could not, no more than they could have overthrown an elephant. If he, or anyone here, were to attempt such a thing now, people would surely die.

The young woman thrust out Dumont's loaf—common

white bread from some grocery store. After a moment she crouched to bring her eyes on a level with the unicorn's.

Anderson heard himself murmur,

"Behold a pale horse:
And his name that sat on him was Death."

Then, when tension had been drawn so fine that it seemed to him that he must break, *it* broke instead. The ivory lance came up; and the shining, impossible lancer trotted forward, nibbled at the bread, nuzzled the young woman's neck. Still quiet, indeed almost hushed, the students surged forward. A boy with a feathery red beard patted the unicorn's withers, and a girl Anderson recognized from one of his classes buried her face in the flowing mane. The young woman herself, the girl with the bread, stroked the fierce horn. Anderson found that he was there too, his hand on a gleaming flank.

Then the magic blew away beneath the threshing of a helicopter, dissolved like a dream at cockcrow. It came in low across the park, a dark blue gunship. (Police, Anderson thought crazily, police and not the Army this time.) A dozen people yelled, and the students began to scatter.

It banked in a tight turn and came back trailing a white plume of tear gas. Anderson ran with the rest then, hearing the thunder of the unicorn's hooves over—no, under—the whicker of the four-bladed prop. There was a sputter of fire from some automatic weapon.

Back in the Liberal Arts Building several hours later, he went to the restroom to wash the traces of the gas from his face and hands and put drops in his faintly burning eyes. The smell of the gas was in his trousers and jacket; they would have to be cleaned. He wished vaguely that he had been prescient enough to keep a change of clothes on campus.

When he opened the door to his office, the young woman was there. Absurdly, she rose when he entered, as though sex roles had not just been eliminated but reversed.

He nodded to her, and she extended her hand. "I'm Julie Coronell, Dr. Anderson."

"It's a pleasure," he said. She might have been quite pretty, he decided, if she were not so thin. And so nervous.

"I—I noticed you out there. With the unicorn. I was the one who fed him bread."

"I know you were," Anderson said. "I noticed you, too. Everyone did."

She actually blushed, something he had not seen in years. "I've some more." She lifted a brown paper sack. "The other wasn't mine, really—I got it from some man there. He's in the Biology Department, I think."

Anderson nodded. "Yes, he is."

"That was white. That bread. This is pumpernickel. I thought he—the unicorn. I thought he might like it better."

Anderson could not keep from grinning at that, and she smiled too.

"Well, anyway, *I* like it better. Do you know the story about the general's horse? Or am I being a pest?"

"Not at all. I'd love to hear the story of the general's horse, especially if it has anything to do with unicorns."

"It doesn't, really. Only with horses, you know, and pumpernickel. The general was one of Napoleon's, I think Bernadotte, and he had a favorite charger named Nicole —we would say Nicholas or Nick. When the Grand Army occupied Germany and the officers ate at the German country inns, they were served the coarse, brown German bread with their meals. All Frenchmen hate it, and none of them would eat it. But the others saw that Bernadotte slipped it into his pockets, and when they asked him about it, he said it was for his horse—*pain pour Nicole,* bread for Nick. After that the others joked about the German 'horse bread,' *pain pour Nicole,* and the Germans thought that was the French name for it, and since anything French has always been very posh on menus, they used it."

Anderson chuckled and shook his head. "Is that what you're going to call him when you find him? Nicholas? Or will it be Nicole?"

"Nick, actually. The story is just folk-etymology, really. But I thought of it, and it seemed to fit. Nick, because we're both Americans now. I was born in New Zealand, and that brings me to one of the things I came to ask you —what nationality are unicorns? I mean originally. Greek?"

"Indian," Anderson told her.

"You're making fun of me."

He shook his head. "Not American Indian, of course. Indian like the tiger. A Roman naturalist called Pliny seemed to have begun the story. He said that people in

India hunted an animal he called the monoceros. Our word *unicorn* is a translation of that. Both words mean 'one-horned.' "

Julie nodded.

"Pliny said this unicorn had a head like a stag, feet like an elephant, a boar's tail, and the body of a horse. It bellowed, it had one black horn growing from its forehead, and it could not be captured alive."

She stared at him. He stared expressionlessly back, and at last she said, "That's not a unicorn! That's not a unicorn at all. That's a rhinoceros."

"Uh-huh. Specifically, it's an Indian rhinoceros. The African ones actually have two horns, one in front of the other. Pliny's description fell into the hands of the scholars of the Dark Ages, who knew nothing about rhinoceroses or even elephants; and the unicorn became a one-horned creature that was otherwise much like a horse. Unicorn horn was supposed to neutralize poisons, but the Indians didn't ship their rhinoceros horns west—China was much closer and much richer, and the Chinese thought rhinoceros horn was an aphrodisiac. Narwhale horns were brought in to satisfy the demand, and narwhale horns succeeded wonderfully, because narwhale horns are so utterly fantastic that no one who hasn't seen one can believe in them. They're ivory, and spiraled, and perfectly straight. You know, of course. You had your hand on one today, only it was growing out of a unicorn's head. Dumont would say out of the head of a genetically re-engineered horse, but I think we both know better."

Julie smiled. "It's wonderful, isn't it? Unicorns are real now."

"In a way, they were real before. As Chesterton says somewhere, to think of a cow with wings is essentially to have met one. The unicorn symbolized masculine purity—which isn't such a bad thing to symbolize, after all. Unicorns were painted on shields and sewn into flags. A unicorn rampant is the badge of Scotland, just as the bald eagle is the badge of this country, and eventually that unicorn became one of the supporters of the British arms. The image, the idea, has been real for a long time. Now it's tangible."

"And I'm glad. I like it like that. Dr. Anderson, the real reason I came to see you was that a friend told me you were the president of an organization that tries to save these animals."

"Most of them are people. All right if I smoke?" She nodded, and Anderson took a pipe from his desk and began to pack it with tobacco. "Many of the creatures of myth were partly human and had human intelligence—lamias, centaurs, fauns, satyrs, and so forth. Often that seems to appeal to the individuals who do this sort of thing. Then too, human cellular material is the easiest of all for them to get—they can use their own."

"Do you mean that I could make one of these mythical animals if I wanted to? Just go off and do it?"

The telephone rang and Anderson picked it up.

"Hello, Andy?" It was Dumont again.

"Yep," Anderson said.

"It seems to have gotten away."

"Uh huh. Our bunch certainly couldn't find it, and our operator said there was nothing on the police radio."

"Well, it gave them the slip. A student—an undergraduate, but I know him, and he's pretty reliable—just came and told me. He saw it over on the far side of the practice field. He tried to get up close, but it ran behind the field house, and he lost it."

Anderson covered the mouthpiece with his hand and said, "Nick's all right. Someone just saw him." He asked Dumont, "You send a bunch to look for him?"

"Not yet. I wanted to talk to you first. I gave the boy the key to my place and asked him to fetch my tranquilizer gun. He's got my van."

"Fine. Come up here and we'll talk. Leave this student a note so he'll know where you are."

"You don't think we ought to send some people out after the unicorn?"

"We've had searchers out after him for a couple of hours, and so have the police. I don't know about you; but while I was beating the bushes, I was wondering just what in the name of Capitoline Jove I was going to do with him if I found him. Try to ride him? Put salt on his tail? We can't do a damn thing until we've got your tranquilizer gun or some other way to control him, and by the time the boy gets back from your house in Brookwood it will be nearly dark."

When he had cradled the telephone, Anderson said, "That should give you an idea how well organized we are."

Julie shrugged sympathetically.

"In the past, you see, it was always a question of letting the creature get away. The soldiers or the police wanted to kill it, we wanted to see it spared. Usually they head for the most lightly populated area they can find. We should have anticipated that sooner or later we'd be faced with one right here in the city, but I suppose we assumed that in a case like that we'd have no chance at all. Now it turns out that we've got a chance—your friend Nick is surprisingly elusive for such a big beast—and we haven't the least idea of what to do."

"Maybe he was born—do you say born?"

"We usually say created, but it doesn't matter."

"Well, maybe he was created here in the city, and he's trying to find his way out of it."

"A creature that size?" Anderson shook his head. "He's come in from outside, from some sparsely settled rural area, or he'd have been turned in by a nosy neighbor long ago. People can—people do—perform DNA engineering in the city. Sometimes in basements or garages or kitchens, more often on the sly in college labs or some big corporation's research and development facility. They keep the creatures they've made, too; sometimes for years. I've got a sea-horse at home in an aquarium, not one of those fish you buy cast in plastic paperweights in the Florida souvenir shops, but a little fellow about ten inches long, with the head and forelegs of a pony and the hindquarters of a trout. I've had him for a year now, and I'll probably have him for another ten. But suppose he were Nick's size—where would I keep him?"

"In a swimming pool, I imagine," Julie said. "In fact, it seems rather a nice idea. Maybe at night, you could take him to Lake Michigan and ride him there, in the lake. You could wear scuba gear. I'm not a terribly good swimmer, but I think I'd do it." She smiled at him.

He smiled back. "It does sound like fun, when you describe it."

"Just the same, you think Nick's escaped from some farm—or perhaps an estate. I should think that would be more likely. The rich must have these poor, wonderful animals made for them sometimes."

"Sometimes, yes."

"Unicorns. A sea-horse—that's from mythology too, isn't it?"

Anderson was lighting his pipe; the mingled fumes of sulfur and tobacco filled the office. "Balios and Xanthos drew the chariot of Poseidon," he said. "In fact, Poseidon was the god of horses as well as of the sea. His herds were the waves, in a mystic sense few people understand today. The whitecaps were the white manes of his innumerable steeds."

"And you mentioned lamias—those were snake women, weren't they?"

"Yes."

"And centaurs. And fauns and satyrs. Are all the animals like that, that the biologists make, from mythology?"

Anderson shook his head. "Not all of them, no. But let me ask you a question, Ms. Coronell—"

"Call me Julie, please."

"All right, Julie. Now suppose that you were a biologist. In genetic engineering they've reached the stage at which any competent worker with a Master's or a Ph.D.—and a lot of bright undergraduates—can do this sort of thing. What would you make for yourself?"

"I have room for it, and privacy, and lots of money?"

"If you like, yes."

"Then I'd make a unicorn, I think."

"You're impressed with them because you saw a beautiful one today. After that. Suppose you were going to create something else?"

Julie paused, looking pensive. "We talked about riding a sea-horse in the lake. Something with wings, I suppose, that I could ride."

"A bird? A mammal?"

"I don't know. I'd have to think about it."

"If you chose a bird, it would have to be much larger, of course, than a natural bird. You'd also find that it could not maintain the proportions of any of the species whose genetic matter you were using. Its wings would have to be much larger in proportion to its body. Its head would not have to be much bigger than an eagle's—and so on. When you were through and you were spotted sailing among the clouds, the newspapers would probably call your bird a roc, after the one that carried Sinbad."

"I see."

"If you decided on a winged horse instead, it would be Pegasus. I've never yet seen one of those that could actually fly, by the way. A winged human being would be an angel, or if it were more birdlike, with claws and tail feathers and so on, perhaps a harpy. You see, it's quite hard to escape from mythological nomenclature, because it covers so much. People have already imagined all these things. It's just that now we—some of us—can make them come true."

Julie smiled nervously. "An alligator! I think I'll choose an alligator with wings. I could make him smarter at the same time."

Anderson puffed out a cloud of smoke. "That's a dragon."

"Wait, I'll—"

The door flew open and Dumont came in. Anderson said, "Here's the man who can tell you about recombinant DNA and that sort of thing. I'd only make a hash of it." He stood. "Julie, may I present Henry A. Dumont of Biology, my good friend and occasionally my rival."

"Friendly rival," Dumont put in.

"Also the treasurer and technical director of our little society. Dumont, this is Julia Coronell, the lady who's hiding the unicorn."

For a moment no one spoke. Julie's face was guarded, expressionless save for tension. Then she said, "How did you know?"

Anderson sat down again, and Dumont took the office's last chair. Anderson said, "You came here because you were concerned about Nick." He paused, and Julie nodded. "But you didn't seem to want to *do* anything. If Nick was running around while the police looked for him, the situation was urgent; but you told me that story about pumpernickel and let me blather on about fauns and centaurs. You were worried, you were under a considerable strain, but you weren't urging me to get busy and reactivate the group we had looking for Nick this afternoon. When Dumont here called, I was very casual about the whole thing and just asked him to come over and talk. You didn't protest, and I decided that you knew where Nick was already. And that he was safe, at least for the time being."

"I see," Julie whispered.

"I don't," Dumont said. "That boy told me he saw the unicorn."

Anderson nodded. "A friend of yours, Julie?"

"Yes . . ."

Dumont said, "Honey, it's nothing to be ashamed of. We're on your side."

"You hid Nick," Anderson continued, "after the police dropped their tear gas. He was tame with you, as we saw earlier. He may even have eaten enough of Dumont's bread to calm him down a bit—there was a sedative in it. For a while after that, you were probably too frightened to do anything more; you just lay low. Then the police went away and our search parties gave up, and you went off campus to buy that bread you're holding. On the way back to give it to Nick, you met someone who told you about me."

Dumont asked, "Was it Ed? The boy who told me he saw the unicorn?"

Julie's voice was nearly inaudible. "Yes, it was."

"And between the two of you, you decided it would be smart to start some rumors indicating that Nick was still free and moving in a direction away from the place where you had him hidden." Anderson paused to relight his pipe. "So the first report had him disappearing behind the field house. The next one would have put him even farther away, I suppose. But more or less on impulse, you decided that we might help you, so you came up here to wait for me. Anyway, it would be safer for you to take that bread to Nick after dark. All right, we will help you. At least, we'll try. Where is Nick?"

Ed was no more a boy, actually, than Julie Coronell was a girl—a studious looking young man of nineteen or twenty. He had brought Dumont's tranquilizer gun, and Dumont had it now, though all of them hoped it would not be needed. Julie led the way, with Anderson beside her and Dumont and Ed behind them. A softness as of rose petals was in the evening air.

Anderson said, "I've seen you around the campus, haven't I? Graduate school?"

Julie nodded. "I'm working on my doctorate, and I teach some freshman and sophomore classes. Ed's one of my students. Most of the people I meet seem to think I'm a sophomore or a junior myself. How did you know I wasn't?"

"The way you're dressed. I guessed, actually. You look young, but you also look like a woman who looks younger than she is."

"You ought to have been a detective," she told him.

"Yes, anything but this."

The sun had set behind the trees of the park, trees whose long shadows had all run together now, flooding the lawns and walks with formless night. Most of the windows in the buildings the four passed were dark.

"What department?" Anderson asked when Julie said nothing more.

"English. My dissertation will be on twentieth century American novelists."

"I should have recognized you, but I'm more than two thousand years behind you."

"I'm easy to overlook."

"Let's hope Nick is too." For a moment, Anderson studied the building looming before them. "Why the library?"

"I've been doing research; they let me have a key. I knew it had just closed, and I couldn't think of anything else." She held up the key.

A minute or two later, it slid into the lock. The interior was dim but not dark—a scattering of lights, lonely and almost spectral, burned in the recesses of the building, as though the spirits of a few geniuses lingered, still awake.

Dumont said, "You'd better let me go in front," and hurried past them with the tranquilizer gun. The doors closed with a hollow boom; suddenly the air seemed stale.

"Isn't there a watchman?" Anderson asked.

Julie nodded. She was near enough for Anderson to smell her faint perfume. "You said Ed was a friend of mine. I don't have a lot, but I suppose Bailey—he's the watchman—is a friend too. I'm the only one who never calls him Beetle. I told you Nick was in the Sloan Fantasy Collection. Have you heard of it?"

"Vaguely. My field is classical literature."

Behind them, Ed said, "That's what fantasy is—classical lit that's still alive. When the people who wrote those stories did it, their books were called fantasy."

"Ed!" Julie protested.

"No," Anderson said. "He's right."

"Anyway," Julie continued, "the Sloan Collection isn't the best in the country, or even a famous collection. But it's a jolly good one. It's got James Branch Cabell in first editions, for example, and a lot of his letters. And there's some wonderful John Gardner material. So that's where I put Nick."

Stamping among the books, Anderson thought to himself. Couchant at the frontiers of Overworld and Oz.

Pity the Unicorn,
Pity the Hippogriff,
Souls that were never born
Out of the land of If!

Somewhere ahead, Dumont called, *"He's dead!"* and suddenly all three of them were running, staggering, stumbling down a dark and narrow corridor, guided by the flame of Dumont's lighter.

Anderson heard Julie whisper, "Nick! Oh, God, Nick!" Then she was quiet. The thing on the floor was no white unicorn.

Dumont rasped, "Hasn't anybody got a light?"

"Just matches," Anderson said. He lit one.

Ed told them, "I've got one," and from the pocket of his denim shirt produced a little, disposable penlight.

Julie was bending over the dead man, trying not to step in his blood. There was a great deal of it, and Dumont had stepped in it already, leaving a footprint. Ed played his light upon the dead man's face—cleanshaven; about sixty, Anderson guessed. He had worn a leather windbreaker. There was a hole in it now, a big hole that welled blood.

"It's Bailey," Julie said. And Dumont, thinking that she spoke to him (as perhaps she did), answered, "Is that his name? Everybody called him Beetle."

Bailey had been gored in the middle of his chest, very near the heart, Anderson decided. No doubt he had died instantly, or almost instantly. His face was not peaceful or frightened or anything else; only twisted in the terrible rictus of death. The match burned Anderson's fingers; he shook it and dropped it.

"Nick . . ." Julie whispered. "Nick did this?"

"I'm afraid so," Dumont told her.

She looked around, first at Dumont, then at Anderson. "He's dangerous. . . . I suppose I always knew it, but I didn't like to think about it. We'll have to let the police . . ."

Dumont nodded solemnly.

"Like hell," Anderson said, and Julie stared at him. "You put him here, in this room"—Anderson glanced at the half open door—"and went away and left him. Is that right?"

"Mr. Bailey was with us. He heard us as soon as I brought Nick inside. Nick's hooves made a lot of noise on the terrazzo floor. We took him to this room, and Mr. Bailey locked it for me."

Ed asked, "Hold this, will you, Dr. Dumont?" and handed Dumont the penlight, then took three steps, stooped, and straightened up with a much larger flashlight. After the near darkness, its illumination seemed almost a glare. Dumont let his lighter go out and dropped it into his pocket.

Ed was grinning weakly. "This must be the old man's flash," he said. "I thought I saw something shine over here."

"Yes." Anderson nodded. "He would have had it in his hand. After Julie left he came here to take another look at the unicorn. He opened the door and turned on his flashlight."

Julie shivered. "It could have been me."

"I doubt it. Even if Nick doesn't have human or almost human intelligence—and I suspect he does—he would have winded the watchman and known it wasn't your smell. No matter what kind of brain his creator gave him, his sensory setup must be basically the one that came with his equine DNA. Am I right, Dumont?"

"Right." The biologist glanced at his wrist. "I wish we had more information about the time Beetle died."

Ed asked, "Can't you tell from the clotting of the blood?"

"Not close enough," Dumont said. "Maybe a forensic technician could, but that's not my field. If this were one of those mysteries on TV, we could tell from the time his watch broke. It didn't, and it's still running. Anybody want to guess how far that unicorn's gone since he did this?"

"I will," Anderson told him. "Not more than about two hundred and fifty feet."

They stared at him.

"The front doors were locked when we came in—Julie had to open them for us. I'd bet the side door is locked too, and this building has practically no windows."

"You mean he's still in here?"

"If he's not, how did he get out?"

Julie said, "We'd hear him, wouldn't we? I told you—his hooves made a racket when I let him in."

"He heard them too," Anderson told her. "He wouldn't have to be a tenth as intelligent as he probably is to keep quiet. Almost any animal will do that by instinct. If it can't run—or doesn't think running's a good idea—it freezes."

Ed cleared his throat. "Dr. Anderson, you said he could tell by the smell that Beetle wasn't Julie. He'll know we aren't Julie too."

"Conversely, he'll know that she is. But if we separate to look for him and the wrong party finds him, there could be trouble."

Dumont nodded. "What do you think we ought to do?"

"To start with, give Ed here the keys to your van so he can bring it around front. If we find Nick, we're going to have to have some way to get him out of town. We'll leave the front doors open—"

"And let him get away?"

"No. But we need unicorn bait, and freedom's about as good a bait as anybody's ever found. Nick's probably hungry by now, and he's almost certainly thirsty. My mind runs to quotations anyway, so how about:

> *One by one in the moonlight there,*
> *Neighing for off on the haunted air,*
> *The unicorns come down to the sea.*

Do you know that one?"

All three looked blank.

"It's Conrad Aiken, and of course he never saw a unicorn. But there may be some truth in it—in the feeling of it—just the same. We'll prop the doors wide. Dumont, you hide in the darkest shadow you can find there; the open doors should let in enough light for you to shoot by, particularly since you'll be shooting at a white animal. Julie and I will go through the building, turning on lights and looking for Nick. If we find him and he's docile with her, we can just lead him out and put him in the van. If he runs, you should get him on the way out."

Dumont nodded.

When the two of them were alone, Julie asked, "That gun of Dr. Dumont's won't really hurt Nick, will it?"

"No more than a shot in the arm would hurt you. Less."

The beam of the dead watchman's flashlight probed the corridor, seeming to leave a deeper twilight where it had passed. A few moments before, Anderson had talked of turning on more lights, but thus far they had failed to find the switches. He asked Julie if it were always this dim when she came to do research after the library had closed.

"Bailey used to take care of the lights for me," she said. "But I don't know where. I'd begin setting up my things on one of the tables, my notebooks and so forth; and the lights would come on." Her voice caught on *lights*.

She sniffled, and Anderson realized she was crying. He put his arm about her shoulders.

"Oh, rot! Why is it that one can—can try to do something fine, and have—have it end . . ."

He chanted softly:

> "*Twist ye, twine ye! Even so,*
> *Mingled shades of joy and woe,*
> *Hope and fear, and peace, and strife,*
> *In the thread of human life.*"

"That's b-beautiful, but what does it mean? That the good and bad are mixed together so we can't pull them apart?"

"And that this isn't the end. Not for men or women or unicorns. Probably not even for poor old Bailey. Threads are long."

She put her arms about his neck and kissed him, and he was so busy pressing those soft, fragrant lips in return that he hardly heard the sudden thunder of the unshod hooves.

He pushed her away just in time. The spiraled horn raked his belly like a talon; the beast's shoulder hit him like a football player's, sending him crashing into a high bookcase.

Julie screamed, "No, Nick! Don't!" and he tried to stand.

The unicorn was rearing to turn in the narrow aisle, tall as a giant on his hind legs. Anderson clawed at the shelves, bringing down an avalanche of books. He found himself somehow grasping the horn, holding on desperately. A hoof struck his thigh like a hammer and he was careening down some dark passage, half carried, half dragged.

Abruptly, there was light ahead. He tried to shout for Dumont to shoot; but he had no breath, grasping the horn, grappling the tossing white head like a bulldogger. If the soft pluff of the gun ever came, it was lost in the clattering hoofbeats, in the roar of the blood in his ears. And if it came, the dart surely missed.

They nearly fell on the steps. Reeling they reached the bottom like kittens tossed from a sack. Anderson managed then to get his right leg under him; and with the unicorn nearly sprawling, he tried to get his left across the broad, white back and found that leg was broken.

He must have shrieked when the ends of splintered bone grated together, and he must have lost his hold. He lay upon his back, on grass, and heard the gallop of approaching death. Saw death, white as bone.

Stallions fight, he thought. Fight for mares, kicking and biting. Only men kill other men for a woman.

He lay without moving, his left leg twisted like a broken doll's. Stallions don't kill—not if the other lies down, surrenders.

The white head was silhouetted against the twinkling constellations now, the colors seemingly reversed as in a negative, the longsword horn both new and ancient to the sky of Earth.

Later, when he told Julie and Dumont about it, Dumont said, "So he was only a horse after all. He spared you."

"A superhorse. A horse armed, with size, strength, grace, and intelligence all augmented." They had wanted to carry him somewhere (he doubted if they themselves knew where), but he had stopped them. Now, after Dumont had phoned for an ambulance, they sat beside him on the grass. His leg hurt terribly.

"Which way did he go? The park again?"

"No, the lake shore. *'The unicorns come down to the sea,'* remember? You'll have to drum up a group and go after him in the morning."

Julie said, "I'll come, and I'm sure Ed will too."

Anderson managed to nod. "We've got a couple of dozen others. Some here, some in town. Dumont has the phone numbers."

She forced a smile. "Andy—can I call you Andy? You like poems. Do you recall this one?

The lion and the unicorn
Were fighting for the crown;
The lion beat the unicorn
And sent him out of town.
Some gave them white bread,
And some gave them brown.
Some gave them plum-cake,
And drummed them out of town.

We've just had it come true, all except for that bit about the plum-cake."

"And the lion," Anderson said.

SERPENTS' TEETH

≈≈≈≈≈≈≈≈≈≈≈≈≈≈≈≈≈≈≈≈≈≈≈≈≈≈≈≈≈≈≈≈

Spider Robinson

Family relationships have been changing slowly but steadily for decades; the time may come when children and parents who don't get along can divorce each other. But children will still need parents, and there will be childless couples who will want to adopt unattached children. Spider Robinson imagines a "pickup bar" where they could meet, and the results of one such meeting.

Spider Robinson's stories of Callahan's Crosstime Saloon are famous in science fiction. The bar he writes about here is very different indeed.

~~~~~~

LOOKOVER LOUNGE

House Rules, Age 16 And Up:

IF THERE'S A BEEF, IT'S YOUR FAULT. IF
YOU BREAK IT, YOU PAY FOR IT, PLUS SALES
TAX AND INSTALLATION. NO RESTRICTED
DRUGS. IF YOU ATTEMPT TO REMOVE ANY
PERSON OR PERSONS FROM THESE PREMISES
INVOLUNTARILY, BY FORCE OR COERCION
AS DEFINED BY THE HOUSE, YOU WILL BE
SURRENDERED TO THE POLICE IN DAM-
AGED CONDITION. THE DECISIONS OF YOUR
BARTENDER ARE FINAL, AND THE MANAGE-
MENT DOESN'T WANT TO KNOW YOU. THE
FIRST ONE'S ON THE HOUSE; HAVE A GOOD
TIME.

Teddy and Freddy both finished reading with slightly
raised eyebrows. Any bar in their own home town might
well have had nearly identical—unofficial—house rules.
But their small town was not sophisticated enough for such
rules to be so boldly committed to printout.

*"You can surrender those sheets at the bar for your
complimentary drink,"* the door-terminal advised them.
"Good luck to you both."

Freddy said "Thank you." Teddy said nothing.

The soft music cut off; a door slid open. New music
spilled out, a processor group working the lower register,

leaving the higher frequencies free for a general hubbub of
conversation. Smells spilled out as well: beer, mostly, with
overlays of pot, tobacco, sweat, old vomit, badly burned
coffee and cheap canned air. It was darker in there; Teddy
and Freddy could not see much. They exchanged a glance,
shared a quick nervous grin.

"Break a leg, kid," Teddy said, and entered the Lounge,
Freddy at her heels.

Teddy's first impression was that it was just what she had
been expecting. The crowd was sizable for this time of
night, perhaps four or five dozen souls, roughly evenly
divided between hunters and hunted. While the general
mood seemed hearty and cheerful, quiet desperation could
be seen in any direction, invariably on the faces of the
hunters.

Teddy and Freddy had certainly been highlighted when
the door first slid back, but by the time their eyes had
adjusted to the dimmer light no one was looking at them.
They located the bar and went there. They strove to move
synchronously, complementarily, as though they were old
dance partners or old cop partners, as though they were
married enough to be telepathic. In point of fact they were
all these things, but you could never have convinced anyone watching them now.

The bartender was a wiry, wizened old man whose hair
had once been red, and whose eyes had once been innocent—perhaps a century before. He displayed teeth half
that age and took their chits. "Welcome to the Big Fruit,
folks."

Freddy's eyebrows rose. "How did you know we're not
from New York?"

"I'm awake at the moment. What'll it be?"

Teddy and Freddy described their liquid requirements.
The old man took his time, punched in their order with one
finger, brought the drinks to them with his pinkies extended. As they accepted the drinks, he leaned forward
confidentially. "None o' my business, but . . . you might
could do all right here tonight. There's good ones in just
now, one or two anyways. Don't push is the thing. Don't
try quite so hard. Get me?"

They stared at him. "Thanks, uh—"

"Pop, everybody calls me. Let them do the talking."

"We will," Freddy said. "Thank you, Pop."

"Whups! 'Scuse me." He spun and darted off at surprising speed toward the far end of the bar, where a patron was in danger of falling off his stool; Pop caught him in time. Teddy would have sworn that Pop had never taken his eyes from them until he had moved. She had smuggled a small weapon past the door-scanner, chiefly to build her morale, but she resolved now not to try it on Pop even in extremis. "Come on, Freddy."

Teddy found them a table near one of the air-circulators, with a good view of the rest of the room. "Freddy, for God's sake quit staring! You heard what the old fart said: lighten up."

"Teddy!"

"I like him too; I was trying to get your attention. Try to look like there isn't shit on your shoes, will you?"

"How about that one?"

"Where?"

"There."

"In the blue and *red?*" Teddy composed her features with a visible effort. "Look, my love: apparently we have 'HICK' written across our foreheads in big black letters. All right. Let's not make it 'DUMB HICK,' all right? Look at her *arms,* for God's sake."

"Oh." Freddy's candidate was brazenly wearing a sleeveless shirt—and a cop should not miss track marks.

"I'm telling you, slow down. Look, let's make an agreement: we're not going to hit on *any*body for the first hour, all right? We're just out for an evening of quiet conversation."

"I see. We spent three hundred and sixty-seven New dollars to come to New York and have a few drinks."

Teddy smiled as though Freddy had said something touching and funny, and murmured, *"God damn it, Freddy, you promised."*

"All right, but I think these people can spot a phony a mile away. The one in pink and yellow, on your left."

"I'm not saying we should be phony, I'm—" Teddy made an elaborate hair-adjusting gesture, sneaked a look, then frankly stared. "Wow. That's more like it. Dancing with the brunette, right?"

"Yes."

Freddy's new choice was golden-haired and heartbreakingly beautiful, dressed daringly by their standards but not shockingly. Ribs showed, and pathetically slender arms,

and long smooth legs. Intelligence showed in the eyes,
above lips slightly curled in boredom.

"Too good to be true," Teddy said sadly. "All these
regulars here, and we walk in our first night and score
that?"

"I *like* wishful thinking. You shoot for the moon, once
in a while you get it."

"And end up wishing you'd settled for a space station.
I'd settle for that redhead in the corner with the ventilated
shoes."

Freddy followed her glance, winced, and made a small
sound of pity. "Don't mock the funny-looking."

"Me? I grew *up* funny-looking. I worked four summers
selling greaseburgers for this chin and nose. I'll settle for
anyone halfway pleasant." She lowered her voice; the
musicians were taking a break.

"I love your chin and nose. I don't like him anyway.
He looks like the secretive type."

"And you aren't? This drink is terrible."

"So's this—"

The voice was startlingly close. "Hey! You're in my seat,
Atlas."

It was the stunning golden-haired youngman. Alone.

Freddy began to move and speak at the same time, but
Teddy kicked him hard in the shin and he subsided.

"No we're not," she said firmly.

There was nothing especially grudging about the respect
that came into the youngman's eyes, but there was nothing
especially submissive about it either. "I always sit by a
circulator. I don't like breathing garbage." He made no
move to go.

Teddy refused her eyes permission to drop from his.
"We would be pleased if you'd join us."

"I accept."

Before Teddy could stop him, Freddy was up after a
chair. He placed it beside the youngman, who moved it
slightly to give himself a better view of the room than of
them, and sat without thanks.

"You're welcome," Freddy said quietly, slouching down
in his own chair, and Teddy suppressed a grin. When she
led firmly, her husband always followed well. For the first
time Teddy became aware that she was enjoying herself.

The youngman glanced sharply at Freddy. "Thanks," he said belatedly.

"Buy you a drink?" Teddy asked.

"Sure. Beer."

Teddy signaled a waiter. "Tell Pop we'd like a couple of horses over here," she said, watching the youngman. The pacification of Mexico had made Dos Equis quite expensive, but his expression did not change. She glanced down at her own glass. "In fact, make it three pair."

"Tab?" asked the waiter.

"Richards Richards, Ted Fred."

When the waiter had left, the blond said, "You people always know how to do that. Get a waiter to come. What is that, how do you do that?"

"Well," Freddy began, "I—"

"Which one of you is which?"

"I'm Freddy."

"Oh God, and you're Teddy, huh?" He sighed. "I hope I die before I get cute. I'm Davy Pangborn.' "

Teddy wondered if it were his legal name, but did not ask. It would not have been polite; Davy had not asked them. "Hello, Davy."

"How long have you been in the city?"

Teddy grinned broadly, annoyed. "Is there hay in my hair or something? Honest to God, I feel like there's a fly unzipped on my forehead."

"There is," Davy said briefly, and turned his attention to the room.

Teddy and Freddy exchanged a glance. Teddy shrugged. "How old are you, Davy?" Freddy asked.

Davy turned very slowly, looked Freddy over with insolent thoroughness. "How many times a week do you folks do the hump?" he asked.

Teddy kept her voice even with some effort. "See here, we're willing to swap data, but if you get to ask questions that personal, so do we."

"You just did."

Teddy considered that. "Okay," she said finally. "I guess I understand. We're new at this."

"Is that so?" Davy said disgustedly and turned back to face the room.

"We make love about three times a week," Freddy said

"I'm nine," Davy said without turning.

*   *   *

The beer arrived, along with a plate of soy crunchies garnished with real peanuts. "Compliments of the house," the waiter said, and rolled away.

Teddy glanced up, craned her head until she could see through the crowd to the bar. Pop's eyes were waiting for hers; he shook his head slightly, winked, and turned away. Total elapsed time was less than a second; she was not sure she had not imagined it. She glanced at Freddy, could not tell from his expression whether he had seen it too.

She examined Davy more carefully. He was obviously bright and quick; his vocabulary and grammar were excellent; his education could not have been too badly neglected. He was clean, his clothes were exotic but neat and well kept. He didn't look like a welfare type; she would have given long odds that he had some kind of job or occupation, perhaps even a legal one. He was insolent, but she decided that in his position he could hardly be otherwise. He was breathtakingly beautiful, and must know it. She was sure he was not and had never been a prostitute, he didn't have that chickie look.

Her cop-sense told her that Davy had potential.

Did Pop know something she didn't? How honest was Davy? How many scars were drawn how deep across his soul, how much garbage had society poured into his subconscious? Would he grow up to be Maker, Taker, or Faker? Everyone in this room was walking wounded; how severe were Davy's wounds?

"How long have you been single, Davy?"

He still watched the roomful of hunters and hunted, face impassive. "How long since *your* kid divorced *you?*"

"Why do you assume we're divorced?"

Davy drank deeply from his beer, turned to face her. "Okay, let's run it down. You're not sterile, or if you are it was postnatal complications. You've had it before, I can see it in your eyes. Maybe you worked in a power plant, or maybe Freddy here got the measles, but once upon a time someone called you Mommy. It's unmistakable. And you're here, so the kid walked out on you."

"Or died," she suggested. "Or got sent up, institutionalized."

"No." He shook his head. "You're hurting, but you're not hurting that bad."

She smiled. "All right. We've been divorced a year last week. And you?"

"Three years."

Teddy blinked. If Davy was telling the truth—and a lie seemed pointless—he had opted out the moment he could, and was in no hurry to remarry. Well, with his advantages he could afford to be independent.

On the other hand—Teddy looked around the room herself, studying only the hunters, the adults, and saw no one who made her feel inferior. *He never met a couple like us before,* she told herself, and she made herself promise not to offer him notarized résumé and net-worth sheets unless and until he offered them his.

"What was your kid like, Atlas?" Davy sipped beer and watched her over the rim of the glass.

"Why do you call us that?" Freddy asked.

Teddy frowned. "It's pretty obvious, darling. Atlas was a giant."

Davy grinned through his glass. "Only half the answer. The least important half. Tell me about your kid—your ex-kid—and I'll tell you the other half."

Teddy nodded. "Done. Well, his name is Eddie, and he's—"

"*'Eddie'?*" the youngman exclaimed. "Oh my God you people are too much!" He began to laugh. "If it'd been a girl it would've been Hedy, right?"

Teddy reddened but held her temper. She waited until he was done laughing, and then two seconds more, and continued, "And he's got dark brown hair and hazel eyes. He's short for his age, and he'll probably turn out stocky. He has . . . beautiful hands. He's got my temper, and Freddy's hands. And he's bright and quick, like you. He'll go far. About the divorce . . ." Teddy paused. She and Freddy had rehearsed this next part for so long that they could make it sound unrehearsed. But Davy had a Bullshit-Detector of high sensitivity. Mentally Teddy discarded her lines and just let the words come. "We . . . I guess we were slow in getting our consciousness raised. Faster than some, slower than most. We, we just didn't realize how misguided our own conditioning had been . . . until it was too late. Until we had our noses rubbed in it." Teddy sipped her beer without tasting it.

Although he had not been fed proper cues, Freddy picked it up. "I guess we had our attention on other things. I don't mean that we fell into parenting. We thought it through—we thought we thought it through—before we decided to conceive. But some of our axioms were wrong. We . . ." He paused, blushed, and blurted it out: "We had plans for Eddie."

"Don't say another word," Davy ordered.

Freddy blinked. Teddy frowned; she was studying Davy's expression.

He finished his beer on one long slow draft, stretching the silence. He set the glass down, put both hands on the table and smiled. The smile shocked Teddy: she had never, not in the worst of the divorce, not in the worst of her work in the streets, seen such naked malice on so young a face. She ordered her own face to be inscrutable. And she took Freddy's hand under the table.

"Let me finish, it'll save time," Davy said. "And I'll still tell you why you're an Atlas." He looked them both up and down with care. "Let's see. You're hicks. Some kind of civil service or social work or both, both of you. Very committed, very concerned. I can tell you what grounds Eddie cited at the hearing, want to hear me?"

"You're doing okay so far," Teddy said tightly.

"On the decree absolute it says 'Conceptual Conditioning, Restraint of Personality, and Authoritarianism.' Guaranteed, sure as God made little green boogers. But it won't have the main reason on it: Delusions of Ownership."

They had not quite visibly flinched on the first three charges, but the fourth got to them both. Davy grinned wickedly.

"Now, the key word for both of you, the word that unlocks you both, is the word *future*. I can even sort of see why. Both of you are the kind that wants to *change* things, to make a better world. You figure like this: the past is gone, unchangeable. The present is here *right now* and it's too late. So the only part you can change is the future. You're both heavy into politics, am I right? Right?"

He knew that he was getting to them both; his grin got bigger. Teddy and Freddy were rigid in their chairs.

"So one day," the youngman went on, "it dawned on you that the best way to change the future is to colonize it. With little xeroxes of yourselves. Of course one of the first concerns of a colonizing country is to properly *condition* the colonists. To ensure their loyalty. Because a

colonist is supposed to give you the things *you* want t
have in exchange for the things *you* want *him* to have
and for this golden opportunity he is supposed to b
properly grateful. It wouldn't do for him to get an
treasonous ideas about his own destiny, his own goals." H
popped a handful of soy crunchies into his mouth. "I
your case, the world needed saving, and Eddie was elected
Like it or not." He chewed the mouthful, washed it down
"Let me see. Don't tell me, now. I see the basic progran
this way: first a solid grounding in math, history, and
languages—I'd guess Japanese Immersion followed b
French. Then by high school begin working toward law
maybe with a minor in Biz Ecch. Then some militar-
service, police probably, and then law school if he sur
vived. With any luck at all old Eddie would have beer
governor of wherever the hell you live—one of the Dako
tas, isn't it?—by the time he was thirty-five. Then Senato
Richards by forty or so."

"Jesus," Teddy croaked.

"I even know what Eddie wants to be instead. *f*
musician. And not even a respectable musician, piano o
electric guitar or something cubical like that, right? He
wants to play that flash stuff, that isn't even proper music
he wants to be in a processor group, right? I saw the wa*
you looked at the band when you came in. There can'
be many things on earth that are as little use to the futur*
as flash. It doesn't even get recorded. It's not supposed
to be: it's for the *present*. I wonder if Eddie's any good.*

"What are you trying to do to us?"

"Now: about why you're Atlases. Atlas isn't just a giant
He's the very worst kind of giant. The one to avoid at al
costs. Because he's got the weight of the whole world or
his shoulders. And he wants you to take it over for him a
soon as you're big enough." Suddenly, finally, the grin wa
gone. "Well stuff you, Atlas! You're not even cured ye*
are you? You're still looking for a Nice Young Kid Wh*
Wants To Make Something Of Himself, you want a god
damned volunteer! You're suddenly childless, and you'r
so fucking lonely you tell each other you'll settle for any
thing just to have a kid around the house again. But i
your secret hearts you can't help hoping you'll find on
with some *ambition,* can you?"

He sat back. He was done. "Well," he said in a differen

voice, knowing the answer, "how'd I do?" and he began eating peanuts.

Teddy and Freddy were speechless for a long time. The blood had drained from both their faces; garish bar lighting made them look like wax mannequins, save that Teddy was swaying slightly from side to side. Her hand crushed Freddy's hand; neither noticed.

It was Teddy who found her voice first, and to her horror it trembled, and would not stop trembling. "You did very damned well. Two insignificant errors. It was going to be Swahili Immersion after the Japanese. Not French."

"And . . . ?"

"Our mutual occupation. You bracketed it, but no direct hit."

"So? All right, surprise me."

"We're cops."

It was Davy's turn to be speechless. He recovered faster. *"Pigs."*

Teddy could *not* get the quaver out of her voice. "Davy, how do you feel when some Atlas calls you 'punk,' or 'kid,' or 'baby'?"

Davy's eyes flashed.

The quaver was lengthening its period. Soon she would be speaking in singsong ululation, and shortly after that (she knew) she would lose the power to form words and simply weep. She pressed on.

"Well, that's how we feel when some punk kid baby calls us 'pigs.' "

He raised his eyebrows, looked impressed for the first time. "Good shot. Fair is fair. Except that you *chose* to be pigs."

"Not at first. We were drafted at the same time, worked together in a black and white. After the Troubles when our hitch was up we got married and went career."

"Huh. Either of you ever worked Juvenile?"

Teddy nodded. "I had a year. Freddy three."

Davy looked thoughtful. "So. Sometimes Juvie cops are all right. Sometimes they get to see things most Atlases don't. And hick cops aren't as bad as New York cops, I guess." He nodded. "Okay, I grant you the provisional status of human beings. Let's deal. I've got no eyes for anything lengthy right at the moment, but I could flash on,

say, a weekend in the country or two. If we're compatible
I like your place and all, maybe we could talk somethin
a little more substantial—*maybe*. So what's your offer?"

Teddy groped for words. "Offer?"

"What *terms* are you offering? We might as well sta⟩
with your résumés and stuff, that'll give us parameters."

She stared.

"Oh, my God," he said, "don't tell me you came *her*
looking for something *permanent*? On a first date? Oh
you people are the Schwartzchild Limit!" He began t
laugh. "I'll bet your own contract with each other is per
manent. Not even ten-year-renewable." When that san
home he laughed even harder. "Unbelievable!" He stoppe
laughing suddenly. "Oh Momma, you have a *lot* to learr
Now how about those résumés?"

"Shut up," Freddy said quietly.

Davy stared at him. *"What did you say?"*

"Shut up. You may not call her that."

Teddy stared as well.

Freddy's voice did not rise in volume, but suddenl
there was steel in it. "You just granted us the provisiona
status of human beings. We do not reciprocate. You ar
cruel, and we would not inflict you on our town, muc
less our home. You can go now."

The enormity of the affront left Davy momentarily at
loss for words, but he soon found some. "How'd you lik
to wake up in the alley with a broken face, old man? Yo
read the house rules, your badges are shit in here. All
have to do is poke you right in the eye, and let the boun⟨
ers do the rest."

Freddy had the habit of sitting slouched low, curle
in on himself. He sat up straight now, and for the fir
time Davy realized that the man topped 185 centimete
and massed well over 90 kilos. Freddy's shoulders seeme
to have swollen, and his eyes were burning with a col
fire. Teddy stared at him round-eyed, not knowing hir
Suddenly it registered on Davy that both of her han⟨
were now visible on the table, and that neither of Freddy
were.

"They'll put us in the same Emergency Room," Fred⟨
said dreamily. "You're a lot younger than I am. But I'
still faster. Leave this table."

Shortly Davy realized that his face was blank wi
shock, and hastily hung a sneer on it. "Hah." He got

his feet. "My pleasure." Standing beside them he was nearly at eye level. "Just another couple of dumb Atlases." He left.

Freddy turned to his wife, found her gaping at him. The fire went out in him; he slumped again in his chair, and finished off his beer. "Stay here, darling," he said, his voice soft again. "I'll get us another round."

Her eyes followed him as he walked to the bar.

Pop had two more beers waiting for him. "Thanks for the munchies, Pop. And the wink."

"My pleasure," Pop said, smiling.

"Can I buy you a drink, Pop?"

The old man's smile broadened. "Thank you." He punched himself up an apricot sour. "You're well shut of that one. Little vampire."

Freddy's eye was caught by graffiti crudely spray-painted on a nearby wall. It said: "TAKE OUT YOUR OWN FUCKIN GARBAGE." On the opposite wall a neater hand had thoughtfully misquoted, "HOW SHARPER THAN A SERPENT'S TOOTH IS A THANKLESS CHILD."

"Why is it that the word 'another' is the cruelest word in the language, Pop?"

"How d'ya mean?"

"Well, when he's alone with himself a man may get real honest and acknowledge—and accept—that he is a fool. But nobody wants to be 'just' *another* fool. 'Another couple of dumb Atlases,' he called us, and of all the things he said that hurt the most."

"Here now—easy! Here, use this here bar rag. Be right back." While Freddy wiped his eyes, the old man quickly filled a tray of orders for the waiter. By the time he returned Freddy was under control and had begun repairing his makeup with a hand mirror. "See here," Pop said, "if you're hip deep in used food, well, maybe you could climb out. But if you see a whole other bunch of people hip deep too, then the chances of you becoming the rare one to climb out seem to go down drastic. But you see, that's a kind of optical illusion. All those others don't affect *your* odds atall. What matters is how bad *you* want to get up out of the shit, and what purchase you can find for your feet."

Freddy took a sip of his new beer, and sighed. "Thanks, Pop. I think you're into something."

"Sure. Don't let that kid throw you. Did he tell you his parents divorced *him*? Mental cruelty, by the Jesus."

Freddy blinked, then roared with laughter.

"Now take that beer on back to your wife, she's looking kind o' shell-shocked. Oh, and I would recommend the redhead over in the corner, the funny-looking boy with the holes in his shoes. He's worth getting to know better, he's got some stuff."

Freddy stared at him, then raised his glass and drank deep. "Thanks again, Pop."

"Any time, son," the old man said easily, and went off to punch up two Scotches and a chocolate ice cream soda.

THE THERMALS OF AUGUST

Edward Bryant

The imaginative ingenuity of science fiction writers isn't confined to figuring out new suggestions for saving the world or escaping from a black hole; sometimes our authors' extrapolations are much more modest, as for instance in this story of a future sport of flying kites. But these are certainly no ordinary kites—nor are the people who fly them quite the sort you meet every day.

Edward Bryant has won two Nebula Awards and his fiction has appeared in all the major SF publications as well as in others such as *National Lampoon* and *Rolling Stone*. He lives in Denver and is, among other things, a novice parachutist.

I SEE THE WOMAN DIE, AND THE INITIAL BEAUTY of the event takes away my breath. Later I will feel the sickness of pain, the weakness of sorrow. But for the moment I sit transfixed, face tilted toward the irregular checkerboard of cumulus. The drama of death has always seemed to me the truest element in life.

The other diners see what I had detected a moment before: a tiny irregularity in the smooth sweep of the newly launched kite. The kite is cobalt blue and dart-shaped, apparently a modified Rogallo wing—not one of the Dragons we'll all be flying later in the week.

Having come to the outdoor café by Bear Creek for a late breakfast, I'd hoped simply to satisfy a necessary but unwanted need. Now, however, the bite of croissant lies dry in my mouth and the cup of coffee cools undrunk. Perhaps I did not really see the minute lurch in the kite's path. I allow myself that one brief luxurious hope, staring at the kite and its pilot more than two thousand feet above the valley floor. The kite is a vivid midge against the lighter blue of the sky.

Then the kite falls.

I see the craft first slip into a stall, then nose downward —no problem for even a moderately experienced pilot. But suddenly half the wing folds back at an unnatural angle. In a little more than a second, we on the ground hear the twang and snap of breaking control wires and twisting aluminium frame.

The kite tumbles.

I am surrounded by babble and one of the other diners begins to whimper.

It seems to take forever to fall.

My brain coolly goes back to work and I know that the descent is far more rapid in terms of feet per second than appears to our eyes.

At first the kite fell like a single piece of confetti pitched from a Wall Street window. Now the collapsed portion of the wing has wrapped around pilot and harness, and the warped mass rotates as it appears to us to grow larger.

The crippled kite twists and spins, flutters and falls like a leaf of aspen. I think I see the shrouded form of the pilot, a pendulum flung outward by centrifugal force.

The kite's fall seems to accelerate as it nears ground, but that also is illusion. Someone screams at us to take cover, evidently thinking that the kite will plunge into the midst of the outdoor diners. It doesn't. The kite makes half a final revolution and spins into the corner of the Conoco Building. The cocooned pilot slams into the brick with the flat smack of a beef roast dropped onto kitchen tile. The wreckage drapes over the temporary barbed-wire fence protecting this building under perpetual reconstruction.

The bit of croissant still lies on my tongue. I feel every sharp edge. I gag and taste bitterness coat my throat.

The dead-moth corpse of the kite is not more than fifty feet away, and the crowd slowly begins to close the distance. I am among them. The others grant me a wide path because most recognize that I too am a pilot. "Let the woman through." Gingerly I approach my fallen comrade.

Her body is almost totally swathed in the cobalt fabric of the kite. I can see her face; her eyes stare open and unpeacefully. The concealed contours of her body are smooth. I suspect most of the bones of her body are splintered.

When I softly touch one of her shoulders, I inadvertently drag one tightly folded flap of kitewing against a steel barb. Pooled blood bursts forth in a brief cataract. Mixed with the scent of her blood is the odor of urine.

This is not death; it is indignity.

My nylon windbreaker is composed of my colors: gold and black. I take it off and cover the dead woman's face. Then I glare around the circle of onlookers. Most of them stare at the ground and mumble, then turn and leave.

I draw back the jacket for a moment and lightly kiss the dead woman's lips.

I love this town between festivals. Living among the stable population of two thousand refreshes me after months of engulfment in the cities of the coasts. I am pleased by the ambivalent socialness of friendly greetings on the street, but without anyone pushing me to respond further. Warm people who hold a fetish of privacy are an impossible paradox elsewhere. This town prides itself on paradox.

The rules do not always hold true in the public downtown, particularly during the festivals. The outsiders flood in at various times of the year for their chamber music and jazz festivals, art symposiums, video circus, and other, more esoteric gatherings.

Although the present festival will not begin until tomorrow at dawn, the town is crowded with both participants and spectators. Tonight people fill the bars downtown and spill out onto the sidewalks along both sides of Main. Though August is not yet ended, the cold crisps the night. The town is at nearly nine thousand feet, and chill is to be expected; but the plumes of breath billow more than one would expect. The stars are clear and icy tonight; I see clouds scudding up the valley from the west.

There is a shifting, vibrant energy in the crowds that runs like quicksilver. I can feel it. The moon tonight is new, so I can't ascribe anything to lunar influence. The magic must generate from the gestalt interaction of the flyers and the watchers. Or, more likely, from the ancient mountains that ring us on three sides.

The air seems most charged in the Club Troposphere, the street-front bar on the ground floor of the Ionic Hotel. I have a table in one of the Trope's raised bay display windows overlooking the sidewalk. The crowd flux continually alters, but at any given moment, at least a dozen others share the table with me. Some stand, some sit, and in the crowd din, body language communicates at least as much as words. I'm stacking empties of imported beers in front of my glass. This early in the evening, my pyramid looks more Aztec than Egyptian.

I continue to taste blood; the thick, dark ale won't wash it away. Before I truly realize what I'm doing, I grasp the latest empty by the neck and slam it down on the hardwood. "God *damn!*" Amber glass sprays across the table and I raise the jagged edges of the neck to the level of my eyes.

"Mairin!" Across the table I see Lark look up from nuzzling Haley's throat. "Mairin, are you all right?" he says. Haley stares at me as well. Everyone at the table is staring at me.

"I dropped it," I say. I set the severed neck down beside my glass.

Lark gets up from Haley's lap and comes around the table to me. I stare from one to the other of the vertices of my present triangle. Lark is small, compact, and dark, with the sense of spatial orientation and imagination and the steel muscles, all of which make him a better Dragon pilot than anyone else here. With the probable exception of me. Haley is tall and light, a woman of the winter with silky hair to her waist and eyes like ice chipped from inaccessible glaciers. But when she smiles, the ice burns.

"Are you okay?" Lark places his fingers lightly on the hand with which I smashed the bottle. I move the hand and pick up my glass. A barmaid hovers beside us, wiping shards into a paper towel.

I nod. "It was an accident."

Lark puts his face very close to mine. "The rookie who died today—you saw the whole thing, right?"

"I saw her get into the truck for the ride up to the point. She was very young. I didn't know her."

"She was good," Lark says. "I know people who flew with her in the Midwest. Today she was very unlucky."

"Obviously."

"That's not what I meant." Lark smiles in the way I've learned to interpret during the long years of competition as all teeth and no mirth. "After the medics took her body away from you practically at gunpoint, I went over her equipment with the officials. She committed a beginner's error, you know—dipped a wingtip when she went off. Clipped an outcropping."

"I saw," I say. "She recovered."

"We did X rays. There was a flaw in the metal. That's why the one wing buckled."

"God." I feel sick, dizzy, as though I'm whirling around in that bright cobalt body bag, waiting for the ground to smash out my life.

"Whoever," Lark says. "Just bad luck." He hesitates.

"I keep thinking about all the times I've inspected my own equipment. You can only check so much."

Haley has come around the table too and stands close to Lark. "I wonder what it felt like."

"I know," I say. I look at Lark's face and realize he knows too. Haley is an artist and photographer who sticks close to her gallery here in town. She has never flown. She can never know.

I'm really not sure how many beers I've drunk tonight. It must be more than I think I've counted, because I do and say what is uncharacteristic of me. With Lark and Haley both standing there, I look into Haley's winter eyes and say, "I need to be with someone tonight."

"I—Mairin—" Haley almost stutters. She gentles her voice. "Lark asked me already. . . ."

"Lark could unask you," I say. I know that's unfair, but I also know my need. Lark is staring studiously out the window, pretending to ignore us both.

Haley says, "Lark was there too. He needs—"

"*I* need." They both stare at me uncomfortably now without speaking. Individually I know how stubborn each can be. Three springs tauten. I want to reach out and be held, to thaw and exhaust myself with body warmth. I want to reach out with the shattered bottleneck and rip both of them until I bathe in steaming blood. Then it all goes out from me and I sink back in my chair. I am so goddamned suspicious of the word *need* and I have heard it too many times.

"I'm sorry," I say. "I'm behaving badly."

"Mairin—" both start to say. Lark touches my shoulder. Haley reaches out.

I shove back my chair and get up unsteadily. My head pounds. Nausea wracks my belly and I am glad there is no competition for me tomorrow. "I'm going to my room. I don't feel . . ." I let the words trail off.

"Do you need help?"

"No, Haley. No, love. I can make it." I push past and leave them at the table. I hope I'm leaving my self-pity there too. The lobby of the Ionic is another zoo of milling humans. I make it to the lone elevator where luck has brought the cage to the first floor. As I enter the car, a bearded flyer-groupie in a yellow down jacket unwisely reaches in from the lobby and grabs my wrist.

"Lady, would you like a drink?" he says.

The spring, still taut, ratchets loose. Luckily for him my knee catches him only in the upper thigh and he flails backward into the lobby as spectators gape. The doors close and the elevator climbs noisily toward my floor. Two young men stand nervously in the opposite corner, just as far from me as four feet will allow.

I'll regret all this tomorrow.

I know the woman who comes to me that night.
I am she.
The cotton sheet slides coolly, rustling, as I restlessly change position. I've pushed the down comforter to my knees. It's too hot for that. The cold will come later, past midnight when the hotel lowers all the thermostats.

Finally I despair of sleeping, lie still, lie on my back with my hands beside me. I can see dimly in the light from the frosted-glass transom, as well as the white glow from the hotel neon outside the single window. I hear the muffled sounds of celebration from the street below.

Then I see the woman standing silently at the foot of the bed. I know her. She is short—five four without shoes. Her body is slender and muscular. The shadows shift as she moves around to the side of my bed. Darkness glides across her eyes, her neck, between her breasts, on her belly and below. Her breasts are small, with dark, prominent nipples. Her muscles, when she moves, are not obtrusive but are clearly delineated.

She steps into the light from the street. There are no crow's-feet visible in chiaroscuro. Her face is delicately boned, heart-shaped, with a chin that misses sharpness by only a degree. Her eyes are wide and as dark as her close-cut hair. In the semidarkness I know I am seeing her as she was when she was twenty and as she will be when she is forty.

I slip the sheet aside as she silently lies in my bed. Slowly, delicately, I slide the fingers of one hand along the side of her face, down the jawline, across her lips. Her lips part slightly and one fingertip touches the firm, moist cushion of her tongue.

Then even more gently I cup her breasts, my palms feeling their warmth long before the skin touches the tips of each erect nipple.

It takes a thousand years.

My hands slide down her flanks and touch all that is

moist and warm between her legs. I know what to seek out and I find it. The warmth builds.

I think of Haley. I think of Lark. I blink him out. Haley leaves of her own accord and abandons me pleading. My pleading, her leaving.

My finger orbits and touches, touches and orbits, touches. The warmth builds and builds, is more than warmth, builds and heats, the heat— The heat coils and expands, ripples outward, ripples across my belly, down my thighs. For a moment, just a bare moment, something flickers like heat lightning on the horizon.

—but it is not sufficient. I am not warm enough.

Heat radiates and is lost, spent. I see Lark and Haley again in my mind and blink away the man. But Haley leaves too.

Only I am left.

I wish the woman would sleep, but I know her too well. I wish I could sleep, but I know me so well.

Dragon Festival.

It is nearly dawn and the roar of dragons splits the chilly air. The tongues of propane burners lick the hearts of twenty great balloons. The ungainly shapes bulk in the near darkness and slowly come erect. The crews hold tight to nylon lines.

As the sun starts to rise above the peaks beyond the two waterfalls, I see that snow dusted the San Juans sometime past midnight. The mountains are topped with weresnow—a sifting that came in the night and will shortly vanish with morning sun. The real storms are yet to come with the autumn.

Mythic creatures rear up in the dawn. These are nothing so simple as the spherical balloons of my childhood. Laboratory-bred synthetics have been sculpted and molded to suggest the shapes of legend. A great golden gargoyle hunches to the east. To the west, a hundred-foot-tall gryphon strains at its handlers' lines. The roaring, rushing propane flames animate a sphinx, a satyr, a kraken with basket suspended from its drooping tentacles, a Cheshire cat, and chimeras of every combination. The giants bob and dip as they distend, but it is a perfect morning with no wind.

I find a perverse delight in not feeling as wretched as I anticipated last night. My mind is clear. My eyes do not ache. Though I was not able to cope with breakfast food, I did manage to drink tea. I realize I'm being caught up in the exhilaration of the first festival day. I know that within the hour I will be flowing with the wind, floating with the clouds.

"How do you feel this morning?" A familiar voice.

"Did you get any rest?" Another familiar voice.

I turn to greet Haley and Lark. "I feel fine. I got some sleep." I determine to leave any qualifications behind.

"I'll see you on the ground," says Lark.

Haley looks at me steadily for several seconds, a time that seems much longer. Finally she draws me close and says, "Good luck. Have a fine flight." Her lips are cool and they touch my cheek briefly.

Lark and she walk toward the balloon called *Cheshire*. I hear fragmented words from a portable public-address system that tell me all flyers should be linking their craft to their respective balloons. I walk across the meadow to *Negwenya*. *Negwenya* is the Zulu word for dragon. *Negwenya* is a towering black-and-scarlet balloon owned by a man named Robert Simms. Robert's eight-times-removed grandparents were Zulu. Robert is a great believer in the mystique of dragons and sees an occult affinity between *Negwenya* and the Dragon Five flyers he ferries up to the sky.

I walk between the serpentine legs of *Negwenya* and feel the sudden chill of entering shadow. The people holding *Negwenya*'s lines, mostly local volunteers, greet me and I answer them back. From where he waits beside my Dragon Five, Robert raises a broad hand in welcome. My gold-and-black glider looks as fragile on the wet grass as it did in the electric glow when I left to watch the coming dawn.

"You ready?" Robert's voice is permanently hoarse from a long-ago accident when a mooring line snapped and lashed around his throat.

"I'm ready." I check the tough lightweight lines that will allow my Dragon to dangle below *Negwenya* as the balloon takes us up to twelve thousand feet. The ends of the lines tuck into safety pressure catches both on the underside of *Negwenya*'s gondola and on my craft's keel tube and wing braces. Either Robert or I can elect at any time to release the catches. Once that happens, *Negwenya* will go on about its own business and I will describe the great descending spiral that eventually brings me back to earth.

More orders blare from the bullhorn across the field. It doesn't matter that none of us can understand the words; we all know what happens next.

"Let's link up," says Robert.

I nod and climb into my harness under the Five as Robert and a helper hold the wings steady on the support stands. It isn't like getting ready to fly a 767; just a few metallic clicks and the appropriate straps are secured. I pull on my helmet and check the instrumentation: the microprocessor-based unit in the liner records air speed, ground speed, and altitude. The figures appear on a narrow band along the inside of the transparent visor. There is an audible stall warning, but I rarely activate that; I'd rather gauge stability directly from the air flutter on the wing fabric.

"Okay, just a few more minutes," says Robert.

I'm glad the Five is resting on the supports. The entire craft may weigh only sixty pounds, but that's half what I weigh. My flight suit feels sticky along the small of my back; I'm sweating. I hear the amplified words of the pageant director continue to fragment on the leading edge of the mountain.

"Time to do it," says Robert. He climbs up to the launch ladder and steps into the gondola. Then he looks back over the edge—I see the reflection in the bulge of my visor—and grins. "Good luck, lady." He displays an erect thumb. "Break a leg."

With a rush and a roar, the twenty lighter-than-air craft embark. The paradox is that with all the fury and commotion, the score of balloons rises so slowly. Our ascension is stately.

Excited as ever by the sight, I watch the images of ground things diminish. I see the takeoff field swarm with video people; the insect eyes of cameras glitter. From beyond the ropes, the sustained note of the crowd swells with the balloons' first rising.

Harpies, genies, furies all, we soar toward a morning clear but for high cirrus. I fill my lungs with chill clean air and feel the exuberance, the climactic anticipation of that moment when each of us cuts loose the tether from our respective balloons and glides into free flight.

Free is the word, free is the key. I know I'm smiling; and then I feel the broad, loose grin. My teeth ache with the cold, but it doesn't matter. I want to laugh madly and I restrain myself only because I know I can afford to waste none of the precious oxygen at this altitude.

The weather's fine!

I raise a gloved hand to Lark as *Cheshire* slowly rises past *Negwenya*. His brown-and-yellow wings bob slightly as he waves back. The grin on *Cheshire*'s cat doesn't seem nearly so wide as mine.

The valley town is a parti-colored patchwork. I glance up and scan the line of red figures along my visor. I'm a thousand feet above the meadow. I look from the comfortable brick and frame of the old town to the newer, wooden, fake Victorian homes rising from the mountain's skirts. Now I'm level with the end of the trees and the beginning of bare rock. To the east I look beyond the old Pandora Mill and see the sun catch the spray from Ingram Falls and Bridal Veil. The waterfalls have not yet been turned off for the winter.

Toward the top of the canyon, light crosswinds buffet the balloons slightly as I expected they would. *Negwenya* rotates slowly and I concentrate on feeling no vertigo. We sweep past a sheer rock face to the waves and shouted greetings of a party of climbers strung like colored beads from their ropes. The balloon pilots yell back.

I can intellectually understand the attraction of technical climbing, but I was never able to appreciate it on a gut level. And I tried. Perhaps the only level on which it communicates to me is: *because it's there. Haley.* I wonder if I should desire Haley so intensely if she were more accessible. Even the anticipation of the coming long flight cannot erase the chill and heat of her from my mind.

"Mairin!"

I hear Robert's shout above the rushing-wind sound of the burner.

"Mairin, are you watching your gauge?"

I hadn't been. *Negwenya*'s at twelve-seven and it won't be long before we're thirteen thousand feet above sea level. While I was thinking about sapphire eyes, like a rank amateur, the other flyers had been cutting loose from their balloons. Below me I see the looping, swarming flight of Dragons.

I glance at the readouts again. Robert has assured my wind direction. I drop.

My Dragon Five drops away from the gondola and *Negwenya*'s roar grows faint; then is gone. The silence of my flight enfolds me. I lie prone in my harness, nothing else between me and the valley but air.

I fly for this moment.

The microprocessor's electronic senses tell me hard information: I am 2,962 feet above the valley floor. My air speed is twenty-two miles per hour, only slightly less than my ground speed. My Dragon Five presently travels nearly twelve feet horizontally for every foot it drops. In a minute I will lose about two hundred feet. Without searching out the thermal currents, I'll reach the ground in about fifteen minutes.

I pay no attention to the readouts. For the moment, the silence and openness, the caress of air on my face, all stir a complex reaction in my mind and body. I feel the throbbing start, far inside.

The slight shift of my body affects the attitude of my flight. The Dragon responds and I sweep into a wide, shallow turn.

No women or men have given me this feeling so fully as has the sky. I spiral down above the land and desire this to last forever. Gravity is the enemy of my love. As well I remind myself that I am part of the pageant; that just as the balloons are now drifting eastward, engaged in their slow-motion behemoth race, so it's demanded of the flyers that all land at about the same time in a live simulation of wide-screen spectacle. The cameras whir. The broadcasts fan out from microwave towers. The spectators watch.

But I want to make it last.

And I realize, first shocked, then amused, how many minutes it's been since I've held Haley's image in my mind.

I wheel the Dragon around in a descending spiral, as silent and graceful as any gull. Catching up with the other Dragons, I hear the mutter of wind rippling the fabric ever closer to the wing's trailing edge. I recognize the proximity of a stall and moderate slightly the angle of the warperons.

There are times when I have thought of gently and irrevocably slipping into the tightest of spirals and hurling myself blackly through the heart of the air. I cannot count the times I have skirted that final edge. Always I've refrained.

The air touches my cheekbones with the soft, tickling touch of Haley's cloudy hair.

There are times . . .

Death in triplicate stands by my elbow at the bar. Three tall shapes in black hooded robes have stepped to the brass rail. Skull faces, obviously sculpted with care, grin from cowled shadows. They say nothing. The trio reminds me of participants in a Mexican holy-day parade.

Two deaths stare around the crowded Trope. The other looks at me. With my beer, I toast it back silently.

"Hey! You people want anything?" The barman tonight is one of the Trope's owners. With the Dragon Festival now started, all possible personnel are needed to service the crowds.

Three bony grins turn to smile at him. There are no words.

After a pause the owner says, "Listen, this is for paying customers. You want something?"

Three shrouded figures lean across the bar toward him. The owner draws back. "Drink," he says, "or get out."

Dead silence.

He apparently decides he's outnumbered. "Shit," the owner mutters, and goes off to wait on newcomers at the end of the bar. I think I hear a giggle from the death figure farthest from me. The nearest turns again to face me. Again I raise a glass in toast.

The figure reaches, hand ivory with makeup, into a pocket beneath the robes and withdraws an object. Then it extends the hand toward me. I accept a small skull made of spun sugar, another relic of Mexican religious celebrations. I incline my head gravely and set the candy skull beside my glass.

The nearest figure turns back to its fellows. I hear a whispered consultation. Then all three leave the bar together. As they reach the door, the barman shouts, "Good goddamn riddance!" He walks past me on the way to the cash register and I hear him say in a lower voice, "Give me the creeps."

"Friends of yours?"

I turn to face Haley and Lark. I hadn't seen them coming. "Friends of ours." I shrug.

"Spooky," says Haley.

"Striking masks," says Lark.

"Want a beer?"

"We're already set," says Lark. "We've got a table back behind the grove of rubber plants. Do you want to join us?"

I toss down the final swallow of beer. "Thanks, no. Not yet. I'm going to get some fresh air before I do any more drinking. You want to come along?"

Lark shakes his head. "We've got to do some drinking before we get some more fresh air."

"Then I'll see you both later. I need the air." I pick up the spun-sugar skull and gnaw on the jaw region as I push through the crowd.

Outside it's warmer than it was last night. There is cloud cover; I suspect the San Juans will be solidly snow-capped by morning. I zip the front of my flight jacket and stick my balled fists into the pockets. Turning right, I head along Main toward the landing meadow. I see the amber lights of trucks still bringing in and unloading the deflated forms of the racing balloons. I heard earlier that Robert Simms and *Negwenya* won. I decide that's a good omen.

"Girl? Hey, stop a moment, girl."

I turn and look toward the source of the voice. I'm in front of the Teller House, the town's lone real department store. I look into the display window and see the life-sized image of an elderly ragged woman staring back at me. It's an argee screen—the name comes from the initials of the people who started setting up these synchronous video arrangements back in the late seventies. One enormous complex of electronic art, the argee screens are spotted in cities and towns around the globe. Each screen shows a live, life-sized, simultaneous transmission of a street scene somewhere else in the world. Sound and video equipment beam my voice and image back to the linked screen. A computer randomly changes the linkages.

Right now the old woman sees and hears me. I see and hear her. I have no idea where she really is. The scene behind her is dark and obviously urban. It could be any nighttime city.

"I'm in Baltimore," she says. "Where are you?"

I tell her.

"Oh, yeah," she says. "I heard about you people. Saw

you on the news. Bunch of fools who jump off cliffs on kites."

I laugh. "Condors launch from cliffs."

"Birds aren't too smart."

"But they fly."

"Yeah." She inspects me seriously. "You one of them?"

"Do I fly?" I nod. "Not exactly on a kite, though."

Her voice is thirsty. "Tell me about it."

For some reason I cannot ignore the imperative in her voice. I tell her about flying. I describe my Dragon Five as the combination of a high-winged monoplane and a bat. I talk of tomorrow's competition. I paint with words the colors of the long, gliding dragon kite I will tow behind my Five. I tell her of the *manjha*, the razor-sharp cutting line with which I will attempt to sever the towline of my opponent's kite. And with which he or she will try to sever mine. But most of all, I describe the flying. I talk religiously of fighting maneuvers in the sky.

And when I pause for breath, she says, "Girl, God bless you." Her image flickers.

The argee screen relinks. I blink a moment at the light. I see a daylight scene under bright sun. In the background is something that looks vaguely like the Taj Mahal. A man in a white linen suit looks out of the screen at me. He inspects me and stares at the colors of my jacket. Slowly he nods his head as though comprehending something. He says, *"Woh kata hai?"*

I smile, spread my hands helplessly, and walk on.

Woh kata hai. I believe that's an Indian kite fighter's challenge.

Dreaming.

It's called a *pench* and I love it more than either soccer or skiing. Each of us stands in a circle about three yards in diameter; the circles are approximately twenty feet apart. The officials have limed the circles on the grass as they would stripe the yard lines for a football game. The breeze is light this morning, but it may kick up. I have brought several different sizes of fighting kites. When I look around at my competition, I generally have to tilt my head back. I am eleven years old.

My gear litters the close-cropped grass around my feet: kites, extra lines, a spare spool. My little brother, eight, sits boredly reading a science-fiction paperback just inside my circle. If I need it, he'll help with the launching.

I love Saturday mornings in general, but this particular one is the Michael Collins Annual Kite Fly. It's the second Saturday in September and it delights everyone except the high-school football coach who wanted to use this field for a practice scrimmage. Luckily the principal has an autographed picture of the Apollo 11 crew and is an old kite fighter himself, so that was that.

The kite-fighting contest isn't the only event today, but it's the only one that interests me. The *pench* should start in a few minutes, at nine, and will continue until noon. Since I've got some sort of reputation, I'm one of the flyers who get to start. Anyone who wants can take a turn standing in the opponent circle. If he loses, someone else takes his place. And if I lose, I'm out. Then I get to stand in line, waiting to challenge the current champions. I don't plan to spend a lot of time waiting in line.

This is an average Indian summer morning. It's cool now, but I'm guessing it's going to get very hot by midday. The nearest referee—Mr. Schindler, the junior-high shop teacher—tells us through his bullhorn that each contestant should be ready. My first opponent steps into the next circle. I don't know his last name, but his first name is Ken and he's really sure of himself. I tell him I wish him luck. Ken snickers. He's in at least eighth grade.

"You want help launching?" says my little brother.

"I can do the first one myself." I adjust the bridle on a middle-sized kite. The breeze is gentle but steady.

"Okay." His attention returns to his Robert Heinlein novel.

Ken's kite looks fourteen inches by a foot—too small. He's overestimating the wind velocity. Too bad.

"Launch 'em," says the referee.

I lightly throw my gold-and-black fighter into the air and pump the cotton string with my right hand: pull in, let out, pull in, let out, until the diamond-shaped kite gains lift in the breeze and begins to climb. I sneak a glance at Ken. His fighter autumnleafs into the ground. I catch his eye and smile. He glares before picking up his kite to launch again.

My kite is solidly airborne. I continue the rhythm of launch; now the pumping motions are longer, smoother, slower. With one handle of the spool anchored at my feet,

I stand at an angle to the nine-pound control line. String sings between thumb and forefinger of my left hand at shoulder level. I brake with right hand at right hip. My fighting kite soars. My mind goes with it and, for a moment, I look down at the field and see myself distantly below. I recognize me because of the colors of my jacket.

Ken has finally launched his kite, and is trying to gain altitude with brute force rather than subtlety. I pay out another hundred feet of line and feel the knot that signals I'm at the preagreed altitude. I practice wind-current turns with my kite and look bored. I know Ken's looking at me, but I studiously ignore him.

"Okay," says the referee. "You both got the altitude? Go to it."

The strategy is fairly simple. Each of us has a flying line of five hundred feet. Then there's one hundred feet of cutting line between that and the kite. The cutting line is *manjha,* ordinary four-stranded string coated with a mixture of egg, starch, and powdered glass. I mixed mine myself. The rules allow us to double-coat the line so that when it's dry, it can slice an opponent's line either from above or below. The winner of the competition is the flyer who has cut loose the greatest number of opponents' kites.

Ken opens the battle ferociously and heavy-handedly, diving his fighter at cross-angles to my string. I dive mine to compensate and am slightly faster. Ken cancels the tactic. That's a mistake too. I see his kite lurch sluggishly for just a moment. I pay out line and let my string rise into his. My index finger detects the slight vibration as the lines touch. I pull in and my fighter rises, tugging the cutting line against Ken's. His kite, severed, spins down with the wind while he reels in loose string. He does not look happy as my next competitor steps up to replace him.

"Good flight," says my little brother, and I'm not sure whether he's being sarcastic to Ken or to me.

My new opponent is a girl in the seventh grade who has just taken up fighting. She has promise, but very little experience. Her kite doesn't fly long after reaching fighting altitude.

It keeps going like that. In the first hour, I destroy five opponents. Next hour, six more. I let the competition keep their defeated kites if they can find them. Where would I store them all in my room?

Each hour we're allowed fifteen minutes out of competition. I use my time to change lines on my kite. Every time I cut someone else's line, my string loses some of its abrasive. I also adjust the bridle angle because the breeze continues to pick up.

The third and final hour gives me some better competition, but no one all that challenging. Not until Lark steps into the circle. He's even smaller than I am, but he's really tough. He's my age. We've grown up in the same small town and gone to school together from the first grade. We both started flying kites about the same time. Lark is the only one whose fighting ability I respect.

He nods to me and smiles, but says nothing as he launches his fighter. Even my little brother is interested in this contest, so he puts his paperback down for the while. "Mairin hasn't lost yet," he says to Lark.

"I'd hate to spoil her morning," Lark says, "but I'm feeling pretty good."

His kite soars on the late-morning heat. Lark's fighter is brown with bright yellow birdwings inset. "Okay," says Mr. Schindler, the referee. "This is the last one. It's almost noon."

At first Lark fights conservatively, not actively countering my spectacular strategies. The trouble is that my kite is all color. I dive on him like a falcon, swoop up from beneath, twirl my fighter across his like the blade of a buzz saw. Nothing happens. I know that much of the abrasive has been scraped from my cutting line by the seven competitions of the past hour. But I'm sure that at least a few feet of cutting edge remain on the line. It's a matter of finding it.

Lark realizes my problem and bides his time.

"Hey," says Mr. Schindler. "I want to go to lunch."

Lark makes his move. His brown-and-yellow fighter crosses the angle of my own string, then drops. My index finger feels the slight vibration as his line touches mine. Lark starts rolling his kite sideways. I compensate by letting out more string and somehow neither line cuts. What does happen, though, each of us discovers simultaneously through fingertips. Our lines have become entangled. Lark's expression is grim.

"Don't worry," I call. I pay out more string as I simultaneously give the line a series of small tugs. Instead of rotating my kite so as to unwind our lines, I rotate to wrap them tighter. Then I pull.

I cut Lark's string, and capture his kite because the upper line is still entwined with mine, all at the same time.

"Mairin!" He sounds furious. My eyes are on the two fighters.

"What?"

His voice moderates as I begin to reel in the kites. "It was a good contest."

I'll keep his kite in my room. For now, I lower my gaze to him and say, "Yes, it was very good." Unaccountably I want to run across to his circle and hug him. I would like to kiss him.

Hug Lark? Kiss him? I sit upright suddenly, supported on my elbows, and stare confusedly at the curtained light. My room in the Ionic Hotel takes on a dawn reality. I glance to the side. Beside me, a humped form snores beneath the comforter. It's not Lark; I know that.

Lark? I didn't grow up with him; we come from opposite sides of the continent. We did not match our kites in childhood. My disorientation causes me to touch my face gently with my fingers to see if I am still who I think I am.

I try to recapture something of the dream. There is an elusive truth I'm missing.

Skyfighters.

We spend our lives riding the thermals, those great columns of heated air that lend lift to our machines and spirits. The thermals rise because they are warmer than the surrounding air. We look for the clues and seek them out, using them as elevators to the sky.

The best thermals generate in this valley from mid to late afternoon. Since there are two competitors remaining in the Dragon festival contests, that time has been reserved for them. The sun has begun its descent into the open western end of the valley and the colors are, as always, spectacular. Crimson tongues lick through the cumulus.

Lark is one competitor; I am the other. All but we have seen our towed Dragon kites spin down the long drop into mountainside, forest, or town, where the children vie to find the many-colored Dragons and rip them to shreds.

Our duel will climax the festival.

Negwenya and *Cheshire* are waiting to ferry us both to a minimal fighting altitude. Then we will ride the thermals. Today Haley walks with me across the staging meadow. Her hand is in mine.

"You do talk in your sleep, you know," Haley says. "Do you know that?" Without an answer, she continues, "Some of the time the words are clear. Sometimes you simply make sounds and your body moves. You're a restless sleeper. I sleep like a lizard on a hot rock." She laughs. "Did you notice?"

I nod.

Her expression turns serious. "I know last night was important to you—at least it was before last night." Her smile is indecipherable. "Now isn't the time to ask you things, I suppose." She hesitates, and her grip tightens in mine. "People don't work well as goals for you. That's my game." Now I see sadness in her face. "You love the sky more."

We have reached *Negwenya*. Robert Simms waits with his assistants by my Dragon Five. Haley enfolds me in her arms and kisses me a long time on the lips. "Fly well," she whispers, then turns and walks across the field toward *Cheshire*.

I realize I'm crying, and I'm not sure yet why.

"Time to link up," says Robert, and his harsh, rope-scarred voice sounds to me softer than usual. I fasten myself into the harness of the Dragon Five. I check to make sure the bridle of my fighting kite is securely fastened to the winch post projecting downward from the Five's keel tube, just behind the point to which my legs extend. The fighting kite is a long, serpentine Dragon of mylar, painted in my colors. It has the oval face and trailing, snakelike body characteristics of Dragon kites. The only differences are the additional lifting surfaces and stabilizing fins.

The flight is ready to begin. I look across to *Cheshire*. Lark gives me a thumbs-up sign and Haley waves. At *Negwenya*, Robert offers me a brilliant smile and his ritual "Break a leg, lady." And we launch.

At twelve thousand feet, *Negwenya* floats almost directly above the immense tailings pond of the moribund Pandora Mine. The bright white tailings heap looks like some malignant thing beached between creek and trees. I think of kids singing their technological jingles when the wind rises and sifts white dust from the tailings down across the town: "Hexa, hexa, hexa-valent chromium!"

I notice that the aspen on the steep sides of the valley are starting to turn prematurely. Great slashes of golden yellow have suddenly appeared within twenty-four hours. No aspen is an island. The root systems of groves are interconnected. When the chlorophyll breaks down in one tree's leaves in the autumn, so goes its extended family.

I had seen broken cumulus above the valley when I linked up to *Negwenya*. Scattered puffy formations are the giveaway signs of thermals, since condensation forms atop the pillars of warm air. The problem is that clouds move with the wind and usually only indicate where the thermals *were*. Extrapolation and a few good guesses should gain my ride up.

At twelve-five, I release the pressure catches and the Five drops away from *Negwenya*. I crane my neck and see that Lark has also dropped. In terms of radiated heat, both of us are more likely to find thermals over the tailings pond or the rooftops of town than above the darker fields or forest. Lark seems to be making for the pond. I stretch my body, feel the muscles loosen, and wheel my Dragon toward the center of town.

The scarlet sunset momentarily dazzles my eyes. I guessed correctly. I feel the left wing rise slightly, indicating I am skirting a thermal. I bring the nose down and turn into it; then feel the mild confirming bump that I am all the way in. Now what I have to do is stay inside the current in a gentle ascending spiral until I've reached the prearranged altitude. In this case, that is fifteen thousand feet. Neither Lark nor I want to try for altitude records today, though kite pilots here have gone above eighteen thousand without oxygen.

Up, up, and the readout on my visor lists off the numbers. As I rise in the thermal column, I touch the button on my control bar that unreels the line tethering my fighter. The black-and-gold dragon shape drops below and behind my Five. The lift ratio of the kite with its fins is excellent, so it takes a few moments before it is gliding behind the Dragon. I pay out the entire hundred feet of line. Dragon follows Dragon like an offspring trailing the parent.

I am allowed fifty feet, half the tether, to be cutting line. But where the abrasive lengths are placed, and indeed *what* lengths are made abrasive, are up to me. Equipment officials carefully checked before launch to ensure that no more than fifty percent of the Dragon's towline is a cutting surface. Like shagreen, the surface cuts only in one direction.

As I swing back across the town, I see that Lark is ascending above the tailings pond. I see his Dragon followed by the brown-and-yellow fledgling that is his fighter.

At fifteen thousand feet, the air is thin and painfully crisp. The sunlight feels as if it's striking my eyes with sharp edges until I polarize my visor. Now that it's time to leave the thermal, I exit on the upwind side to minimize altitude loss in the cooler surrounding air.

Lark and I stalk each other like soaring birds. These Dragons are not the Indian fighting kites of childhood. There are no sudden moves—or rarely. Maneuvers tend to be graceful and conservative, to minimize loss of altitude.

We sweep by each other in a wide pass and I estimate I'm about one hundred feet higher than Lark. From one point of view, we might seem to be tracing arabesques across the sky. From a more realistic referent, we circle each other like hungry, cautious predators.

Lark loops back in a figure eight and sails along still below, but parallel to me. I assume he is offering bait and try to guess how many moves ahead he's thinking. My craft and I are slightly heavier than he and his; my sink rate is higher and so I'm gradually descending to his altitude. I'm in a position to wing over and pounce, but that's the expectable thing. Lark doesn't expect me to do the expected: so I do it.

I hit the warperons hard; the ends of my wings deform and peel me into a steep, descending bank. I'm losing vertical advantage fast, but my Dragon is cutting down hard behind Lark's tail. It should have been an easy victory except that Lark reacts as though anticipating me—and I have the bemused thought that he probably was. The brown-and-yellow Dragon matches me move for move. If he's not duplicating the exact angle of bank and degree of dive, I can't tell the difference.

Damn it! Frustration moderates my caution as I slam the Dragon into a reverse-angle bank. Stabilized fabric crackles like firecrackers; the aluminum skeleton groans.

Lark predicted that one too. I know the long lenses on the ground are taking all this in. I hope the viewers are enjoying it.

The hell with this. I tighten my downward spiral, knowing that sooner or later I'll suck him out of the tactic. Either that or we'll hit the ground together.

Any others would have pulled out of this falling-moth spiral in some sort of sane maneuver that should have allowed me to use the slim remaining margin of altitude to cross their fighter's tether with my cutting line. At times I must remind myself that Lark is no saner than I. One moment I'm aware that I'm still sinking closer to Lark and in a relatively short time am going to be right on top of him. The next moment Lark reverses the pitch of his spiral in an aching, crushing maneuver that neither rips off his wings nor puts him into a stall. I see brown fabric rush past my right eye, so close that I recoil slightly. *Jesus!* One track of my mind wonders how close his cutting line came to severing my wing—or my head.

I don't know what he's planning, but I won't equal his suicide maneuver. As I level off less precipitously, I see Lark to my right, apparently fleeing. I look beyond his Dragon and know this is not an abdication of the field. Lark is making for what appears to be a great funnel of birds soaring upward. They're in a thermal.

Rather than seek out my own thermal, I pursue Lark, hoping to catch him before he reaches the elevator. The epinephrine surge from Lark's spectacular maneuver starts to abate, leaving tinglings in my chest and hands. I will the Dragon to fly faster; other than that I can do nothing but let the craft sail serenely along. I enjoy the silence. I remember the network coverage of a previous Dragon tourney in which, as a novelty, audio technicians had dubbed in the wasp-buzz sounds of old, piston-engined fighter planes. It was amusing at first, but ultimately offensive.

I am close to Lark, but not close enough as he enters the thermal and begins his ascent. I glance at my altimeter readout: ten-seven. That means we were about a thousand feet above the town when Lark pulled out of the spiral. I trust all the groundlings were suitably thrilled. At a thousand feet, people truly *do* look like ants.

The gentle bump of entering the warmer air rocks the Dragon's nose and I start to follow Lark vertically. As I go into the ascending bank, I sneak a look behind and see that my black-and-gold fighter is still trailing. Good. It hasn't occurred to me in these past minutes to check. It's an article of faith that I won't lose the Dragon kite through mechanical accident or chance.

Again because he's lighter, Lark rises faster in the thermal than I. I resign myself fatalistically to the ride up and start to think like a tourist. I never, *never* think like a tourist. But now I look at the aspen, or I stare down at the checkerboard town, or I think about the act of flight rather than feeling it. Or something.

Something!

I look up and stare and react—try to do all those things at once. Lark hasn't done as I anticipated. He has not waited until achieving the fighting altitude. No need—no rule that says he must. Instead he swoops upon me like a hawk at prey.

His Dragon grows in my vision. I watch. I know I must choose a maneuver, but something else bids me wait. By now I should be reacting unconsciously. If my conscious is at work, it's now too late. There are several possible defensive maneuvers. So far today, Lark has correctly anticipated my every movement.

—large, so large. Brown and—

I must choose, I must—I do nothing.

That is my choice.

Lark does not anticipate it. Our vectors merge. His Dragon slams into mine with a force I could probably calculate, except—except I cannot think. I don't know if I'm hurt or if I'm in shock. I feel nothing. I simply know a buffeting like a great wind has seized us. I realize we are flying a ragged craft composited of bits and pieces of our two Dragons: snapped, flailing wires, twisted tubing, rent fabric. Lark hangs in his harness only a few feet from me, but he doesn't look up.

My vision skips like the frames in a badly spliced film. I see the golden aspen and the town spread out in the valley below us. I see Lark start to raise his head. Blood covers one side of his face. Droplets fly backward from his head like a fan.

I see the truth in that scarlet spray.

It is a long moment suspended in time.

Then it falls.

We fall—as bits of shattered Dragon spin away from us like colored confetti. I try to reach out toward Lark, but I can move only one arm. He stares back at me and I think he's alive. The sky, I try to tell him. At least we're in the sky. There could have been so many other ways. But the sky— Those who fly there are more important than any others.

Wind sucks the breath from my lungs. Lark, I try to say. Friend. I was wrong, I think Haley knows. Lovers. I should have—

I see green fields below.

Lark, it should have been us. We know the sky—

And the ground rises up like a fist.

GOING UNDER

≈≈≈≈≈≈≈≈≈≈≈≈≈≈≈≈

Jack Dann

From future sports we turn to future vacations
—how about a trip on the maiden voyage of
the *Titanic?* You can bring along a robot recreation of your late father's head for company
and advice. (Despite that description, this is
anything but a frivolous story.)

Jack Dann, who lives in Johnson City, New
York, is well known as both author and an-
thologist. His latest novel is *The Man Who
Melted;* his new anthology, coedited with Gardner Dozois, is *Unicorns.*

SHE WAS BEAUTIFUL, HUGE, AS GRACEFUL AS A racing liner. She was a floating Crystal Palace, as magnificent as anything J. P. Morgan could conceive. Designed by Alexander Carlisle and built by Harland and Wolff, she wore the golden band of the company along all nine hundred feet of her. She rose one hundred and seventy-five feet like the side of a cliff, with nine steel decks, four sixty-two-foot funnels, over two thousand windows and sidelights to illuminate the luxurious cabins and suites and public rooms. She weighed forty-six thousand tons, and her reciprocating engines and Parsons-type turbines could generate over fifty-thousand horsepower and speed the ship over twenty knots. She had a gymnasium, a Turkish bath, squash and racket courts, a swimming pool, libraries and lounges and sitting rooms. There were rooms and suites to accommodate seven hundred and thirty-five first-class passengers, six hundred and seventy-four in second class, and over a thousand in steerage.

She was the *RMS Titanic,* and Stephen met Esme on her Promenade Deck as she pulled out of her Southampton dock, bound for New York on her maiden voyage.

Esme stood beside him, resting what appeared to be a cedar box on the rail, and gazed out over the cheering crowds on the docks below. She was plain-featured and quite young. She had a high forehead, a small, straight nose, wet brown eyes which peeked out from under plucked, arched eyebrows, and a mouth that was a little too full. Her blonde hair, although clean, was carelessly brushed and tangled in the back.

316

To Stephen she seemed beautiful.

"Hello," he said. Colored ribbons and confetti snakes were coiling through the air, and anything seemed possible.

Esme glanced at him. "Hello you," she said.

"Pardon?"

"I said 'hello, you.' That's an expression that was in vogue when this boat first sailed, if you'd care to know. It means, 'Hello, I think you're interesting and would consider sleeping with you if I were so inclined.' "

"You must call it a ship," Stephen said.

She laughed and for an instant looked at him intently, as if in that second she could see everything about him— that he was taking this voyage because he was bored with his life, that nothing had ever *really* happened to him. He felt his face become hot. "Okay, 'ship,' does that make you feel better?" she asked. "Anyway, I *want* to pretend that I'm living in the past. I don't ever want to return to the present. I suppose you do, want to return, that is."

"What makes you think that?"

"Look how you're dressed. You shouldn't be wearing modern clothes on this ship. You'll have to change later, you know." She was perfectly dressed in a powder-blue walking suit with matching jacket, a pleated, velvet-trimmed front blouse, and an ostrich-feather hat. She loked as if she had stepped out of another century.

"What's your name?" Stephen asked.

"Esme." She turned the box that she was resting on the rail and opened the side facing the deck. "You see," she said to the box, "we really *are* here."

"What did you say?" Stephen asked.

"I was just talking to Poppa," she said, closing and latching the box.

"Who?"

"I'll show you later if you like." Bells began to ring and the ship's whistles cut the air. There was a cheer from the dock and on board, and the ship moved slowly out to sea. To Stephen it seemed that the land, not the ship, was moving. The whole of England floated peacefully away while the string band on the ship's bridge played Oskar Straus.

They watched until the land had dwindled to a thin line on the horizon, then Esme reached for Stephen's hand, squeezed it for a moment and hurried away.

*   *   *

Stephen found her again in the Café Parisien, sitting in a large wicker chair beside an ornately trellised wall.

"Well, hello you," Esme said, smiling. She was the model of a smart, stylish young lady.

"Does that mean you're still interested?" Stephen asked, standing before her. Her smile was infectious, and Stephen felt himself losing his poise, as he couldn't stop grinning.

"But *mais oui*," she said. "That's French, which no one uses anymore, but it was *the* language of the world when this ship first sailed." She relaxed suddenly in her chair, slumped down as if she could revert instantly to being a child, and looked around the room as though Stephen had suddenly disappeared.

"I believe it was English," he said.

"Well," she said, looking up at him, "whatever, it means that I might be interested *if* you'd kindly sit down instead of looking at me from the heights." Stephen sat beside her. "It took you long enough to find me," Esme said.

"Well, I had to dress. Remember? You didn't find my previous attire—"

"I agree and I apologize," she said quickly, as if suddenly afraid of hurting his feelings. She folded her hands behind the box that she had centered perfectly on the damask-covered table. Her leg brushed his; indeed, he did look fine dressed in gray-striped trousers, spats, black morning coat, blue vest, and a silk cravat tied under a butterfly collar. "Now don't you feel better?"

Stephen was taken with her; this had never happened to him before. A tall waiter disturbed him by asking if he wished to order cocktails, but Esme asked for a Narcodrine instead.

"I'm sorry, madam, but Narcodrines or inhalers are not publicly sold on the ship."

"Well, that's what I *want*."

"One would have to ask the steward for more modern refreshments."

"You did say you wanted to live in the past," Stephen said. He ordered a Campari for her and a Drambuie for himself.

"Right now I would prefer a robot to take my order," Esme said.

"I'm sorry, but we have no robots on this ship either," the waiter said before turning away.

"Are you going to show me what's inside the box?" Stephen asked.

"It might cause a stir if I opened it here."

"I would think you'd like that," Stephen said.

"You see, you know me intimately already." Esme smiled and winked at someone four tables away. "Isn't he cute?"

"Who?"

"The little boy with the black hair parted in the middle." She waved at him, but the boy ignored her and made an obscene gesture at a woman who looked to be his nanny. Then Esme opened the box, which drew the little boy's attention. She pulled out a full-sized head of a man and placed it gently beside the box.

"Jesus," Stephen said.

"Stephen, I'd like you to meet Poppa. Poppa, this is Stephen."

"Who is Stephen?" Poppa said. "Where am I? Why is this going on? I'm frightened."

Esme leaned toward the head and whispered into its ear. "He sometimes gets disoriented on awakening," she said to Stephen confidentially. "He still isn't used to it yet. But he'll be all right in a moment."

"I'm scared," Poppa said in a fuller voice. "I'm alone in the dark."

"Not anymore," Esme said positively. "Poppa, this is my friend, Stephen."

"Hello, Poppa," Stephen said awkwardly.

"Hello, Stephen," the head said. Its voice was powerful now, commanding. "I'm pleased to meet you." It rolled its eyes and then said to Esme, "Turn me a bit now so I can see your friend without eyestrain." The head had white hair, which was a bit yellowed on the ends. It was neatly trimmed at the sides and combed into a rather seedy pompadour in the front. The face was strong, although dissipated. It was the face of a man in his late sixties, lined and tanned.

"My given name is Elliott," the head said. "Call me that, please."

"Hello, Elliott," Stephen said. He had heard of such things, but had never seen one before.

"These are going to be all the rage in the next few months," Esme said. "They aren't on the mass market yet, but you can imagine their potential for both adults and children. They can be programmed to talk and react very realistically."

"So I see," Stephen said.

The head smiled, accepting the compliment.

"He also learns and thinks quite well," Esme continued.

"I should hope so," said the head.

"Is your father alive?" Stephen asked.

"I *am* her father," the head said, its face betraying impatience. "At least give me *some* respect."

"Be civil, Poppa, or I'll close you up," Esme said, piqued. She looked at Stephen. "Yes, he died recently. That's the reason I'm taking this trip and that's the reason—" She nodded at the head. "He's marvelous, though. He *is* my father in every way." Mischievously she added, "Well, I *did* make a few changes. Poppa was very demanding."

"You're ungrateful—"

"Shut up, Poppa."

Poppa shut his eyes.

"That's all I have to say," Esme said, "and he turns himself off."

The little boy who had been staring unabashedly came over to the table just as Esme was putting Poppa back in the box. "Why'd you put him away?" he asked. "I want to talk to him. Take him out."

"No," Esme said firmly, "he's sleeping now. And what's your name?"

"Michael, and can I please see the head, just for a minute?"

"If you like, Michael, you can have a private audience with Poppa tomorrow," Esme said. "How's that?"

"I want to talk to him now."

"Shouldn't you be getting back to your nanny?" Stephen asked, standing and indicating that Esme do the same. They would have no privacy here.

"Stuff it," Michael said. "She's not my nanny, she's my sister." Then he pulled a face at Stephen; he was able to contort his lips, drawing the right side toward the left and left toward the right as if they were made of rubber. Stephen and Esme walked out of the café and up the staircase to the Boat Deck, and Michael followed them.

The Boat Deck was not too crowded at least; it was brisk out and the breeze had a chill to it. Looking forward, Stephen and Esme could see the ship's four huge smokestacks to their left and a cluster of four lifeboats to their right. The ocean was a smooth, deep green expanse turning to blue toward the horizon. The sky was empty, except for a huge, nuclear-powered airship that floated high over the *Titanic* . . . this was the dirigible *California,* a French luxury liner capable of carrying two thousand passengers.

"Are you two married?" Michael asked.

"No we are not," Esme said impatiently. "Not yet, at least," and Stephen felt exhilarated at the thought of her really wanting him. Actually, it made no sense for he could have any young woman he wanted. Why Esme? Simply because just now she was perfect.

"You're quite pretty," Michael said to Esme.

"Well, thank you," Esme replied, warming to him. "I like you, too."

"Are you going to stay on the ship and die when it sinks?"

"No!" Esme said, as if taken aback.

"What about your friend?"

"You mean Poppa?"

Vexed, the boy said, "No, *him,*" giving Stephen a nasty look.

"Well, I don't know," Esme said. Her face was flushed. "Have you opted for a lifeboat, Stephen?"

"Yes, of course I have."

"Well, *we're* going to die on the ship."

"Don't be silly," Esme said.

"Well, we are."

"Who's we?" Stephen asked.

"My sister and I. We've made a pact to go down with the ship."

"I don't believe it," Esme said. She stopped beside one of the lifeboats, rested the box containing Poppa on the rail, and gazed downward at the ocean spume curling away from the side of the ship.

"He's just baiting us," Stephen said. "Anyway, he's too young to make such a decision, and his sister, if she is his sister, couldn't decide such a thing for him, even if she were his guardian. It would be illegal."

"We're at sea," Michael said in the nagging tone children use. "I'll discuss the ramifications of my demise with Poppa tomorrow. I'm sure *he's* more conversant with these things than you."

"Shouldn't you be getting back to your sister now?" Stephen asked.

Michael made the rubber-lips face at him and then walked away, tugging at the back of his shorts as if his undergarments had bunched up beneath. He only turned around to wave good-bye to Esme, who blew him a kiss.

"Intelligent little brat," Stephen said to be ingratiating.

But Esme looked as if she had just now forgotten all about Stephen and the little boy. She stared at the box as tears rolled from her eyes.

"Esme?"

"I love him and now he's dead," she said. She seemed to brighten then. She took Stephen's hand and they went inside, down the stairs, through several noisy corridors— stateroom parties were in full swing—to her suite. Stephen was a bit nervous, but all things considered, everything was progressing at a proper pace.

Esme's suite had a parlor and a private promenade deck with Elizabethan half-timbered walls. She led him directly into the plush-carpeted, velour-papered bedroom, which contained a huge four-poster bed, an antique night table, and a desk and stuffed chair beside the door. The ornate, harp-sculpture desk lamp was on, as was the lamp just inside the bedcurtains. A porthole gave a view of sea and sky, but to Stephen it seemed that the bed overpowered the room.

Esme pushed the desk lamp aside, and then took Poppa out of the box and placed him carefully in the center of the desk. "There," she said. At rest the head seemed even more handsome and quite peaceful although now and then an eyelid twitched. Then she undressed quickly, looking shyly away from Stephen who was taking his time. She slipped between the parted curtains of the bed and complained that she could hear the damn engines thrumming right through these itchy pillows—she didn't like silk. After a moment, she sat up in bed and asked him if he intended to get undressed or just stand there.

"I'm sorry," Stephen said, "but it's just—" He nodded toward the head.

"Poppa *is* turned off you know," Esme said.

The head's left eyelid fluttered.

Michael knocked on Esme's door at seven-thirty the next morning.

"Good morning," Michael said, looking Esme up and down. She had not bothered to put anything on before answering the door. "I came to see Poppa. I won't disturb you."

"Jesus, Michael, it's too early—"

"Early bird gets the worm."

"Oh," Esme said, "and what the hell does that mean?"

"I calculated that my best chance of talking with Poppa was if I woke you up. You'll go back to bed and I can talk with him in peace. My chances would be greatly diminished if—"

"Come in."

"The steward in the hall just saw you naked."

"Big deal. Look, why don't you come back later, I'm not ready for this, and I don't know why I let you in the room."

"You see, it worked." Michael looked around. "He's in the bedroom, right?"

Esme nodded and followed him in. Michael was wearing the same wrinkled shirt and shorts that he had worn yesterday; his hair was not combed, just tousled.

"Is *he* with you, too?" Michael asked.

"If you mean Stephen, yes."

"I thought so," said Michael. Then he sat down at the desk. "Hello Poppa," he said.

"I'm frightened," the head said. "It's so dark; I'm scared."

Michael gave Esme a look.

"He's always like that when he's been shut off for a while," Esme said. "Talk to him a bit more."

"It's Michael," the boy said. "I came in here to talk to you. We're on the *Titanic*."

"Oh Michael," the head said, more confidently. "I think I remember you. Why are you on the *Titanic?*"

"Because it's going to sink."

"That's a silly reason," the head said confidently. "There must be others."

"There are lots of others."

"Can't we have *any* privacy?" Stephen said, sitting up in the bed. Esme sat beside him, shrugged, and took a pull at her inhaler. Drugged, she looked even softer, more vulnerable. "I thought you told me that Poppa was turned off all night," he continued angrily.

"But he *was* turned off," Esme said. "I just now turned him back on for Michael."

"I'll tell you all about the *Titanic*," Michael said confidentially to the head. He leaned close to it and whispered intensely.

"He *was* turned off," Esme said. "I just now turned him back on for Michael." She cuddled up to Stephen, as intimately as if they had been in love for days. That seemed to mollify him.

"Do you have a spare Narcodrine in there?" Michael shouted.

Stephen looked at Esme who laughed. "No," Esme said, "you're too young for such things." She pulled the curtain so that the bed was now shut off from Michael and the head. "Let him talk to Poppa," she said. "He'll be dead soon, anyway."

"You mean you believe him?" Stephen said. "I'm going to talk to his sister or whoever she is about this."

Michael peered through the curtain. "I heard what you said. I have very good hearing, I heard everything. Go ahead and talk to her, talk to the captain if you like. It won't do you any good. I'm an international hero if you'd like to know. That girl who wears the camera in her hair already did an interview for me for the poll." He closed the curtain.

"What does he mean?" Esme asked.

"The woman reporter from *Interfax*," Stephen said.

Michael opened the curtain again. "Her job is to guess which passengers will opt to die and why. She interviews the most interesting passengers, then gives her predictions to her viewers, and she has a lot of them. They respond immediately to a poll taken several times every day. Keeps us in their minds, and everybody loves the smell of death." The curtain closed.

"Well, she hasn't tried to interview *me*," Esme said, pouting.

"Do you really want her to?"

"And why not? I'm for conspicuous consumption, and I want so much for this experience to be a success. Goodness, let the whole world watch us sink if they want. They might just as well take bets." Then, in a conspiratorial whisper, she said, "None of us knows who's really opted to die. *That's* part of the excitement."

"I suppose," Stephen said.

"Oh you're such a prig," Esme said. "One would think you're a doer."

"A what?"

"A doer. All of us are either doers or voyeurs, isn't that right? But the doers mean business," and to illustrate she cocked her head, stuck out her tongue, and made gurgling noises as if she were drowning. "The voyeurs, however, are just along for the ride. Are you *sure* you're not a doer?"

Michael, who had been eavesdropping again, said, referring to Stephen, "He's not a doer, you can bet on that! He's a voyeur of the worst sort. He takes it all seriously."

"Now that's enough disrespect from both of you," Poppa said richly. "Michael, stop goading Stephen. Esme says she loves him. Esme, be nice to Michael. He just made my day. And you don't have to threaten to turn me off. I'm turning myself off. I've got some thinking to do." Poppa closed his eyes.

"*Well,*" Esme said to Michael who was now standing before the bed and trying to place his feet as wide apart as possible, "he's never done that before. He's usually so afraid of being afraid when he wakes up. What did you say to him?"

"Nothing much."

"Come on, Michael, *I* let you into the room, remember?"

"I remember. Can I come into bed with you?"

"Hell, no," Stephen said.

"He's only a child," Esme said as she moved over to make room for Michael, who climbed in between her and Stephen. "Be a sport. *You're* the man I love."

Stephen moved closer to Esme so that Michael could come into the bed. They discussed the transmigration of souls. Michael was sure of it, but Esme thought it all too confusing. Stephen had no real opinion.

They finally managed to lose Michael by lunchtime. Esme seemed happy enough to be rid of the boy, and they spent the rest of the day discovering the ship. They tried a quick dip in the pool, but the water was too cold and it was chilly outside. If the dirigible was floating above, they did not see it because the sky was covered with heavy, gray clouds. They changed clothes, strolled along the glass-enclosed lower Promenade Deck, looked for the occa-

sional flying fish, and spent an interesting half hour being
interviewed by the woman from *Interfax*. Then they took a
snack in the opulent first-class smoking room. Esme loved
the mirrors and stained-glass windows. After they ex-
plored cabin and tourist class, Esme talked Stephen into a
quick game of squash, which he played rather well. By
dinnertime they found their way into the garish, blue-
tiled Turkish bath. It was empty and hot, and they made
gentle but exhausting love on one of the Caesar couches.
Then they changed clothes again, danced in the lounge,
and took a late supper in the café.

He spent the night with Esme in her suite. It was about
four in the morning when he was awakened by a hushed
conversation. Rather than make himself known, Stephen
feigned sleep and listened.

"I can't make a decision," Esme said as she carefully
paced back and forth beside the desk upon which Poppa
rested.

"I'm still scared," Poppa said in a weak voice. "Just give
me a minute, this was so *sudden*. Where did you say I am?"

"The *Titanic*," Esme said angrily, "and I have to make
a decision. Come to your senses."

"You've told me over and over what you know you must
do, haven't you?" Poppa said. His voice sounded better; the
disorientation was leaving him. "Now you change your
mind?"

"I think things have changed."

"And how is that?"

"Stephen. He—"

"Ah," Poppa said, "so now *love* is the escape. But do
you know how long that will last?"

"I didn't expect to meet him, to feel better about everything."

"It will pass."

"But right now I don't want to die."

"You've spent a fortune on this trip, and on me. And
now you want to throw it away. Look, the way you feel
about Stephen is all for the better, don't you understand?
It will make your passing away all the sweeter because
you're happy, in love, whatever you want to claim for it.
But now you want to throw everything away that we've
planned and take your life some other time, probably
when you're desperate and unhappy and don't have me

around to help you. You wish to die as mindlessly as you were born."

"That's not so, Poppa. But it's up to *me* to choose."

"You've made your choice, now stick to it or you'll drop dead like I did."

"Esme, what the hell are you talking about?" Stephen said.

Esme looked startled in the dim light and then said to Poppa, "You were purposely talking loudly to wake him up, weren't you?"

"*You* had me programmed to help you. I love you and I care about you. You can't undo that!"

"I can do whatever I wish," Esme said petulantly.

"Then let me help you, as I always have. If I were alive and had my body I would tell you exactly what I'm telling you now."

"What *is* going on?" Stephen asked.

"She's fooling you," Poppa said gently to Stephen. "She's using you because she's frightened. She's grasping at anyone she can find."

"What the hell is he telling you?" Stephen asked.

"The truth," Poppa said. "I know all about fear, don't you know that?"

Esme sat beside Stephen on the bed and began to cry, then, as if sliding easily into a new role, she looked at him and said, "I did program Poppa to help me die. Poppa and I talked everything over very carefully, we even discussed what to do if something like this came about."

"You mean if you fell in love and wanted to live."

"And she decided that under no circumstances would she undo what she had done," Poppa said. "She has planned the best possible death for herself, a death to be experienced and savored. She's given everything up and spent all her money to do it. She's broke. She can't go back now, isn't that right, Esme?"

Esme folded her hands, swallowed, and looked at Stephen. "Yes," she said.

"But you're not sure," Stephen said. "I can see that."

"I will help her as I always have," Poppa said.

"Jesus, shut that thing up," Stephen shouted.

"He's not a——"

"Please," Stephen said, "at least give us a chance. You're the first authentic experience I've ever had, I love you, I don't want it to end. . . ."

Poppa pleaded his own case eloquently until Esme told him to shut up.

The great ship hit an iceberg on the fourth night of her voyage, exactly one day earlier than scheduled. Stephen and Esme were standing by the rail of the Promenade Deck. Both were dressed in the early twentieth-century accouterments provided by the ship—he in woolen trousers, jacket, motoring cap, and caped overcoat with a long scarf; she in a fur coat, a stylish 'Merry Widow' hat, high-button shoes, and a black-velvet, two-piece suit edged with white silk. She looked ravishing and very young, despite the clothes.

"Throw it away," Stephen said authoritatively. "Now."

Esme brought the cedar box containing Poppa to her chest, as if she were about to throw it forward, then slowly placed it atop the rail again. "I *can't.*"

"Do you want me to do it?"

"I don't see why I must throw him away."

"Because we're starting a new life together."

At that moment someone shouted, and as if in the distance, a bell rang three times.

"Could there be another ship nearby?" Esme asked.

"Esme, throw the box away!" Stephen snapped; and then he saw it. He pulled Esme backward, away from the rail. An iceberg as high as the forecastle deck scraped against the side of the ship; it almost seemed that the bluish, glistening mountain of ice was another ship passing, that the ice rather than the ship was moving. Pieces of ice rained upon the deck, slid across the varnished wood, and then the iceberg was lost in the darkness astern. It must have been at least one hundred feet high.

"Oh my God!" Esme screamed, rushing to the rail.

"What is it?"

"Poppa! I dropped him when you pulled me away from the iceberg."

"It's too late for that—"

Esme disappeared into the crowd, crying for Poppa.

It was bitter cold and the Boat Deck was filled with people, all rushing about, shouting, scrambling for the lifeboats, and, inevitably, those who had changed their minds at the last moment about going down with the ship were shouting the loudest, trying the hardest to be permitted into the boats, not one of which had been lowered yet. There were sixteen wooden lifeboats and four canvas Engelhardts, the collapsibles. But they could not be lowered away until the davits were cleared of the two forward boats. "We'll let you know when it's time to board," shouted an officer to the families crowding around him.

The floor was listing. Esme was late, and Stephen wasn't going to wait. At this rate, the ship would be bow down in the water in no time.

She must be with Michael, he thought. The little bastard has talked her into dying.

Michael had a stateroom on C-Deck. Stephen knocked, called to Michael and Esme, tried to open the door, and finally kicked the lock free.

Michael was sitting on the bed, which was a Pullman berth. His sister lay beside him, dead.

"Where's Esme?" Stephen said, repelled by the sight of Michael sitting so calmly beside his dead sister.

"Not here. Obviously." Michael smiled and made the rubber-lips face.

"Jesus," Stephen said. "Put your coat on, you're coming with me."

Michael laughed and patted down his hair. "I'm already dead, just like my sister, almost. I took a pill too, see?" He held up a small brown bottle. "Anyway, they wouldn't let me on a lifeboat. I didn't sign up for one, remember?"

"You're a baby—"

"I thought Poppa explained all that to you." Michael lay down beside his sister and watched Stephen like a puppy with its head cocked at an odd angle.

"You do know where Esme is, now tell me."

"You never understood her. She came here to die."

An instant later, Michael stopped breathing.

Stephen searched the ship, level by level, broke in on the parties where those who had opted for death were having a last fling, looked into the lounges where many old couples sat, waiting for the end. He made his way down to F-Deck, where he had made love to Esme in the Turkish bath. The water was up to his knees; it was green and soapy. He was afraid, for the list was becoming worse minute by minute. The water rose even as he walked.

He had to get to the stairs, had to get up and out, onto

a lifeboat, away from the ship, but on he walked, looking for Esme, unable to stop. He had to find her. She might even be on the Boat Deck right now, he thought, wading through a corridor. But he had to satisfy himself that she wasn't down here.

The Turkish bath was filling with water, and the lights were still on, giving the room a ghostly illumination. Oddments floated in the room: blue slippers, a comb, scraps of paper, cigarettes, and several seamless, plastic packages. On the farthest couch, Esme sat meditating, her eyes closed and hands folded on her lap. She wore a simple white dress. Overjoyed, he shouted to her. She jerked awake, looking disoriented, and without a word waded toward the other exit, dipping her hands into the water as if to speed her on her way.

"Esme, where are you going?" Stephen called, following. "Don't run from *me*."

An explosion pitched them both into the water and a wall gave way. A solid sheet of water seemed to be crashing into the room, smashing Stephen, pulling him under and sweeping him away. He fought to reach the surface and tried to swim back, to find Esme. A lamp broke away from the ceiling, just missing him. "Esme," he shouted, but he couldn't see her, and then he found himself choking, swimming, as the water carried him through a corridor and away from her.

Finally, Stephen was able to grab the iron curl of a railing and pull himself onto a dry step. There was another explosion, the floor pitched. He looked down at the water, which filled the corridor, the Turkish bath, the entire deck, and he screamed for Esme.

The ship shuddered, then everything was quiet. In the great rooms, chandeliers hung at angles; tables and chairs had skidded across the floors and seemed to squat against the walls like wooden beasts. Still the lights burned, as if all was quite correct, except gravity, which was misbehaving. Stephen walked and climbed, followed by the sea, as if in a dream.

Numbed, he found himself back on the Boat Deck. Part of the deck was already submerged. Almost everyone had moved aft, climbing uphill as the bow dipped farther into the water.

The lifeboats were gone, as were the crew. There were a few men and women atop of the officers' quarters. They were working hard, trying to launch Collapsibles C and D, their only chance of getting safely away from the ship.

"Hey," Stephen called to them, just now coming to his senses. "Do you need any help up there?"

He was ignored by those who were pushing one of the freed collapsibles off the port side of the roof. Someone shouted, "Damn!" The boat had landed upside down in the water.

"It's better than nothing," a woman shouted, and she and her friends jumped after the boat.

Stephen shivered; he was not yet ready to leap into the twenty-eight-degree water, although he knew there wasn't much time left, and he had to get away from the ship before it went down. Everyone on or close to the ship would be sucked under. He crossed to the starboard side, where some other men were trying to push the boat to the edge of the deck. The great ship was listing heavily to port.

This time Stephen just joined the work. No one complained. They were trying to slide the boat over the edge on planks. All these people looked to be in top physical shape—Stephen noticed that about half of them were women wearing the same warm coats as the men. This was a game to all of them, he suspected, and they were enjoying it. Each one was going to beat the odds, one way or another; the very thrill was to outwit fate, opt to die and yet survive.

But then the bridge was under water.

There was a terrible crashing and Stephen slid along the floor as everything tilted. Everyone was shouting. "She's going down!" someone screamed. Indeed, the stern of the ship was swinging upward. The lights flickered. There was a roar as the entrails of the ship broke loose: anchor chains, the huge engines and boilers. One of the huge, black funnels fell, smashing into the water amid sparks. But still the ship was brilliantly lit, every porthole afire. The crow's nest before him was almost submerged, but Stephen swam for it nevertheless. Then he caught himself and tried to swim away from the ship, but it was too late. He felt himself being sucked back, pulled under. He was being sucked into the ventilator, which was in front of the forward funnel; he gasped, swallowed water, and felt the wire mesh, the air-shaft grating that prevented him from being sucked under. He held his breath desperately.

Water was surging all around him, and then there was another explosion. Stephen felt warmth on his back, as a blast of hot air pushed him upward. Then he broke out into the freezing air. He swam for his life, away from the ship, away from the crashing and thudding of glass and wood, away from the debris of deck chairs, planking, and ropes, and especially away from the other people who were moaning, screaming at him, and trying to grab him as a buoy, trying to pull him down as the great ship sank.

Swimming, he heard voices nearby and saw a dark shape. For a moment it didn't register, then he realized that he was near an overturned lifeboat, the collapsible he had seen pushed into the water. There were almost thirty men and women standing on it. Stephen tried to climb aboard and someone shouted, "You'll sink us, we've too many already." A woman tried to hit Stephen with an oar, just missing his head. Stephen swam around to the other side of the boat. He grabbed hold again, found someone's foot, and was kicked back into the water.

"Come on," a man said, "take my arm and I'll pull you up."

"There's no *room!*" someone else said.

"There's enough room for one more."

"No there's not."

The boat began to rock.

"We'll all be in the water if we don't stop this," shouted the man who was holding Stephen afloat. Then he pulled Stephen aboard. He stood with the others; truly there was barely enough room. Everyone had formed a double line now, facing the bow, and leaned in the direction opposite the swells. Slowly the boat inched away from the site where the ship had gone down, away from the people in the water, all begging for life, for one last chance. As he looked back to where the ship had once been, Stephen thought of Esme. He couldn't bear to think of her as dead, floating through the corridors of the ship.

Those in the water could be easily heard; in fact the calls seemed magnified, as if meant to be heard clearly by everyone who was safe as a punishment for past sins.

"We're all deaders," said a woman standing beside Stephen. "I'm sure no one's coming to get us before dawn, when they have to pick up survivors."

"We'll be the last pickup, that's if they intend to pick us up at all."

"Those in the water have to get their money's worth. And since we opted for death——"

"I didn't," Stephen said, almost to himself.

"Well, you've got it anyway."

Stephen was numb but no longer cold. As if from far away, he heard the splash of someone falling from the boat, which was very slowly sinking as air was lost from under the hull. At times the water was up to Stephen's knees, yet he wasn't even shivering. Time distended or contracted. He measured it by the splashing of his companions as they fell overboard. He heard himself calling Esme, as if to say good-bye, or perhaps to greet her.

By dawn, Stephen was so muddled by the cold that he thought he was on land, for the sea was full of debris . . . cork, steamer chairs, boxes, pilasters, rugs, carved wood, clothes, and of course the bodies of those unfortunates who could not or would not survive——and the great icebergs and the smaller ones called growlers looked like cliffs and mountainsides. The icebergs were sparkling and many-hued, all brilliant in the light, as if painted by some cheerless Gauguin of the north.

"There," someone said, a woman's hoarse voice. "It's coming down, it's coming down!" The dirigible, looking like a huge white whale, seemed to be descending through its more natural element, water, rather than the thin, cold air. Its electric engines could not be heard.

In the distance, Stephen could see the other lifeboats. Soon the airship would begin to rescue those in the boats, which were now tied together in a cluster. As Stephen's thoughts wandered and his eyes watered from the reflected morning sunlight, he saw a piece of carved oak bobbing up and down near the boat, and noticed a familiar face in the debris that seemed to surround the lifeboat. There, just below the surface in his box, the lid open, eyes closed, floated Poppa. Poppa opened his eyes and looked at Stephen. Stephen screamed, lost his balance on the hull, and plunged like a knife into the cold black water.

The Laurel Lounge of the dirigible *California* was dark and filled with survivors. Some sat in the flowered, stuffed chairs; others just milled about. But they were all watching the lifelike, holographic tapes of the sinking of the *Titanic*. The images filled the large room.

Stephen stood in the back, away from the others who cheered each time there was a close-up of someone jumping overboard or slipping under the water. He pulled the scratchy woolen blanket around him and shivered. He had been on the dirigible for over twenty-four hours, and he was still chilled. A crewman had told him it was because of the injections he had received when he boarded the airship.

There was another cheer and, horrified, he saw that they were cheering for *him*. He watched himself being sucked into the ventilator and then blown upward to the surface. His body ached from the battering. But he had saved himself. He had survived and that had been an actual experience. It was worth it for that, but poor Esme. . . .

"You had one of the *most* exciting experiences," a woman said to him as she touched his hand. He recoiled and she shrugged, then moved on.

"I wish to register a complaint," said a stocky man dressed in period clothing to one of the *Titanic*'s officers, who was standing beside Stephen and sipping a cocktail.

"Yes?"

"I was saved against my wishes. I specifically took this voyage that I might pit myself against the elements."

"Did you sign one of our protection waivers?"

"I was not aware that we were required to sign any such thing."

"All such information was provided," the officer said, looking disinterested. "Those passengers who are truly committed to taking their chances sign, and we leave them to their own devices. Otherwise, we are responsible for every passenger's life."

"I might just as well have jumped into the ocean at the beginning and gotten pulled out," the passenger said bitterly.

The officer smiled. "Most want to test themselves as long as they can. Of course, if you want to register a formal complaint . . ."

The passenger stomped away.

"The man's trying to save face," the officer said to Stephen. "We see quite a bit of that. But *you* seemed to have an interesting ride. You gave us quite a start; we thought you were going to take a lifeboat with the others,

but you disappeared below deck. It was a bit more difficult
to monitor you, but we managed—that's the fun for *us*.
You were never in any danger, of course. Well, maybe a
little."

Stephen was shaken. He had felt that his experiences
had been authentic, that he had really saved himself. But
none of that had been *real*. Only Esme . . .

And then he saw her step into the room.

"Esme?" He couldn't believe it. "Esme!"

She walked over to him and smiled as she had the first
time they'd met. She was holding a water-damaged, cedar
box. "Hello, Stephen. Wasn't it exciting?"

Stephen threw his arms around her, but she didn't respond. She waited a proper time, then disengaged herself.

"And look," she said, "they've even found Poppa." She
opened the box and held it up to him.

Poppa's eyes fluttered open. For a moment his eyes were
vague and unfocused, then they fastened on Esme and
sharpened. "Esme . . ." Poppa said, uncertainly, and then
he smiled. "Esme, I've had the strangest dream." He
laughed. "I dreamed I was a head in a box. . . ."

Esme snapped the box closed. "Isn't he marvelous?" she
said. She patted the box and smiled. "He almost had me
talked into going through with it this time."

THE QUIET

≈≈≈≈≈≈≈≈≈≈≈≈≈≈≈≈≈≈≈≈≈≈

George Florance-Guthridge

The progress of civilization inevitably brings
with it a decline and often extinction of various
local tribes, which often means the loss of their
ways, knowledge, beliefs, even whole languages. If future anthropologists were to move
the last members of such a tribe to a simulated
"natural" environment on the moon, just how
much could be saved?

George Florance-Guthridge was born and
currently lives in the state of Washington.

KUARA, MY SON, THE WHITES HAVE STOLEN
the moon.

Outside the window the sky is black. A blue-white disc
hangs among the stars. It is Earth, says Doctor Stefanko.
I wail and beat my fists. Straps bind me to a bed. Doctor
Stefanko forces my shoulders down, swabs my arm.
"Since you can't keep still, I'm going to have to put you
under again," she says, smiling. I lie quietly.

It is not Earth. Earth is brown. Earth is Kalahari.

"You are on the moon," Doctor Stefanko says. It is the
second or third time she has told me; I have awakened
and slept, awakened and slept until I am not sure what
voices are dream and what are real, if any. Something
pricks my skin. "Rest now. You have had a long sleep."

I remember awakening the first time. The white room,
white cloth covering me. Outside, blackness and the blue-
white disc.

"On the moon," I say. My limbs feel heavy. My head
spins. Sleep drags at my flesh. "The moon."

"Isn't it wonderful?"

"And you say my husband, Tuka—dead."

Her lips tighten. She looks at me solemnly. "He did not
survive the sleep."

"The moon is hollow," I tell her. "Everyone knows that.
The dead sleep there." I stare at the ceiling. "I am alive
and on the moon. Tuka is dead but is not here." The
words seem to float from my mouth. There are little dots
on the ceiling.

338

"Sleep now. That's a girl. We'll talk more later."

"And Kuara. My son. Alive." The dots are spinning. I close my eyes. The dots keep spinning.

"Yes, but. . . ."

"About a hundred years ago a law was formulated to protect endangered species—animals which, unless humankind was careful, might become extinct," Doctor Stefanko says. Her face is no longer blurry. She has gray hair, drawn cheeks. I have seen her somewhere—long before I was brought to this place. I cannot remember where. The memory slips away.

Gai, wearing a breechclout, stands grinning near the window. The disc Doctor Stefanko calls Earth haloes his head. His huge, pitted tongue sticks out where his front teeth are missing. His shoulders slope like those of a hartebeest. His chest, leathery and wrinkled, is tufted with hair beginning to gray. I am not surprised to see him, after his treachery. He makes num pulse in the pit of my belly. I look away.

"Then the law was broadened to include endangered peoples. Peoples like the Gwi." Doctor Stefanko smiles maternally and presses her index finger against my nose. I toss my head. She frowns. "Obviously, it would be impossible to save entire tribes. So the founders of the law did what they thought best. They saved certain representatives. You. Your family. A few others, such as Gai. These representatives were frozen."

"Frozen?"

"Made cold."

"As during gum, when ice forms inside the ostrich-egg containers?"

"Much colder."

It was not dream, then. I remember staring through a blue, crinkled sheen. Like light seen through a snakeskin. I could not move, though my insides never stopped shivering. *So this is death,* I kept thinking.

"In the interim you were brought here to the moon. To Carnival. It is a fine place. A truly international facility; built as a testament to the harmony of nations. Here we have tried to recreate the best of what used to be." She pauses, and her eyes grow keen. "This will be your home now, U," she says.

"And Kuara?"

"He will live here with you, in time." Something in her voice makes fear touch me. Then she says, "Would you like to see him?" Some of the fear slides away.

"Is it wise, Doctor?" Gai asks. "She has a temper, this one." His eyes grin down at me. He stares at my pelvis.

"Oh, we'll manage. You'll be a good girl, won't you, U?" My head nods. My heart does not say yes or no.

The straps leap away with a loud click. Doctor Stefanko and Gai help me to my feet. The world wobbles. The Earth-disc tilts and swings. The floor slants one way, another way. Needles tingle in my feet and hands. I am helped into a chair. More clicking. The door hisses open and the chair floats out, Doctor Stefanko leading, Gai lumbering behind. We move down one corridor after another. This is a place of angles. No curves, except the smiles of Whites as we pass. And they curve too much.

Another door hisses. We enter a room full of chill. Blue glass, the inside laced with frost, stretches from floor to ceiling along each wall. Frozen figures stand behind the glass. I remember this place. I remember how sluggish was the hate in my heart.

"Kuara is on the end," Doctor Stefanko says, her breath white.

The chair floats closer. My legs bump the glass; cold shocks my knees. The chair draws back. I lean forward. Through the glass I can see the closed eyes of my son. Ice furs his lashes and brows. His head is tilted to one side. His little arms dangle. I touch the glass in spite of the cold. I hear Gai's sharp intake of breath and he draws back my shoulders, but Doctor Stefanko puts a hand on Gai's wrist and I am released. There is give to the glass. Not like that on the trucks in the tsama patch. My num rises. My heart beats faster. Num enters my arms, floods my fingers. "Kuara," I whisper. Warmth spreads upon the glass. It makes a small, ragged circle.

"He'll be taken from here as soon as you've settled into your new home," Doctor Stefanko says.

Kuara. If only I could dance. Num would boil within me. I could kia. I would shoo away the ghosts of the cold. Awakening, you would step through the glass and into my arms.

Though we often lacked water we were not unhappy. The tsama melons supported us. It was a large patch, and by conserving we could last long periods without journeying to the waterholes. Whites and tame Bushmen had taken over the Gam and Gautscha Pans, and the people there, the Kung, either had run away or had stayed for the water and now worked the Whites' farms and ate mealie meal.

There were eleven of us, though sometimes one or two more. Gai, unmated, was one of those who came and went. Tuka would say, "You can always count us on three hands, but never on two or four hands." He would laugh, then. He was always laughing. I think he laughed because there was so little game near the Akam Pan, our home. The few duiker and steenbok that had once roamed our plain had smelled the coming of the Whites and the fleeing Kung, and had run away. Tuka laughed to fill up the empty spaces.

Sometimes, when he wasn't trapping springhare and porcupine, he helped me gather wood and tubers. We dug xwa roots and koa, the water root buried deep in the earth, until our arms ached. Sometimes we hit the na trees with sticks, making the sweet berries fall, and Tuka would chase me round and round, laughing and yelling like a madman. It was times like those when I wondered why I had once hated him so much.

I wondered much about that during kuma, a hot season when starvation stalked us. During the day I would take off my kaross, dig a shallow pit within what little shade an orogu bush offered, then urinate in the sand, cover myself with more sand and place a leaf over my head. The three of us—Tuka, Kuara, and I—lay side by side like dead people. "My heart is sad from hunger," I sang to myself all day. "Like an old man, sick and slow." I thought of the bad things, then. My parents marrying me to Tuka before I was ready because, paying bride service, he brought my mother a new kaross. Tuka doing the marrying thing to me before I was ready. Everything before I was ready! Sometimes I prayed into the leaf that a paouw would fly down and think his penis a fat caterpillar.

Then one night Tuka snared a honey badger. A badger, during kuma! Everyone was excited. Tuka said, "Yesterday, when we slept, I told the land that my U was hungry, and I must have meat for her and Kuara." The badger was very tender. Gai ate his share and went begging, though he had never brought meat to the camp. When the meat was gone we roasted ga roots and sang and danced while

Tuka played the gwashi. I danced proudly. Not for Tuka but for myself. Num uncurled from the pit of my belly and came boiling up my spine. I was afraid, because when num reaches my skull I kia. Then I see ghosts killing people, and I smell the rotting smell of death, like decaying carcasses.

Tuka took my head in his hands. "You must not kia," he said. "Not now. Your body will suffer too much for the visions." For other people, kia brings healing—of self, of others; for me it only brings pain.

Tuka held me beside the fire and stroked me, and num subsided. "When I lie in the sand during the day, I dream I have climbed the footpegs in a great baobab tree," he said. "I look out from the treetop, and the land is agraze with animals. Giraffe and wildebeest and kudu. 'You must kill these beasts and bring them to U and Kuara before the Whites kill them,' my dream says."

Then he asked, "What do you think of when you lie there, U?"

I did not answer. I was afraid to tell him; I did not want him to feel angry or sad after his joy from catching the honey badger. He smiled. His eyes, moist, shone with firelight. Perhaps he thought num had stopped my tongue.

The next day the quiet came. Lying beneath the sand, I felt num pulse in my belly. I fought the fear it always brought. I did not cry out to Tuka. The pulsing increased. I began to tremble. Sweat ran down my face. Num boiled within me. It entered my spine and pushed toward my throat. My eyes were wide and I kept staring at the veins of the leaf but seeing dread. I felt myself going rigid and shivering at the same time. My head throbbed; it was as large as a ga root. I could hear my mouth make sputtery noises, like Kuara used to at my breast. The pressure inside me kept building, building.

And suddenly was gone. It burrowed into the earth, taking my daydreams with it. I went down and down into the sand. I passed ubbee roots and animals long dead, their bones bleached and forgotten. I came to a waterhole far beneath the ground. Tuka was in the water. Kuara was too. He looked younger, barely old enough to toddle. Tuka, smiling, looked handsome. *He is not a bad person,* I told myself; *he just wants his way too much. But he has brought meat to our people, I cannot forget that. And some day*

*perhaps he will bring me a new kaross. Perhaps he will
bring many things. Important things.*

I took off my kaross, and the three of us held hands and
danced, naked, splashing. There was no num to seize me.
No marrying-thing urge to seize Tuka. Only quiet, and
laughter.

"This will be your new home, U," Doctor Stefanko says
as she opens a door. She has given me a new kaross; of
genuine gemsbok, she tells me, though I am uncertain why
she speaks of it that way. When she puts her hand on my
back and pushes me forward, the kaross feels soft and
smooth against my skin. "We think you'll like it, and if
there's anything you need. . . ."

I grab the sides of the door and turn my face away. I
will not live in nor even look at the place. But her push
becomes firmer, and I stumble inside. I cover my face with
my hands.

"There, now," Doctor Stefanko says. I spy through my
fingers.

We are in Kalahari.

I turn slowly, for suddenly my heart is shining and singing. No door. No walls. No angles. The sandveld spreads
out beneath a cloudless sky. Endless pale-gold grass sur-
rounds scattered white-thorn and tsi; in the distance lift
several flat-topped acacias and even a mongongo tree. A
dassie darts in and out of a rocky kranze.

"Here might be a good place for you tshushi—your
shelter," Doctor Stefanko says, pulling me forward. She
enters the tall grass, bends, comes up smiling, holding
branches in one hand, gui fibers in the other. "You see?
We've even cut some of the materials you'll need."

"But how—"

"The moon isn't such a horrible place, now is it." She
strides back through the grass. "And we here at Carnival
are dedicated to making your stay as pleasant as possible.
Just look here." She moves a rock. A row of buttons
gleams. "Turn this knob, and you can control your weather;
no more suffering through those terrible hot and cold
seasons. Unless you want to, of course," she adds quickly.
"And from time to time some nice people will be looking
down . . . *in* on you. From up there, within the sky." She
makes a sweep of her arm. "They want to watch how you
live; you—and others like you—are quite a sensation, you

know." I stare at her without understanding. "Anyway, if you want to see them, just turn this knob. And if you want to hear what the monitor's saying about you, turn this one." She looks up, sees my confusion. "Oh, don't worry; the monitor translates everything. It's a wonderful device."

Standing, she takes hold of my arms. Her eyes almost seem warm. "You see, U, there is no more Kalahari on Earth—not as you knew it anyhow—so we created another. In some ways it won't be as good as what you were used to, in a lot of ways it'll be better." Her smile comes back. "We think you'll like it."

"And Kuara?"

"He's waking now. He'll join you soon." She takes hold of my hands. "Soon." Then she walks back in the direction we came, quickly fading in the distance. Suddenly she is gone. A veil of heat shimmers above the grass where the door seemed to have been. For a moment I think of following. Finally I shrug. I work at building my tshushi. I work slowly, methodically, my head full of thoughts. I think of Kuara, and something gnaws at me. I drop the fiber I am holding and begin walking toward the opposite horizon, where a giraffe is eating from the mongongo tree.

Grasshoppers, kxon ants, dung beetles hop and crawl among the grasses. Leguaan scuttle. A mole snake slithers for a hole beneath a uri bush. I walk quickly, the sand warm but not hot beneath my feet. The plain is sun-drenched, the few small omirimbi water courses parched and cracked, yet I feel little thirst. A steenbok leaps for cover behind a white-thorn. This is a good place, part of me decides. Here will Kuara become the hunter Tuka could not be. Kuara will never laugh to shut out sadness.

The horizon draws no closer.

I measure the giraffe with my thumb, walk a thousand paces, remeasure, walk another thousand paces, remeasure.

The giraffe does not change size.

I will walk another thousand. Then I will turn back and finish the tshushi.

A hundred paces further I bump something hard.

A wall.

Beyond, the giraffe continues feeding.

The Whites with the Land Rovers came during ga, the hottest season. The trucks bucked and roared across the sand. Tuka took Kuara and hurried to meet them. I went too, though I walked behind with the other women. There were several white men and some Bantu. Gai was standing in the lead truck, waving and grinning.

A white, blond-haired woman climbed out. She was wearing white shorts and a light brown shirt with rolled-up sleeves. I recognized her immediately. Doctor Morse, come to study us again. Tuka had said the Whites did not wonder about their own culture, so they liked to study ours.

She talked to us women a long time, asking about our families and how we felt about SWAPO, the People's Army. Everyone spoke at once. She kept waving her hands for quiet. "What do you think, U?" she would ask. "What's your opinion?" I said she should ask Tuka; he was a man and understood such things. Doctor frowned, so I said SWAPO should not kill people. SWAPO should leave people alone. Doctor Morse wrote in her notebook as I talked. I was pleased. The other women were very jealous.

Doctor Morse told us the war in South Africa was going badly; soon it would sweep this way. When Tuka finished looking at the engines I asked him what Doctor Morse meant by "badly." Badly for Blacks, or Whites. Badly for those in the south, or those of us in the Kalahari. He did not know. None of us asked Doctor Morse.

Then she said, "We have brought water. Lots of water. We've heard you've been without." Her hair caught the sunlight. She was very beautiful for a white woman.

We smiled but refused her offer. She frowned but did not seem angry. Maybe she thought it was because she was white. If so, she was wrong; accept gifts, and we might forget the ones Kalahari gives us. "Well, at least go for a ride in the trucks." she said, beaming. Tuka laughed and, taking Kuara by the hand, scrambled for the two Land Rovers. I shook my head. "You really should go," Doctor Morse said. "It'll be good for you."

"That is something for men to do," I told her. "Women do not understand those things."

"All they're going to do is ride in the back!"

"Trucks. Hunting. Fire. Those are men's things," I said.

Only one of the trucks came back. Everyone but Tuka, Kuara, and some of the Bantu returned. "The truck's stuck in the sand; the Whites decided to wait until dawn to pull it out," Gai said. "Tuka said he'd sleep beside it. You know how he is about trucks!" Everyone laughed. Except me. An empty space throbbed in my heart; that I wanted him home angered me.

Then rain came. It was ga go—male rain. It poured down strong and sudden, not even and gentle, the female rain that fills the land with water. Rain, during ga! Everyone shouted and danced for joy. Even the Whites danced. A miracle! people said. I thought about the honey badger caught during kuma, and was afraid. I felt alone. In spite of my fear, perhaps because of it, I did a foolish thing. I slept away from the others.

In the night the quiet again touched me. Num uncurled in my belly. I did not beckon it forth. I swear I didn't. I wasn't even thinking about it. As I slept I felt my body clench tight. In my dreams I could hear my breathing— shallow and rapid. Fear seized me and shook me like the twig of a ni ni bush. I sank into the earth. Tuka and Kuara were standing slump-shouldered in steaming, ankle-deep water at the waterhole where we had danced. Kuara was wearing the head of a wildebeest; the eyes had been carved out and replaced with smoldering coals. "Run away, mother," he kept saying.

I awoke to shadows. A fleeting darkness came upon me before I could move. I glimpsed Gai grinning beneath the moon. Then a hand was clapped over my mouth.

Doctor Stefanko returns after I've finished the hut. She and Gai bring warthog and kudu hides, porcupine quills, tortoise shells, ostrich eggs, a sharpening stone, an awl, two assagai blades, pots of Bantu clay. Many things. Gai grins as he sets them down. Doctor Stefanko watches him. "Back on Earth, he might not have remained a bachelor if your people hadn't kept thinking of him as one," she tells me as he walks away. Then she also leaves.

Later, she brings Kuara.

He comes sprinting, gangly, the grass nearly to his chin. "Mama," he shouts, "mama, mama," and I take him in my arms, whirling and laughing. I put my hands upon his cheeks; his arms are around my waist. Real. Oh, yes. So very real, my Kuara! Tears roll down my face. He looks hollow-eyed, and his hair has been shaved. But I do not let concern stop my heart. I weep from joy, not pain.

Doctor Stefanko leaves, and Kuara and I talk. He babbles about a strange sleep, and Doctor Stefanko, and Gai, as I show him the camp. We play with the knobs Doctor Stefanko showed me; one of them makes a line of small windows blink on in the slight angle between wall-sky and ceiling-sky. The windows look like square beads. There, faces pause and peer. Children. Old men. Women with smiles like springhares. People of many races. I tell him not to smile or acknowledge their presence. Not even that of the children. Especially not the children. The faces are surely ghosts, I warn. Ghosts dreaming of becoming Gwi.

We listen to the voice Doctor Stefanko calls the monitor. It is singsong, lulling. A woman's voice, I think. "U and Kuara, the latest additions to Carnival, members of the last Gwi tribal group, will soon become accustomed to our excellent accommodations," the voice says. The voice floats with us as we go to gather roots and wood.

A leguaan pokes its head from the rocky kranze, listening. Silently I put down my wood. Then my hand moves slowly. So slowly it is almost not movement. I grab. Caught! Kuara shrieks and claps his hands. "Notice the scarification across the cheeks and upper legs," the voice is saying. "The same is true of the buttocks, though like any self-respecting Gwi, U will not remove her kaross in the presence of others except during the Eland Dance." I carry the leguaan wiggling to the hut. "Were she to disrobe, you would notice tremendous fatty deposits in the buttocks, a phenomenon known as steatopygia. Unique to Bushmen (or 'Bushwomen,' we should say), this anatomical feature aids in food storage. It was once believed that. . . ."

After breaking the leguaan's neck, I take off the kaross of genuine gemsbok and, using gui fiber, tie it in front of my hut. It makes a wonderful door. I have never had a door. Tuka and I slept outside, using the tshushi for storage. Kuara will have a door. A door between him and the watchers.

He will have fire. Fire for warmth and food and U to sing beside. I gather kane and ore sticks and carve male and female, then use galli grass for tinder. Like Tuka did. "The Gwi are marked by a low, flattened skull, tiny mastoid processes, a bulging or vertical forehead, peppercorn hair, a nonpragnathous face. . . ." I twirl the sticks between my palms. It seems to take forever. My arms grow sore. I am ready to give up when smoke suddenly curls.

Gibbering, Kuara leaps about the camp. I gaze at the fire and grin with delight. But it is frightened delight. I will make warmth fires and food fires, I decide as I blow the smoke into flame. Not ritual fires. Not without Tuka.

I roast the leguaan with eru berries and the tsha-cucumber, which seems plentiful. But I am not Tuka, quick with fire and laughter; the fire-making has taken too long. Halfway through the cooking, Kuara seizes the lizard and, bouncing it in his hands as though it were hot dough, tears it apart. "Kuara!" I blurt out in pretended anger. He giggles as, the intestines dangling, he holds up the lizard to eat. I smile sadly. Kuara's laughing eyes and ostrich legs . . . so much like Tuka!

"The Gwi sing no praises of battles or warriors," the voice sing-says. I help Kuara finish the leguaan. "They have no history of warfare; ironically, it was last century's South African War, in which the Gwi did not take part, that assured their extinction. Petty arguments are common (even a nonviolent society cannot keep husbands and wives from scrapping), but fighting is considered dishonorable. To fight is to have failed to. . . ." When I gaze up there are no faces in the windows.

At last, dusk dapples the grass. Kuara finds a guinea-fowl feather and a reed; leaning against my legs, he busies himself making a zani. The temperature begins to drop. I decide the door would fit better around our shoulders than across the tshushi.

A figure strides out of the setting sun. I shield my eyes with my arm. Doctor Stefanko. She smiles and nods at Kuara, now tying a nut onto his toy for a weight, and sits on a log. Her smile remains, though it is drained of joy. She looks at me seriously.

"I do hope Kuara's presence will dissuade you from any more *displays* such as you exhibited this afternoon," she tells me. "Surely you must realize that he is here with you on a . . . a trial basis, shall we say. If you create problems, we'll have to take the boy back to the prep rooms until . . . until you become more accustomed to your surroundings." She taps her forefinger against her palm. "This impetuousness of yours has got to cease." Another tap. "And cease now."

Head cocked, I gaze at her, not understanding.

"Taking off your kaross simply because the monitor

said you do not." She nods knowingly. "Oh, yes, we're aware when you're listening. And that frightful display with the lizard!" She makes a face and appears to shudder. "Then there's the matter of the fire." She points toward the embers. "You're supposed to be living here like you did back on Earth. At least during the day. Men *always* started the fires."

"Men were always present." I shrug.

"Yes. Well, arrangements are being made. For the time being stick to foods you don't need to cook. And use the heating system." She goes to the rock and, on hands and knees, turns one of the knobs. A humming sounds. Smiling and rubbing her hands over the fire, she reseats herself on the log, pulls a photograph from her hip pocket and hands it to me. I turn the picture right-side-up. Doctor Morse is standing with her arm across Gai's shoulders. His left arm is around her waist. The Land Rovers are in the background.

"Impetuous," Doctor Stefanko says, leaning over and clicking her fingernail against the photograph. "That's exactly what Doctor Morse wrote about you in her notebooks. *She* considered it a virtue." Again the eyebrow lifts. "We do not." Then she adds proudly, "She was my grandmother, you know. As you can imagine, I have more than simply a professional interest in our Southwest African section here at Carnival."

I start to hand back the photograph. She raises her hand, halting me. "Keep it," she says. "Think of it as a wedding present. The first of many."

That night, wrapped in the kaross, Kuara and I sleep in one another's arms, in the tshushi. He is still clutching the zani, though he has not thrown it once into the air to watch it spin down. Perhaps he will tomorrow. Tomorrow. An ugly word. I lie staring at the dark ground, sand clenched in my fists. I wonder if, somehow using devices to see in the dark, the ghosts in the sky-windows are watching me sleep. I wonder if they will watch the night Gai climbs upon my back and grunts throughout the marrying-thing.

Sleep comes. A tortured sleep. I can feel myself hugging Kuara. He squirms against the embrace but does not awaken. In my dreams I slide out of myself and, stirring up the fire, dance the Eland Dance. My body is slick with eland fat. My eyes stare rigidly into the darkness and my head is held high and stiff. Chanting, I lift and put down my feet, moving around and around the fire. Other women clap and sing the kia-healing songs. Men play the gwashi and musical bows. The music lifts and lilts and throbs. Rhythm thrums within me. Each muscle knows the song. Tears squeeze from my eyes. Pain leadens my legs. And still I dance.

Then, at last, num rises. It uncurls in my belly and breathes fire-breath up my spine. I fight the fear. I dance against the dread. I tremble with fire. My eyes slit with agony. I do not watch the women clapping and singing. My breaths come in shallow, heated gasps. My breasts bounce. I dance. Num continues to rise. It tingles against the base of my brain. It fills my head. My entire body is alive, burning. Thorns are sticking everywhere in my flesh. My breasts are fiery coals. I can feel ghosts, hot ghosts, ghosts of the past, crowding into my skull. I stagger for the hut; Kuara and U, my old self, await me. I slide into her flesh like someone slipping beneath the cool, mud-slicked waters of a year-round pan. I slide in among her fear and sorrow and the anguished joy of Kuara beside her.

She stirs. A movement of a sleeping head. A small groan; denial. I slide in further. I become her once again. My head is aflame with num and ghosts. "U," I whisper, "I bring the ghosts of all your former selves, and of your people." Again she groans, though weaker; the pleasure-groan of a woman making love. Her body stretches, stiffens. Her nails rake Kuara's back. She accepts me, then; accepts her self. I fill her flesh.

And bring the quiet, for the third time in her life. Down and down into the sand she seeps, leaving nothing of her self behind, her hands around Kuara's wrists as she pulls him after her, the zani's guinea-fowl feather whipping behind him as if in a wind. She passes through sand, Carnical's concrete base, moonrock, moving ever downward, badger-burrowing. She breaks through into a darkness streaked with silver light: into the core of the moon, where live the ancestral dead, the ghosts of kia. She tumbles downward, crying her dismay and joy, her kaross fluttering. In the center of the hollow, where water shines like cold silver, awaits Tuka, arms outstretched. He is laughing—a shrill, forced cackle. Such is the only laughter a ghost can know whose sleep has been disturbed. They will dance this night, the three of them: U, Tuka, Kuara.

Then he will teach her the secret of oa, the poison squeezed from the female larvae of the dung beetle. Poison for arrows he will teach her to make. Poison for which Bushmen know no antidote.

She will hunt when she returns to Gai and to Doctor Stefanko.

She will not hunt animals.

SWARMER, SKIMMER

≋≋≋≋≋≋≋≋≋≋≋≋≋≋≋≋≋≋≋≋

Gregory Benford

Invasions from space have been a common
theme in science fiction almost since the beginning. Xenophobia is not the only reason; writers
have always been intrigued by the thought of
unknown beings with strange powers pitted
against the entrenched strengths of our entire
world. Here Gregory Benford brings the theme
to life once more, in a thoughtful and taut adventure story.

Gregory Benford, a physicist by primary pro-
fession, last year won (for his novel *Timescape*)
the Nebula Award, the John W. Campbell
Memorial Award, the British Fantasy Award . . .
indeed, every major award in science fiction except the Hugo. At least two magazines were so
impressed that they credited him with having
won the Hugo too.

I

WARREN WATCHED THE MANAMIX GOING DOWN. The ocean was in her and would smother the engines soon, swamping her into silence. Her lights still glowed in the mist and rain.

She lay on her starboard side, down by the head, and the swell took her solidly with a dull hammering. The strands that the Swarmers cast had laced across her decks and wrapped around the gun emplacements and over the men who had tended them.

The long green and yellow strands still licked up the sides and over the deck, seeking and sticking. They were spun out from the swollen belly pouches of the Swarmers. Their green bodies clustered in the dark water at the bows.

A long finger of tropical lightning cracked. It lit the wedge of space between the close black storm clouds and the rain-pocked, wrinkled skin of the sea. The big aliens glistened in the glare.

Warren treaded water and floated. He tried to make no noise. A strand floated nearby and a wave brushed him against it but there was no sting. The Swarmer it came from was probably dead and drifting down now. But there were many more in the crashing surf near the ship and he could hear screams from the other crewmen who had gone over the side with him.

The port davits on the top deck dangled, trailing ropes, and the lifeboats hung from them unevenly, useless. Warren had tried to get one down but the winch and cabling fouled and he had finally gone over the side like the rest.

Her running lights winked and then came on steady again. The strands made a tangled net over the decks now. Once they stunned a man, the sticky yellow nerve sap stopped coming and they lost their sting. As he watched, bobbing in the waves, one of the big aliens amidships rolled and brought in its strand and pulled a body over the railing. The man was dead and when the body hit the water there was some quick fighting over it.

Wisps of steam curled from the engine-room hatch. He thought he could hear the whine of the diesels. Her port screw was clear and spinning like a metal flower. In the hull plates he could see the ragged holes punched by the packs of Swarmers. She was filling fast now.

Warren knew the jets the Filipinos had promised the captain would never get out this far. It was a driving, splintering storm and to drop the canisters of poison that would kill the Swarmers would take low and dangerous flying. The Filipinos would not risk it.

She went without warning. The swell came over her bows and the funnel slanted down fast. The black water poured into her and into the high hoods of her ventilators and the running lights started to go out. The dark gully of her forward promenade and bay filled and steam came gushing up from the hatches like a giant thing exhaling.

He braced himself for it, thinking of the engine he had tended, and the sudden deep booming came as the sea reached in and her boilers blew. She slid in fast. Lightning crackled and was reflected in a thousand shattered mirrors of the sea. The waters accepted her and the last he saw was a huge rush of steam as great chords boomed in her hull.

In the quiet afterward, calls and then screams came to him, carried on the gusts. There had been so many men going off the aft deck the Swarmers had missed him. Now they had coiled their strands back in and would find him soon. He began to kick, floating on his back, trying not to splash.

Something brushed his leg. He went limp.

It came again.

He pressed the fear back, far away from him. The thing was down there in the blackness, seeing only by its phosphorescent stripes along the jawline. If it caught some movement—

A wave rolled him over. He floated face down and did nothing about it. A wave rocked him and then another and his face came out for an instant and he took a gasp of air. Slowly he let the current turn him to the left until a slit of his mouth broke clear and he could suck in small gulps of air.

The cool touch came at a foot. A hip. He waited. He let the air bubble out of him slowly when his chest started to burn so that he would have empty lungs when he broke surface. A slick skin rubbed against him. His throat began to go tight. His head went under again and he felt himself in the black without weight and saw a dim glimmering, a wash of silvery light like stars—and he realized he was staring at the Swarmer's grinning phosphorescent jaw.

The fire in his throat and chest was steady and he struggled to keep them from going into spasm. The grin of gray light came closer. Something cold touched his chest, nuzzled him, pushed—

A wave broke hard over him and he tumbled and was in the open, face up, gasping, ears ringing. The wave was deep and he took two quick breaths before the water closed over him again.

He opened his eyes in the dark water. Nothing. No light anywhere. He could not risk a kick to take him to the air. He waited to bob up again, and did, and this time saw something riding down the wave near him. A lifeboat.

He made a slow easy stroke toward it. Nothing touched him. If the Swarmer had already eaten it might just have been curious. Maybe it was not making its turn and coming back.

A wave, a stroke, a wave— He stretched and caught the trailing aft line. He wrenched himself up and sprawled aboard, rattling the oars in the gunwale. Quietly he paddled toward the weakening shouts. Then the current took him to starboard. He did not use the oars in the locks because they would clank and the sound would carry. He pulled toward the sounds but they faded. A fog came behind the rain.

There was a foot of water in the boat and the planking was splintered where a Swarmer tried to stove it in. A case of supplies was still clamped in the gunwale.

Awhile later he sighted a smudge of yellow. It was the woman, Rosa, clinging to a life jacket she had got on wrong. He had been staying down in the boat to keep hidden from the Swarmers but without thinking about it he pulled her aboard.

She was a journalist he had seen before on the *Manamix*. She was covering the voyage for Brazilian TV and wanted to take this fast run down from Taiwan to Manila. She had said she wanted to see a Swarm beaten off and her camera crew was on deck all day bothering the crew.

She sat aft and huddled down and then after a time started to talk. He covered her mouth. Her eyes rolled from side to side, searching the water. Warren paddled slowly. He wore jeans and a long-sleeved shirt, and even soaked they kept off the night chill. The fog was thick. They heard some distant splashes and once a rifle shot. The fog blotted out the sounds.

They ate some of the provisions when it got light enough to see. Warren felt the planking for seepage and he could tell it was getting worse.

A warm dawn broke over them. Wreckage drifted nearby. There were uprooted trees, probably carried out to sea by the storm. The rain had started just as the first packs struck the bows. That had made it harder to hit them with the automatic rifles on deck and Warren was pretty sure the Swarmers knew that.

There was smashed planking from other boats near them, an empty box, some thin twine, life jackets, bottles. No one had ever seen Swarmers show interest in debris in the water, only prey. The things had no tools. Certainly they had not made the ships that dropped into the atmosphere and seeded the oceans. Those craft would have been worth looking at but they had broken up on the seas and sunk before anyone could get to them.

The wreckage would not attract Swarmers but they might be following the current to find survivors. Warren knew no school of Swarmers was nearby because they always broke surface while in a Swarm and you could see the mass of them from a long way off. There were always the lone Swarmers that some people thought were scouts, though. Nobody really knew what they did but they were just as dangerous as the others.

He could not steer well enough to pick up wreckage. The boat was taking on more water and he did not think they had much time. They needed the drifting wood and he had to swim for it. Five times he went in the water and each time he had to push the fear away from him and swim as smoothly and quietly as he could until finally the fear came strongly and he could not do it anymore.

He skinned the bark from two big logs, using the knife from the provisions case, and made lashings. The boat was shipping water now as it rolled in the swell. He and Rosa cut and lashed and built. When they had a frame of logs they broke up the boat and used some of the planks for decking. The boat sank before they could save most of it but they got the case onto the raft.

He pried nails out of some of the driftwood. By now his vision was blurring in the bright sunlight and he was clumsy. They cleared a space in the frame to lie on and Rosa fell asleep while he was pounding in the last board. Each task he had now was at the end of a tunnel and he peered through it at his hands doing the job and they were dumb and thick as though he was wearing gloves. He secured the case and other loose pieces and hooked his right arm over a limb to keep from falling overboard. He fell asleep face down.

II

The next day as he got more driftwood and lashed it into the raft there was a slow, burning, pointless kind of anger in him. He could have stayed on land and lived off the dole. He had known the risks when he signed on as engineer.

It had been six years since the first signs of the aliens. With each year more ships had gone down, hulled in deep water and beyond protection from the air. The small craft, fishermen and the like, had been first to go. That did not change things much. Then the Swarmers multiplied and cargo vessels started going down. Trade across open seas was impossible.

The oceanographers and biologists said they were starting to understand the Swarmer mating and attack modes by that time. It was slow work. Studying them on the open water was dangerous. When they were captured they hammered themselves against the walls of their containers until the jutting bone of their foreheads shattered and drove splinters into their brains.

Then the Swarmers began taking bigger ships. They

found a way to mass together and hull even the big super-tankers.

By then the oceanographers were dying, too, in their reinforced-hull research ships. The Swarmers could sink anything then and no one could explain how they had learned to modify their tactics. The things did not have particularly large brains.

There were reports of strange-looking Swarmers, of strays from the schools, of massed Swarmers who could take a ship down in minutes. Then came photographs of a totally new form, the Skimmers, who leaped and dove deep and were smaller than the Swarmers. The specimens had been killed by probots at depths below 200 fathoms, where Swarmers had never been seen.

The automatic stations and hunters were the only way men could study the Swarmers by that time. Large cargo vessels could not sail safely. Oil did not move from the Antarctic or China or the Americas. Wheat stayed in the farm nations. The intricate world economy ground down.

Warren had been out of work and stranded in the chaos of Tokyo. His wife had left him years before, so he had no particular place to go. When the *Manamix* advertised that it had special plates in her hull and deck defenses, he signed into a berth. The pay was good and there was no other sea work anyway. He could have run on the skim-ships that raced across the Taiwan Straits or to Korea, but those craft did not need engineers. If their engines ever went out they were finished before any repair could get done because the loud motors always drew the Swarmers in their wake.

Warren was an engineer and he wanted to stick to what he knew. He had worked hard for the rating. The heavy plates in the fore and aft holds had looked strong to him. But they had buckled inside of half an hour.

Rosa held up well at first. They never saw any other survivors of the *Manamix*. They snagged more wreckage and logs and lashed it together. Floating with the wood they found a coil of wire and an aluminum railing. He pounded the railing into nails and they made a lean-to for protection from the sun.

They were drifting northwest at first. Then the current shifted and took them east. He wondered if a search pattern could allow for that and find them.

One night he took Rosa with a power and confidence he had not felt since years before, with his wife. It surprised him.

They ate the cans of provisions. He used some scraps for bait and caught a few fish but they were small. She knew a way to make the twine tight and springy. He used it to make a bow and arrow and it was accurate enough to shoot fish if they came close.

Their water began to run out. Rosa kept their stores under the lean-to and at seven days Warren found the water was almost gone. She had been drinking more than her share.

"I had to," she said, backing away from him at a crouch. "I can't stand it, I . . . I get so bad. And the sun, it's too hot, I just . . ."

He wanted to stop but he could not and he hit her several times. There was no satisfaction in it.

Through the afternoon Rosa cringed at a corner of the raft and Warren lay under the lean-to and thought. In the cool, orderly limits of the problem he found a kind of rest. He squatted on a plank and rocked with the swell and inside, where he had come to live more and more these past years, the world was not just the gurgle and rush of waves and the bleaching raw edge of salt and sun. Inside there were the books and the diagrams and things he had known. He struggled to put them together.

Chemistry. He cut a small slit in the rubber stopper of a water can and lowered it into the sea on a long fishing line.

The deeper water was cold. He pulled the can up and put it inside a bigger can. It steamed like a champagne bucket. Water beaded on the outside of the small can. The big can held the drops. It was free of salt but there was not much.

Nine days out the water was gone. Rosa cried. Warren tried to find a way to make the condensing better but they did not have many cans. The yield was no more than a mouthful a day.

In the late afternoon of that day Rosa suddenly hit him and started shouting filthy names. She said he was a sailor and should get them water and get them to land and when they finally did get picked up she would tell everybody how bad a sailor he was and how they had nearly died because he did not know how to find the land.

He let her run down and stayed away from her. If she scratched him with her long fingernails the wound would heal badly and there was no point in taking a risk. They had not taken any fish on the lines for a long time now and they were getting weaker. The effort of hauling up the cans from below made his arms tremble.

The next day the sea ran high. The raft groaned, rising sluggishly and plunging hard. Waves washed them again and again so it was impossible to sleep or even rest. At dusk Warren discovered jelly seahorses as big as a thumbnail riding in the foam that lapped over the raft. He stared at them and tried to remember what he had learned of biology.

If they started drinking anything with a high salt content the end would come fast. But they had to have something. He put a few on his tongue, tentatively, and waited until they melted. They were salty and fishy but seemed less salty than sea water. The cool moisture seemed right and his throat welcomed it. He spoke to Rosa and showed her and they gathered handfuls of the seahorses until nightfall.

On the eleventh day there were no seahorses and the sun pounded at them. Rosa had made hats for them, using cloth from the wreckage. That helped with the worst of the day but to get through the hours Warren had to sit with closed eyes under the lean-to, carefully working through the clear hallways of his mind.

The temptation to drink sea water was festering in him, flooding the clean places inside him where he had withdrawn. He kept before him the chain of things to keep himself intact.

If he drank sea water he would take in a quantity of dissolved salt. The body did not need much salt so it had to get rid of most of what he took in. The kidneys would sponge up the salt from his blood and secrete it. But doing that took pure water, at least a pint a day.

The waves churned before him and he felt the rocking of the deck and he made it into a chant.

Drink a pint of sea water a day. The body turns it into about twenty cubic centimeters of pure water.

But the kidneys need more than that to process the salt. They react. They take water from the body tissues.

The body dries out. The tongue turns black. Nausea. Fever. Death.

He sat there for hours, reciting it, polishing it down to

a few key words, making it perfect. He told it to Rosa and she did not understand but that was all right.

In the long afternoon he squinted against the glare and the world became one of sounds. The rattling of their cans came to him against the murmur of the sea and the hollow slap of waves against the underside of the raft. Then there was a deep thump. He peered to starboard. A rippling in the water. Rosa sat up. He gestured for silence. The planks and logs creaked and worked against each other and the thump came again.

He had heard dolphins knocking under the raft before and this was not their playful string of taps. Warren crawled out from the lean-to and into the yellow sunlight and a big green form broke surface and rolled belly-over, goggling at them with a bulging eye. Its mouth was like a slash in the blunt face. The teeth were narrow and sharp.

Rosa cried in terror and the Swarmer seemed to hear her. It circled the raft, following her awkward scuttling. She screamed and moved faster but the big thing flicked its tail and kept alongside her.

His concentration narrowed to an absolute problem that took in the Swarmer and its circling and the closed geometry of the raft. If they let it come in when it chose, it would lunge against the raft and catch them off balance and have a good chance of tumbling them into the water or breaking up the raft.

The green form turned and dove deep under the raft.

"Rosa!" He tore off his shirt. "Here! Wave it in the water on the side." He dipped the shirt, crouching at the edge. "Like this."

She hung back. "I . . . but . . . no, I . . ."

"Damn it! I'll stop it before it gets to you."

She gaped at him and the Swarmer broke water on the far side of the raft. It rolled ponderously, as if it was having trouble understanding how to attack a thing so much smaller than a ship, and attack it alone.

Rosa took the shirt hesitantly. He encouraged her and she bent over and swished a tip of it in the surf. "Good."

Warren brought out the crude arrow he had made with a centimeter-thick slat from the *Manamix* lifeboat. He had tapered it down and driven a nail in the head. He tucked the arrow into the rubber strip of his bow and tested it. The arrow had a line on it and did not fly very straight. Not much good for fish.

He slitted his eyes against the glare and looked out at the shallow troughs. The sea warped and rippled where the thing had just disappeared. Warren sensed that it had judged them now and was gliding back in the blue shadows under the raft, coming around for its final pass. It would not see the shirt until it turned and that would bring it up and near the corner where Warren now stood, between its path and Rosa. He drew the arrow back in a smooth motion, sighting, straining, sighting—

Rosa saw the dim shape first. She flicked the rag out of the water with a jerk. Warren saw something dart up, seeming to come up out of the floor of the ocean itself, catching the refracted bands of light from the waves.

Rosa screamed and stepped back. The snout broke water and the mouth like a cut was leering at them, and Warren let go the arrow *thunk* and followed it forward, scrabbling on all fours. The thing had the arrow in under the gills and the big flaps of green flesh bulged and flared open in spasms as it rolled to the side.

Warren snatched at the arrow line and missed. "Grab the end!" he called. The arrow was enough to stun the Swarmer but that was all. The thing was stunned with the nail driven deep in it but Warren wanted more of it now, more than just the killing of it, and he splashed partway off the raft to reach the snout and drag it in. He got a slippery grip on a big blue ventral fin. The mouth snapped. It thrashed and Warren used the motion to haul it toward the raft. He swung himself, the wood cutting into his hip, and levered the body partway onto the deck. Rosa took a fin and pulled. He used the pitch of the deck and his weight to flip the thing over on its side. It arched its back, twisting to gain leverage to thrash back over the side. Warren had his knife out and as the thing slid away from him he drove the blade in, slipping it through soft tissue at the side and riding up against the spine. Warren slashed down the body, feeling the Swarmer convulse in agony. Then it straightened and seemed to get smaller.

The two stood back and looked at the scaly green body, three meters long. Its weight made the raft dip in the swell.

Something sticky was beginning to drain from the long cut. Warren fetched a can and scooped up the stuff. It was a thin, pale yellow fluid. He did not hear Rosa's whimpering, stumbling approach as he lifted the can to his lips.

He caught the cool, slightly acrid taste of it for an instant. He opened his mouth wider to take it in. She struck the can from his hands. It clattered on the deck.

His punch drove her to her knees. "Why?" he yelled. "What do you care—"

"Wrong," she sputtered out. "Ugly. They're not . . . not *normal* . . . to . . . to eat."

"You want to drink? Want to live?"

She shook her head, blinking. "Na . . . ah, yeah, but . . . not that. Maybe . . ."

He looked at her coldly and she moved away. The carcass was dripping. He wedged it against a log and propped cans under it. He drank the first filled can, and the second.

The dorsal and ventral fins sagged in death. In the water he had seen them spread wide as wings. The bulging brain case and the goggle eyes seemed out of place, even in the strange face with its squeezed look. The rest of the body was sleek like the large fish. He had heard somebody say that evolution forced the same slim contours on any fast thing that lived in an ocean, even on submarines.

The Swarmer had scaly patches around the forefins and at each ventral fin. The skin looked like it was getting thick and hard. Warren did not remember seeing that in the photographs of dead ones but then the articles and movies had not said anything about the Swarmer scouts either until a year ago. They kept changing.

Rosa crouched under the lean-to. Once, when he drank, she spat out some word he could not understand.

The third can he set down on the boards halfway between them. He cut into the body and found the soft pulpy places where it was vulnerable to an arrow. He learned the veins and arteries and ropes of muscle. There were big spaces in the head that had something to do with hearing. In the belly pouch the strand was shriveled and laced with a kind of blue muscle. Around the fins where the skin became scaly there were little bones and cartilage that did not seem to have any use.

Rosa edged closer as he worked. The heat weighed on her. She licked her lips until they were raw and finally she drank.

He kept track of the days by making a cut each morning in a tree limb. The ritual sawing became crucial, part of the struggle. The itching salt spray and the hammering of the sun blurred distinctions. In the simple counting he found there was some order, the beauty of number that existed outside the steady rub of the sea's green sameness.

Between the two of them they made the killing of the Swarmers a ritual as well. The scouts came at random intervals now, with never more than three days of waiting until the next thumping probes at the planking. Then Rosa would stoop and wave the shirt in the water. The thing would make a pass to look and then turn to strike, coming by the jutting corner, and Warren would drive the arrow into the soft place.

Rosa would crouch under the shelter then and mumble to herself and wait for him to gut it and bleed the watery pouches of fin fluid and finally take the sour syrup from behind the eyes.

With each fresh kill he learned more. They cut up some cloth and made small bags to hold the richer parts of the carcass and then chewed it for each drop. Sometimes it made them sick. After that he twisted chunks of the flesh in a cloth bag and let the drops air in the sun. That was not so bad. They ate the big slabs of flesh but it was the fluid they needed most.

With each kill Rosa became more distant. She sat dreamily swaying at the center of their plank island, humming and singing to herself, coiling inward. Warren worked and thought.

On the twenty-first day of drifting she woke him. He came up reluctantly from the vague, shifting sleep. She was shouting.

Darting away into the bleak dawn was something lean and blue. It leaped into the air and plunged with a shower of foam and then almost in the same instant was flying out of the steep wall of a wave, turning in the gleaming fresh sun.

"A Skimmer," he murmured. It was the first he had ever seen.

Rosa cried out. Warren stared out into the hills and valleys of moving water, blinking, following her finger. A gray cylinder the size of his hand floated ten meters away.

He picked up the tree limb they used for marking the days. His hands were puffed up now from the constant damp and the bark of the limb scraped them. No green shapes moved below. He rocked with the swell, waiting at the edge of the raft for a random current to bring the gray thing closer.

A long time passed. It bobbed sluggishly and came no closer. Warren leaned against the pitch of the deck and stretched for it. The limb was short at least a meter.

He swayed back, relaxing, letting the clenching in his muscles ease away. His arms trembled. He could swim to it in a few quick strokes, turn and get back in a few—

No. If he let go he would be sucked into the same endless caverns that Rosa was wandering. He had to hold on. And take no risks.

He stepped back. The thing to do was wait and see if—

White spray exploded in front of him. The lean form shot up into the air and Warren rolled back away from it. He came up with the knife held close to him.

But the Skimmer arced away from the raft. It cut back into a wave and was gone for an instant and then burst up and caught the cylinder in its slanting mouth. In the air it rolled and snapped its head. The cylinder clunked onto the raft. The Skimmer leaped again, blue-white, and was gone into the endlessly shifting faces of green marble.

Rosa was huddled in the shelter. Warren picked up the cylinder carefully. It was smooth and regular but something about it told him it had not been made with tools. There were small flaws in the soft, foamy gray, like the blotches on a tomato. At one end it puckered as though a tassel had fallen away.

He rubbed it, pulled at it, turned the ends— It split with a moist pop. Inside there curled a thick sheet of the same softly resistant gray stuff. He unrolled it.

SECHTON XMENAPU DE AN LANSDORFKOPPEN SW BY W ABLE SAGON MXIL VESSE L ANSAGEN MANLATS WIR UNS? FTH ASDØLENGS ERTY EARTHN PROFUILEN CO NISHI NAGARE KALLEN KOPFT EARTHN UMI

He studied the combinations and tried to fit them together so there was some logic to it. It was no code, he guessed. Some of the words were German and there was some English and Japanese, but most of it was either meaningless or no language he knew. VESSE L might be *vessel.* ANSAGEN—to say? He wished he remembered more of the German he had picked up in the merchant marine.

The words were in a clear typeface like a newspaper and were burned into the sheet.

He could make no more of it. Rosa did not want to look at the sheet. When he made her, she shook her head, no, she could not pick out any new words.

A Swarmer came later that day. Rosa did not back away fast enough and the big shape shot up out of the water. It bit down hard on the shirt as Warren's arrow took it and the impact made the blunt head snap back. Rosa was not ready for it and she stumbled forward and into the sea. The Swarmer tried to flip away. Warren caught her as she went into the water. The alien lunged at her but he heaved her back onto the deck. He had dropped the bow. The Swarmer rolled. The bow washed overboard and then the tail fins caught the edge of the raft and it twisted and came tumbling aboard. Warren hit it with the tree limb. It kept thrashing but the blows stunned it. He waited for the right angle and then slipped the knife in deep, away from the snapping jaws, and the thing went still.

Rosa helped with the cutting up. She started talking suddenly while he looked for the bow. He was intent on seeing if it was floating nearby and at first did not notice that she was not just muttering. He spotted the bow and managed to fetch it in. Rosa was discussing the Swarmers, calmy and in a matter-of-fact voice he had not heard from her before.

"The important thing, *ja*, is to not let one get away," she concluded.

"Guess so," Warren said.

"They know about the raft, the Swarm comes."

"If they can find us, yeah."

"They send out these scouts. The pack, it will follow where the lone ones tell it."

"We'll get 'em."

"Forever? No. Only solution is land."

"None I've seen. We're drifting west, could be—"

"I thought you are sailor."

"Was."

"Then sail us to land."

"Not that easy," Warren said, and went on to tell her how hard it was to get any control of a raft, and anyway he didn't know where they were, what the landfalls were out here. She sniffed contemptuously at this news. "Find an island," she repeated several times. Warren argued, not because he had any clear reason, but because he knew how to survive here and a vague fear came when he thought about the land. Rosa was speaking freely and easily now and she thought fast, sure of herself. Finally he broke off and set to work storing away the slabs of Swarmer meat. The talk confused him.

The next day a Skimmer came and leaped near the raft and there was another cylinder. It swam away, a blur of silvery motion. He read the sheet.

GEFAHRLICH GROSS HIRO ADFIN SOLID MNX 8 SHIO NISHI. KURO NAGARE. ANAXLE UNS NORMEN 286 W SCATTER PORTLINE ZERO NAGARE. NISHI.

He could not make any sense of it. Rosa worked on it, not much interested, and shrugged. He tried to scratch marks on the sheets, thinking that he could send them something, ask questions. The sheet would not take an impression.

A Swarmer surfaced to the west the next day. Rosa shrieked. It circled them twice and came in fast toward Rosa's lure. Warren shot at it and hit too far back. The tip buried itself uselessly in a spot where he knew there was only fatty tissue. The Swarmer lunged at Rosa. She was ready though, falling back from the edge, and it missed. Warren yanked on the line and freed the arrow. The Swarmer flinched as the arrow came out and rolled off the raft. It sank and was gone.

"Don't let it get away!" Rosa cried.

"It's not coming up."

"You hit it in the wrong place."

"Went in pretty deep, though. Might die before it can get back to the pack."

"You think so?"

Warren didn't but he said, "Might."

"You, you have *got* to find us an island. *Now.*"

"I still think we're safe here."

"Incredible! You are no kind of sailor at all and you are afraid to admit it. Afraid to say you don't know how to find land."

"Bullshit. I—" but she interrupted him with a flood of words he couldn't keep up with. He heard her out, nodding finally, not knowing himself why he wanted to stay on the raft, on the sea. It just *felt* better, was all, and he did not know how to tell her that.

When the argument was finally over, he went back to thinking about the second message. Some of it was German and he knew a little of that, but not those particular words. He had never learned any Japanese even though he had lived in Tokyo.

The next morning at dawn he woke suddenly and thought there was something near the raft. The swell was smooth and orange as the sun caught it. On the glassy horizon he saw nothing. He was very hungry and he remembered the Swarmer from yesterday. He had used the meat from the first kills to bait their lines but nothing bit. He wondered if that was because the fish would not take Swarmer meat or if there were no fish down there to have. The aliens had been changing the food chain in the oceans, he had read about that.

Then he saw the gray dot floating far away. The raft was drifting toward it and in a few minutes he snagged it. The message said:

CONSQUE KPOF AMN SOLID. DA ØLEN MACHEN SMALL YOUTH SCHLECHT UNS. DERINGER CHANGE DA. UNS B WSW. SAGEN ARBEIT BEI MOUTH. SHIMA CIRCLE STEIN NONGO NONGO UMI DRASVITCH YOU.

He peered at the words and squatted on the deck and felt the long dragging minutes go by. If he could—

"Warren! Wa—Warren!" Rosa called. He followed her gesture.

A blur on the horizon. It dipped and rose among the ragged waves. Warren breathed deeply. "Land."

Rosa's eyes swelled and she barked out a sharp cackling laughter. Her lips went white with the laughing and she cried, "Yeah! Yeah! Land!" and shook her fists in the air.

Warren blinked and measured with his eyes the current and the angle the brown smudge ahead made with their course. They would not reach it by drifting.

He worked quickly.

He took the tree limb and knocked away the supports of the lean-to. In the center of the raft he knelt and measured out the distances with hands and fingers and worked a hole in between two planks. He could wedge the limb into it. He made a collar out of strips of bark. The limb was crooked but it made a vertical beam.

He took the plywood sheet of the lean-to and lashed it to the limb. With the knife he dug stays in the plywood. The wire that held the logs in place in the deck would have been good to use but he could not risk unlashing them. He used the last of their twine instead, passing it through the stays in the plywood and making them into trailing lines. The plywood was standing up now like a sail catching the wind; and by pulling the twine he could tack. The raft took the waves badly but by turning the plywood sheet he could take the strain off the weak places where the logs and boards met.

The wind backed into the east in late morning. They could not make much headway and the land was still a dark strip on the horizon. Warren broke off a big piece of wood at the raft corner. He hacked at it with the knife. A Swarmer surfaced nearby and Rosa started her screeching. He hit her and watched the Swarmer but he never stopped whittling at the wood in his lap. The Swarmer circled once and then turned and swam away to the south.

He finished with the wood. He made a housing for it with the rest of the bark strips. It sat badly at the end of the raft but the broad part dug into the water and by leaning against the top of it he could hold the angle. He got Rosa to hold two blocks of wood against the shaft for leverage and that way the thing worked something like a rudder. The raft turned to the south, toward the land.

Noon passed. Warren fought the wind and the rudder and tried to estimate the distance and the time left. If dark came before they reached it the current would take them past the land and they would never be able to beat back against the wind to find it again. He had been so long away from firm ground that he felt a need for it that was worse than his hunger. The pitch of the deck took the energy out of you day and night, you could not sleep for holding on to the deck when the sea got high, and you would do anything for something solid under you, for just—

Solid.

The message had said *solid*. Did that mean land? *Gefahrlich gross* something something *solid*. *Gefahrlich* had some kind of feel to it, something about bad or dangerous, he thought. *Gross* was *big*. Dangerous big blank blank land? Then some Japanese and other things and then *scatter portline zero. Scatter.* Make to go away?

Warren sweated and thought. Rosa brought him an old piece of Swarmer but he could not eat it. He thought about the words and saw there was some key to them, some beauty in it.

The rudder creaked against the wooden chocks. The land was a speck of brown now and he was pretty sure it was an island. The wind picked up. It was coming on to late afternoon.

Rosa moved around the raft when he did not need her, humming to herself, the Swarmers forgotten, eating from the pieces of meat still left. He did not try to stop her. She was eating out of turn but he needed all his thought now for the problem.

They were coming in on the northern shore. He would bring them in at a graze, to have a look before beaching. The current fought against them but the plywood was enough to sweep them to the south.

South? What was there . . .

WSW. West south west?

UNS B WSW.

Uns was *we* in German, he was pretty sure of that. We be WSW? On the WSW part of the land? The island? Or WSW of the island? We—the Skimmers.

He noticed Rosa squatting in the bow of the raft, eager, her weight dipping the boards into the blue-green swell and bringing hissing foam over the planks. It slowed them but she did not seem to see that. He opened his mouth to yell at her and then closed it. If they went slow, he would have more time.

The Skimmers were all he had out here and they had tried to tell him. . . .

Portline. Port was left. A line to the left? They were coming in from the northeast as near as he could judge. Veering left would take them around and to the southwest. Or WSW.

The island seemed to grow fast now as the sun set behind it. Warren squinted against the glare on the waves. There was something between them and the island. At the top of a wave he strained to see and could make out a darker line against pale sand. White rolls of surf broke on it.

A reef. The island was going to be harder to reach. He

would have to bring the raft in easy and search for a passage. Either that or smash up on it and swim the lagoon, if there was no way through the circle of coral around—

Circle stein nongo. He did not know what *stein* was, something to drink out of or something, but the rest might say *don't go in the circle.*

Warren slammed the tiller over full. It groaned and the collar nearly buckled but he held it, throwing his shoulder into it.

Rosa grunted and glared at him. The raft tacked to port. He pulled the twine and brought the plywood further into the wind.

Small youth schlecht uns. The Swarmers were bigger than the Skimmers but they might mean smaller in some other way. Smaller development? Smaller brain? *Schlecht uns.* Something about *us* and the Swarmers. If they were younger than the Skimmers, maybe their development was still to come. Something told him that *schlecht* was a word like *gefahrlich* but what the difference was he did not know. *Swarmers dangerous us?* There was nothing in the words to show action, to show who *us* was. Did *us* include Warren?

Rosa stumbled toward him. The swell was coming abaft now and she clutched at him for support. "Wha'? Land! Go!"

He rubbed his eyes and focused on her face but it looked different in the waning light. He saw that in all the days they had been together he had never known her. The face was just a face. There had never been enough words between them to make the face into something else. He . . .

The wind shifted and he shrugged away the distraction and worked the twine. He studied the dark green mass ahead. It was thickly wooded and there were bare patches and a beach. The white curves of breaking surf were clear now. The thick brown reef—

Things moved on the beach.

At first he thought they were driftwood, logs swept in by a storm. Then he saw one move and then another and they were green bodies in the sand. They crawled inland. A few had made it to the line of trees.

Small youth. Young ones who were still developing.

He numbly watched the island draw near. Dimly he felt Rosa pounding on his chest and shoulder. "Steer us in! You hear me? Make this thing—"

"Wha—what?"

"You afraid of the rocks, that it?" she spit out something in Spanish or Portuguese, something angry and full of scorn. Her eyes bulged unnaturally. "No *man* would—"

"Shut up." His lips felt thick. They were rushing by the island now, drawn by the fast currents.

"You fool, we're going to *miss*."

"Look . . . look at it. The Skimmers, they're telling us not to go there. You'll see . . ."

"See what?"

"The things. On the beach.

She followed his pointing. She peered at it, shook her head, and said fiercely, "So? Nothing there but logs."

Warren squinted and saw logs covered with green moss. The surf broke over some of them and they rolled in the swell, looking like they were crawling.

"I . . . I don't . . ." he began.

Rosa shook her head impatiently. "Huh!" She bent down and found a large board that was working loose. Grunting, she pried it up. Warren peered at the beach and saw stubs on the logs, stubs where there had once been fins. They began to work against the sand again. The logs stirred.

"You can stay here and die," Rosa said clearly. "Me, *no*." The reef swept by only meters away. Waves slapped and muttered against its flanks. The gray shelves of coral dipped beneath the water. Its shadowy mass below thinned and a clear sandy spot appeared. A passage. Shallow, but maybe enough . . .

"Wait . . ." Warren looked toward the beach again. *If he was wrong* . . . The logs had fleshy stubs now that pushed at the sand, crawling up the beach. What he had seen as knotholes were something else. Sores? He strained to see. . . .

Rosa dived into the break in the reef. She hit cleanly and wallowed onto the board. Resolutely she stroked through the water, battling the swells of waves refracted into the opening.

"Wait! I think the Swarmers are—" She could not hear him over the slopping of waves on the reef.

He remembered distantly the long days . . . the Skimmers . . . "Wait!" he called. Rosa was through the passage and into the calm beyond. "Wait!" She went on.

Where he had seen logs he now saw something bloated and grotesque, sick. He shook his head. His vision cleared

—*or did it?* he wondered—and how he could not tell what waited for Rosa on the glimmering sand.

He lost sight of her as the raft followed deflected currents around the island. The trade wind was coming fresh. He felt it on his skin like a reminder, and the sunset sat hard and bright on the west. Automatically he tacked out free of the reef and turned WSW. When he looked back in the soft twilight it was hard to see the forms struggling like huge lungfish up onto their new home. Under the slanted light the wind broke the sea into oily facets that became a field of mirrors reflecting shattered images of the burnt orange sky and the raft. He peered at the mirrors.

The logs on the beach . . . He felt the tug of the twine and made a change in heading to steady a yaw.

He gathered speed. When the thin scream came out of the dusk behind him he did not turn around.

III

The wind had backed into the northeast and was coming up strong again. Warren watched the sullen clouds moving in. He shook his head. It was still hard for him to leave his sleep.

It was three days now since he had passed the island. He had thought much about the thing with Rosa. When his head was clear he was certain that he had made no mistake. He had let her do what she wanted and if she had not understood it was because he could not find a way to tell her. It was the sea itself which taught and the Skimmers too, and you had to listen. Rosa had listened only to herself and her belly.

On the second day past the island the air had become thick and a storm came down from the north. He had thought it was a squall until the deck began to pitch at steep angles and a piece broke away with a groan. Then he had lashed himself to the log and tried to pull the plywood sheet down. He could reach it but the collar he had made out of his belt was slippery with rain. He pulled at the cracked leather. He thought of using the knife to cut the sheet free but then the belt would be no good. He twisted at the stiff knot and then the first big wave broke into foam over the deck and he lost it. The waves came fast then and he could not get to his feet. When he looked up it was dark overhead and the plywood was wrenched away from the mast. The wind battered it against the mast and the collar at the top hung free. A big wave slapped him and when next he saw the sheet it had splintered. A piece fell to the deck and Warren groped for it and slipped on the worn planking. A wave carried the piece over the side. The boards of the deck worked against each other and there was more splintering among them. Warren held on to the log. The second collar on the mast broke and the sheet slammed into the deck near him. He reached for it with one hand and felt something cut into his arm. The deck pitched. The plywood sheet fell backward and then slid and was over the side before he could try to get to it.

The storm lasted through the night. It washed away the shelter and the supplies. He clung to the log and the lashing around his waist cut into him in the night. Warren let the water wash freely over the cuts, the salt stinging across his back and over his belly, because it would heal faster that way. He tried to sleep. Toward dawn he dozed and woke only when he sensed a shift in the currents. The wind had backed into the northeast. Chop still washed across the deck and a third of the raft had broken away, but the sea was lessening as dawn came on. Warren woke slowly, not wanting to let go of the dreams.

There was nothing left but the mast, some poles he had lashed to the center log, and his knife and arrow. From a pole and a meter of twine he made a gaff with the knife. The twine had frayed. It was slow work and the twine slipped in his raw fingers. The bark of the log had cut them in the night. The sun rose quickly and a heat came into the air that worked at the cuts in him and made them sweat. He could feel that the night had tired him and he knew he would have to get food to keep his head clear. The Skimmers would come to him again he knew, and if there was a message he would have to understand it.

He made the knife fast to the pole with the twine but it was not strong and he did not want to risk using it unless he had to. A green patch of seaweed came nearby and he hooked it. He meant to use it for bait if he could but as he shook it out small shrimps fell to the planking. They jumped and kicked like sand fleas, and without thinking Warren pinched off their heads with his fingernails and ate them. The shells and tails crunched in his teeth and filled his mouth with a salty moist tang.

He kept a few for bait even though they were small. The twine was too heavy for a good line but he used it as he had before, in the first days after the *Manamix* went down when he had tried with some of their food as bait and had never caught anything. He was a sailor but he did not know how to fish. He set three trailing lines and sat to wait, wishing he had the shelter to stop the sun. The current moved well now and the chop was down. Warren hefted the gaff and hoped for a Swarmer to come. He thought of them as moving appetites, senseless alone but dangerous if enough came at once and butted the raft.

He bent over and looked steadily at a ripple of water about twenty meters from the raft. Something moved. Shifting prisms of green light descended into the dark waters. He thought about a lure. With Rosa it had been simple, a movement to draw them in and a quick shot. Warren turned, looking for something to rig to coax with, and he saw the trailing line on the left strengthen and then the line hissed and water jumped from it.

He reached to take some of the weight off and play in the line. It snapped. To the right something leaped from the water. The slim blue form whacked its tail noisily three times. Another sailed aloft on the other side of the raft as the first crashed back in a loud white splash. A third leaped and shone silver-blue in the sun and another and another and they were jumping to all sides at once, breaking free of the flat sea, their heads tilted sideways to see the raft. Warren had never seen Skimmers in schools and the way they rippled the water with their quick rushes. They were not like the Swarmers in their grace and the way they glided in the air for longer than seemed right until you looked closely at the two aft tails that beat the water and gave the look of almost walking.

Warren stood and stared. The acrobatic swivel of the Skimmers at the peak of their arc was swift and deft, a dash of zest. Their markings ran downward toward the tail. There were purplings and then three fine white stripes that fanned into the aft tails. There was no hole in the gut like the place where the Swarmers spun out their strands. Warren guessed the smallest of them was three meters long. Bigger than most marlin or sharks. Their thin mouths parted at the top of the arc and sharp narrow teeth showed white against the slick blue sky.

It was easy to see why his clumsy fishing had never hooked any big fish. These creatures and the Swarmers had teeth for a reason. There were many of them in the oceans now and they had to feed on something.

They leaped and leaped and leaped again. Their forefins wriggled in flight. The fins separated into bony ridges at their edge and rippled quickly. Each ridge made a stubby projection. The rear fins were the same. They smacked the water powerfully and filled the air with so much spray that he could see a rainbow in one of the fine white clouds.

Just as suddenly they were gone.

Warren waited for them to return. After a while he licked his lips and sat down. He began to think of water without wanting to. He had to catch a Swarmer. He wondered if the Skimmers drove them away.

In the afternoon he saw a rippling to the east but it passed going north. The high hard glare of the sun weighed on him. Nothing tugged at his lines. The mast traced an ellipse in the sky as the waves came.

A white dab of light caught his eye. It was a blotch on the flat plane of the sea. It came steadily closer. He squinted.

Canvas. Under it was a blue form tugging at a corner. Warren hauled it aboard and the alien leaped high, showering him, the bony head slanted to bring one of the big elliptical white eyes toward the figure on the deck. The Skimmer plunged, leaped again, and swam away fast, taking short leaps. Warren studied the soggy bleached canvas. It looked like a tarp used to cover the gun emplacements on the *Manamix* but he could not be sure. There were copper-rimmed holes along one edge. He used them to hoist it up the mast, lashing it with wire and punching new holes to fasten the boom. He did not have enough lines to get it right but the canvas filled with the quickening breeze of late afternoon.

He watched the bulging canvas and patiently did not think about his thirst. A splash of spray startled him. A Skimmer—the same one?—was leaping next to the raft. He licked his swollen lips and thought for a moment of fetching the gaff and then put the idea away. He watched the Skimmer arc and plunge and then speed away. It went a few tens of meters and then leaped high and turned and came back. It splashed him and then left and did the same thing again. Warren frowned. The Skimmer was heading southwest. It cut a straight line in the shifting waters.

To keep that heading he would need a tiller. He tore up a plank at the raft edge and lashed a pole to it. Fashioning a collar that would seat in the deck was harder. He finally wrapped strips of bark firmly into a hole he had punched with the gaff. They held for a while and he had to keep replacing them. The tiller was weak and he could not turn it quickly for fear of breaking the lashing. It was impossible to perform any serious maneuver like coming about if the wind shifted, but the sunset breeze usually held steady and anyway he could haul down the canvas if the wind changed too much. He nodded. It would be enough.

He brought the bow around on the path the Skimmer was marking. The current tugged him sideways and he could feel it through the tiller but the raft steadied and began to make a gurgle where it swept against the drift. The canvas filled.

The clouds were fattening again and he hoped there would not be another storm. The raft was weaker. The boards creaked with the rise and fall of each wave. He would not last an hour if he had to cling to a log in the water. He could feel a heavy fatigue settle in him.

The sea was calming, going flat. He scratched his skin where the salt had caked and stung. He slitted his eyes and looked toward the sunset. Banks of clouds were reflected in the ocean that now at sunset was like a lake. Waves made the image of the clouds into stacked bars of light. Pale cloud, then three washes of blue, then rods of cloud again. The reflection made light seem bony, broken into beams and angles. Square custard wedges floated on the glassy skin. He looked up into the empty sky, above the orange ball of sun, and saw a thin streak of white. At first he tried to figure out how this illusion was made but there was nothing in optics that would give a line of light that stood up into the sky rather than lying in it. It was no jet or rocket trail.

After describing it to himself this way Warren knew what it had to be. The Skyhook. He had forgotten the project, had not heard it mentioned in years. He supposed they were still building it. The strand started far out in orbit and lowered toward the earth as men added to it.

It would be more years before the tip touched the air and began the worst part of the job. If they could lower it through the miles of air and pin it to the ground, the thing would make a kind of elevator. People and machines would ride up it and into orbit and the rockets would not streak the sky anymore. Warren had thought years ago about trying to get a job working on the Skyhook but he knew only how engines worked and they did not use any of that up there, nothing that needed air to burn. It was a fine thing where it caught the sun like a spider thread. He watched it until it turned red against the black and then faded as the night came on.

IV

He woke in the morning with the first glow of light. His left arm was crooked around the tiller to hold it even though he had moored it with a wire. The first thing he checked was the heading. It had drifted some and he sat up to correct it and then found that his left arm was cramped. He shook it. It would not loosen so he gave it a few minutes to come right while he unlashed the tiller and brought them around to the right bearing. He was pretty sure he knew the setting even though he could feel that the current had changed. The raft cut across the shallow waves more at this new angle. Foam broke over the deck and the swell was deeper, the planking groaned, but he held to it.

The left arm would not uncramp. The cold of the night and sleeping on it had done this. He hoped the warmth later would loosen the muscles though he knew it was probably because his body was not getting enough food or the right food. The arm would just have to come loose on its own. He massaged it. The muscles jumped under his right hand and after a while he could feel a tingling all down the arm although that was probably from rubbing the salt in, he knew.

There was nothing on his lines. He drew in the bait but it had been nibbled away. He kept himself busy gathering seaweed with the gaff and resetting the lines with the weed but he knew it was not much use and he was trying to keep his mind off the thirst. It had been bad since he woke up and was getting worse as the sun rose. He searched for the Skyhook to take his mind off his throat and the raw puffed-up feel in his mouth but he could not see it.

He checked the bearing whenever he remembered it but there was a buzzing in his head that made it hard to tell how much time had passed. He thought about the Swarmers and how much he wanted one. The Skimmers were different but they had left him here now and he was not sure how much longer he could hold the bearing or even remember what the bearing was. The steady hollow slap of the waves against the underside of the raft soothed him and he closed his eyes against the sun.

He did not know how long he slept but when he woke his face burned and his left arm had come free. He lay there feeling it and noticed a new kind of buzzing. He looked around for an insect even though he had not seen any for many days and then cocked his head up and heard the sound coming out of the sky. Miles away a dot drifted across a cloud. The airplane was small and running on props, not jets. Warren got to his feet with effort and waved his arms. He was sure they would see him because there was nothing else in the sea and he would stick out if he could just keep standing. He waved and the plane kept going straight and he thought he could see under it something jumping in the water after its shadow had passed. Then the plane was a speck and he lost the sound of it and finally stopped waving his arms although it had not really come to him yet that they had not seen him. He sat down heavily. He was panting from the waving and then without noticing it for a while he began crying.

After a time he checked the bearing again, squinting at the sun and judging the current. He sat and watched and did not think.

The splash and thump startled him out of a fever dream.

The Skimmer darted away, plunging into a wave and out the other side with a turning twist of its aft fins.

A cylinder like the others rolled across the deck. He scrambled to catch it. The rolled sheet inside was ragged and uneven.

WAKTPL   OGO SHIMA
  WSW WSW CIRCLE ALAPMTO GUNJO
  GEHEN WSW WSW
SCHLECT SCHLECT YOUTH UNSSTOP NONGO
LUCK LOTS

Now instead of NONGO there was OGO. Did they think this was the opposite? Again WSW and again CIRCLE. Another island? The misspelled SCHLECHT, if that was what it was, and repeated. A warning? What point could there be in that when he had not seen a Swarmer in days? If UNS was the German *we,* then UNSSTOP might be *we stop.* The line might mean *bad youth we stop not go.* And it might not. But GEHEN WSW WSW meant *go west south west* or else everything else made no sense at all and he had been wrong ever since the island. There was Japanese in it too but he had never crewed on a ship where it was spoken and he didn't know any. SHIMA. He remembered the city, Hiroshima, and wondered if *shima* was *town* or *river* or something geographical. He shook his head. The last line made him smile. The Skimmers must have been in contact with something well enough to know a salute at the end was a human gesture. Or was that what they meant? The cold thought struck him that this might be *goodbye.* Or, looking at it another way, that they were telling him he needed lots of luck. He shook his head again.

That night he dreamed about the eyes and blood and fin-fluid of the Swarmers, about swimming in it and dousing his head in it and about water that was clear and fresh. When he woke the sun was already high and hot. The sail billowed west. He got the heading close to what he could remember and then crawled into the shadow of the sail, as he had done the days before. He had kept his clothes on all the time on the raft and they were rags now. They kept off the sun still but were caked with salt and rubbed at the cuts and stung when he moved. At his neck and on his hands were black patches where the skin had peeled away and then burned again. He had worn a kind of hat he made before from Swarmer skin and bone and it was good shade but it had gone overboard in the storm.

Warren thought about the message but could make no more sense of it. He scratched his beard and found it had a crust of salt in it like hoarfrost. The salt was in his eyebrows too and he leaned over the side face down in the water and scrubbed it away. He peered downward at the descending blades of green light and the dark shadow of the raft tapering away like a steep pyramid into the shifting murky darkness. He thought he saw something moving down there but he could not be sure.

He was getting weak now. He caught some more sea-weed and used it as bait on the lines. The effort left him trembling. He set the heading and sat in the shade.

He woke with a jerk and there was splashing near the raft. Skimmers. They leaped into the noonday glare and beyond them was a brown haze. He blinked and it was an island. The wind had picked up and the canvas pulled full-bellied toward the land.

He sat numb and tired at the tiller and brought the raft in toward the island, running fast before the wind and cutting the waves and sending foam over the deck. There was a lagoon. Surf broke on the coral reefs hooking around the island. The land looked to be about a kilometer across, wooded hills and glaring white beaches. The Skimmers moved off to the left and Warren saw a pale space in the lagoon that looked like a passage. He slammed the tiller over full and the raft yawed and bucked against the waves that were coming harder now. The deck groaned and the canvas luffed but the raft came into the pocket of the pale space and then the waves took it through powerfully and fast. Beyond the crashing of surf on the coral he sailed close to the wind to keep away from the dark blotches in the shallows and then turned toward shore. The Skimmers were gone now, but he did not notice until the raft snagged on a sandbar and he looked around, judging the distance to the beach. He was weak and it would be stupid to risk anything this close. He stood up with a grunt and jumped heavily on the free side of the raft. It slewed and then broke free of the sandbar and the wind blew it fifty meters more. He got his tools and stood on the raft, hesitating as if leaving it after all this time was hard to imagine and then he swore at himself and stepped off. He swam slowly until his feet hit sand and then took slow steps up to the beach, careful to keep his balance, so he did not see the man come out of the palms.

Warren pitched forward onto the sand and tried to get up. The sand felt hard and hot against him. He stood again with pains in his legs and the man was standing nearby, Chinese or maybe Filipino. He said something to Warren and Warren asked him a question and they stared at each other. Warren waited for an answer and when he saw there was not going to be one he held out his right hand, palm up. In the silence they shook hands.

V

For a day he was weak and could not walk far. The Chinese brought him cold food in tin cans and coconut milk. They talked at each other but neither one knew a single word the other did, and soon they stopped. The Chinese pointed to himself and said "Gijan" or something close to it so Warren called him that.

It looked as though Gijan had drifted to the island in a small lifeboat. He wore clothes like gray pajamas and had two cases of canned food.

Warren slept deeply and woke to a distant booming. He stumbled down to the beach, looking around for Gijan. The Chinese was standing waist-deep in the lagoon and he pointed a pistol into the water and fired, making a loud bang but not kicking up much spray. Warren watched as slim white fish floated up, stunned. Gijan picked them from the water and put them in a palm frond he carried. He came ashore smiling and held out one of the fish to Warren. Its eyes bulged.

"Raw?" Warren shook his head. But Gijan had no matches.

Warren pointed to the pistol. Gijan took the medium-caliber automatic and hefted it and looked at him. "No. I mean, give me a shell." He realized it was pointless talking. He made a gesture of things coming out of the muzzle and Gijan caught it and fished a cartridge out of his pockets. Gijan took the fish up on the sand as they started flopping in the palm frond, waking up from the stunning. Warren gathered dry brush and twigs and mixed them and dug a pit for the mixture with his hands. He still had his knife and some wire. He forced open the cartridge with them. He mixed the gunpowder with the wood. He had been watching Gijan the night before and the man was not using fire, just eating out of cans. Warren found some hardwood and rubbed the wire along it quickly while Gijan watched, frowning at first. The fish were dead and gleamed in the sun. Warren was damned if he was going to eat raw fish now that he was on land. He rubbed the wire harder, bracing the wood between his knees and drawing the wire quickly back and forth. He felt it get warm in his hands. When he was sweating and the wire was both burning and biting into his hands he knelt beside the wood and pressed the searing wire into it. The powder fizzled and sputtered for a moment and then with a rush it caught, the twigs snapped, and the fire made its own pale yellow glow in the sun. Gijan smiled.

Warren had felt a dislike of Gijan's using the gun to get the fish. He thought about it as he and Gijan roasted them on sticks, but the thought went away as he started eating them and the rich crisp flavor burst in his mouth. He ate four of them in a row without stopping to drink any of the coconut milk Gijan had in tin cans. The hunger came on him suddenly as if he had just remembered food and it did not go away until he finished six fish and ate half of the coconut meat. Then he thought again about using the gun that way but it did not seem so bad now.

Gijan tried to describe something by using his hands and drawing pictures in the sand. A ship, sinking. Gijan in a boat. The sun coming into the sky seven times. Then the island. Boat broken up on the coral, but Gijan swimming beside it and getting it to shore, half sunken.

Warren nodded and drew his own story. He did not show the Swarmers or the Skimmers except at the shipwreck because he did not know how to tell the man what it was like and also he was not sure how Gijan would like the idea of eating Swarmer. Warren was not sure why this hesitation came into his head but he decided to stick with it and not tell Gijan too much about how he survived.

In the afternoon Warren made a hat for himself and walked around the island. It was flat most of the way near the beach with a steep outcropping of brown rock where the ridgeline of the island ran down into the sea. There were palms and scrub brush and sea grass and dry stream beds. He found a big rocky flat space on the southern flank of the island and squinted at it awhile. Then he went back and brought Gijan to it and made gestures of picking out some of the pale rocks and carrying them. The man caught the idea on the second try. Warren scratched out SOS in the sand and showed it to him. Gijan frowned, puzzled. He made his own sign with a stick and Warren could not understand it. There were four lines like the outline of a house and a cross bar. Warren thumped the sand next to the SOS and said "Yes!" and thumped it again. He was pretty sure SOS was an international symbol but the other man simply stared at him. The silence got longer. There was tension in the air. Warren could not understand where it had come from. He did not move. After a moment Gijan shrugged and went off to collect more of the light-colored rocks.

They laid them out across the stony clearing, letters fifty meters tall. Warren suspected the airplane he had seen was searching for survivors of Gijan's ship, which had gone down nearby, and not the *Manamix*. It was funny Gijan had not thought of making a signal but then he did not think of making a fire either.

The next morning Warren drew pictures of fishing and found that Gijan had not tried it. Warren guessed the man was simply waiting to be picked up and was a little afraid of the big silent island and even more of the empty sea. Gijan's hands were softer than Warren's and he guessed maybe the man had been mainly a desk worker. When the canned food ran out Gijan would have tried fishing but not before. So far all he had done was climb a few palms and knock down coconuts. The palms were stunned here though and there was not much milk in the coconuts. They would need water.

Warren worked the metal in the leftover cans and made fishhooks. Gijan saw what he was doing and went away into the north part of the island.

Warren was surveying the lagoon, looking for deep spots near the shore, when he found the raft moored in a narrow cove. Gijan must have found it drifting and tied it there. The boards looked worn and weak and the whole thing—cracked tiller, bleached canvas, rusted wire lashings —carried the feel of an old useless wreck. Warren studied it for a while and then turned away.

Gijan found him at a rough shelf of rock that stuck out over the lagoon. Gijan was carrying a box Warren had not seen. He put the box down and gestured to it, smiling slightly, proud. Warren looked inside. There was a tangle of fishing line inside, some hooks, a rod, a diving mask, fins, a manual in Chinese or something like it, a screwdriver, and some odds and ends. Warren looked at the man and wished he knew how to ask a question. The box was the same kind that the canned food was in, so Warren guessed Gijan had brought all this in the boat.

They went down to the beach and Gijan drew some more pictures and that was the story that came out of it. He did not draw anything about hiding the box away but Warren could guess that he had. Gijan must have seen the raft coming, and in a hurry, afraid, he would snatch up what he could and hide it. Then when he saw that Warren was no trouble he came out and brought the food. He left the rest behind just to be careful. He was still being careful when he used the pistol to fish. Maybe that was a way to show Warren he had it without making any threats.

Warren smiled broadly and shook his hand and insisted on carrying the box back to their camp. Land crabs skittered away from their feet as they walked, two men with a strange silence between them.

Warren fished in the afternoon. The canned goods would not last long with two of them eating and Warren was more hungry than he could ever remember. His body was waking up after being half dead and it wanted food and water, more water than they could get out of the coconuts. He would have to do something about that. He thought about it while he fished, using worms from the shady parts of the island, and then he saw moving shadows in the lagoon. They were big fish but they twisted on their turns in a way he remembered. He watched and they did not break water but he was sure.

He began to notice the thirst again after he had caught two fish. He left a line with bait and went inland and knocked down three coconuts but they did not yield much of the sweet milk. He took the fish back to camp where Gijan was keeping the fire going. Warren sat and watched him gut the fish, not making a good job of it. He felt the way he had in the first days on the raft. New facts, new problems. This island was just a bigger raft with more to take from but you had to learn the ways first.

Gijan's odd box of equipment had some rubber hose that had sheared off some missing piece of equipment. Warren stared at the collection in the box for a while. He began idly making a cover for one of the large tin cans, fitting pieces of metal together. Crimping them over the lip of the can and around the edge of the hose he found that they made a pretty fair seal. He made a holder for the can, working patiently. Gijan watched him with interest. Warren sent him to get sea water in a big can. He rigged the hose to pass through a series of smaller cans. With the sea water he filled the big can and sealed the tight cover and put it on the fire. The men watched the water boil and then steam came out of the hose. Gijan saw the idea and put sea water into the small cans. It

cooled the hose so that in the end the thin steam faded
into a dribble of fresh water. They smiled at each other
and watched the slow drip. By late afternoon they had
their first drink. It was brackish but not bad.

Warren used gestures and sketches in the sand to ask
Gijan about the assortment of equipment. Had he been on
a research vessel? A fast skimship?

Gijan drew the profile of an ordinary freighter, even
adding the loading booms. Gijan pointed at Warren so he
drew an outline of the *Manamix*. With pantomime and
gestures and imitating sounds they got across their trades.
Warren worked with machines and Gijan was some kind of
trader. Gijan drew a lopsided map of the Pacific and
pointed to a speck not big enough or in the right place to
be any island Warren knew about. Gijan sketched in nets
and motor boats and Warren guessed they had been using
a freighter to try for tuna. It sounded stupid. Until now
he had not thought about the islands isolated for years
now and how they would get food. You could not support
a population by fishing from the shore. Most crops were
thin in the sandy soil. So he guessed Gijan's island had
armored a freighter and sent it out with nets, desperate.
If it was a big enough island they might have an airplane
and some fuel left and maybe that was the one he saw.

Gijan showed him the stuff in the box again. It was
pretty banged up and salt-rusted and Warren guessed it
had been left years ago when the freighter was still working. In the years when the Swarmers were spreading Warren had had a gun like everybody else in the crew, not
in his own duffle where somebody might find it, but in a
locker of spare engine parts. Now that he thought about it
a lifeboat was a better place to stow a weapon, down in
with some old gear nobody would want. When you needed
a gun you would be on deck already and you could get to
it easy.

He looked at Gijan's pinched face and tried to read it
but the man's eyes were blank, just watching with a puzzled frown. It was hard to tell what Gijan meant by some
of his drawings and Warren got tired of the whole thing.

They ate coconuts at sundown. The green ones were
like jelly inside. Gijan had a way of opening them using a
stake wedged into the hardpacked ground. The stake was
sharp and Gijan slammed the coconut down on it until

the green husk split away. The hard-shelled ones had the tough white meat inside but not much milk. The palms were bent over in the trade winds and were short. Warren counted them up and down the beach and estimated how long the two men would take to strip the island. Less than a month.

Afterward Warren went down to the beach and waded out. A current tugged at his ankles and he followed with his eyes the crinkling of the pale water where a deep current ran. It swept around the island toward the passage in the coral, the basin of the lagoon pouring out into the ocean under the night tide. Combers snarled white against the dark wedge of the coral ring and beyond was the jagged black horizon.

They would have to get fish from the lagoon and lines from shore would not be enough. But that was only one of the reasons to go out again.

In the dim moonlight he went back, past the fire where Gijan sat watching the hissing distiller and then into the scrub. Uphill he found a tree and stripped bark from it. He cut it into chips and mashed them on a rock. He was tired by the time he got a sour-smelling soup going on the fire. Gijan watched. Warren did not feel like trying to tell the man what he was doing. Warren tended the simmering and fell asleep and woke when Gijan bent over him to taste the can's thick mash. Gijan made a face. Warren roughly yanked the can away, burning his own fingers. He shook his head abruptly and set the can where it would come to a rolling boil. Gijan moved off. Warren ignored him and fell back into sleep.

This night mosquitoes found them. Warren woke and slapped his forehead and each time in the fading orange firelight his hand was covered by a mass of squashed redbrown. Gijan grunted and complained. Toward morning they trudged back into the scrub and the mosquitoes left them and they curled up on the ground to sleep until the sun came through the canopy of fronds above.

The lines he had left overnight were empty. The fishing was bound to be bad when you had no chance to play the line. They had more coconuts for breakfast and Warren checked the cooling mash he had made. It was thick and it stained wood a deep black. He put it aside without thinking much about how he could use it.

In the cool of the morning he repaired the raft. The slow working of the tide had loosened the lashings and some of the boards were rotting. It would do for the lagoon, but as he worked he thought of the Swarmers crawling ashore at the last island. The big things had been slow and clumsy and with Gijan's pistol the men would have an advantage, but there were only two of them. They could not cover the whole island. If the Swarmers came, the raft might be the only escape they had.

He brought the fishing gear aboard and cast off. Gijan saw him and came running down the hard white sand. Warren waved. Gijan was excited and jabbering and his eyes rolled back and forth from Warren to the break in the reef. He pulled out his pistol and waved it in the air. Warren ran up the worn canvas sail and swung the boom around so that the raft peeled away from the passage and made headway along the beach, around the island. When he looked back Gijan was aiming the pistol at him. Warren frowned. He could not understand the man but after a moment when Gijan saw that he was running steady in the lagoon the pistol came down. Warren saw the man put the thing back in his pocket and then he set to work laying his lines. He kept enough wind in the sail to straighten the pull and move the bait so it would look like it was swimming.

Maybe he should have drawn a sketch for Gijan. Warren thought about it a moment and then shrugged. An aft line jerked as something hit it and Warren forgot Gijan and his pistol and played in the catch.

He took four big fish in the morning. One had the striped back and silvery belly of a bonito and the others he did not recognize. He and Gijan ate two and stripped and salted the others and in the afternoon he went out again. Standing on the raft he could see the shadows of the big fish as they came into the lagoon. A Skimmer darted in the distance and he stayed away from it, afraid it would come for the trailing lines. After a while he remembered that they had never hit the lines in the ocean so he did not veer the raft when the Skimmer leaped high nearby, rolling over in that strange way. Gijan was standing on the glaring white beach, he noticed, watching. Another leap, splashing foam, and then a tube rattled on the boards of the raft.

SHIMA STONES CROSSING SAFE YOUTH
WORLD NEST UNSSPRACHEN
SHIGANO YOU SPRACHEN
    YOUTH UMI HIRO SAFE NAGARE CIRCLE UNS SHIO
WAIT WAIT YOU   LUCK

Warren came ashore with it and Gijan reached for the
slick sheet. The man moved suddenly and Warren stepped
back, bracing himself. The two stood still for a moment
looking at each other, Gijan's face compressed and intent.
Then in a controlled way Gijan relaxed, making a careless
gesture with his hands, and helped moor the raft. Warren
moved the tube and sheet from one hand to the other and
finally, feeling awkward, handed them to Gijan. The man
read the words slowly, lips pressed together. "Shima," he
said. "Shio. Nagare. Umi." He shook his head and looked
at Warren, his lips forming the words again silently.

They drew pictures in the sand. For *shima* Gijan
sketched the island and for *umi* the sea around it. In the
lagoon he drew wavy lines in the water and said several
times, "Nagare." Across the island he drew a line and then
made swooping motions of bigness and said, "Hiro."

Warren murmured, "Wide island? Hiro shima?" but
aside from blinking Gijan gave no sign that he understood.
Warren showed him a rock for *stone* and drew the Earth
for *world* but he was not sure if that was what the words
on the sheet meant jammed in with the others. What did
the dark W of *world* mean?

The men spoke haltingly to each other over the booming of the reef. The clusters of words would not yield to
a sensible plan and even if it had, Warren was not sure
he could tell Gijan his part of it, the English smattering
of words, or that Gijan could get across to him the foreign ones. He felt in Gijan a restless energy now, an impatience with the crabbed jumble of language. *Wait wait
you* and then *luck*. It seemed to Warren he had been waiting a long time now and even though this message had
more English and was clearer there was no way for the
Skimmers to know what language Warren understood, not
unless he told them. Frowning over a diagram Gijan was
drawing in the floury sand, he saw suddenly why he had
made the bark mash last night.

It took hours to write a message on the back of the
sheet. A bamboo quill stabbed the surface and if you held

it right it did not puncture. The sour black ink dripped
and ran but by pinning the sheet flat in the sun he got it
to dry without a lot of blurring.

SPEAK ENGLISH. WILL YOUTH COME HERE? ARE WE SAFE
FROM YOUTH ON ISLAND? SHIMA IS ISLAND IN ENGLISH.
WHERE ARE YOU FROM? CAN WE HELP YOU? WE ARE
FRIENDLY.

LUCK

Gijan could not understand any of it or at least he gave
no sign. Warren took the raft out again at dusk as the
wind backed into the north and ebbed into fitful breezes.
The sail luffed and he had trouble bringing the raft out
of the running lagoon currents and toward the spot where
flickering shadows played on the white expanse of a sandbar. A Skimmer leaped and turned as he came near. He
held the boom to catch the last gusts of sunset wind and
when the shadows were under the raft he threw the tube
into the water. It bobbed and began to drift out toward
the passage to the sea as Warren waited, watching the
shadows, wondering if they had seen it, knowing he could
not catch the tube now with the raft before it reached the
reef, and then a quick flurry of motion below churned
the pale sand and a form came up, turning, then ripping
the smooth water as it leaped. The Skimmer flexed in air
and hung for an instant, rolling, before it fell with a smack
and was gone in an upwash of bright foam. The tube was
gone.

That night the mosquitoes came again and drove them
onto the rocky ground near the center of the island. In
the morning their hands were blood-streaked where they
had slapped their faces and legs in the night and caught
the fat mosquitoes partway through the feeding.

In the morning Warren went out again and laid his lines
as early as possible. Near the sandbar there were many
fish. One of them hit a line and when Warren pulled it in
the thing had deep-set eyes, a small mouth like a parrot's
beak, slimy gills and hard blue scales. He pressed at the
flesh and a dent stayed in it for a while, the way it did if
you squeezed the legs of a man with leprosy or dropsy.
The thing smelled bad as it lay on the planks and the sun
warmed it so he threw it back, pretty sure it was poison-

ous. It floated and a Skimmer leaped near it and then took the thing and was gone. Warren could see more Skimmers moving below. They were feeding on the poison fish.

He caught two skipjack tuna and brought them ashore for Gijan to clean. The man was watching him steadily from the beach and Warren did not like it. The thing between him and the Skimmers was his and he did not want any more of the stupid drawing and hand-waving of trying to explain it to Gijan.

He went into the palm grove where the fire crackled and got the diving mask he had seen in Gijan's box. It was made for a smaller head but with the rubber strap drawn tight he could ride it up against the bridge of his nose and make it fit. As he came back down to the beach, Gijan said something but Warren went on to the raft and cast off, bearing in the southerly wind out toward the sandbar. He grounded the raft on the bar to hold it steady.

He lay on the raft and peered down at the moving shapes. They were at least twenty fathoms down and they had finished off the poison fish. Seven Skimmers hovered over a dark patch, rippling their forefins where the bony ridges stuck out like thick fingers. Sunlight caught a glint from the thing they were working on and suddenly a gout of gray mist came up from it and broke into bubbles. It was steam. He lay halfway over the side of the raft and watched the regular puffs of steam billow up from the machine. Without thinking of the danger he slipped overboard and dove, swimming hard, pushing as deep as he could despite the tightness and burning in his chest. The Skimmers moved as they saw him and the machine became clearer. It was like a pile of junk, pieces of a ship's hull and deck collars and fittings of all sizes. Four batteries were mounted on one side and rust-caked cables led from them into the machine. There were other fragments and bits of worked metal and some of it he was sure had not been made by men. Knobs of something yellow grew here and there and in the wavering, rippling green light there was something about the form and shape of the thing that Warren recognized as right and yet he knew he had never seen anything like it before. There is a logic to a piece of equipment that comes out of the job it has to do and he felt that this machine was well shaped. Then his lungs at last burned too much and he fought upward, all thought leaving him as he let the air burst from him and followed the silvery bubbles up toward the shifting slanting blades of yellow-green sun.

VI

In the lagoon the water shaded from pale blue at the beach to emerald in the deep channel where the currents ran with the tides. Beyond the snarling reef the sea was a hard gray.

Warren worked for five days in the slow dark waters near the sandbar. He double-anchored the raft so the deck was steady and he could write well on it with the bark mash and then dry the sheets the Skimmers brought up to him.

Their first reply was not much better than the earlier messages but he printed out in capital letters a simple answer and gradually they learned what he could not follow. Their next message had more English in it and less Japanese and German and fewer of the odd words made up out of parts of languages. There were longer stretches in it, too, more like sentences now than strings of nouns.

The Skimmers did not seem to think of things acting but instead of things just being, so they put down names of objects in long rows as though the things named would react on each other, each making the other clearer and more specific and what the things did would be obvious because of the relations between them. It was a hard way to learn to think and Warren was not sure he knew what the impacted knots of words meant most of the time. Sometimes the chains of words said nothing to him and the blue forms below would flick across the bone-white sand in elaborate looping arabesques, turning over and over with their ventral fins flared, in designs that escaped him. When the sun was low at morning or at dusk he could not tell the Skimmers from their shadows and the gliding long forms merged with their dark echoes on the sand in a kind of slow elliptical dance. He lay halfway off the raft and watched them when he was tired from the messages, and peered through the mask, and something in their quick darting glide would come through to him. He would try then to ask a simple question. He would write it out and dry it and throw it into the lagoon. Sometimes that was enough to cut through the jammed lines of endless nouns they had offered him and he would see a small thought that hung between the words in a space each word allowed but did not define. It was as if the words packed together still left a hole between them and the job was to see the hole instead of the blurred lumpy things that made the edges of the hole. That was a part of what it was like to think about the long strings of letters and to watch the skimming grace they had down in the dusky emerald green. There was more to it than that but he could not sort it out.

He went ashore at dusk each day. The catch from the trailing lines was good in the morning and went away in the afternoon. Maybe it had something to do with the Skimmers. The easy morning catch left him most of the day to study the many sheets they brought up to him and to work on his own halting answers.

Gijan stood on the beach most of the day and watched. He did not show the pistol again when Warren went out. He kept the fire and the distiller going and they ate well. Warren brought the finished sheets ashore and kept them in Gijan's box but he could not tell the man much of what was in them, at first because lines in the sand and gestures were not enough and later because Warren did not know himself how to tell it.

Gijan did not seem to mind not knowing. He tended the fire and knocked down coconuts and split them and gutted the catch and after a while asked nothing more. At times he would leave the beach for hours and Warren guessed he was collecting wood or some of the pungent edible leaves they had at supper.

To Warren the knowing was all there was and he was glad Gijan would do the work and not bother him. At noon beneath the high hard dazzle of the sky he ate little because he wanted to keep his head clear. At night though he filled himself with the hot moist fish and tin-flavored water. He woke to a biting early sun. The mosquitoes still stung but he did not mind it so much now.

On the third day like this he began to write down for himself a kind of patchwork of what he thought they meant. He knew as soon as he read it over that it was not right. He had never been any good with words. When

he was married he did not write letters to his wife when
he shipped out even if he was gone half a year. But this
writing was a way of getting it down and he liked the act
of scratching out the blunt lines on the backs of the
Skimmer sheets.

*In the long times before, the early forms went easy
in the World, then rose up leaping out of the
bottom of the World, to the land, made the tools
we knew, struck the fire, made the fire-hardened
sand we could see through so that we could cup the
light. The clouds open, we can see lights, learn
the dots above, we see lights we cannot reach, even
the highest jumper of us cannot touch the lights that
move. We cup the light, scoop it up, and find
the lights in the sky are small and hot, but there is
one light that we cup to us and find it is a stone in
the sky, we think other lights are stones in the sky but
far away, we see no other place like the World, we
swim at the bottom of everything, in the World,
the place where stones want to fall, but the flow
takes the stones in the sky, makes them circle us, circle
forever like the hunters in the World before they
close for the killing, so the stones cannot strike us in
the nest of us, the World of the people. We thought
that ours was the only World and that all else was
cold stone or burning stone. And as we cupped
the light not thinking of it we saw the cold stone in
the sky grow a light which went on, then off, then
on, again and again, moving now strangely in the
sky and then growing more stones, moving, stones
falling into the World, stones smaller than the big sky
stone, hitting killing bringing big animals that stink,
eating every piece of the World that comes before
them, taking some of us in them, big stones making
big animals that are not alive but swallow, keeping
us in them in water, sour water that brings pain, we
live there, light coming from land that is not land,
a World that is not the World, no waves no land
but there is the glowing stone on all sides that we
cannot climb, no land for the youth to crawl to,
long time passing, we sing over and over the
soon-birthing but it does not come, the song does
not make it stir out of this red World, this small*

*World that one of us can cross in the time of a
single singing. The youth change their song slowly
then more and then more, their song goes away
from us, they sing strangely but do not crawl, hot red
things bubble in the small World where we live and
the youth drink it. The smooth stone on all sides
makes this World glow with light that never grows
and never dims, we keep some of our tools and can
feel the time going, many songs pass, we do not let
the youth sing or crawl but then they do not know
us and sing their own noise, drinking in the foul
currents of the big animal we inhabit, the smooth
stone oozing light, always rumbling, the currents not
right, we move thickly, lose our tides, the red currents
suck and bring food sweet and bitter, wrong,
through long times the walls humming and no waves
for us to fly through and splash white. Then the
smooth stone grows slowly hot, cracks open, some
of us die, the song dims among us, bitter blue
currents drive us down, more of us fall from the
song, long cold sounds stab us, and more fall, from
the sour streams come now waves, fresh streams, we
taste, sing weakly, speak, it is a World like the one
World, the smooth stone on all sides is gone, we break
water. There are waves cutting white, sharp, we find
salt foods, leap into hot airs, waves hard fast, we
cup the light and see big stone in sky, far stones
moving across the many stones, like our World but
not of our World. The song is weak, we seek to cross
this World but cannot, we know we will lose ourselves in
this World if our song is stretched farther. But the
youth have a strange song and they go out. They find
food, they find big animals in the waves and bigger
animals that crush the waves, they strike at them in
the way we once did long times past, throw their
webs to bring down the crushers of waves. These
crushers are not the big animals we knew in the
World and when the youth drag them down closer
to the center they are not ripe, do not burst with fruit,
are fiery to the mouth and kill some youth without
releasing the pods that would drive the youth to
the land, drive them to the air to suck, drive the
change to make the youth into the form that would be
us. These things that float and crush the waves we fear*

*and flee but the youth eat of them and yet do not go
to the land to crawl, we lose the song with them
forever, they fly the waves no more, they take the big
animals that walk above the waves, the youth have
become able to kill the bitter wave-walkers, they
feast on the things in them. We see from a distance
that it is you the youth eat, even if you are sick
and death-causing, you are killed in the skins that
carry you walking the waves. The youth do not sing,
they split your skins, they grow and eat all that
comes before them. Now you are gone like us, nearly
chewed. We come to here, we drive the youth
away, the act chews us but does not finish us. We
find you in the skins you love and we cannot sing
with you. We find you one and in one you can sing,
together you are deaf. You are the twenty-fourth we
have sung with on the waves. Your kind cannot
hear unless you are one and cannot sing to each other
but many of the others who sang with us are now
chewed but we can keep the youth away for a time
we grow weak the youth run with sores and leave
stink in the currents foul where they go we smell
them the World that was false World made them this
way not as they were when we knew them in the
World that was ours. They can not sing but know of
the places where you sing to each other and some
now go there with their sores they may be chewed by
you but there are many many of them they ache
now for the skins-that-sink but they are madness
they are coming and they chew you others last.*

Each night after it got too dark for Warren to write in
the yellow firelight they would move inland. The mosquitoes stayed near the beach and there were a lot of other
insects, too. Warren listened to fish in the lagoon leaping
for the insects and the splashing as the Skimmers took the
fish in turn. He could see their phosphorescent wakes in
the water.

They smeared themselves with mud to keep off the mosquitoes but it did not keep off the ticks that dropped from
the trees. There was no iodine in Gijan's box of random
items. Putting a drop of iodine on the tick's tail was the
best treatment and second best was burning them off.

Each morning the men inspected each other and there were always a few black dots where the ticks burrowed in. An ember from the fire pressed against the tick's hindquarters made it let go and then Warren could pull the tick out with his fingernails. He knew that if the head came off in the skin it would rot and the whole area would become a boil. He noticed that Gijan got few ticks and he wondered if it had anything to do with the oriental skin.

The next morning he got a good catch and when he brought it in he was sore from the days of work on the raft. After eating the fish he went for more coconuts. The softer fronds were good too for rubbing the skin to take away the sting of mosquito bites and to get the salt out. Finding good coconuts was harder now and he worked his way across the island, up the ridgeline and down to a swampy part on the southern side. There were edible leaves there and he chewed some slowly as he made his way back, thinking. He was nearly across a bare stretch of soil when he saw it was the place they had laid out the SOS. The light-colored rocks were there but they were scattered. The SOS was broken up.

Gijan was looking in the storage box when Warren came back into the camp. "Hey!" he called. Gijan looked at him, calm and steady, and then stood up, taking his time.

Warren pointed back to the south and glared at the man and then bent down and drew the SOS in the sand. He rubbed it out and pointed at Gijan.

Warren had expected the man to give him a blank look or a puzzled expression. Instead, Gijan put a hand in a pocket.

Then Gijan said quite clearly, "It does not matter."

Warren stood absolutely still. Gijan pulled the pistol casually out of his pocket but he did not aim it at anything.

Warren said carefully, "Why?"

"Why deceive you? So that you would go on with your—" he paused—"your good work. You have made remarkable progress."

"The Skimmers."

"Yes."

"And the SOS . . ."

"I did not want anyone to spot the island who should not."

"Who would that be?"

"Several. The Japanese. The Americans. There are reports of Soviet interest."

"So you are—"

"Chinese, of course."

"Of course."

"I would like to know how you wrote that summary. I read the direct messages you got from them, read them many times. I could not see in them very much."

"There's more to it than what they wrote."

"You are sure that you brought all their messages ashore?"

"Sure. I kept them all."

"How do you discover things that are not in the messages?"

"I don't think I can tell you that."

"Cannot? Or will not?"

"Can't."

Gijan became pensive, studying Warren. Finally he said, "I cannot pass judgment on that. Others will have to decide that, others who know more than I do." He paused. "Were you truly in a shipwreck?"

"Yeah."

"Remarkable that you survived. I thought you would die when I saw you first. You are a sailor?"

"Engine man. What're you?"

"Soldier. A kind of soldier."

"Funny kind, seems to me."

"This is not the duty I would have chosen. I sit on this terrible place and try to talk to those things."

"Uh huh. Any luck?"

"Nothing. They do not answer me. The tools I was given do not work. Kinds of flashlights. Sound makers. Things floating in the water. I was told they are drawn to these things."

"What would happen if they did answer?"

"My job is over then."

"Well, I guess I've put you out of work. We're still going to need something to eat, though." He gestured at the raft and turned toward it and Gijan leveled the pistol.

"You can rest," the man said. "It will not be long."

VII

In mid-afternoon six delta-planes came in low, made a pass and arced up, one at a time, to land in V-mode. They came down in the rocky area to the south and a few minutes after the shrieking engines shut down three squads' of fast, lean-looking infantry came double-timing onto the beach.

Warren watched them from the shade where he sat within clear view of Gijan. The man had made him carry the radio and power supply from its concealment in the scrub and onto the beach, where he could talk down the planes. Gijan shouted at the men and they backed away from the beach where the Skimmers might see them. A squad took Warren and marched him south, saying nothing. At the landing site men and forklifts were unloading and building and no one looked at him twice. The squad took him to a small building set down on rocky soil and locked him inside.

It was light durablock construction, three meters square with three windows with heavy wire mesh over them. There was a squat wooden chair, a thin sleeping pad on the floor, and a fifty-watt glow plate in the ceiling that did not work. Warren tasted the water in a gallon jug and found it tepid and metallic. There was a bucket to use as a toilet.

He could not see much through the windows but the clang and rumble of unloading went on. Darkness came. A motor started up nearby and he tried to tell if it was going or coming until he realized it was turning over at a steady rpm. He touched the wall switch and the soft glow above came on so he guessed the generator had started. In the dim light everything in the room stood out bleak and cold.

Later a muscular soldier came with a tin plate of vegetable stew. Warren ate it slowly, tasting the boiled onions and carrots and spinach and tomatoes, holding back his sudden appetite so that he got each taste separately. He licked the pan clean and drank some water and rather than sit and think fruitlessly he laid down and slept.

At dawn the same guard came again with more of the stew, cold this time. Warren had not finished it when the guard came back and took it away and yanked him to his feet. The soldier quick-marched him across a compound in the pale morning light. He memorized the sizes and distances of the buildings as well as he could. The guard took him to the biggest building in the compound, a prefab that was camouflage-speckled for the jungle. The front room was an office with Gijan sitting in one of the four flimsy chairs and a tall man, Chinese or Japanese, standing beside a plywood desk.

"You know Underofficer Gijan? Good. Sit." The tall man moved quickly to offer Warren a chair. He turned and sat behind the desk and Warren watched him. Each motion of the man had a kind of sliding quality to it, as though he was keeping his body centered and balanced at all times to take a new angle of defense or attack if needed.

"Please relax," the man said. Warren noticed that he was sitting on the edge of the chair. He settled back in it, using the moment to locate the guard in a far corner to his right, an unreachable two meters away.

"What is your name?"

"Warren."

"You have only one name?" the man asked, smiling.

"Your men didn't introduce themselves either. I didn't think I had to be formal."

"I am sure you understand the circumstances, Warren. In any case, my name is Tseng Wong. Since we are using only single names, call me Tseng." His words came out separately like smooth round objects forming in the still air.

"I can see that conditions have been hard on you."

"Not so bad."

Tseng pursed his lips. "The evidence given by your little—" he searched for the word—"spasm in the face, is enough to show me—"

"What spasm?"

"Perhaps you do not notice it any longer. The left side, a tightening in the eyes and the mouth."

"I don't have anything like that."

Tseng looked at Gijan, just a quick glance, and then back at Warren. There was something in it Warren did not like and he found himself focusing his attention on his own face, waiting to see if there was anything wrong with it he had not noticed. Maybe he—

"Well, we shall let it pass. A casual remark, that is all.

I did not come to criticize you but to, first, ask for your help, and second, to get you off this terrible island."

"You coulda got me off here days ago. Gijan had the radio."

"His task came first. You are fascinated by the same problem, are you, Warren?"

"Seems to me my big problem is you people."

"I believe your long exposure out here has distorted your judgment, Warren. I also believe you overestimate your ability to survive for long on this island. With Under-officer Gijan the two of you did well enough but in the long run I—" Tseng stopped when he saw the slight upward turn of Warren's mouth that was clearly a look of disdain.

"I saw that case of rations Gijan had stashed back in the brush," Warren said. "None of you know nothing about living out here."

Tseng stood up, tall and straight, and leaned against the back wall of the office. It gave him a more casual look but put him so that Warren had to look up to talk to him.

"I will do you the courtesy of speaking frankly. My government—and several others, we believe—has suspected for some time that there are two distinct populations among the aliens. One—the Swarmers—is capable of mass actions, almost instinctive actions, which are quite effective against ships. The others, the Skimmers, are far more intelligent. They are also verbal. Yet they did not respond to our research vessels. They ignored attempts to communicate."

Warren said, "You still have ships?"

For the first time Gijan spoke. "No. I was on one of the last that went down. They got us off with helicopters, and then—"

"No need to go into that," Tseng cut him off smoothly.

"It was the Swarmers who sank you. Not Skimmers," Warren said. It was not a question.

"Skimmer intelligence was really only an hypothesis," Tseng said, "until we had reports that they had sought out single men or women. Usually people adrift, though sometimes even at the shore."

"Safer for them," Warren said.

"Apparently. They avoid the Swarmers. They avoid ships. Isolated contact is all that is left to them. It was really quite stupid of us not to have thought of that earlier."

"Yeah."

Tseng smiled slightly. "Everything is of course clearer in, as you say, the rearview mirror."

"Uh huh."

"It seems they learned the bits of German and Japanese and English from different individual encounters. The words were passed among the Skimmers so that each new contact had more available vocabulary."

"But they didn't know the words were from different languages," Gijan added.

"Maybe they only got one," Warren said.

"So we gather," Tseng said. "I have read your, ah, summary. Yours is the most advanced contact so far."

"A lot of it doesn't make much sense," Warren said. He knew Tseng was drawing him into the conversation but it did not matter. Tseng would have to give information to get some.

"The earlier contacts confirm part of your summary."

"Uh huh."

"They said that Swarmers can go ashore."

"Uh huh."

"How do you know that?"

"It's in the stuff I wrote. The stuff Gijan stole."

Gijan said sharply, "You showed it to me."

Warren looked at him without expression and Gijan stared back and after a moment looked away.

"Let us not bother with that. We are all working on the same problem, after all."

"Okay," Warren said. He had managed to get the talk away from how he knew about the Swarmers going on the land. Tseng was good at talking, a lot better than Warren, so he would have to keep the man away from some things. He volunteered, "I guess going up on the shore is part of their, uh, evolution."

"You mean their development?"

"They said something, the last day I saw them, about a deathlight. A deathlight coming on the land and only the Swarmers could live through it."

"Light from their star?"

"Guess so. It comes sometimes and that's why the Skimmers don't go up onto the land."

Tseng stood and began pacing against the back wall.

Warren wondered if he knew that Swarmers had already gone inland on an island near here. Tseng gave no sign of it and said out of his concentration, "That agrees with the earlier survivors' reports. We think that means their star is irregular. It flares in the UV. The Swarmers have simple nervous systems, smaller brains. They can survive a high UV flux."

"For about two of their planet's years, the Skimmers said," Warren murmured. "But you're wrong—the Swarmers aren't dumb."

"They have heads of mostly bone."

"That's for killing the big animals, the ones that float on the surface of their sea. Something like whales, I guess. Maybe they stay at the top to use the UV or something."

"The Swarmers ram them, throw those webs over them? Sink them?"

"Yeah. Just what they did to our ships."

"Target confusion. They think ships are animals."

"The Swarmers, they drag the floaters under, eat some kind of pods inside 'em. That's what triggers their going up on the land."

"If we could find a way to prevent their confusing our ships with—"

Gijan said, "But they are going to the land now. They are in the next mode."

"Uh huh." Warren studied the two men, tried to guess if they knew anything he could use. "Look, what're they doing when they get ashore?"

Tseng looked at him sharply. "What do the Skimmers say?"

"Far as I can tell, the Swarmers aren't dumb, not once they get on land. They make the machines and stuff for the Skimmers. They're really the same kind of animal. They grow hands and feet and the Skimmers have some way to tell them—singing—how to build stuff, make batteries, tools, that stuff."

Tseng stared at Warren for a long moment. "A break in the evolutionary ladder? Life trying to get out of the oceans, but turned back by the solar flares?" Tseng leaned forward and rested his knuckles on the gray plywood. He had a strange weight and force about him. And a desperate need.

Warren said, "Maybe it started out with the Swarmers

crawling up on the beaches to lay eggs or something. Good odds they'd be back in the water before a flare came. Then the Skimmers invented tools and saw they needed things on the land, needed to make fire or something. So they got the Swarmers, the younger form of their species, to help. Maybe—"

"The high UV speeded up their evolutionary rate. Perhaps the Swarmers became more intelligent, in their last phase, on land, where the intelligence would be useful in making the tools. Um, yes."

Tseng gave Gijan an intense glance. "Possible. But I think there is more than that. These creatures are here for some purpose beyond this charming little piece of natural history we have been told. Or sold."

Tseng turned back to Warren. "We have our partially successful procedures of communication, as you have probably guessed. I have been ordered to carry out systematic methods of approach." He was brisk and sure, as though he had digested Warren's information and found a way to classify it. "Yours will be among them. But it is an idiosyncratic technique and I doubt we could teach it to our field men. Underofficer Gijan, for example." The contempt in his voice for Gijan was obvious. "Meanwhile, I will call upon you for help if we need it, Warren."

"Uh huh."

Tseng took a map of the ocean from his desk drawer and flipped it across to Warren. "I trust this will be of help in writing your report."

"Report?"

"An account of your interactions with the aliens. I must file it with my superior. I am sure it will be in your own interests to make it as accurate as possible." He made a smile without any emotion behind it. "If you can fix the point where your ship went down, we might even be able to find some other survivors."

Warren could see there was nothing in this last promise. He thought and then said, "Mr. Wong, I wondered if I could, you know, rest a little. And when the guard there brings me my food, I'd like a long time to eat it. My stomach, being out on the ocean so long, it can't take your food unless I kind of take it easy."

"Of course, of course." Tseng smiled with genuine emotion this time. Warren could see that he was glad to be dispensing favors and that the act made him sure he had judged the situation and had it right.

"Sure do appreciate that, Mr. Wong," he said, getting the right tone into the words so that the man would classify him and file him away and forget him.

VIII

He worked for two days on the report. The guard gave him a pad of paper and a short stubby little pen and Tseng told him to write it in English. Warren smiled at that. They thought any seaman had to speak a couple of languages but he had never any trouble getting around with one and a few words picked up from others. You learned more from watching people than from listening to all their talk anyway.

He had never been any good at writing and a lot of the things about the Skimmers he could not get down. He worked on the writing in his cell, listening all the time for the sound of new motors or big things moving. It was hard to tell anything about what the teams were doing. He was glad he could rest in the shadows of the cell and think, eating the food they brought him as quickly as he could while still getting the taste of it.

The same chinless guard he had from the first came once a day to take him down to the shore. Warren carried the waste bucket. The guard would not let him take the time to bury the waste and instead made him throw it into the surf. The guard stayed back in the sea-grape bushes while Warren went down to the lagoon. The man was probably under orders not to show himself on the beach, Warren guessed. On the windward side of the island there was a lot of dry grass and some gullies. Dried-up streambeds ran down into little half-moon beaches and Warren could see the teams had moored catboats and other small craft there. Some of the troops had pitched tents far back in the gullies but most of them were empty. The guard marched him back that way. On one of the sandy crescents Warren's raft was beached, dragged up above the tide line but not weighted down or moored.

Coming back on the second day some sooty terns were hanging in the wind, calling with long low cries. Some were nested in the rocks up at the windward and others in

the grass of the lee. The terns would fall off the wind and
swoop down over the heads of the men gathering the eggs
out of the rocky nests. The birds cawed and dipped down
through the wind but the men did not look up.

The next morning the chinless soldier came too soon
after the breakfast tin and Warren had to straighten his
sleeping pad in a hurry. The guard never came into the
shadowy cell because of the smell from the bucket which
Warren kept next to the door. The man had discovered
that Warren knew no Chinese and so instead of giving
orders he shoved Warren in whatever direction he wanted.
This time they went north.

Tseng was surveying a work team at a point halfway up
the ridge at the middle of the island. He nodded to Warren and signaled that the guard should remain nearby.
"Your report?"

"Nearly done with it."

"Good. I will translate it myself. Be sure it is legible."

"I printed it out."

"Just as do the Skimmers."

"Yeah."

"We duplicated your methods, you know, and dropped
several messages into the lagoon." From here on the ridge
moving shadows were plain against the sand. The soft green
of the lagoon was like a ring and beyond it was the hard
blue that went to the horizon. "No reply."

"How'd you deliver them?"

"Three men, two armed for safety. After so many incidents they are afraid to go out unprotected."

"They go in that?" Warren pointed to a skiff beached
below them.

"Yes. I'm going to supplement their work with a set of
acoustics. They should be—yes, here we are." A buzz
came from the south and a motorboat came up the lagoon
leaving a white wake. It cut in among the shoals and sand-
bars and a big reel on the back of it was spinning in the
sun, throwing quick darts of yellow into Warren's eyes.

"We will have a complete acoustic bed. A very promising method."

"You make any sense out of that?"

Tseng shaded his eyes against the glare and turned to
smile at Warren. "Their high-frequency 'songs' are their
basic method of communication. We already have much
experience with the dolphins. We can converse freely with

them. Only on simpleminded subjects, of course. Much of what we know about Swarmer and Skimmer movements comes from the dolphins."

Warren said sharply, "Look, why fool with that stuff. Let me go out and I'll ask them what you want."

Tseng nodded. "Eventually I might. But you must understand that the Skimmers have reasons of their own for not telling you everything that is important."

"Such as?"

"Here." Tseng snapped his fingers at an aide standing nearby. The soldier brought over a document pouch. Tseng took out a set of photographs and handed them to Warren. The top one was a color shot of a woman's stomach and breasts. There were small bumps on them, white mounds on the tan skin. One lump was in her left nipple.

Warren went on to the next, and the next. The lumps got bigger and whiter. "They are quite painful," Tseng said distantly. "Some kind of larva burrows into a sweatsore and in a day this begins. The larva is biggest near the skin, armed with sharp yellow spines. The worm turns as it feeds. Spines grate against the nerves. The victim feels sudden, deep pain. Within another day the victim is hysterical and tries to claw the larva out. These are small larvae. There are reports of larger ones."

In one photograph the open sores were bleeding and dripping a white pus. "Like a tick," Warren said. "Burn it out. Use iodine. Or cover it with tape so it can't get air."

Tseng sighed. "Any such attack and the larva releases something, we are unsure what, into the victim's bloodsteam. It paralyzes the victim so he cannot treat himself further."

"Well, if you—"

"The larva apparently does not breathe. It takes oxygen directly from the host. If anything dislodges the spines, once they are hooked in, the larva releases the paralyzer and something else, something that carries a kind of egg so that other larvae can grow elsewhere. All this in minutes."

Warren shook his head. "Never heard of any tick or bug like that."

"They come from the Swarmers. When they are ashore."

Warren watched the motorboat methodically crisscrossing the lagoon, the reel spinning. He shook his head.

"Something to do with their mating? Don't know. The Skimmers—"

"They said nothing about it. Interesting, eh?"

"Maybe they don't know."

"It seems unlikely."

"So you're listening for what?"

"Contact between the Skimmers and the Swarmers. Some knowledge of how they interact."

"Can't you treat this bug, get rid of it?"

"Possibly. The European medical centers are at work now. But there are other diseases. They are spreading rapidly from contact points near Ning-po and Macau."

"Maybe you can block them off."

"The things are everywhere. They come ashore and the larvae are carried by the birds, by animals—somehow. That is why we burn our reserves of fuel to come this far."

"To the islands?"

"Only in isolation do they make contact. The reported incidents are from the Pacific basin. That is why there are Japanese aircraft near here, Soviet, American—you are an American, aren't you?"

"No."

"Oh? Somehow I thought—but never mind. The other powers are desperate. They do not know what is happening and they envy our lead in information. You will notice the installation to the south?"

Tseng gestured. Warren saw at the rocky tip of the island a fan of slender shapes knifing up at the sky. "Anti-air missiles. We would not want anyone else to exploit this opportunity."

"Uh huh."

The motorboat droned, working its way up the eastern shore. Warren studied the island, noticing where the tents were pitched and where the men moved in work teams and where the scrub jungle cut off visibility.

"If you're smart you won't use a motor in the lagoon."

"The men will not go out without some way of returning quickly. I understand their fear. I have seen—"

An aide approached. He spoke quickly and Tseng answered with anxiety creeping into his voice. Warren watched the motorboat cross near the sandbar and saw the shadows dart and twist and turn, swift black shapes in the watery green light.

*   *   *

That night he felt a dark hammering thing above him that wove and wove, rippling the sunlight, swimming badly, and dropped metal that settled on him, heavy and foul. The steady dead rasp from above cut and burned and he turned on his side. Then he was above the motor and saw the fuel line backfilled and heard the sluggish rumble as they blew the lines out and heard the plugs not running right either. That was it: nothing ran right. Humans were great talkers but down here, lofting in the salty murk, he could see that they worked their mouths a lot but said damned little to each other. In Tokyo he'd never learned a word of Japanese, and here Gijan had played a mute without Warren's minding, and now the Chinese were trying to talk to Skimmers—who wanted something they couldn't say either—and each life form had its own private language. He turned over again and felt his wife sleeping against him warm and moist and then on top of him the way she liked. She was heavy too, like the falling spreading metal the hammering machine laid in the lagoon, heavy and yet soft, and her hair lay silky on his face and in his eyes. In shadows her face was intersecting planes, lean and white the way he had always liked, and he took her hair in his mouth and tasted it. The salt and musk was like her sex below. He touched the canted planes of her and remembered that she had fallen away from him when more than anything he had wanted her weight. And her hair swinging across his face and the taste of it.

When he woke the pad was damp with sweat. He felt in the blackness for the table turned over on its side to conceal the far wall. This reassuring flat plane of wood gave him back the present so he did not have to think about the past. But he remembered the hammering from above and the falling cold metal and knew how much they hated what was happening to them out in the lagoon.

Before dawn his cell rattled and there was a booming that rolled down from the sky. He woke and looked out the windows through the heavy wire mesh. High up in the black, luminous things tumbled and exploded into auras of blue and crimson and then gutted into nothing. Distant hollow boomings came long after the lights were gone and then the sounds faded into the crashing on the reef.

In the morning the chinless soldier came again and took the tin dish that Warren had rubbed clean. The soldier did not like this job and he cuffed Warren twice to show him where to walk. First they went to the beach with the waste bucket, which had more in it now because Warren's body no longer absorbed almost everything he was fed. From the beach he watched the small motor ketches and cats that stayed near the shore while they laid something into the water, dropping boxes off the stern where they would lie on the bottom and, Warren was sure, send back reports on the passing sounds and movements.

The guard took him north and inland, just out of view of the reef. Tseng was there with a crowd and they were all watching the green water from far back among the trees.

"See them?" Tseng said to Warren when he had worked his way through the group of men and women. Warren looked out past the brilliant white sand that stung the eyes and saw silver-blue forms leaping.

"What's . . . why are they doing that?" he asked.

"We are returning their acoustic signals to them. As a kind of test."

"Not smart."

"Oh?" Tseng turned with interest. "Why?"

"I can't really tell you but—"

"It is a technique of progression. We give them back their songs. We see how they react. The dolphins eventually did well with this approach."

"These aren't dolphins."

"So. Yes." Tseng seemed to lose interest in the splashing forms in the lagoon. He turned, hands placed neatly behind his back, and led Warren through the group of advisers around them. "But you must admit they are giving a kind of response."

Warren swore. "Would you talk to somebody if they kept poking you in the eye?"

"Not a good analogy."

"Yeah?"

"Still . . ." Tseng slowed, peering out through the brush and palm trees at the glistening water. "You are the only one who got the material about how they came here. Getting scooped up and going on a long voyage and then being dumped into the ocean—you got that. I had not heard it before.

"It does make a certain kind of sense. Fish like that—they might make printed messages, yes. They have shown they can put together our own wreckage and make a kind of electrostatic printing press—underwater, even. But to build a rocket? A ship that goes between stars? No."

"Somebody brought them."

"I am beginning to believe that. But why? To spread these diseases?"

"I dunno. Let me go out and—"

"Later, when we are more sure. Yes, then. But tomorrow we have more tests."

"Have you counted the number of them out there?"

"No. They are hard to keep track of. I—"

"There are a lot less of 'em now. I can see. You know what happens when you drive them away?"

"Warren, you will get your turn." Tseng put a restraining hand on his sleeve. "I know you have had a hard time here and on that raft but believe me, we are able to—"

Gijan approached, carrying some pieces of paper. He rattled off something in Chinese and Tseng nodded. "I am afraid we are being interrupted once more. Those incidents last night—you saw them?—have involved us, a research party, in— Well, the Americans have been humiliated again. Their missiles we knocked down with ease."

"You're sure that stuff was theirs?"

"They are the ones complaining—isn't the conclusion obvious? I believe they and perhaps too their lackeys, the Japanese, have discovered how much progress we are making. They would very much like to turn the Swarmers and their larvae to their own nationalistic advantage. These messages—" he waved the pack of them—"are more diplomatic notices. The Japanese have given my government an ultimatum of sorts. I am sure even you understand that this is part of a larger game. Of course China does not wish to use the Swarmers against other powers, even if we did understand the creatures."

"I don't know about that."

"But I thought you were American." Tseng smiled without mirth.

"No."

"I see. I think it is perhaps time to have Underofficer Gijan take you back to your little room, then."

The guard took Warren down the center of the island, along a path worn smooth in the last few days by the troops. They passed a dozen technicians working on acoustic equipment and playing back the high-pitched squeals of Skimmer song. The troops were making entries on computer screens and chattering to each other, breaking down the problem into bits that could be cross-referenced and reassembled to make patterns that people could understand. It would have to be good because they wanted to eavesdrop. But the way the Skimmers talked to the Swarmers might not be anything like the songs the Skimmers sang among themselves.

It made no sense that the Skimmers had much control over the Swarmers, Warren thought to himself as he marched down the dirt path. No sense at all. Something had brought them all to Earth and given the Swarmers some disease and the answer lay in thinking about that fact, not playing stupid games with machines in the water.

The troops were spread out more now, he saw. There were nests of high-caliber cannon strung out along the ridge and down near the beaches men were digging in where they could set up a cross fire over the natural clearings.

The men and women he passed were talking among themselves now, not silent and efficient the way they had been at first. They looked at him with suspicion. He guessed the missile attack in the night had made them nervous and even the hot work of clearing fields of fire in the heavy humidity did not take it out of them.

Coming down the rocky ridgeline Warren slipped on a stone and fell. The guard hit him to get him to hurry. Warren went on and saw ahead one of the bushes with leaves he knew he could eat and when he went by it he pulled some off and started to stuff them into his pockets for later. The guard shouted and hit him in the back with the butt of his rifle and Warren went down suddenly, banging his knee on a big tree root. The guard kicked him in the ribs and Warren saw the man was jumpy and bored at the same time. That was dangerous. He carefully got up and moved along the path, limping from the dull pain spreading in his knee. The guard pushed him into his cell and kicked him again. Warren fell and lay there, not moving, waiting, and the guard finally grunted and slammed the door.

Noon came and went and he got no food. He ate the leaves. He did not blame the Chinese for the way they treated him. The great powers all acted the same, independent of what they said their politics were, and it was easier to think of them as big machines that did what they were designed to do rather than as bunches of people.

Night came. Warren had gotten used to not thinking about food when he was on the raft and he was just as glad the guard did not bring food. Eventually the squat chinless soldier would come all the way into the cell and look behind the table which was overturned and would see the dirt mounds. Warren lay on the rocky ground that was the floor and wondered if he would dream of his wife again. It was a good dream because it took away all the pain they both had caused and left only her smells and taste. But when he dozed off he was in the deep place where clanking came from above, a metallic sound that blended with the dull buzzing he had heard all that afternoon from the motorboat in the lagoon, the sounds washing together until he realized they were the same but the loud clanking one was the way the Skimmers heard it. It was hard to think with the ringing hammering sound in his head and he tried to swim up and break water to get away from it. The clanking went on and then was a roar, louder, and he woke up suddenly and felt the sides of the cell tremble with the sound. Two abrupt crashes came down out of the sky and then sudden blue light.

Warren looked out through the mesh on the windows and saw women running. There was no moon but in the starlight he could see they were carrying rifles. A sudden rattling came from the north and west and then answering fire from up on the ridge.

He used the flickering light from the windows to find the map Tseng had given him. He pulled back the sleeping pad to expose the hole he had dug and without hesitation crawled in. He knew the feel of it well and in the complete dark found the stone at the end he used. He had estimated that there was only a foot of dirt left above. Using the pan to scrape away the last few feet of dirt had left him with a feel for how strong the earth was above but when he hit it with the stone it did not give. There was not much room to swing and three more solid hits did not even shake loose clods of it. Warren was sweating in the closeness of the tunnel and the dirt stuck to his face as he chipped away at the hard soil over him. It was hardpacked and filled with rocks that struck him in the face and rolled onto his chest. His arm started to ache and then tire but he did not stop. He switched the stone to his left hand and felt a softness give above and then was hitting nothing. The stone broke the crust and he could see stars.

He studied the area carefully: A soldier ran by carrying a tripod for an automatic rifle. The sharp cracking fire still came from north and west.

There was a spark of light high up and Warren snapped his head away to keep his night vision. Then the glare was gone and a hollow roar rolled over the camp. Mortars, not far away. He struggled up out of the tunnel and ran for the trees nearby. Halfway there his knee folded under him and he cursed it silently as he went down. It was worse than he had thought from the fall, and lying on the hard cell floor had made it go stiff. He got up and limped to the trees, each moment feeling a spot between his shoulder blades where the slug would come if any of the running men in the camp behind him saw the shadow making its painful way. The slug did not come but a flare went up as he reached a clump of bushes. He threw himself into them and rolled over so he could see the clearing. The flare had taken away most of his night vision. He waited for it to come back and smelled the wind. There was something heavy and musky in it. It was the easterly trade, blowing steady, which meant the tide was getting ready to shift and it was past midnight. Coming from the east the wind should not have picked up the smell of the fire fight so the musky smell was something else. Warren knew the taste but could not remember what it was and what it might mean about the tide. He squinted, moving back into the bush, and saw a man in the camp coming straight toward him.

The figure stopped at the door of Warren's cell. It fumbled at the door and a banging of automatic-weapons fire came from the other side of camp. The man jumped back and yelled to someone and then went back to trying to unlock the door. Warren glanced into the distance where sudden flashes lit the camp in pale orange light. The firing got heavier, and when he looked back at the cell there were two men there and the first one was opening the door. Warren crawled out of the dry bushes, moving when a burst of machine-gun fire covered any sound he might make. He got to a thin stand of trees and turned. A flare went up, burning yellow. It was the chinless soldier. He had the door open and Gijan was coming out, waving a hand, pointing north. They shouted at each other for a moment. Warren edged back further into the trees. He was about fifty meters away now and could see each man unshoulder the slim rifles they carried. They held them at the ready. Gijan pointed again and the two men separated, moving apart about thirty meters. They were going to search. They turned and walked into the brush. Gijan came straight at Warren.

It would be easy to give himself up now. Wait for a flare and come forward with his hands held high. He had counted on getting further away than this before anyone came after him. Now in the dark and with the fighting going there was a good chance they were jumpy and would shoot him if they saw some movement. But as he thought this Warren moved back, sinking into the shadows. He had faced worse than this on the raft. He limped away, going by feel in the shadows.

He reached a line of palms and moved along them toward the north. He was still about five hundred meters from the beach but there was a big clearing in the way so he angled in toward the ridge. Muffled thuds from the west told him that the Chinese were using mortars against whoever was coming into the beaches. Five spaced screeches cut through the deep sounds of distant battle.

Warren guessed the Japanese or the Americans had decided to take the island and try to speak to the Skimmers themselves. Maybe they would try their own machines and codes.

They might know about him, though. The Chinese wanted to keep him or else Gijan would not have come with the soldier. Warren stumbled and slammed his knee into a tree. He paused, panting and trying to see if the men were within sight. With a moment to think he saw that Gijan might want to kill him to keep him out of the hands of the others. He could not be sure that giving himself up was safe anymore.

The five shrill notes came again and he recognized them as an emergency signal blown on a whistle. They were from close by. Gijan was calling for help. With the Chinese fighting other troops on the other side of the island, Gijan might not get a quick answer. But help would come and then they would box him in.

Warren turned toward the beach. He moved as fast as he could without making a lot of noise. His knee went out from under him again and as he got up he realized he was not going to give them much trouble. They had him bracketed already; they had good knees, and help was coming. He could not outrun them. The only chance he had was to circle around and ambush one of them, ambush an armed, well-trained man, using his bare hands. Then get away before the other one found out.

He picked up a rock and put it in his pocket. It banged against his leg with each step. A rustling came from behind him and he hurried and stumbled at the edge of a gully.

A shout. He jumped down into the gully. As he landed there was a sharp crack and something zipped by overhead. It chunked into a tree on the other bank. Warren knew there was no point in going back now.

He trotted down the deepening water-carved wash. It was too narrow for two men. He tried to think how Gijan would figure it. The smartest thing was to wait for the other troops and then comb the area.

But Warren might reach the beach by then. Better to send one man down the gully and another through the trees, to cut him off.

Warren went what felt like a hundred meters before he stopped to listen. The crack of a twig snapping came from far back in the blackness. To the left? He could not be sure. The gully was rocky and it slowed him down. There were some good places to hide in the shadows and then try to hit the following man as he came by. Better than in the scrub, anyway. But by then the other man would have gotten between him and the beach.

A pebble rattled faintly behind him. He stopped. The hard clay of the gully was three meters high here and steep. He found some thick roots sticking out and carefully pulled himself up. He stuck his head above the edge and looked around. Nothing moving. He crawled over the lip and a rock came loose under his foot. He lunged and caught it. A stabbing pain came in his knee and he bit his tongue to keep from making a noise.

The scrub was thicker here. He rolled into a stand of trees, keeping down and out of the starlight. Twigs snagged at his clothes.

There was an even chance the man would come on

this side of the gully. If he didn't Warren could slip off to the north. But Gijan had probably guessed where he was headed and he would not have much of a lead when he reached the beach. On the open sand he would be exposed, easy to pick off.

Warren crawled into the dark patches under the trees and waited, rubbing his leg. The wind smelled bad here, damp and heavy. He wondered if the tide had changed.

He leaned his head on his hands to rest and felt a muscle jump in his face. It startled him. He could not feel it unless he put his hand to it. So Tseng had been right and he did have a spasm without knowing it. Warren frowned. He did not know what to think about that. It was a fact he would have to understand. For now, though, he put the thought away from him and watched the darkness.

He pulled the rock out of his pocket and hefted it and a pale form moved in the trees forty meters inland. It was a short soldier, the chinless one. Warren crouched low to follow. The pain that shot through his knee reminded him of how the chinless man had kicked him but the memory did not make him feel anything about what he was going to do. He moved forward.

In the dry brush he kept as quiet as he could. The dull claps and crashes that came over the ridge were muffled now, just when he needed them to be loud. Under the trees it was quieter, and he was surprised to hear the rasping of the soldier breathing. The man moved slowly, rifle at the ready, the weapon looking big in the starlight. The man kept in the starlight and watched the shadows. That was smart.

The breathing got louder. Warren moved, favoring his knee. He would have to jump up fast and take the soldier from behind.

The figure came closer. Suddenly Warren saw that the man wore a helmet. To use the rock now he would have to hit him in the face. That made the odds a lot worse. But he would have to try.

The man stopped, turned, looked around. Warren froze and waited. The head turned away and Warren eased forward, closing, the pain shooting in his knee. The leg would try to give way when he came up for the rush. He would watch for that and force it to hold. The air was still and heavy under the trees and the smell was worse, something from the beach. The soldier's was the only visible movement.

In the quilted pattern of shadows and light it was hard to follow the silhouette. Warren put his hand out and gathered his feet under him and felt something wet and slick ahead and suddenly knew that the slow rasping laboring breath did not come from the chinless soldier but from something between them. He felt the ground and brought his hand up to his face and smelled the strong reek he had tasted on the wind. Ahead in the faint light that fell between two palms he saw the long form struggling, pulling itself forward on blunt legs. It sucked in the air with each step. It was thick and heavy and the skin was a gunmetal gray, pocked with inch-wide round holes. Warren felt a whirring in the air and something brushed against his face, lingered, and was gone. Another whirring followed, so quiet he could barely hear it. The stubby fin-legs of the Swarmer went mechanically forward and back, dragging its bloated body. In the starlight he could see the glistening where fluid seeped from the moist holes.

* the young run with sores *

Another small whirring sound came and he saw from one of the dark openings a thing as big as a finger spring out, slick with moisture, and spread its wings. It beat against the thick and reeking air and then lifted its heavy body, coming free of its hole, wings fluttering. It lifted into the air and hovered, seeking. It darted away, missing Warren, passing on into the night. He did not move. The Swarmer pulled itself forward. Its dry rattling gasps caught the attention of the soldier and the man turned and took a step. The Swarmer gathered itself and kicked with its hind leg. It reached the man's leg and the massive head turned to take the calf between its jaws. It seized and twisted and Warren heard the sharp intake of breath before the soldier went down. He screamed and the Swarmer turned itself and rolled over the man. The long blunt head came up and nuzzled down into the belly of the man and the sharp shrill scream cut off suddenly. Warren stood, the smell stronger now, and watched the two forms struggle on the open sand. The man pawed for his rifle where it had fallen and the thick leg of the Swarmer pinned his arm. They rolled to the side. The thing wallowed on him, covering him with a slick sheen, cutting off the low moans he made. Warren ran toward them and picked up the rifle. He backed away, thumbing off the safety. The man went limp and the air rushed out of him as the alien settled into place. Its head turned toward Warren and held there for a moment and then it turned back and dipped down to the belly of the man. It began feeding.

The soldier was dead. Gijan had heard the screams and would be here soon. There was no point in shooting the Swarmer and giving Gijan a sound to follow. Warren turned and limped away from the licking and chewing sounds.

He walked silently through brush, hobbling. The rifle had a bayonet on the muzzle. If a Swarmer came at him he would use that instead of firing. He stayed in the open, watching the shadows.

Abruptly from behind him came a loud hammering of automatic fire. Warren dodged to the side and then realized that no bullets were thumping into the trees near him. It was Gijan, killing the Swarmer a hundred meters or more away.

Warren was sure the Chinese did not know the Swarmers were crawling ashore or else they would have come after him in a group. Now Gijan would be shaken and uncertain. But in a few minutes he would recover and know what he had to do. Gijan would run to the beach, moving faster than Warren could, and try to cut him off.

Warren heard a light humming. He looked up between the trees where the sound came and could see nothing against the stars.

* the World that was false World made them this way not as they were when we knew them in the World that was ours they cannot sing but know of the places where you sing to each other and some now go there with their sores they may be chewed by you but there are many many *

Something smacked into his throat. It was wet and it attached itself with a sudden clenching thrust like a ball of needles. Warren snatched at it. He stopped an inch short of grabbing at the thing when he caught the musty sea stench full in his nostrils. The moist lump dripped something down his throat. He brought the rifle up quickly and pointed the bayonet at his throat and jabbed, aiming by instinct in the dark. He felt the tip go into the thing and turned the blade so it scraped, pulling the wet centimeter-long larva out. It came away before the spines had sunk in. Blood seeped out and trickled down his throat. He sopped it up with his sleeve and held the bayonet up in the starlight. The thing was white as a maggot and twisted feebly on the blade. One wing fluttered. The other was gone. The skin of it peeled back some more and the wing fell off. He stuck the blade into the sand to clean it and stepped on the thing that moved in spasms on the ground. Something still stuck on his neck. He scraped it off. The other wing was on the blade and some thin dark needles. He wiped them on the sand and with a sudden rushing fear slammed his heel down on them again and again.

He was breathing hard by the time he reached the beach. The fear had gone away when he had concentrated on staying away from the shadows, not thinking about what could be in them. The stabbing pain in his knee helped. He listened for the deep rasping and the humming and tasted the wind for their smell.

He hobbled out from the last line of palms and onto the white glow of the beach beneath the stars. He could see maybe fifty meters and there were no dark forms struggling up from the water. To the north he could hear faint shouts. That did not bother him because he did not have far to go. He stumbled toward the shouts, ignoring the quick rippling flashes of yellow light from a mortar barrage and the long *crump* that came after them. There were motorboats moored in the shallows with the big reels in the stern but no one in them. He took an oar out of one.

He came around the last horn of a crescent beach and saw ahead the dark blotch of the raft far up on the sand. He threw his rifle aboard and began dragging the raft toward the water. Big combers boomed on the reef.

He got it into the shallows and rolled aboard without looking back. He pushed off with the oar and kept pushing until he felt the current catch him. Speed, now. Speed.

The tide had just turned. It was slow but it would pick up in a few minutes and take him toward the pass in the reef. When he was sure of that he sat down and felt for the rifle. Sitting, he would be harder to see and he could steady the rifle against his good knee. His throat had nearly stopped bleeding but his shirt was heavy with blood. He wondered if the flying things would smell it and find him. The Skimmers had never said anything about the things like maggots with wings and he was sure now it was because they did not know about it. There was no reason the Swarmers would have evolved a thing like that to help them live on the land. And with the Skimmers driven from the lagoon by the men there was nothing to keep the Swarmers from bringing the things ashore.

He saw something move on the land and he lay down on the raft and Gijan came out onto the sand, running. Gijan stopped and looked straight out at Warren and then turned and ran north. Warren picked up his rifle. Gijan was carrying his weapon at the ready. Was the man trying to cut him off but keep him alive? Then he should have run south, toward the motorboats. But there might be boats to the north, too. Maybe Gijan had heard the shouts in that direction and was running for help.

Warren thumbed off the safety and put the rifle on automatic fire. He would know what to do if Gijan would tell him by some action what he intended to do. If he could just shout to the man, ask him— But maybe Gijan had not seen him after all. And the man might lie even if he answered.

Suddenly the running figure dropped his rifle and slapped at his neck and then fell heavily on the sand. He twisted and brought both hands to his neck and struggled for a moment. Then he brought something out from his neck and threw it into the water and made a sound of fear. Gijan lurched up and staggered. He still clutched his neck with one hand but turned and looked for his weapon. He seemed dazed. His head came up and his gaze swept past Warren and then came back again. Gijan had seen the raft for sure this time.

Warren wished he could read the man's face. Gijan hesitated only a moment. Then he picked up his weapon and turned to the north. He took some steps and Warren relaxed, and then there was something about the way Gijan moved his arm. Warren aimed quickly, with no pause for conscious thought, and Gijan was bringing the rifle around. It made a bright yellow flash, firing on automatic, as Gijan swept the muzzle, fanning, and Warren fired a burst. It took Gijan high in the shoulder and then in the chest, spinning him.

Warren slowly put down the rifle, panting. He had not thought at all about killing Gijan but had just done it, not stopping for the instant of balancing the equation and seeing if it had to be that way, and that was what had saved him.

He peered shoreward again. Voices, near. There was some sea still running against the ebb but now the tide was taking hold and carrying him out. The pass was a dark patch in the snarling white of the combers. He had to get away fast now because the men to the north would be coming toward the gunfire. Hoisting the sail would just give them a target. He had to wait for the slow steady draw to take him through.

Something thumped against the bottom of the raft. It came again. Warren stood and cradled the rifle. The boards worked against each other as they came into the chop near the pass. A big dark thing broke water and rolled hugely. Eyes looked at him and legs that had grown from fins kicked against the current. The Swarmer turned and wallowed in the wash from the passage and then sank, the great head turning toward shore.

Warren used the oar to turn the raft free of the rocks. The surf broke to each side and the deep bands of current sucked the raft through with a sudden rush. Behind him Warren heard a cry, lonely and harsh and full of surprise. The warring rumbled beyond the ridge and was lost in the crashing of the waves running hard before an east wind and he went out into the dark ocean, the raft rising fast and plunging as it came into the full sea swell.

A sharp crack. A motorboat was coming fast behind. Warren lay flat on the raft and groped for his rifle.

They would get him out here for sure. He aimed at the place where the pilot would be but in the fast chop he knew he would miss. There came a short, stuttering bark of automatic-weapons fire.

The raft slewed to port and the boat turned to follow. Warren crawled to the edge of the raft, ready to slip overboard when they got too close. It would be better than getting cut down, even with the Swarmers in the water.

The boat whined and bounced on the swell, bearing down. He lifted the rifle to take aim and knew the odds were damn long against him. He saw a muzzle flash and the deck spat splinters at him where the shots hit. Warren squeezed carefully and narrowed his eyes to frame the target and saw something leap suddenly across the bow of the boat. It was big and another followed, landing in front of the pilot and wriggling back over the windshield in one motion. It crashed into the men there. Shouts. A blue-white shape flicked a man overboard and knocked another sprawling. The boat veered to starboard. From this angle Warren could see the pilot holding to the wheel and crouched to avoid the flicking tail of the Skimmer.

A hammering of the automatic weapon. The Skimmer jumped and slashed at the man with its tail. Warren leaped up and rocked against the swell to improve his aim. He got off two quick shots at the man. The figure staggered and the Skimmer struck him solidly and he pitched over the side. The pilot glanced back and saw he was alone. The Skimmer stopped thrashing and went still. Warren did not give the man time to think. He fired at the dark splotch at the wheel until it was gone.

Distant shouts came from shore but no sounds of another boat. The boat drifted away. Warren thought of the Skimmer who lay dead in it. He tried to reach the boat, but the currents separated them further. In moments it was gone in the darkness and the island itself faded into a mere looming shadow on the sea.

IX

At noon the next day three jets split the sky with their roaring and passed over the south. All morning the sky had been streaked with the trails of craft that flew high and made no sound. He had rounded the island in the night and run up his worn sail and then run before the wind to get distance. He had the map from Tseng and the fishing lines were still on the raft with their hooks so he could try for something. The rifle had no rounds left in its clip but with the bayonet it made a good gaff. He had a strike in the morning from a small tuna. It had got away when he hauled it in. But there would be more now that the Swarmers were going to land and would not be taking the fish.

The Skimmers came in the afternoon. They leaped in crystal showers that glinted in the raw sunlight.

In the night there was a sudden distant glare of orange light reflected off clouds near the horizon. It became a glow and the color seeped out of it, and then it was gone. Afterward a rolling hammer blow of sound came. Later there were more huge bursts of light, faint and far away.

High up, silvery specks coasted smoothly across the dark. One by one they vanished in bright firefly glows— yellow, blue, orange. Satellite warfare. Soon they were gone.

At dawn he woke and searched the sky and found the thin silver thread that reached up into the dark bowl overhead.

But now it curled about itself. Warren looked down the sky toward the dawn and found another pale streak far below, where nothing should be. The Skyhook was broken. Part of it was turning upward while the other fell. Somebody had blown it in two.

For long moments he watched the faint band fall. Finally he lost it in the glare as the sun rose. There had been men and women working on the lower tip of the Skyhook, and he tried to imagine what it was to fall hopeless that far and that long and then to burn quick and high in the air like a shooting star.

His knee had swollen up now and he could not stand so he laid in the shade of the sail. The wound in his neck had a crusted blue scab and did not hurt so much. He thought it would be all right. He would ask the Skimmers about the larvae that flew but he was sure that they were not natural to the Swarmers. Something had changed the Swarmers so that the Skimmers did not know them anymore.

He remembered the sheets he had written on, the tangled sentences and thoughts, things he had not been able to understand. He had known that the Skimmers hated the machines that intruded into the water. They had learned that through the long years of voyaging, when they had been in ships, carried like cargo, moved and fed and poked at by things that hummed and jerked and yet had no true life, things they had never seen before: machines. Computers and robots that could span the stars. A civilization of nothing but devices and remorseless logic. Things that had evolved, because the same laws of selection operated on them as did on living matter. Things that came out of those laws and would kill to survive, to protect themselves from any enemy. And life, arising from nothing at all, flowering and blooming wherever chemicals met and sunlight boomed through a blanket of gas—life was constant competition. The machines must have come from long-dead civilizations whose computer nets survived, but in time the machines would come to fear the rivalry of life that burst forth from every possible corner of the galaxy. And fear would, by evolution's logic, kindle something that could stir the machines to action when necessary, something like hatred.

In the long years of their voyage, that would become clear to the ripe cargo the machines carried. So the Swarmers and Skimmers had come to hate them in return. And when they saw the simple, noisy machines of men, they hated those, too.

He fished through the day without success.

That night there were more orange flashes to the west.

Then, in the hours before dawn, things moved in the sky. Shapes glided through the black, catching the sunlight as they moved out of the earth's shadow. They were in close orbit, moving fast, the orbits repeating in less than an hour. They were huge and irregular, their surfaces grainy and blotched. For Warren to be able to see the features on them, they had to be far bigger than the ships that had brought the Swarmers and Skimmers.

No defenses rose to meet these shapes. There were no military satellites left, no high-energy lasers, no particle-beam weapons. The ships absorbed the sunlight and gave back a strange glowing gray. As Warren watched they began to split. Chunks broke away and fell, separating again and again as they streaked across the sky.

With dawn came three Skimmers.

They stayed deep. Warren leaned over and put his head in the water. He let his eyes adjust until he could see the quick, darting movements they made. There was something in the elaborate twistings that recalled some passages from the lagoon. He watched them and when he thought he understood, he lay back on the raft and thought.

The gray ships were bigger than the earlier ones, but they had the same aim. To set one kind of life against another. To cause a war that looked to men like a simple fight with aliens from the sea.

So the men had done the same things they always did when they were in groups. The Swarmers were a threat, but there were always humans who would use the situation against each other, to get the advantage, and somehow the thing had gotten away from them, and in these last nights the terrible weapons had at last been used. And they had killed the Skyhook, too.

Nuclear war, once ignited, was a runaway instability. Life at this stage of development was vulnerable to it. The machines probably knew that. They understood that the humans, carried away by passions, would miss the fact that the Swarmers and Skimmers were only a piece of a bigger puzzle. That somewhere something wanted life to cancel other life and for each form to pull the other down. An efficient way to eliminate competitors.

But this morning, watching the intricate turns of the Skimmers, seeing it in a blurred way through the water that would always separate him from them, he had understood new things. The gray ships were hurling themselves into the sea, far from the battles raging on the continents.

The Skimmers knew these machines, had lived for generations in them. **The gray things float deep beneath the waves**, the Skimmers had said. **They mine the sea; their factories clank; we can hear them for great distances. They make copies of themselves. The Swarmers are gone to the land and the gray things think they are safe.**

He caught some small fish in the afternoon and used them to bait the lines. He got two hits immediately and brought them in. The meat was tough and strong-flavored. The sea was gathering itself again after the long time of the Swarmers, blossoming, growing, the schools of fish returning. He was sure he could live here now.

They think they are safe. They think there is only us, trapped in this new _W_orld. We cannot make tools. But we know the waters and the machines do not, cannot know them, cannot taste the essence of them.

He watched the long rolling waves, squinting. The Skimmers had spoken of other men and women who had learned to live on the sea. Remnants. They would have little to work with, just the wreckage of the mainlands where the death was spreading, and of old ships, but with the Skimmers they could fashion things.

To reach the land the gray machines would have to come up finally. They would be prepared to take the solid ground. They would not be ready for life that had lasted and fought battles and lost them and endured and fought again because it did not know it was defeated, and went on silently, still peering forward and by instinct seeking other life, and still waiting when the gray things began to move again, still powerful and still asking as life always does, and still dangerous and still coming.

He finished the fish he had caught and lay there letting the sun warm him. As dusk came he could see more of the gray shapes in orbit but they did not fill him with the fear he had known before. He was tired. He fell asleep early. He lay face down on the worn deck, rolling gently with the steady swell. He did not wake at first when a Skimmer leaped near the raft. He was dreaming of his wife.

THE SCIENCE FICTION YEAR

Charles N. Brown

1981 WAS, BOTH COMMERCIALLY AND ARTISTI-
cally, a mediocre year in science fiction. The total number
of books published, including original titles, reprints, and
reissues, dropped for the second year in a row, but there
were still about 1,000 books done, compared with the
record 1,300 in 1979 and 1,200 in 1980. The drop was
mostly in hardcover publishing. Paperback publishing kept
up with both new and reprint titles.

Prices of books jumped again. By the end of the year,
the average paperback had gone to $2.50 and the standard
hardcover to $14.95. 1982 will probably be worse. Each
time the price goes up, average sales go down. This tends
to make editors more conservative, since only well-known
authors and well-worn plots are relatively sure sellers.

There were more trade paperbacks published, and more
complaints about them from booksellers and readers because of the prices. (The trade paperback edition of
Anatomy of Wonder, an important reference book, sold
for $22.95!) Sales were mixed. Popular items such as
Expanded Universe by Robert A Heinlein, *Little, Big* by
John Crowley, and *Dream Park* by Larry Niven and
Steven Barnes sold well, but others, even by well-known
authors, bombed. The publishers are caught in a squeeze
and will probably stick with these high-price paperbacks
because hardcover SF is just too expensive to produce.
Berkley Books, once a major publisher of hardcovers, will
be doing trade paperbacks instead in 1982. Simon and
Schuster will keep the Timescape line of hardcovers but
will be doing fewer titles. They will also do trade paper-

backs. Ace, Avon, and Del Rey, despite mixed reactions, will do more of them.

God Emperor of Dune by Frank Herbert (Putnam) was a general hardcover bestseller with 175,000 copies in print. Nothing else came close. At least half a dozen books sold in the 10,0000- to 20,000-copy range—once considered an incredible sale, but, with large advances and advertising budgets, now considered barely adequate for a mid-range seller. The old bread-and-butter hardcovers, which used to have low or zero advances and made money by selling 2,000 to 3,000 copies, are no longer financially feasible.

Paperback bestsellers were all first mass-market reprints of 1980 hardcovers: *Timescape* by Gregory Benford, *Lord Valentine's Castle* by Robert Silverberg, *The Magic Labyrinth* by Philip José Farmer, *The Wounded Land* by Stephen Donaldson, *The Snow Queen* by Joan D. Vinge, and *The Ringworld Engineers* by Larry Niven. All sold over 150,000 copies.

Unfortunately, the low end of the scale has suffered. Just the words "science fiction" on the book were once good for a 60,000 copy sale. Now there are books by unknowns (and even by some well-known authors) which sell under 15,000 copies and are economic disasters.

It was a terrible year for quality novels, and I had to struggle to come up with five outstanding books. *The War Hound and The World's Pain* (Timescape) by Michael Moorcock is the year's best novel. It's a realistic, urbane fantasy in the style of James Branch Cabell, set in the seventeenth century but, thanks to its logical structure, reads more like SF than fantasy. *The Claw of the Conciliator* (Timescape) by Gene Wolfe, on the other hand, is a science-fiction novel (according to the author) written in a fantasy style. In any case, the writing is marvelous and the book is highly recommended even though it's a middle volume in a tetralogy. *The Cool War* by Frederik Pohl (Del Rey) is a fine satire, while *The Many-Colored Land* by Julian May (Houghton Mifflin) is the best adventure novel of the year. My fifth choice is a tie between *Project Pope* by Clifford D. Simak (Del Rey), a low-key book about robots and religion, and *At the Eye of the Ocean* by Hilbert Schenck (Timescape), a powerful study of strange powers in nineteenth-century New England.

Good first novels are always a pleasure to discover. The Schenck book was a first novel and easily the best, but there were also some others you should go out of your way to find: *Radix* by A. A. Attanasio (Morrow), *Tintagel* by Paul H. Cook (Berkley), *Starship & Haiku* by Somtow Sucharitkul (Timescape), and *The Breaking of Northwall* by Paul O. Williams (Del Rey).

It was a good year for collections. Ace reprinted the short fiction of H. Beam Piper in several volumes; *Paratime* was probably the best one. Piper, who died in the sixties, was a fine short-story writer. Several other authors had their shorter works collected for the first time. I was particularly impressed by *Far From Home* by Walter Tevis (Doubleday), *A Life in the Day of . . .* by Frank M. Robinson (Bantam), and *The Woman Who Loved the Moon* by Elizabeth A. Lynn (Berkley).

It was also a good year for bibliography, biography, and critical books. Urge your local library to get *Twentieth Century Science Fiction Writers* edited by Curtis C. Smith (St. Martin's) and *Twentieth-Century American Science Fiction Writers* edited by David Coward and Thomas L. Wymer (Gale Research). The former is the better critical book, but the latter is better for literary biography and survey articles. *Anatomy of Wonder* edited by Neil Barron (Bowker) has been thoroughly revised and is an excellent book with descriptions of all the important SF titles.

Art lovers should not miss *The Art of Leo and Diane Dillon* edited by Byron Preiss (Ballantine), which contains not only gorgeous reproductions but a complete course in commercial art.

Robert A. Heinlein, Arthur C. Clarke, and Isaac Asimov all signed contracts for new novels. The Heinlein book, *Friday*, is completely written and will appear in mid-1982. The Clarke book, *2010: Odyssey Two*, a sequel to *2001: A Space Odyssey*, received a million-dollar advance. It will appear in 1983. The Asimov book, *Lightning Rod*, a sequel to *The Foundation Trilogy*, is partially written and may appear in late 1982.

Carl Sagan set the new record for an advance when Simon and Schuster offered him $2,000,000 for *Contact*, a novel about our first encounter with an alien civilization. The book sold from a 115-page outline. Larry Niven and Jerry Pournelle managed to get two six-figure ad-

vances in the same month. They got $600,000 from Faw-
cett for *The Foot,* an alien-invasion novel, and "another
six-figure sum" for *The Moat Around Murchison's Eye,*
a sequel to *The Mote in God's Eye.* Niven also got
$100,000 by himself for *Smoke Ring.* There were far
fewer advances in the $10,000 to $100,000 range. There
seems to be a complete split between low-advance genre
fiction and high-advance potential best sellers.

Two new magazines appeared in 1981. *Science Fiction
Digest,* edited by Shawna McCarthy, which does excerpts
from new novels, has published two issues so far. It's too
early to tell how the magazine is doing, but I don't hold
out too high a hope for its success: there seems to be
little overlap between those who buy books and those who
buy magazines. The other new magazine, *The Twilight
Zone,* edited by T.E.D. Klein, is mostly fantasy/horror.
It's large-sized, and it gets better newsstand display, but
it has no subscriptions or direct sales yet. Four surviving
digest magazines, *Analog, Isaac Asimov's, F & SF,* and
Amazing, all experienced drops in newsstand sales. *Analog*
and *Asimov's* were redesigned for the worse. *Amazing,*
which went to reprint artwork on its covers, looks much
better, but its circulation is down to 14,000—the lowest of
any nationally distributed SF magazine in living memory.
George Scithers, the editor of *Asimov's* since its first issue,
quit. *Amazing* ended the year by going quarterly.

Omni cut its SF to a couple of short stories per issue,
but *Playboy, Penthouse,* and a number of other general
magazines picked up the slack. Robert Sheckley quit as
Omni fiction editor. He was replaced by his assistant, Ellen
Datlow.

There were more semiprofessional magazines, such as
the new *Rigel,* and more specialty books published in
1981. Perhaps the future of magazines and hardcovers lies
in that direction.

Gregg Press, which specialized in hardcover reprints of
rare books or those only available in paperback, suspended
its publication of new titles. It produced too many titles in
too short a time.

Dell dropped its science-fiction line and SF editor because it wasn't profitable enough. On the other hand,
Pinnacle expanded its line because its SF was very profitable. The new Pinnacle line, Tor Books, is edited by Jim
Baen, ex-Ace editor. Ace expanded its monthly list to

an amazing ten titles. Doubleday cut its list from two to one title per month. Holt and Houghton Mifflin announced expanded SF publishing programs for 1982.

Several of the SF specialty stores went out of business in 1981. The economic climate is against any small operation.

Paramount announced a second *Star Trek* movie.

DAW Books, the only purely SF mass-market publisher, celebrated its tenth birthday.

F&SF announced a hardcover copublishing venture with Charles Scribner's Sons.

The most famous unpublished book in the SF field, *The Last Dangerous Visions,* edited by Harlan Ellison, was postponed again.

The last few years have provided a relatively new phenomenon in which the more successful science-fiction writers have protected themselves from the tax man by becoming corporations. Thus Alan Dean Foster is now Thranx, Inc.; Robert Silverberg is Agberg Ltd.; Robert Zelazny is The Amber Corporation; Isaac Asimov is Nightfall, Inc.; Gregory Benford is Abbenford, Associates; and Peter Straub is Seafront Corporation. Frank Herbert, Arthur C. Clarke, and a number of others have also developed corporations.

James H. Schmitz, 69, died of congestive lung failure on April 18, 1981. Schmitz will be remembered for fast-paced adventure stories featuring strong, non-stereotyped female protagonists of all ages. His output was not large, but was influential because his successful combination of the hard-boiled story and science fiction was used as a model by many other writers. Some of his best works are *The Witches of Karres* (1966), *The Universe Against Her* (1966), and *Agent of Vega* (1960).

George O. Smith, 70, was found dead of an apparent heart attack on May 27, 1981. His technical-problem stories for *Astounding* in the forties, later collected as *Venus Equilateral,* were extremely popular. He also wrote a number of good space operas plus one outstanding modern SF novel, *The Fourth "R"* (1959).

Other losses to the field in 1981 included Robert Aickman, Lee Brown Coye, Nicholas Stuart Gray, Marjorie Hope Nicolson, Kit Pedler, R. S. Richardson, Lou Tabakow, and Stephen Tall.

The 1980 Nebula Awards were presented at the sixteenth annual Nebula Banquet at the Waldorf-Astoria in New York on April 25, 1981. Winners were: Best Novel, *Timescape* by Gregory Benford; Best Novella, "Unicorn Tapestry" by Suzy McKee Charnas; Best Novelette, "The Ugly Chickens" by Howard Waldrop; Best Short Story, "Grotto of the Dancing Deer" by Clifford D. Simak; Grand Master Award, Fritz Leiber.

The 1981 *Locus* Awards were announced on July 4 in Sacramento. Winners were: Best SF Novel, *The Snow Queen* by Joan D. Vinge; Best Fantasy Novel, *Lord Valentine's Castle* by Robert Silverberg; Best First Novel, *Dragon's Egg* by Robert L. Forward; Best Novella, "Nightflyers" by George R. R. Martin; Best Novelette, "The Brave Little Toaster" by Thomas M. Disch; Best Short Story, "Grotto of the Dancing Deer" by Clifford D. Simak; Best Anthology, *The Magazine of Fantasy and Science Fiction: A 30 Year Retrospective,* edited by Edward L. Ferman; Best Single Author Collection, *The Barbie Murders* by John Varley; Best Related Nonfiction Book, *In Joy Still Felt* by Isaac Asimov; Best Artist, Michael Whelan; Best Magazine, *The Magazine of Fantasy and Science Fiction;* Best Publisher, Ballantine/Del Rey.

Timescape by Gregory Benford won the ninth annual John W. Campbell Memorial Award.

The 1981 Hugo Awards were presented in Denver on September 6, 1981. Winners were: Best Novel, *The Snow Queen* by Joan D. Vinge; Best Novella, "Lost Dorsai" by Gordon R. Dickson; Best Novelette, "The Cloak and the Staff" by Gordon R. Dickson; Best Short Story, "Grotto of the Dancing Deer" by Clifford D. Simak; Best Nonfiction Book, *Cosmos* by Carl Sagan; Best Pro Editor, Edward L. Ferman; Best Fanzine, *Locus;* Best Fan Artist, Victoria Poyser; Best Pro Artist, Michael Whelan; Best Fan Writer, Susan Wood; Best Dramatic Presentation, *The Empire Strikes Back.* The John W. Campbell Award for best new writer went to Somtow Sucharitkul.

Denvention II, the Thirty-ninth World Science-Fiction Convention, was held September 3–7 in Denver, Colorado. More than 3,800 people attended the festivities, which included the Hugo Awards extravaganza orchestrated by Edward W. Bryant, the largest dealers' room ever, a science-fictional version of "The Dating Game," a chance to meet authors in hot tubs, and the Howard Waldrop history of SF movies. The guests of honor, Clifford D.

Simak and Catherine L. Moore, were dually honored in what turned out to be a relaxed, low-key gathering. Simak's warm, personal guest-of-honor speech was one of the most moving given at a convention.

The Fortieth World Science-Fiction Convention will be held in Chicago, September 2–6, 1982. Guests of honor include A. Bertram Chandler, Lee Hoffman, and Frank Kelly Freas. For information on membership, write ChiCon IV, P.O. Box A 3120, Chicago, Illinois 60690.

The Forty-first World Science-Fiction Convention will be held in Baltimore, September 1–5, 1983. Guests of honor include John Brunner and Dave Kyle. For information on membership, write Worldcon Forty-one, Box 1046, Baltimore, Maryland 21203.

CHARLES N. BROWN is the editor of *Locus,* the newspaper of the science-fiction field. Copies are $1.75 each. Subscriptions in the United States are $18.00 for twelve issues, $34.00 for twenty-four issues via second-class mail. First-class subscriptions in the U.S. or Canada are $25.00 for twelve issues, $48.00 for twenty-four issues. Overseas subscriptions are $20.00 for twelve issues, $38.00 for twenty-four issues via sea mail. Airmail overseas subscriptions are $32.00 for twelve issues, $60.00 for twenty-four issues. All subscriptions are payable only in U.S. funds to *Locus Publications,* P.O. Box 3938, San Francisco, California 94119.

RECOMMENDED READING— 1981

≈≈≈≈≈≈≈≈≈≈≈≈≈≈≈≈≈≈≈≈≈≈≈≈≈≈

Terry Carr

GREGORY BENFORD: "Exposures." *Isaac Asimov's Science Fiction Magazine,* July 6.

MICHAEL BISHOP: "Vox Olympica." *Omni,* December.

REGINALD BRETNOR: "These Stones Will Remember." *Isaac Asimov's Science Fiction Magazine,* February 16.

PAUL BRIANS: "The Day They Tested the Rec Room." *Co-Evolution Quarterly,* Summer.

F. M. BUSBY: "Backup System." *Isaac Asimov's Science Fiction Magazine,* October 26.

MICHAEL CASSUTT: "The Free Agent." *Fantasy and Science Fiction,* August.

DAVID DRAKE: "Time Safari." *Destinies,* Volume 3, Number 2.

GEORGE ALEC EFFINGER: "Breakaway." *Fantasy and Science Fiction,* January.

PHYLLIS EISENSTEIN: "In the Western Tradition." *Fantasy and Science Fiction,* March.

JOHN M. FORD: "Intersections." *Isaac Asimov's Science Fiction Magazine,* October 26.

WILLIAM GIBSON: "The Gernsback Continuum." *Universe 11.* "Johnny Mnemonic." *Omni,* May.

PHYLLIS GOTLIEB: "Blue Apes." *Berkley Showcase,* Volume 4.

RICHARD GRANT: "Drode's Equations." *New Dimensions 12.*

JAMES GUNN: "The North Wind." *Isaac Asimov's Science Fiction Magazine,* October 26.

JOE HALDEMAN: "A !Tangled Web." *Analog,* September 14.

IRA HERMAN: "The Two Tzaddiks." *Stellar #7.*

NANCY KRESS: "Casey's Empire." *Fantasy and Science Fiction,* November. "Shadows on the Cave Wall." *Universe 11.*

R. A. LAFFERTY: "In Deepest Glass: An Informal History of Stained-Glass Windows." *Berkley Showcase*, Volume 4.

GEORGE R. R. MARTIN: "Guardians." *Analog*, October 12.

TED REYNOLDS: "Through All Your Houses Wandering." *Isaac Asimov's Science Fiction Magazine*, March 16.

SPIDER ROBINSON: "Chronic Offender." *The Twilight Zone*, May.

WARREN M. SALOMON: "Time and Punishment." *Isaac Asimov's Science Fiction Magazine*, May 11.

ROBERT SILVERBERG: "A Thief in Ni-Moya." *Isaac Asimov's Science Fiction Magazine*, December 21.

D. D. STORM: "Mud/Aurora." *Isaac Asimov's Science Fiction Magazine*, November 23.

MICHAEL SWANWICK: "Mummer Kiss." *Universe 11*.

CHERRY WILDER: "The Dreamers of Deliverance." *Distant Worlds*.

KATE WILHELM: "The Winter Beach." *Redbook*, September.

NICHOLAS YERMAKOV: "Crash Course for the Ravers." *Berkley Showcase*, Volume 3.